COMMONWEALTH SHORT STORIES

Commonwealth short stories

Edited by
ANNA RUTHERFORD
and
DONALD HANNAH

EDWARD ARNOLD

First published 1971 by Edward Arnold (Publishers) Ltd.,
41 Maddox Street, London, WIR OAN

ISBN 0 7131 5584 1

Printed in Great Britain by
Billing & Sons Limited, Guildford and London

Acknowledgements

The editors wish to acknowledge the contribution of Hena Maes-Jelinek of the University of Liège, who is at present engaged on a full-length critical study of Wilson Harris's work and who has kindly written the introduction to "Kanaima".

We also wish to express our grateful thanks to Miss Ann Draycon, Staff Tutor in the Department of Extra-Mural Education, University of Glasgow; Miss G. Wiles, librarian, New Zealand House, London; Mr. Peter Saunders, Liaison Officer, National Library of Australia, London; Mr. Andrew Salkey, and Mr. Edwin Thumboo, English Department, University of Singapore, for help in obtaining some of the material.

We also grateful to Mrs. Hoffer and Miss B. Møgelberg for their help in typing the manuscript.

The Publishers' thanks are due to the following who granted permission for the use of these stories:

The New Yorker and the Bodley Head for R. K. Narayan's "A Horse and Two Goats" from *A Horse and Two Goats:* Curtis Brown Ltd. for Patrick White's "Down at the Dump" from *The Burnt Ones;* George Lamming for "A Wedding in Spring"; Angus & Robertson (U.K.) Ltd. for Peter Cowan's "The Tractor" and Hal Porter's "Francis Silver"; A. P. Watt & Son and Mordecai Richler for "The Summer my Grandmother was Supposed to Die"; Heinemann Educational Books (Asia) Ltd. for Lee Kok Liang's "When the Saints Go Marching By" from *Twenty-two Malaysian Stories;* Wilson Harris for "Kanaima" which appeared in *Black Orpheus*, Nigeria; Granada Publishing Ltd. for Frank Sargeson's "A Man and His Wife" from *Collected Stories;* Faber & Faber Ltd. for an extract entitled "The Complete Gentleman" from Amos Tutuola's *The Palm-Wine Drinkard;* Randolph Stow for "Magic"; A. M. Heath & Co. Ltd. for Janet Frame's "Two Sheep" from *The Reservoir and Other Stories;* Janet Frame and *Landfall* for "A Boy's Will"; Andrew Salkey for "Anancy"; East African Pub-

lishing House for Ezekiel Mphahlele's "The Living and the Dead";
Mavis Gallant and the New Yorker Magazine Inc, © 1965, for
"Orphan's Progress"; André Deutsch Ltd. for V. S. Naipaul's
"Man-Man" from *Miguel Street*; James Ngugi for "A Meeting in
the Dark" and The Atlantic Monthly Company, Boston, Mass. for
Chinua Achebe's "The Sacrificial Egg", © 1959.

Contents

Introduction

Anyone compiling an anthology feels caught between two fires since the reader's reaction is almost bound to alternate between questioning the reason why a particular work has been included to one of surmising why another has been omitted. Consequently a few words should perhaps first be said about the principles determining which stories were finally included in this selection. At the outset we were faced with two possibilities: either we could choose to include a single story from each country in the Commonwealth (in some cases mainly because the author came from a country that would otherwise remain unrepresented), or we could be guided in our selection by more purely literary standards. Tempting in many ways as the first possibility was, we finally decided to follow the latter course, even though, regrettably, this has meant that some countries have been omitted altogether. We can only hope that the reader will feel convinced that the merit of each story is sufficient in itself to justify this principle.

Our aim in the critical introduction to each one has been to try to summarize very briefly the major themes in the writer's work as a whole, especially those that have a direct bearing on the story. In this way we hope to have provided a general context within which the particular story can better be understood, as well as offering some assistance to any reader who wishes to read further works by the same author using the story as a starting-point.

The anthology is primarily intended for use by students and for teaching purposes in schools; however we have also attempted to keep in mind the requirements of the common reader who may already be familiar with that part of the field of Commonwealth literature which writing in his own country constitutes, but who may wish to explore other areas. Consequently we have, wherever possible, drawn comparisons and established parallels with other writers represented in the collection. Thus the book may serve as a basis for a comparative study of texts drawn from various cultures, since, used in this way, the reader is also exploiting one of the great advantages of a study of Commonwealth literature in that it makes such a type of approach possible without the barriers of several different languages having first to be surmounted.

The fact that this can be done is possibly alone sufficient to illustrate the wealth of literature and experience that can be drawn upon both by the reader and writer who share the common heritage of the English language. It is our hope that this anthology will at least indicate something of the extent of these resources even within the comparatively limited field of the short story.

ANNA RUTHERFORD
DONALD HANNAH

Department of English
Aarhus University, Denmark

R. K. Narayan

R. K. Narayan is undoubtedly the greatest of the Indian writers in English, and he must rank amongst the finest of the world's story-tellers today. His imaginary town, Malgudi, and its inhabitants have become known to readers all over the world. Narayan has told us that he writes his stories out of the impact of life and persons around him. He has spent almost all his life in India, and with his sharp eye for detail, character and incident he has been able to create what is perhaps the best picture we have of a way of life that has changed but little over the centuries. The setting of this story is a village in Southern India, a village which Narayan has described elsewhere as 'somewhat isolated from the main stream of life'. By choosing this tiny village instead of the larger Malgudi, Narayan is able to place an even greater stress on the distance between old and new and the inability of either to comprehend one another, which is a frequent concern in his writing.

From the moment the screech of brakes intrudes upon the tran-quillity we are presented with a comic confrontation between East and West, ancient and modern. Graham Greene has remarked that 'the juxtaposition of the age old conventions and modern characters provides much of the comedy' in Narayan's works. There can be no doubt that the meeting between the old Indian villager and the brash, red-faced American "doing" India creates a rich comic situation. But we are aware of the underlying seriousness of purpose. It is an excellent example of William Walsh's comment in *A Human Idiom*, that Narayan has 'an affectionately ridiculing eye with that kind of humour in which the jokes are also species of moral insight'. Beneath the comedy we feel Narayan's deep concern for values which he upholds and which he feels are in danger of being destroyed. The inability of the two to communicate is symbolic of the clash be-tween two ways of thinking. They are symbols of two different worlds, of two attitudes to life; one ponders the great mysteries of life, the other the problem of transportation.

Pervading all Narayan's works is a deep sense of the spiritual: to our modern scientific age he opposes the ancient beliefs and culture of India, symbolized by a goddess, a shrine, or in this case, the statue of the horse. Narayan is not concerned with the poverty of the village but with the poverty of modern man bereft of all spiritual values and beliefs. The village is rich as long as it has the statue and a belief in what it symbolizes. To the outside world it may appear poor; the peasant's dream is one we would laugh at. Narayan would question our values.

Narayan, like so many other writers in this anthology, senses the danger to man's spirit in this man-eating world of ours but he is never in any doubt that the spirit will eventually triumph. In his novel, *The Man-Eater of Malgudi*, Vasu, the man-eater, the rakshasas, scornful of the old ways finally destroys himself. Sastri comments on this:

> Yet the universe has survived all the 'rakshasas' that were ever born. Every demon carries within him, unknown to himself, a tiny seed of self-destruction, and goes up in thin air at the most unexpected moment. Otherwise what is to happen to humanity?

Sastri is expressing here what Narayan has described in *Gods, Demons, and Others* as the sustaining philosophy of the Indian people. It is the philosophy of his novels and stories, this faith, that as in the epics, 'everything is bound to come out right in the end; if not immediately, at least in a thousand or ten thousand years; if not in this world, at least in other worlds'. It is a belief implicit in this story. The westerly sun touching off the ancient faded colours of the statue with a fresh splendour reminds us of this.

The clash between the ancient beliefs and modern rationalism often leads to a division in Narayan's work between old and young, father and son, man and the machine, and, as in this story, between India and America. In his novel *The Sweet Vendor* Jagan's son returns from America with a machine that can write novels: one knob for characters, one for plot situations, one for climax and one for right combinations. Ridiculous you say. No more so than the contention of Dr. Leavis's luncheon companion that 'a computor can write a poem' (*Times Literary Supplement*, 23.4.70). Both Dr. Leavis and Narayan remind us that it is no more possible to manufacture culture than it is to buy it. 'The "work", in the first place, was not 'written'; it arose within the writer. The 'character' was not conceived but revealed himself in a vision.' (*Gods, Demons, and Others*.)

Because of his deep belief in the visionary nature of a work of art Narayan places great emphasis on the myths. These he believes are prototypes of human characters, aspirations and defeats; 'moulds in which humanity is cast and remains valid for all time'. He believes that they engender in the listener 'an ever deepening understanding of life, death and destiny'. You may notice that Narayan has said 'listener'. He places great emphasis on the oral nature of the myths and on the role of the story-teller, for it is through him that the stories are conveyed to every man, woman and child. Narayan believes that 'literature is not a branch of study to be placed in a separate compartment, for the edification only of scholars, but a comprehensive and artistic medium of expression to benefit the literate and illiterate alike' (*Gods, Demons, and Others*). To ensure that this is accomplished he has produced works which abound in concrete images and which are remarkable for their simplicity and purity of language. It has been said that Narayan can pin down a whole society in two pages of dialogue. In this story he has managed to pin down not one society but two. *A. R.*

A Horse and Two Goats

The village was so small that it found no mention in any atlas. On the local survey map it was indicated by a tiny dot. It was called Kiritam, which in the Tamil language means "crown" (preferably diamond-studded)—a rather gorgeous conception, readily explained by any local enthusiast convinced beyond doubt that this part of India is the apex of the world. In proof thereof, he could, until quite recently, point in the direction of a massive guardian at the portals of the village, in the shape of a horse moulded out of clay, baked, burnt, and brightly coloured. The horse reared his head proudly, prancing, with his forelegs in the air and his tail looped up with a flourish. Beside the horse stood a warrior with scythe-like moustaches, bulging eyes, and an aquiline nose. The image-makers of old had made the eyes bulge out when they wished to indicate a man of strength, just as the beads around the warrior's neck were meant to show his wealth. Blobs of mud now, before the ravages of sun and rain they had had the sparkle of emerald, ruby, and diamond. The big horse looked mottled, but at one time it was white as a dhobi-washed sheet, its back enveloped in a checkered brocade of pure red and black. The lance in the grip of the warrior had been covered with bands of gay colour, and the multicoloured sash around his waist contrasted with every other colour in these surroundings. This statue, like scores of similar ones scattered along the countryside, was forgotten and unnoticed, with lantana and cactus growing around it. Even the youthful vandals of the village left the statue alone, hardly aware of its existence. On this particular day, an old man was drowsing in the shade of a nearby cactus and watching a pair of goats graze in this arid soil; he was waiting for the sight of a green bus lumbering down the hill road in the evening, which would be the signal for him to start back home, and he was disturbed by a motorist, who jammed on his brakes at the sight of the statue, and got out of his car, and went up to the mud horse.

"Marvellous!" he cried, pacing slowly around the statue. His face was sunburned and red. He wore a khaki-coloured shirt and shorts. Noticing the old man's presence, he said politely in English, "How do you do?"

The old man replied in pure Tamil, his only means of communication, "My name is Muni, and the two goats are mine and mine only; no one can gainsay it, although the village is full of people ready to slander a man."

The red-faced man rested his eyes for a moment in the direction of the goats and the rocks, took out a cigarette, and asked, "Do you smoke?"

"I never even heard of it until yesterday," the old man replied nervously, guessing that he was being questioned about a murder in the neighbourhood by this police officer from the government, as his khaki dress indicated.

The red-faced man said, "I come from New York. Have you heard of it? Have you heard of America?"

The old man would have understood the word "America" (though not "New York") if the name had been pronounced as he knew it—"Ah Meh Rikya"—but the red-faced man pronounced it very differently, and the old man did not know what it meant. He said respectfully, "Bad characters everywhere these days. The cinema has spoiled the people and taught them how to do evil things. In these days anything may happen."

"I am sure you must know when this horse was made," said the red-faced man, and smiled ingratiatingly.

The old man reacted to the relaxed atmosphere by smiling himself, and pleaded, "Please go away, sir. I know nothing. I promise I will hold him for you if I see any bad character around, but our village has always had a clean record. Must be the other village."

"Please, please, I will speak slowly. Please try to understand me," the red-faced man said. "I arrived three weeks ago and have travelled five thousand miles since, seeing your wonderful country."

The old man made indistinct sounds in his throat and shook his head. Encouraged by this, the other went on to explain at length, uttering each syllable with care and deliberation, what brought him to this country, how much he liked it, what he did at home, how he had planned for years to visit India, the dream of his life and so forth—every now and then pausing to smile affably. The old man smiled back and said nothing, whereupon the red-faced man finally said, "How old are you? You have such wonderful teeth. Are they real? What's your secret?"

The old man knitted his brow and said mournfully, "Sometimes our cattle, too, are lost; but then we go and consult our astrologer.

He will look at a camphor flame and tell us in which direction to search for the lost animals. . . . I must go home now." And he turned to go.

The other seized his shoulder and said earnestly, "Is there no one —absolutely no one—here to translate for me?" He looked up and down the road, which was deserted on this hot afternoon. A sudden gust of wind churned up the dust and the dead leaves on the roadside into a ghostly column and propelled it toward the mountain road. "Is this statue yours? Will you sell it to me?"

The old man understood that the other was referring to the horse. He thought for a second and said, "I was an urchin of this height when I heard my grandfather explain this horse and warrior, and my grandfather himself was of this height when he heard his grandfather, whose grandfather . . ." Trying to indicate the antiquity of the statue, he got deeper and deeper into the bog of reminiscence, and then pulled himself out by saying, "But my grandfather's grandfather's uncle had first-hand knowledge, although I don't remember him."

"Because I really do want this statue," the red-faced man said, "I hope you won't drive a hard bargain."

"This horse," the old man continued, "will appear as the tenth avatar at the end of the Yuga."

The red-faced man nodded. He was familiar with the word "avatar."

"At the end of this Kali Yuga, this world will be destroyed, and all the worlds will be destroyed, and it is then that the Redeemer will come, in the form of a horse called Kalki, and help the good people, leaving the evil ones to perish in the great deluge. And this horse will come to life then, and that is why this is the most sacred village in the whole world."

"I am willing to pay any price that is reasonable——"

This statement was cut short by the old man, who was now lost in the visions of various avatars. "God Vishnu is the highest god, so our pandit at the temple has always told us, and He has come nine times before, whenever evil-minded men troubled this world."

"But please bear in mind that I am not a millionaire."

"The first avatar was in the shape of a fish," the old man said, and explained the story of how Vishnu at first took the form of a little fish, which grew bigger each hour and became gigantic, and supported on its back the holy scriptures, which were about to be lost in the ocean. Having launched on the first avatar, it was inevitable that he should go on with the second one, a tortoise, and the third, a boar on whose tusk the world was lifted up when it had been carried off and hidden at the bottom of the ocean by an extraordinary vicious conqueror of the earth.

"Transportation will be my problem, but I will worry about that later. Tell me, will you accept a hundred rupees for the horse only? Although I am charmed by the moustached soldier, I will have to come next year for him. No space for him now."

"It is God Vishnu alone who saves mankind each time such a thing has happened. He incarnated himself as Rama, and He alone could destroy Ravana, the demon with ten heads who shook all the worlds. Do you know the story of Ramayana?"

"I have my station wagon, as you see. I can push the seat back and take the horse in. If you'll just lend me a hand with it."

"Do you know Mahabharata? Krishna was the eighth avatar of Vishnu, incarnated to help the Five Brothers regain their kingdom. When Krishna was a baby, he danced on the thousand-hooded, the giant serpent, and trampled it to death. . . ."

At this stage the mutual mystification was complete. The old man chattered away in a spirit of balancing off the credits and debits of conversational exchanges, and said, in order to be on the credit side, "Oh, honourable one, I hope God has blessed you with numerous progeny. I say this because you seem to be a good man, willing to stay beside an old man and talk to him, while all day I have none to talk to except when somebody stops to ask for a piece of tobacco. . . . How many children have you?"

"Nothing ventured, nothing gained," the red-faced man said to himself. And then, "Will you take a hundred rupees for it?" Which encouraged the other to go into details.

"How many of your children are boys and how many girls? Where are they? Is your daughter married? Is it difficult to find a son-in-law in your country also?"

The red-faced man thrust his hand into his pocket and brought forth his wallet, from which he took a hundred rupee currency note.

The old man now realized that some financial element was entering their talk. He peered closely at the currency note, the like of which he had never seen in his life; he knew the five and ten by their colours, although always in other people's hands. His own earning at any time was in coppers and nickels. What was this man flourishing the note for? Perhaps for change. He laughed to himself at the notion of anyone's coming to him to change a thousand- or ten-thousand-rupee note. He said with a grin, "Ask our village headman, who is also a money-lender; he can change even a lakh of rupees in gold sovereigns if you prefer it that way. He thinks nobody knows, but dig the floor of his *puja* room and your head will reel at the sight of the hoard. The man disguises himself in rags just to mislead the public."

"If that's not enough, I guess I could go a little higher," the red-faced man said.

"You'd better talk to him yourself, because he goes mad at the sight of me. Someone took away his pumpkins with the creeper and he thinks it was me and my goats. That's why I never let my goats be seen anywhere near the farms," the old man said, with his eyes travelling to his goats as they were nosing about, attempting to wrest nutrition out of minute greenery peeping out of rock and dry earth.

The red-faced man followed his look and decided it would be a sound policy to show an interest in the old man's pets. He went up to them casually and stroked their backs.

Now the truth dawned on the old man. His dream of a lifetime was about to be realized: the red-faced man was making him an offer for the goats. He had reared them up in the hope of selling them some day and with the capital opening a small shop on this very spot; under a thatched roof he would spread out a gunny sack and display on it fried nuts, coloured sweets, and green coconut for thirsty and hungry wayfarers on the highway. He needed for this project a capital of twenty rupees, and he felt that with some bargaining he could get it now; they were not prize animals worthy of a cattle show, but he had spent his occasional savings to provide them some fancy diet now and then, and they did not look too bad.

Saying, "It is all for you, or you may share it if you have a partner," the red-faced man placed on the old man's palm one hundred and twenty rupees in notes.

The old man pointed at the station wagon.

"Yes, of course," said the other.

The old man said, "This will be their first ride in a motor car. Carry them off after I get out of sight; otherwise they will never follow you but only me, even if I am travelling on the path to the

Underworld." He laughed at his own joke, brought his palms together in a salute, turned round, and was off and out of sight beyond a clump of bushes.

The red-faced man looked at the goats grazing peacefully and then perched himself on the pedestal of the horse, as the westerly sun touched off the ancient faded colours of the statue with a fresh splendour. "He must be gone to fetch some help," he remarked, and settled down to wait.

Patrick White

In an article entitled "The Prodigal Son' (*Australian Letters*, I, 3, April, 1958), Patrick White tells us that on his return to Australia the thing that made him panic most 'was the exaltation of the *average*'. It is in suburbia more than anywhere else that one finds this exaltation, and it is Australian suburbia, its narrowness, its hypocrisy, its materialism, its reluctance to explore, that has been the object of White's sharpest criticism. But White was not contented with criticism alone. For he believed that behind this façade of mediocrity there was a brilliance. 'I wanted', he said, 'to discover the extraordinary behind the ordinary, the mystery and the poetry which alone could make bearable the lives of such people, and incidentally, my own since my return.' This is what White has attempted and achieved in this story.

The setting is Sarsaparilla, White's imaginary suburb, inhabited by the Mrs. Hogbens, Jollys and Flacks, all characterized by their mediocrity, their falsity, their malice and their hate. These champions of conformity ruthlessly persecute and isolate all those who fail to conform, unshakeably self-righteous in their belief that, in the words of the mother in White's short story "Clay", ' "no-one is different without they have something wrong with them" '. In all of White's work we find an opposition between conformist society valuing its material possessions and the nonconformist individual, poor in earthly possessions but rich in knowledge. In this story also, we find a set of polarities between good and evil, love and hate, material and spiritual, the living and the dead. The rich, earthy, riotous world of the Whalley's who 'did the dumps' and whose 'faces were lit by the certainty of life' is contrasted with the barren, antiseptic, respectable world of Mrs. Hogben, councillor's wife, with her 'Breath-o'-Pine' and a face 'selected' for the funeral. Daise Morrow, preaching her message of love is opposed by Myrtle Hogben preaching her message of hate.

Most of the story takes place at the dump or the cemetery, both symbols of death and decay. But like the serpent in *Voss*, White uses them as symbols of eternal repetition, of the continuous process of renewal in decay, of life in death, symbols that the life-giving forces will triumph over the forces of destruction and death. In the dump it may appear that 'trash might win. . . . But in many secret, steamy pockets, a rout was in progress.' It may also appear that Daise Morrow was dead. Certainly her body had been committed to the earth. But she 'had not altogether died'. For ' "death isn't death, unless it's the death of love"', and it was Christ's message of love that Daise preached and practised, and which her spirit, transmitted to, and, living on in her niece, will continue to practise.

Meg's consciousness of the need to explore, her realization that 'she had not yet looked enough', mark her out as one of White's chosen ones. Exploration is part of White's obsession with the need of man to know himself, for he believes that it is in the knowledge of ourselves that we will find knowledge of God. He believes that each of us contains 'a little of Christ' but it takes inward looking eyes to realize this; normally it is in the depths of the mind 'the part a decent person ignores'. The reluctance to explore is one of the marks of White's conformist society for suburbia has bred agoraphobia, a fear of the open spaces of the mind. White insists that we must be prepared to look into the depths, to come to terms with the paradoxical nature of man, to recognize the co-existence in man of good and evil, of the divine and human. He constantly reminds us that the agony and the ecstasy go hand in hand, that we must accept and acknowledge the grub within the rose, for it is only when we have acknowledged and accepted the human with all its frailties that we will find the divine. This is the lesson that Voss had to learn, 'when man is truly humbled, when he has learnt that he is not God, then he is nearest to becoming so. In the end, he may ascend.'

This exploration is all part of the quest to become that mysterious identity which Jung calls "the whole Man"; it is the quest of all of White's visionaries. The exploration not only leads to the discovery of the divine spark within oneself but also to the discovery of God within others, of the brilliant shapes behind the common forms. This in turn leads to a realization of one's brotherhood with all living things, to a reconciliation with life, which can be accepted as it is and not as it ought to be. We don't see Daise Morrow on her journey of exploration but we know by her actions that she has undertaken it and reached her goal.

The Lum–Meg relationship is another aspect of this quest for totality. "Every man carries within him his own Eve" is the German proverb that White seeks to illustrate. Meg and Lum are drawn to one another and White stresses their complementary natures: male–female; light–dark; mind–matter; spirit–earth. It is the relationship between male and female, anima and animus that White explores more fully in *Voss* and *The Solid Mandala*.

At the conclusion of *Voss* Willie Pringle, White's spokesman, comments on the inherent mediocrity of the people and then says:

> 'I am confident that the mediocrity . . . is not a final and irrevocable state; rather it is a creative source of endless variety and subtlety. The blow fly on its bed of offal is but a variation of the rainbow. Common forms are continually breaking into brilliant shapes. If we will explore them.'

This is the message of "Down at the Dump". It is a tribute to White's genius that he has been able, through the exploration of the lives of these most ordinary people, to present us with his own metaphysical vision of life, a vision in which in White's own words from "The Prodigal Son", 'Even the ugliness, the bags and iron of Australian life, [acquire] a meaning.' *A. R.*

Down at the Dump

"Hi!"

He called from out of the house, and she went on chopping in the yard. Her right arm swung, firm still, muscular, though parts of her were beginning to sag. She swung with her right, and her left arm hung free. She chipped at the log, left right. She was expert with the axe.

Because you had to be. You couldn't expect all that much from a man.

"Hi!" It was Wal Whalley calling again from out of the home.

He came to the door then, in that dirty old baseball cap he had shook off the Yankee disposals. Still a fairly appetizing male, though his belly had begun to push against the belt.

"Puttin' on yer act?" he asked, easing the singlet under his armpits; easy was policy at Whalleys' place.

"'Ese!" she protested. "Waddaya make me out ter be? A lump of wood?"

Her eyes were of that blazing blue, her skin that of a brown peach. But whenever she smiled, something would happen, her mouth opening on watery sockets and the jags of brown, rotting stumps.

"A woman likes to be addressed," she said.

No one had ever heard Wal address his wife by her first name. Nobody had ever heard her name, though it was printed in the electoral roll. It was, in fact, Isba.

"Don't know about a dress," said Wal. "I got a idea, though."

His wife stood tossing her hair. It was natural at least; the sun had done it. All the kids had inherited their mother's colour, and when they stood together, golden-skinned, tossing back their unmanageable hair, you would have said a mob of taffy brumbies.

"What is the bloody idea?" she asked, because she couldn't go on standing there.

"Pick up a coupla cold bottles, and spend the mornun at the dump."

"But that's the same old idea," she grumbled.

"No, it aint'. Not our own dump. We ain't done Sarsaparilla since Christmas."

She began to grumble her way across the yard and into the house. A smell of sink strayed out of grey unpainted weatherboard, to oppose the stench of crushed boggabri and cotton pear. Perhaps because Whalleys were in the bits-and-pieces trade their home was threatening to give in to them.

Wal Whalley did the dumps. Of course there were the other lurks besides. But no one had an eye like Wal for the things a person needs: dead batteries and musical bedsteads, a carpet you wouldn't notice was stained, wire, and again wire, clocks only waiting to jump back into the race of time. Objects of commerce and mystery littered Whalleys' back yard. Best of all, a rusty boiler into which the twins would climb to play at cubby.

"Eh Waddaboutut?" Wal shouted, and pushed against his wife with his side.

She almost put her foot through the hole that had come in the kitchen boards.

"Waddabout what?"

Half-suspecting, she half-sniggered. Because Wal knew how to play on her weakness.

"The fuckun *idea*!"

So that she began again to grumble. As she slopped through the house her clothes irritated her skin. The sunlight fell yellow on the grey masses of the unmade beds, turned the fluff in the corners of the rooms to gold. Something was nagging at her, something heavy continued to weigh her down.

Of course. It was the funeral.

"Why, Wal," she said, the way she would suddenly come round, "you could certainly of thought of a worse idea. It'll keep the kids out of mischief. Wonder if that bloody Lummy's gunna decide to honour us?"

"One day I'll knock 'is block off," said Wal.

"He's only at the awkward age."

She stood at the window, looking as though she might know the hell of a lot. It was the funeral made her feel solemn. Brought the goose-flesh out on her.

"Good job you thought about the dump," she said, out-staring a red-brick propriety the other side of the road. "If there's anythun gets me down, it's havin' ter watch a funeral pass."

"Won't be from 'ere," he consoled. "They took 'er away same evenun. It's gunna start from Jackson's Personal Service."

"Good job she popped off at the beginnun of the week. They're not so personal at the week-end."

She began to prepare for the journey to the dump. Pulled her frock down a bit. Slipped on a pair of shoes.

"Bet *She*'ll be relieved. Wouldn't show it, though. Not about 'er sister. I bet Daise stuck in 'er fuckun guts."

Then Mrs. Whalley was compelled to return to the window. As if her instinct. And sure enough there She was. Looking inside the letter-box, as if she hadn't collected already. Bent above the brick pillar in which the letter-box had been cemented, Mrs. Hogben's face wore all that people expect of the bereaved.

"Daise was all right," said Wal.

"Daise was all right," agreed his wife.

Suddenly she wondered: What if Wal, if Wal had ever. . . .?

Mrs. Whalley settled her hair. If she hadn't been all that satisfied at home—and she was satisfied, her recollective eyes would admit—she too might have done a line like Daise Morrow.

Over the road Mrs. Hogben was calling.

"Meg?" she call. "Mar*gret*?"

Though from pure habit, without direction. Her voice sounded thinner today.

Then Mrs. Hogben went away.

"Once I got took to a funeral," Mrs. Whalley said. "They made me look in the coffun. It was the bloke's wife. He was that cut up."

"Did yer have a squint?"

"Pretended to."

Wal Whalley was breathing hard in the airless room.

"How soon do yer reckon they begin ter smell?"

"Smell? They wouldn't let 'em!" his wife said very definite. "You're the one that smells, Wal. I wonder you don't think of takin' a bath."

But she liked his smell for all that. It followed her out of the shadow into the strong shaft of light. Looking at each other their two bodies asserted themselves. Their faces were lit by the certainty of life.

Wal tweaked her left nipple.

"We'll slip inter the Bull on the way, and pick up those cold bottles."

He spoke soft for him.

Mrs. Hogben called another once or twice. Inside the brick entrance the cool of the house struck at her. She liked it cool, but not cold, and this was if not exactly cold, anyway, too sudden. So now she whimpered, very faintly, for everything you have to suffer, and death on top of all. Although it was her sister Daise who had died, Mrs. Hogben was crying for the death which was waiting to carry her off in turn. She called: "Me-ehg?" But no one ever came to your rescue. She stopped to loosen the soil round the roots of the aluminium plant. She always had to be doing something. It made her feel better.

Meg did not hear, of course. She was standing amongst the fuchsia bushes, looking out from their greenish shade. She was thin and freckly. She looked awful, because Mum had made her wear her uniform, because it was sort of a formal occasion, to Auntie Daise's funeral. In the circumstances she not only looked, but was thin. That Mrs. Ireland who was all for sports had told her she must turn her toes out, and watch out—she might grow up knock-kneed besides.

So Meg Hogben was, and felt, altogether awful. Her skin was green, except when the war between light and shade worried her face into scraps, and the fuchsia tassels trembling against her unknowing cheek, infused something of their own blood, brindled her with shifting crimson. Only her eyes resisted. They were not exactly an ordinary grey. Lorrae Jensen, who was blue, said they were the eyes of a mopey cat.

A bunch of six or seven kids from Second-Grade, Lorrae, Edna, Val, Sherry, Sue Smith and Sue Goldstein, stuck together in the holidays, though Meg sometimes wondered why. The others had come around to Hogbens' Tuesday evening.

Lorrae said: "We're going down to Barranugli pool Thursday. There's some boys Sherry knows with a couple of Gs. They've promised to take us for a run after we come out."

Meg did not know whether she was glad or ashamed.

"I can't," she said. "My auntie's died."

"Arrr!" their voices trailed.

They couldn't get away too quick, as if it had been something contagious.

But murmuring.

Meg sensed she had become temporarily important.

So now she was alone with her dead importance, in the fuchsia bushes, on the day of Auntie Daise's funeral. She had turned fourteen. She remembered the ring in plaited gold Auntie Daise had promised her. When I am gone, her aunt had said. And now it had really happened. Without rancour Meg suspected there hadn't been time to think about the ring, and Mum would grab it, to add to all the other things she had.

Then that Lummy Whalley showed up, amongst the camphor laurels opposite, tossing his head of bleached hair. She hated boys with white hair. For that matter she hated boys, or any intrusion on her privacy. She hated Lum most of all. The day he threw the dog poo at her. It made the gristle come in her neck. Ugh! Although the old poo had only skittered over her skin, too dry to really matter, she had gone in and cried because well, there were times when she cultivated dignity.

Now Meg Hogben and Lummy Whalley did not notice each other even when they looked.

'Who wants Meg Skinny-leg?
I'd rather take the clothes-peg . . .'

Lum Whalley vibrated like a comb-and-paper over amongst the camphor laurels they lopped back every so many years for firewood. He slashed with his knife into bark. Once in a hot dusk he had carved I LOVE MEG, because that was something you did, like on lavatory walls, and in the trains, but it didn't mean anything of course. Afterwards he slashed the darkness as if it had been a train seat.

Lum Whalley pretended not to watch Meg Hogben skulking in the fuchsia bushes. Wearing her brown uniform. Stiffer, browner than for school, because it was her auntie's funeral.

"Me-ehg?" called Mrs. Hogben. "Meg!"

"Lummy! Where the devil are yer?" called his mum.

She called all around, in the woodshed, behind the dunny. Let her!

"Lum? Lummy, for Chris*sake*!" she called.

He hated that. Like some bloody kid. At school he had got them to call him Bill, halfway between, not so shameful as Lum, nor yet as awful as William.

Mrs. Whalley came round the corner.

"Shoutin' me bloody lungs up!" she said. "When your dad's got a nice idea. We're going down to Sarsaparilla dump."

"Arr!" he said.

But didn't spit.

"What gets inter you?" she asked.

Even at their most inaccessible Mrs. Whalley liked to finger her children. Touch often assisted thought. But she liked the feel of them as well. She was glad she hadn't had girls. Boys turned into men, and you couldn't do without men, even when they took you for a mug, or got shickered, or bashed you up.

So she put her hand on Lummy, tried to get through to him. He was dressed, but might not have been. Lummy's kind was never ever born for clothes. At fourteen he looked more.

"Well," she said, sourer than she felt, "I'm not gunna cry over any sulky boy. Suit yourself."

She moved off.

As Dad had got out the old rattle-bones by now, Lum began to clamber up. The back of the ute was at least private, though it wasn't no Customline.

The fact that Whalleys ran a Customline as well puzzled more unreasonable minds. Drawn up amongst the paspalum in front of Whalleys' shack, it looked stolen, and almost was—the third payment overdue. But would slither with ease a little longer to Barranugli, and snooze outside the Northern Hotel. Lum could have stood all day to admire their own two-tone car. Or would stretch out inside, his fingers at work on plastic flesh.

Now it was the ute for business. The bones of his buttocks bit into the boards. His father's meaty arm stuck out at the window, disgusting him. And soon the twins were squeezing from the rusty boiler. The taffy Gary—or was it Barry? had fallen down and barked his knee.

"For Chrissake!" Mrs. Whalley shrieked, and tossed her identical taffy hair.

Mrs. Hogben watched those Whalleys leave.

"In a brick area, I wouldn't of thought," she remarked to her husband once again.

"All in good time, Myrtle," Councillor Hogben replied as before.

"Of course," she said, "if there are *reasons*."

Because councillors, she knew, did have reasons.

"But that home! And a Customline!"

The saliva of bitterness came in her mouth.

It was Daise who had said: I'm going to enjoy the good things of life—and died in that pokey little hutch, with only a cotton frock to her back. While Myrtle had the liver-coloured brick home—not a single dampmark on the ceilings—she had the washing machine, the septic, the TV, and the cream Holden Special, not to forget her husband. Les Hogben, the councillor. A builder into the bargain.

Now Myrtle stood amongst her things, and would have continued to regret the Ford the Whalleys hadn't paid for, if she hadn't been regretting Daise. It was not so much her sister's death as her life Mrs. Hogben deplored. Still, everybody knew, and there was nothing you could do about it.

"Do you think anybody will come?" Mrs. Hogben asked.

"What do you take me for?" her husband replied. "One of these cleervoyants?"

Mrs. Hogben did not hear.

After giving the matter consideration she had advertised the death in the *Herald*:

> MORROW, Daisy (Mrs.), suddenly, at her residence,
> Showground Road, Sarsaparilla.

There was nothing more you could put. It wasn't fair on Les, a public servant, to rake up relationships. And the *Mrs.*—well, everyone had got into the habit when Daise started going with Cunningham. It seemed sort of natural as things dragged on and on. Don't work yourself up, Myrt, Daise used to say; Jack will when his wife dies. But it was Jack Cunningham who died first. Daise said: It's the way it happened, that's all.

"Do you think Ossie will come?" Councillor Hogben asked his wife slower than she liked.

"I hadn't thought about it," she said.

Which meant she had. She had, in fact, woken in the night, and lain there cold and stiff, as her mind's eye focused on Ossie's runny nose.

Mrs. Hogben rushed at a drawer which somebody—never herself —had left hanging out. She was a thin woman, but wiry.

"Meg?" she called. "Did you polish your shoes?"

Les Hogben laughed behind his closed mouth. He always did when he thought of Daise's parting folly: to take up with that old scabby deadbeat Ossie from down at the showground. But who cared?

No one, unless her family.

Mrs. Hogben dreaded the possibility of Ossie, a Roman Catholic for extra value, standing beside Daise's grave, even if nobody, even if only Mr. Brickle saw.

Whenever the thought of Ossie Coogan crossed Councillor Hogben's mind he would twist the knife in his sister-in-law.

Perhaps, now, he was glad she had died. A small woman, smaller than his wife, Daise Morrow was large by nature. Whenever she dropped in she was all around the place. Yarn her head off if she got the chance. It got so as Les Hogben could not stand hearing her laugh. Pressed against her in the hall once. He had forgotten that, or almost. How Daise laughed then. I'm not so short of men I'd pick me own brother-in-law. Had he pressed? Not all that much, not intentional, anyway. So the incident had been allowed to fade, dim as the brown-linoleum hall, in Councillor Hogben's mind.

"There's the phone, Leslie."

It was his wife.

"I'm too upset," she said, "to answer."

And began to cry.

Easing his crutch Councillor Hogben went into the hall.

It was good old Horrie Last.

"Yairs . . . yairs . . ." said Mr. Hogben, speaking into the telephone which his wife kept swabbed with Breath-o'-Pine. "Yairs . . . Eleven, Horrie . . . from Barranugli . . . from Jackson's Personal . . . Yairs, that's decent of you, Horrie."

"Horrie Last," Councillor Hogben reported to his wife, "is gunna put in an appearance."

If no one else, a second councillor for Daise, Myrtle Hogben was consoled.

What could you do? Horrie Last put down the phone. He and Les had stuck together. Teamed up to catch the more progressive vote. Hogben and Last had developed the shire. Les had built Horrie's home. Lasts had sold Hogbens theirs. If certain people were spreading the rumour that Last and Hogben had caused a contraction of the Green Belt, then certain people failed to realize the term itself implied flexibility.

"What did you tell them?" asked Mrs. Last.

"Said I'd go," her husband said, doing things to the change in his pocket.

He was a short man, given to standing with his legs apart.

Georgina Last withheld her reply. Formally of interest, her shape suggested she had been made out of several scones joined together in the baking.

"Daise Morrow," said Horrie Last, "wasn't such a bad sort."

Mrs. Last did not answer.

So he stirred the money in his pocket harder, hoping perhaps it would emulsify. He wasn't irritated, mind you, by his wife—who had brought him a parcel of property, as well as a flair for real estate —but had often felt he might have done a dash with Daise Morrow on the side. Wouldn't have minded betting old Les Hogben had tinkered a bit with his wife's sister. Helped her buy her home, they said. Always lights on at Daise's place after dark. Postman left her mail on the veranda instead of in the box. In summer, when the men went round to read the meters, she's ask them in for a glass of beer. Daise knew how to get service.

Georgina Last cleared her throat.

"Funerals are not for women," she declared, and took up a cardigan she was knitting for a cousin.

"You didn't do your shoes!" Mrs. Hogben protested.

"I did," said Meg. "It's the dust. Don't know why we bother to clean shoes at all. They always get dirty again."

She stood there looking awful in the school uniform. Her cheeks were hollow from what she read could only be despair.

"A person must keep to her principles," Mrs. Hogben said, and added: "Dadda is bringing round the car. Where's your hat, dear? We'll be ready to leave in two minutes."

"Arr, Mum! The hat?"

That old school hat. It had shrunk already a year ago, but had to see her through.

"You wear it to church, don't you?"

"But this isn't church!"

"It's as good as. Besides, you owe it to your aunt," Mrs. Hogben said, to win.

Meg went and got her hat. They were going out through the fuchsia bushes, past the plaster pixies, which Mrs. Hogben had trained her child to cover with plastic at the first drops of rain. Meg Hogben hated the sight of those corny old pixies, even after the plastic cones had snuffed them out.

It was sad in the car, dreamier. As she sat looking out through the window, the tight panama perched on her head lost its power to humiliate. Her always persistent, grey eyes, under the line of dark fringe, had taken up the search again: she had never yet looked enough. Along the road they passed the house in which her aunt, they told her, had died. The small, pink, tilted house, standing amongst the carnation plants, had certainly lost some of its life. Or the glare had drained the colour from it. How the mornings used to sparkle in which Aunt Daise went up and down between the rows, her gown dragging heavy with dew, binding with bast the fuzzy flowers by handfuls and handfuls. Auntie's voice clear as morning. No one, she called, could argue they look stiff when they're bunched tight eh Meg what would you say they remind you of? But you never knew the answers to the sort of things people asked. Frozen fireworks, Daise suggested. Meg loved the idea of it, she loved Daise. Not so frozen either, she dared. The sun getting at the wet flowers broke them up and made them spin.

And the clovey scent rose up in the stale-smelling car, and smote Meg Hogben, out of the reeling heads of flowers, their cold stalks dusted with blue. Then she knew she would write a poem about Aunt Daise and the carnations. She wondered she hadn't thought of it before.

At that point the passengers were used most brutally as the car entered on a chain of potholes. For once Mrs. Hogben failed to invoke the Main Roads Board. She was asking herself whether Ossie could be hiding in there behind the blinds. Or whether, whether. She fished for her second handkerchief. Prudence had induced her to bring two—the good one with the lace insertion for use beside the grave.

"The weeds will grow like one thing," her voice blared, "now that they'll have their way."

Then she began to unfold the less important of her handkerchiefs.

Myrtle Morrow had always been the sensitive one. Myrtle had understood the Bible. Her needlework, her crochet doilys had taken prizes at country shows. No one had fiddled such pathos out of the pianola. It was Daise who loved flowers, though. It's a moss-rose, Daise had said, sort of rolling it round on her tongue, while she was still a little thing.

When she had had her cry, Mrs. Hogben remarked: "Girls don't know they're happy until it's too late."

Thus addressed, the other occupants of the car did not answer. They knew they were not expected to.

Councillor Hogben drove in the direction of Barranugli. He had arranged his hat before leaving. He removed a smile the mirror reminded him was there. Although he no longer took any risks in a re-election photograph by venturing out of the past, he often succeeded in the fleshy present. But now, in difficult circumstances, he was exercising his sense of duty. He drove, he drove, past the retinosperas, heavy with their own gold, past the lagerstroemias, their pink sugar running into mildew.

Down at the dump Whalleys were having an argument about whether the beer was to be drunk on arrival or after they had developed a thirst.

"Keep it, then!" Mum Whalley turned her back. "What was the point of buyin' it cold if you gotta wait till it hots up? Anyways," she said, "I thought the beer was an excuse for comin'."

"Arr, stuff it!" says Wal. "A dump's business, ain't it? With or without beer. Ain't it? Any day of the week."

He saw she had begun to sulk. He saw her rather long breasts floating around inside her dress. Silly cow! He laughed. But cracked a bottle.

Barry said he wanted a drink.

You could hear the sound of angry suction as his mum's lips called off a swig.

"I'm not gunna stand by and watch any kid of mine," said the wet lips, "turn 'isself into a bloody dipso!"

Her eyes were at their blazing bluest. Perhaps it was because Wal Whalley admired his wife that he continued to desire her.

But Lummy pushed off on his own. When his mum went crook, and swore, he was too aware of the stumps of teeth, the rotting brown of nastiness. It was different, of course, if you swore yourself. Sometimes it was unavoidable.

Now he avoided by slipping away, between the old mattresses, and boots the sun had buckled up. Pitfalls abounded: the rusty traps of open tins lay in wait for guiltless ankles, the necks of broken bottles might have been prepared to gash a face. So he went thoughtfully, his feet scuffing the leaves of stained asbestos, crunching the torso of a celluloid doll. Here and there it appeared as though trash might win. The onslaught of metal was pushing the scrub into the gully. But in many secret, steamy pockets, a rout was in progress: seeds had been sown in the lumps of grey, disintegrating kapok and the laps of burst chairs, the coils of springs, locked in the spirals of wirier vines, had surrendered to superior resilience. Somewhere on the edge of the whole shambles a human ally, before retiring, had lit a fire, which by now the green had almost choked, leaving a stench of smoke to compete with the sicklier one of slow corruption.

Lum Whalley walked with a grace of which he himself had never been aware. He had had about enough of this rubbish jazz. He would have liked to know how to live neat. Like Darkie Black. Everything in its place in the cabin of Darkie's trailer. Suddenly his throat yearned for Darkie's company. Darkie's hands, twisting the wheel, appeared to control the whole world.

A couple of strands of barbed wire separated Sarsaparilla dump from Sarsaparilla cemetery. The denominations were separated too, but there you had to tell by the names, or by the angels and things the RIPs went in for. Over in what must have been the Church of England Alf Herbert was finishing Mrs. Morrow's grave. He had reached the clay, and the going was heavy. The clods fell resentfully.

If what they said about Mrs. Morrow was true, then she had lived it up all right. Lum Whalley wondered what, supposing he had met her walking towards him down a bush track, smiling. His skin tingled. Lummy had never done a girl, although he pretended he had, so as to hold his own with the kids. He wondered if a girl, if that sourpuss Meg Hogben. Would of bitten as likely as not. Lummy felt a bit afraid, and returned to thinking of Darkie Black, who never talked about things like that.

Presently he moved away. Alf Herbert, leaning on his shovel, could have been in need of a yarn. Lummy was not prepared to yarn. He turned back into the speckled bush, into the pretences of a shade. He lay down under a banksia, and opened his fly to look at himself. But pretty soon got sick of it.

The procession from Barranugli back to Sarsaparilla was hardly what you would have called a procession: the Reverend Brickle, the Hogbens' Holden, Horrie's Holden, following the smaller of Jackson's hearses. In the circumstances they were doing things cheap— there was no reason for splashing it around. At Sarsaparilla Mr. Gill joined in, sitting high in that old Chev. It would have been practical, Councillor Hogben sighed, to join the hearse at Sarsaparilla. Old Gill was only there on account of Daise being his customer for years. A grocer lacking in enterprise. Daise had stuck to him, she said, because she liked him. Well, if that was what you put first, but where did it get you?

At the last dip before the cemetery a disembowelled mattress from the dump had begun to writhe across the road. It looked like a kind of monster from out of the depths of somebody's mind, the part a decent person ignored.

"Ah, dear! At the cemetery too!" Mrs. Hogben protested. "I wonder the Council," she added, in spite of her husband.

"All right, Myrtle," he said between his teeth. "I made a mental note."

Councillor Hogben was good at that.

"And the Whalleys on your own doorstep," Mrs. Hogben moaned.

The things she had seen on hot days, in front of their kiddies too.

The hearse had entered the cemetery gate. They had reached the bumpy stage toppling over the paspalum clumps, before the thinner, bush grass. All around, the leaves of the trees presented so many grey blades. Not even a magpie to put heart into a Christian. But Alf Herbert came forward, his hand dusted with yellow clay, to guide the hearse between the Methoes and the Presbyterians, onto Church of England ground.

Jolting had shaken Mrs. Hogben's grief up to the surface again. Mr. Brickle was impressed. He spoke for a moment of the near and dear. His hands were kind and professional in helping her out.

But Meg jumped. And landed. It was a shock to hear a stick crack so loud. Perhaps it was what Mum would have called irreverent. At the same time her banana-coloured panama fell off her head into the tussocks.

It was really a bit confusing at the grave. Some of the men helped with the coffin, and Councillor Last was far too short.

Then Mrs. Hogben saw, she saw, from out of the lace handkerchief, it was that Ossie Coogan she saw, standing the other side of the grave. Had old Gill given him a lift? Ossie, only indifferently buttoned, stood snivelling behind the mound of yellow clay.

Nothing would have stopped his nose. Daise used to say: You don't want to be frightened, Ossie, not when I'm here, see? But she wasn't any longer. So now he was afraid. Excepting Daise, Protestants had always frightened him. Well, I'm nothing, she used to say, nothing that you could pigeonhole, but love what we are given to love.

Myrtle Hogben was ropeable, if only because of what Councillor Last must think. She would have liked to express her feelings in words, if she could have done so without giving offence to God.

Then the ants ran up her legs, for she was standing on a nest, and her body cringed before the teeming injustices.

Daise, she had protested the day it all began, whatever has come over you? The sight of her sister had made her run out leaving the white sauce to burn. Wherever will you take him? He's sick, said Daise. *But you can't*, Myrtle Hogben cried. For there was her sister Daise pushing some old deadbeat in a barrow. All along Showground Road people had come out of homes to look. Daise appeared smaller pushing the wheelbarrow down the hollow and up the hill. Her hair was half uncoiled. *You can't! You can't!* Myrtle called. But Daise could, and did.

When all the few people were assembled at the graveside in their good clothes, Mr. Brickle opened the book, though his voice soon suggested he needn't have.

'*I am the resurrection and the life*,' he said.

And Ossie cried. Because he didn't believe it, not when it came to the real thing.

He looked down at the coffin, which was what remained of what he knew. He remembered eating a baked apple, very slowly, the toffee on it. And again the dark of the horse-stall swallowed him up, where he lay hopeless amongst the shit, and her coming at him with the barrow. What do you want? he asked straight out. I came down to the showground, she said, for a bit of honest-to-God manure, I've had those fertilizers, she said, and what are you, are you sick? I live 'ere, he said. And began to cry, and rub the snot from his snivelly nose. After a bit Daise said: We're going back to my place, What's-yer-Name—Ossie. The way she spoke he knew it was true. All the way up the hill in the barrow the wind was giving his eyes gyp, and blowing his thin hair apart. Over the years he had come across one or two lice in his hair, but thought, or hoped he had got rid of them by the time Daise took him up. As she pushed and struggled with the barrow, sometimes she would lean forward, and he felt her warmth, her firm diddies pressed against his back.

'*Lord, let me know mine end, and the number of my days: that I may be certified how long I have to live*,' Mr. Brickle read.

Certified was the word, decided Councillor Hogben looking at that old Ossie.

Who stood there mumbling a few Aspirations, very quiet, on the strength of what they had taught him as a boy.

When all this was under way, all these words of which, she knew, her Auntie Daise would not have approved, Meg Hogben went and got beneath the strands of wire separating the cemetery from the dump. She had never been to the dump before, and her heart was lively in her side. She walked shyly through the bush. She came across an old suspender-belt. She stumbled over a blackened primus.

She saw Lummy Whalley then. He was standing under a banksia twisting at one of its dead heads.

Suddenly they knew there was something neither of them could continue to avoid.

"I came here to the funeral," she said.

She sounded, well, almost relieved.

"Do you come here often?" she asked.

"Nah," he answered, hoarse. "Not here. To dumps, yes."

But her intrusion had destroyed the predetermined ceremony of his life, and caused a trembling in his hand.

"Is there anything to see?" she asked.

"Junk," he said. "Same old junk."

"Have you ever looked at a dead person?"

Because she noticed the trembling of his hand.

"No," he said. "Have you?"

She hadn't. Nor did it seem probable that she would have to now. Not as they began breathing evenly again.

"What do you do with yourself?" he asked.

Then, even though she would have liked to stop herself, she could not. She said: "I write poems. I'm going to write one about my Aunt Daise, like she was, gathering carnations early in the dew."

"What'll you get out of that?"

"Nothing," she said, "I suppose."

But it did not matter.

"What other sorts of pomes do you write?" he asked, twisting at last the dead head of the banksia off.

"I wrote one," she said, "about the things in a cupboard. I wrote about a dream I had. And the smell of rain. That was a bit too short."

He began to look at her then. He had never looked into the eyes of a girl. They were grey and cool, unlike the hot, or burnt-out eyes of a women.

"What are you going to be?" she asked.

"I dunno."

"You're not a white-collar type."

"Eh?"

"I mean you're not for figures, and books, and banks and offices," she said.

He was too disgusted to agree.

"I'm gunna have me own truck. Like Mr. Black. Darkie's got a trailer."

"What?"

"Well," he said, "a semi-trailer."

"Oh," she said, more diffident.

"Darkie took me on a trip to Maryborough. It was pretty tough goin'. Sometimes we drove right through the night. Sometimes we slept on the road. Or in places where you get rooms. Gee, it was good though, shootin' through the country towns at night."

She saw it. She saw the people standing at their doors, frozen in the blocks of yellow light. The rushing of the night made the figures for ever still. All around she could feel the furry darkness, as the semi-trailer roared and bucked, its skeleton of coloured lights. While in the cabin, in which they sat, all was stability and order. If she glanced sideways she could see how his taffy hair shone when raked by the bursts of electric light. They had brought cases with tooth-brushes, combs, one or two things—the pad on which she would write the poem somewhere when they stopped in the smell of sunlight dust ants. But his hands had acquired such mastery over the wheel, it appeared this might never happen. Nor did she care.

"This Mr. Black," she said, her mouth getting thinner, "does he take you with him often?"

"Only once interstate," said Lummy, pitching the banksia head away. "Once in a while short trips."

As they drove they rocked together. He had never been closer to anyone than when bumping against Darkie's ribs. He waited to experience again the little spasm of gratitude and pleasure. He would have liked to wear, and would in time, a striped sweat-shirt like Darkie wore.

"I'd like to go in with Darkie," he said, "when I get a trailer of me own. Darkie's the best friend I got."

With a drawnout shiver of distrust she saw the darker hands, the little black hairs on the backs of the fingers.

"Oh well," she said, withdrawn, "p'raps you will in the end," she said.

On the surrounding graves the brown flowers stood in their jars of browner water. The more top-heavy, plastic bunches had been slapped down by a westerly, but had not come to worse grief than to lie strewn in pale disorder on the uncharitable granite chips.

The heat made Councillor Last yawn. He began to read the carved names, those within sight at least, some of which he had just about forgot. He almost laughed once. If the dead could have sat up in their graves there would have been an argument or two.

'*In the midst of life we are in death,*' said the parson bloke.

JACK CUNNINGHAM
BELOVED HUSBAND OF FLORENCE MARY,

read Horrie Last.

Who would have thought Cunningham, straight as a silky-oak, would fall going up the path to Daise Morrow's place. Horrie used to watch them together, sitting a while on the veranda before going in to their tea. They made no bones about it, because everybody knew. Good teeth Cunningham had. Always a white, well-ironed shirt. Wonder which of the ladies did the laundry. Florence Mary was an invalid, they said. Daise Morrow liked to laugh with men, but for Jack Cunningham she had a silence, promising intimacies at which Horrie Last could only guess, whose own private life had been lived in almost total darkness.

Good Christ, and then there was Ossie. The woman could only have been at heart a perv of a kind you hadn't heard about.

'*Forasmuch as it hath pleased Almighty God of his great mercy to take unto himself the soul . . .*' read Mr. Brickle.

As it was doubtful who should cast the earth, Mr. Gill the grocer did. They heard the handful rattle on the coffin.

The the tears truly ran out of Ossie's scaly eyes. Out of darkness. Out of darkness Daise had called: What's up Ossie, you don't wanta cry. I got the cramps, he answered. They were twisting him. The cramps? she said drowsily. Or do you imagine? If it isn't the cramps it's something else. Could have been. He'd take Daisie's word for it. He was never all that bright since he had the meningitis. Tell you what, Daise said, you come in here, into my bed, I'll warm you, Os, in a jiffy. He listened in the dark to his own snivelling. Arr, Daise, I couldn't he said, I couldn't get a stand, not if you was to give me the jackpot, he said. She sounded very still then. He lay and counted the throbbing of the darkness. Not like that, she said—she didn't laugh at him as he had half expected—besides, she said, it only ever really comes to you once. That way. And at once he was parting the darkness, bumping and shambling to get to her. He had never known it so gentle. Because Daise wasn't afraid. She ran her hands through his hair, on and on like water flowing. She soothed the cramps out of his legs. Until in the end they were breathing in time. Dozing. Then the lad Ossie Coogan rode again down from the mountain, the sound of the snaffle in the blue air, the smell of sweat from under the saddle-cloth, towards the great, flowing river. He rocked and flowed with the motion of the strong, never-ending river, burying his mouth in brown cool water, to drown would have been worth it.

Once during the night Ossie had woken, afraid the distance might have come between them. But Daise was still holding him against her breast. If he had been different, say. Ossie's throat had begun to wobble. Only then, Daise, might have turned different. So he nuzzled against the warm darkness, and was again received.

"If you want to enough, you can do what you want," Meg Hogben insisted.

She had read it in a book, and wasn't altogether convinced, but theories sometimes come to the rescue.

"If you want," she said, kicking a hole in the stony ground.

"Not everything you can't."

"You can!" she said. "But you can!"

She who had never looked at a boy, not right into one, was looking at him as never before.

"That's a lot of crap," he said.

"Well," she admitted, "there are limits."

It made him frown. He was again suspicious. She was acting clever. All those pomes.

But to reach understanding she would have surrendered her cleverness. She was no longer proud of it.

"And what'll happen if you get married? Riding around the country in a truck. How'll your wife like it? Stuck at home with a lot of kids."

"Some of 'em take the wife along. Darkie takes his missus and kids. Not always, like. But now and again. On short runs."

"You didn't tell me Mr. Black was married."

"Can't tell you everything, can I? Not at once."

The women who sat in the drivers' cabins of the semi-trailers he saw as predominantly thin and dark. They seldom returned glances, but wiped their hands on Kleenex, and peered into little mirrors, waiting for their men to show up again. Which in time they had to. So he walked across from the service station, to take possession of his property. Sauntering, frowning slightly, touching the yellow stubble on his chin, he did not bother to look. Glanced sideways perhaps. She was the thinnest, the darkest he knew, the coolest of all the women who sat looking out from the cabin windows of the semi-trailers.

In the meantime they strolled a bit, amongst the rusty tins at Sarsaparilla dump. He broke a few sticks and threw away the pieces. She tore off a narrow leaf and smelled it. She would have liked to smell Lummy's hair.

"Gee, you're fair," she had to say.

"Some are born fair," he admitted.

He began pelting a rock with stones. He was strong, she saw. So many discoveries in a short while were making her tremble at the knees.

And as they rushed through the brilliant light, roaring and lurching, the cabin filled with fair-skinned, taffy children, the youngest of whom she was protecting by holding the palm of her hand behind his neck, as she noticed women do. Occupied in this way, she almost forgot Lum at times, who would pull up, and she would climb down, to rinse the nappies in tepid water, and hang them on a bush to dry.

"All these pomes and things," he said, "I never knew a clever person before."

"But clever isn't any different," she begged, afraid he might not accept her peculiarity and power.

She would go with a desperate wariness from now. She sensed that, if not in years, she was older than Lum, but this was the secret he must never guess: that for all his strength, all his beauty, she was, and must remain the stronger.

"What's that?" he asked, and touched.

But drew back his hand in self-protection.

"A scar," she said. "I cut my wrist opening a tin of condensed milk."

For once she was glad of the paler seam in her freckled skin, hoping that it might heal a breach.

And he looked at her out of his hard blue Whalley eyes. He liked her. Although she was ugly, and clever, and a girl.

"Condensed milk on bread," he said, "that's something I could eat till I bust."

"Oh yes!" she agreed.

She did honestly believe, although she had never thought of it before.

Flies clustered in irregular jet embroideries on the backs of best suits. Nobody bothered any longer to shrug them off. As Alf Herbert grunted against the shovelfuls, dust clogged increasingly, promises settled thicker. Although they had been told they might expect Christ to redeem, it would have been no less incongruous if He had appeared out of the scrub to perform on altars of burning sandstone, a sacrifice for which nobody had prepared them. In any case, the mourners waited—they had been taught to accept whatever might be imposed— while the heat stupefied the remnants of their minds, and inflated their Australian fingers into foreign-looking sausages.

Myrtle Hogben was the first to protest. She broke down—into the wrong handkerchief. *Who shall change our vile body?* The words were more than her decency could bear.

"Easy on it," her husband whispered, putting a finger under her elbow.

She submitted to his sympathy, just as in their life together she had submitted to his darker wishes. Never wanting more than peace, and one or two perquisites.

A thin woman, Mrs. Hogben continued to cry for all the wrongs that had been done her. For Daise had only made things viler. While understanding, yes, at moments. It was girls who really understood, not even women—sisters, sisters. Before events whirled them apart. So Myrtle Morrow was again walking through the orchard, and Daise Morrow twined her arm around her sister; confession filled the air, together with a scent of crushed fermenting apples. Myrtle said: Daise, there's something I'd like to do, I'd like to chuck a lemon into a Salvation Army tuba. Daise giggled. You're a nut, Myrt, she said. But never *vile*. So Myrtle Hogben cried. Once, only once she thought how she'd like to push someone off a cliff, and watch their expression as it happened. But Myrtle had not confessed that.

So Mrs. Hogben cried, for those things she was unable to confess, for anything she might not be able to control.

As the blander words had begun falling, *Our Father*, that she knew by heart, *our daily bread*, she should have felt comforted. She should of. Should of.

Where was Meg, though?

Mrs. Hogben separated herself from the others. Walking stiffly. If any of the men noticed, they took it for granted she had been overcome, or wanted to relieve herself.

She would have liked to relieve herself by calling: "Margaret Meg wherever don't you hear me Me-ehg?" drawing it out thin in anger. But could not cut across a clergyman's words. So she stalked. She was not unlike a guinea-hen, its spotted silk catching on a strand of barbed-wire.

When they had walked a little farther, round and about, anywhere, they overheard voices.

"What's that?" asked Meg.

"Me mum and dad," Lummy said. "Rousin' about somethun or other."

Mum Whalley had just found two bottles of unopened beer. Down at the dump. Waddayaknow. Must be something screwy somewhere.

"Could of put poison in it," her husband warned.

"Poison? My arse!" she shouted. "That's because *I* found it!"

"Whoever found it," he said, "who's gunna drink a coupla bottlesa hot beer?"

"I am!" she said.

"When what we brought was good an' cold?"

He too was shouting a bit. She behaved unreasonable at times.

"Who wanted ter keep what we brought? Till it got good an' hot!" she shrieked.

Sweat was running down both the Whalleys.

Suddenly Lum felt he wanted to lead this girl out of earshot. He had just about had the drunken sods. He would have liked to find himself walking with his girl over mown lawn, like at the Botanical Gardens, a green turf giving beneath their leisured feet. Statues pointed a way through the glare, to where they finally sat, under enormous shiny leaves, looking out at boats on water. They unpacked their cut lunch from its layers of fresh tissue-paper.

"They're rough as bags," Lummy explained.

"I don't care," Meg Hogben assured.

Nothing on earth could make her care—was it more, or was it less? She walked giddily behind him, past a rusted fuel-stove, over a field of deathly feltex. Or ran, or slid, to keep up. Flowers would have wilted in her hands, if she hadn't crushed them brutally, to keep her balance. Somewhere in their private labyrinth Meg Hogben had lost her hat.

When they were farther from the scene of anger, and a silence of heat had descended again, he took her little finger, because it seemed natural to do so, after all they had experienced. They swung hands for a while, according to some special law of motion.

Till Lum Whalley frowned, and threw the girl's hand away.

If she accepted his behaviour it was because she no longer believed in what he did, only in what she knew he felt. That might have been the trouble. She was so horribly sure, he would have to resist to the last moment of all. As a bird, singing in the prickly tree under which they found themselves standing, seemed to cling to the air. Then his fingers took control. She was amazed at the hardness of his boy's body. The tremors of her flinty skin, the membrane of the white sky appalled him. Before fright and expectation melted their mouths. And they took little grateful sips of each other. Holding up their throats in between. Like birds drinking.

Ossie could no longer see Alf Herbert's shovel working at the earth.

"Never knew a man cry at a funeral," Councillor Hogben complained, very low, although he was ripe enough to burst.

If you could count Ossie as a man, Councillor Last suggested in a couple of noises.

But Ossie could not see or hear, only Daise, still lying on that upheaval of a bed. Seemed she must have burst a button, for her breasts stood out from her. He would never forget how they laboured against the heavy yellow morning light. In the early light, the flesh turned yellow, sluggish. What's gunna happen to me, Daisy? It'll be decided, Os, she said, like it is for any of us. I ought to know, she said, to tell you, but give me time to rest a bit, to get me breath. Then he got down on his painful knees. He put his mouth to Daise's neck. Her skin tasted terrible bitter. The great glistening river, to which the lad Ossie Coogan had ridden jingling down from the mountain, was slowing into thick, yellow mud. Himself an old, scabby man attempting to refresh his forehead in the last pothole.

Mr. Brickle said: '*We give thee hearty thanks for that it hath pleased thee to deliver this our sister out of the miseries of this sinful world.*'

"No! No!" Ossie protested, so choked nobody heard, though it was vehement enough in its intention.

As far as he could understand, nobody wanted to be delivered. Not him, not Daise, anyways. When you could sit together by the fire on winter nights baking potatoes under the ashes.

It took Mrs. Hogben some little while to free her *crêpe de Chine* from the wire. It was her nerves, not to mention Meg on her mind. In the circumstances she tore herself worse, and looked up to see her child, just over there, without shame, in a rubbish tip, kissing the Whalley boy. What if Meg was another of Daise? It was in the blood, you couldn't deny.

Mrs. Hogben did not exactly call, but released some kind of noise from her extended throat. Her mouth was too full of tongue to find room for words as well.

Then Meg looked. She was smiling.

She said: "Yes, Mother."

She came and got through the wire, tearing herself also a little.

Mrs. Hogben said, and her teeth clicked: "You chose the likeliest time. Your aunt hardly in her grave. Though, of course, it is only your aunt, if anyone, to blame."

The accusations were falling fast. Meg could not answer. Since joy had laid her open, she had forgotten how to defend herself.

"If you were a little bit younger"—Mrs. Hogben lowered her voice because they had begun to approach the parson—"I'd break a stick on you, my girl."

Meg tried to close her face, so that nobody would see inside.

"What will they say?" Mrs. Hogben moaned. "What ever will happen to us?"

"What, Mother?" Meg asked.

"You're the only one can answer that. And someone else."

Then Meg looked over her shoulder and recognized the hate which, for a while, she had forgotten existed. And at once her face closed up tight, like a fist. She was ready to protect whatever justly needed her protection.

Even if their rage, grief, contempt, boredom, apathy, and sense of injustice had not occupied the mourners, it is doubtful whether they would have realized the dead woman was standing amongst them. The risen dead—that was something which happened, or didn't happen, in the Bible. Fanfares of light did not blare for a loose woman in floral cotton. Those who had known her remembered her by now only fitfully in some of the wooden attitudes of life. How could they have heard, let alone believed in, her affirmation? Yet Daise Morrow continued to proclaim.

Listen, all of you, I'm not leaving, except those who want to be left, and even those aren't so sure—they might be parting with a bit of themselves. Listen to me, all you successful no-hopers, all you who wake in the night, jittery because something may be excaping you, or terrified to think there may never have been anything to find. Come to me, you sour women, public servants, anxious children, and old scabby, desperate men. . . .

Physically small, words had seemed too big for her. She would push back her hair in exasperation. And take refuge in acts. Because her feet had been planted in the earth, she would have been the last to resent its pressure now, while her always rather hoarse voice continued to exhort in borrowed syllables of dust.

Truly, we needn't experience tortures, unless we build chambers in our minds to house instruments of hatred in. Don't you know, my darling creatures, that death isn't death, unless it's the death of love? Love should be the greatest explosion it is reasonable to expect. Which sends us whirling, spinning, creating millions of other worlds. Never destroying.

From the fresh mound which they had formed unimaginatively in the shape of her earthly body, she persisted in appealing to them.
I will comfort you. If you will let me. Do you understand?
But nobody did, as they were only human.
For ever and ever. And ever.
Leaves quivered lifted in the first suggestion of a breeze.
So the aspirations of Daise Morrow were laid alongside her small-boned wrists, smooth thighs and pretty ankles. She surrendered at last to the formal crumbling which, it was hoped, would make an honest woman of her.
But had not altogether died.
Meg Hogben had never exactly succeeded in interpreting her aunt's messages, nor could she have witnessed the last moments of the burial, because the sun was dazzling her. She did experience,

however, along with a shiver of recollected joy, the down laid against her cheek, a little breeze trickling through the moist roots of her hair, as she got inside the car, and waited for whatever next.

Well, they had dumped Daise.

Somewhere the other side of the wire there was the sound of smashed glass and discussion.

Councillor Hogben went across to the parson and said the right kind of things. Half-turning his back he took a note or two from his wallet, and immediately felt disengaged. If Horrie Last had been there Les Hogben would have gone back at this point and put an arm round his mate's shoulder, to feel whether he was forgiven for unorthodox behaviour in a certain individual—no relation, mind you, but. In any case Horrie had driven away.

Horrie drove, or flew, across the dip in which the dump joined the cemetery. For a second Ossie Coogan's back flickered inside a spiral of dust.

Ought to give the coot a lift, Councillor Last suspected, and wondered, as he drove on, whether a man's better intentions were worth, say, half a mark in the event of their remaining unfulfilled. For by now it was far too late to stop, and there was that Ossie, in the mirror, turning off the road towards the dump, where, after all, the bugger belonged.

All along the road, stones, dust, and leaves, were settling back into normally unemotional focus. Seated in his high Chev, Gill the grocer, a slow man, who carried his change in a little, soiled canvas bag, looked ahead through thick lenses. He was relieved to realize he would reach home almost on the dot of three-thirty, and his wife pour him his cup of tea. Whatever he understood was punctu l, decent, docketed.

As he drove, prudently, he avoided the mattress the dump had spewed, from under the wire, half across the road. Strange things had happened at the dump on and off, the grocer recollected. Screaming girls, their long tight pants ripped to tatters. An arm in a sugar-bag, and not a sign of the body that went with it. Yet some found peace amongst the refuse: elderly derelict men, whose pale, dead, fish eyes never divulged anything of what they had lived, and women with blue, metho skins, hanging around the doors of shacks put together from sheets of bark and rusty iron. Once an old down-andout had crawled amongst the rubbish apparently to rot, and did, before they sent for the constable, to examine what seemed at first a bundle of stinking rags.

Mr. Gill accelerated judiciously.

They were driving. They were driving.

Alone in the back of the ute, Lum Whalley sat forward on the empty crate, locking his hands between his knees, as he forgot having seen Darkie do. He was completely independent now. His face had been reshaped by the wind. He liked that. It felt good. He no longer resented the junk they were dragging home, the rust flaking off at his feet, the roll of mouldy feltex trying to fur his nostrils up. Nor his family—discussing, or quarrelling, you could never tell— behind him in the cabin.

The Whalleys were in fact singing. One of their own versions. They always sang their own versions, the two little boys joining in.

> Show me the way to go home,
> I'm not too tired for bed.
> I had a little drink about an hour ago,
> And it put ideas in me head . . .

Suddenly Mum Whalley began belting into young Garry—or was it Barry?

"Wadda *you* know, eh? Wadda *you*?"

"What's bitten yer?" her husband shouted. "Can't touch a drop without yer turn nasty!"

She didn't answer. He could tell a grouse was coming, though. The little boy had started to cry, but only as a formality.

"It's that bloody Lummy," Mrs Whalley complained.

"Why pick on Lum?"

"Give a kid all the love and affection, and waddayaget?"

Wal grunted. Abstractions always embarrassed him.

Mum Whalley spat out of the window, and the spit came back at her.

"Arrrr!" she protested.

And fell silenter. It was not strictly Lum, not if you was honest. It was nothing. Or everything. The grog. You was never ever gunna touch it no more. Until you did. And that bloody Lummy, what with the caesar and all, you was never ever going again with a man.

"That's somethink a man don't understand."

38

"What?" asked Wal.

"A caesar."

"Eh?"

You just couldn't discuss with a man. So you had to get into bed with him. Grogged up half the time. That was how she copped the twins, after she had said never ever.

"Stop cryun, for Chrissake!" Mum Whalley coaxed, touching the little boy's blowing hair.

Everything was sad.

"Wonder how often they bury someone alive," she said.

Taking a corner in his cream Holden Councillor Hogben felt quite rakish, but would restrain himself at the critical moment from skidding the wrong side of the law.

They were driving and driving, in long, lovely bursts, and at the corners, in semi-circular swirls.

On those occasions in her life when she tried to pray, begging for an experience, Meg Hogben would fail, but return to the attempt with clenched teeth. Now she did so want to think of her dead aunt with love, and the image blurred repeatedly. She was superficial, that was it. Yet, each time she failed, the landscape leaped lovingly. They were driving under the telephone wires. She could have translated any message into the language of peace. The wind burning, whenever it did not cut cold, left the stable things alone: the wooden houses stuck beside the road, the trunks of willows standing round the brown saucer of a dam. Her too candid, grey eyes seemed to have deepened, as though to accommodate all she still had to see, feel.

It was lovely curled on the back seat, even with Mum and Dad in front.

"I haven't forgotten, Margret," Mum called over her shoulder.

Fortunately Dadda wasn't interested enough to inquire.

"Did Daise owe anything on the home?" Mrs. Hogben asked. "She was never at all practical."

Councillor Hogben cleared his throat.

"Give us time to find out," he said.

Mrs. Hogben respected her husband for the things which she, secretly, did not understand: Time the mysterious, for instance, Business, and worst of all, the Valuer General.

"I wonder Jack Cunningham," she said, "took up with Daise. He was a fine man. Though Daise had a way with her."

They were driving. They were driving.

When Mrs. Hogben remembered the little ring in plaited gold.

"Do you think those undertakers are honest?"

"Honest?" her husband repeated.

A dubious word.

"Yes," she said. "That ring that Daise."

You couldn't very well accuse. When she had plucked up the courage she would go down to the closed house. The thought of it made her chest tighten. She would go inside, and feel her way into the back corners of drawers, where perhaps a twist of tissue-paper. But the closed houses of the dead frightened Mrs. Hogben, she had to admit. The stuffiness, the light strained through brown holland. It was as if you were stealing, though you weren't.

And then those Whalleys creeping up.

They were driving and driving, the ute and the sedan almost rubbing on each other.

"No one who hasn't had a migraine," cried Mrs. Hogben, averting her face, "can guess what it feels like."

Her husband had heard that before.

"It's a wonder it don't leave you," he said. "They say it does when you've passed a certain age."

Though they weren't passing the Whalleys he would make every effort to throw the situation off. Wal Whalley leaning forward, though not so far you couldn't see the hair bursting out of the front of his shirt. His wife thumping his shoulder. They were singing one of their own versions. Her gums all watery.

So they drove and drove.

"I could sick up, Leslie," Mrs. Hogben gulped, and fished for her lesser handkerchief.

The Whalley twins were laughing through their taffy forelocks.

At the back of the ute that sulky Lum turned towards the opposite direction. Meg Hogben was looking her farthest off. Any sign of acknowledgement had been so faint the wind had immediately blown it off their faces. As Meg and Lummy sat, they held their sharp but comforting knees. They sank their chins as low as they would go. They lowered their eyes, as if they had seen enough for the present, and wished to cherish what they knew.

The warm core of certainty settled stiller as driving faster the wind paid out the telephone wires the fences the flattened heads of grey grass always raising themselves again again again.

George Lamming

In a B.B.C. talk Stuart Hall discussed the collective memories of the West Indians:

> The first is the peasant and village memory. . . . The second is the incredible jumble and scurry of life in the downtown section of any of the bigger towns and cities of the Caribbean. . . . The third is not of the West Indies at all. It is the memory of the freezing bed-sitter in Earls Court or W.10; it is the sad, bitter-sweet memory of emigration.

It is with the third of these memories that this story deals.

Since 1945 there has been a steady flow of emigrants from the New World to the Old. Prior to leaving their homes the West Indians regarded England as the mother country, as a home across the sea where they were always welcome. They were soon to realize that they had been living in an illusion. Instead of a welcome they were met with open hostility, rejection, exploitation and racial prejudice. Quite often they discovered they had exchanged a warm slum for a cold one; it was not only the warmth of climate that was lost but of community as well. For even if they lived in a slum in the West Indies they were sustained by the collective life such as we find in Naipaul's *Miguel Street*. But no such community existed in London. Another West Indian writer, Sam Selvon, describes the life in London through the eyes of one of his characters:

> 'It have people living in London who don't know what happening in the room next to them, far more the street, or how other people living. London is a place like that.'
>
> (from *The Lonely Londoners*)

Such a way of living is completely alien to the West Indians and to counteract its loneliness they have formed their own smaller communities within the larger one. This of course has the effect of isolating them still further from the community as a whole.

It is not only the West Indian's colour that sets him apart; it is his temperament as well. The coldness and aloofness of the Englishman is one of the first impressions that the West Indians receive. One of the newly arrived emigrants in a novel of Lamming's comments:

> 'Look Lilian look de ol' geyser in de corner like de whole worl' come to a standstill—he eyes don't wink when he pull that pipe an' he lookin' only Gawd knows where he lookin' like he ain't got eyes in his head—is the way they is in dis country—no talk till you talk, no speak till you speak. No notice till you notice, no nothin' till you somethin'—'tis what ah mean when ah says England.'

(from The Emigrants)

The first of the collective memories mentioned by Stuart Hall, suggests a major reason for the temperamental differences; the question of origins. It is on this that Lamming places much emphasis. He believes that the basic feature of the West Indian background is the peasant origin and he regards this contact with the soil as a source of life. The characters of his novels and stories are invariably of peasant origin and display all the simplicity, directness and honesty of men close to the soil. They may lack the sophistication of the Englishman but to compensate they have an energy, a sheer delight in life. 'The soil may be unrefined," Lamming says, "but it is good warm fertile earth.' These people are not afraid of expressing their emotions; they have vivid imaginations and will readily let them run wild; they are adept at living in a fantasy world, perhaps because that of reality so often proves uncongenial.

The events of this story, the exotic names, the richness of the language, all bear witness to the truth of the above statements. Lamming's opening paragraph places us in the world of the West Indian exile, the huge lonely city, the basement rooms where they are huddled together for emotional warmth. Beresford is getting married because '"he don't want to roam like a bush beast in this London jungle"'. On the other hand, foreign and remote as it is from his immediate experience, he still wants to show that he belongs to England and therefore tries to "do it as the done thing is doed".

In his book *The Pleasures of Exile*, Lamming tells of an incident that occurred at Westminster Abbey during the celebration of the coronation. He and another West Indian, Thomasos, had been sent by the B.B.C. to report the ceremony:

He [Thomasos] saw a black man coming towards him. The man was a member of an official party from the West Indies. The people of his island had chosen him as the leader who would represent their feeling; tell by his presence alone their delight on this day. And he was dressed to match the fantasy of the morning. It is not clear why or how he selected the articles of his regalia; but it must have struck the English eye as a most 'extraordinary innovation'. To Thomasos, who had now halted, this man was simply playing the ass. That hilarious get-up might have been perfect on carnival day in Port-of-Spain. But in the Abbey!

The black man in question was not only wearing a morning suit, but like Lice-Preserver, he also wore a sword. What was Thomasos' reaction? He fled for he 'wasn't going to let any of these English people think that this sword-man and me come from the same part of the world'. The "arrows of civilization" had pierced Thomasos' pride and he ran.

The parallels to this story are obvious. Beresford and Knickerbocker desired like the representative to express their delight in the day, they too dressed to match the fantasy of the event. Snooker's and Flo's first reactions were the same as Thomasos'. But here the parallel ends. For the "arrows of civilization" were unable to pierce these people. Unlike Thomasos, they had not been corrupted by a "superior" culture whose values, Lamming maintains, are gravely in doubt. The reactions of Flo, of the boys from "back home" bear witness to the peasant virtues that Lamming is extolling.

Lamming believes that it is in the West Indian novel that:

> For the first time the West Indian peasant became other than a cheap source of labour. He became, through the novelist's eye, a living existence, living in silence and joy and fear, involved in riot and carnival. It is the West Indian novel that has restored the West Indian peasant to his true and original status of personality.
>
> (from *The Pleasures of Exile*)

It would be quite true to say that in this story Lamming has contributed much to the restoration. "A Wedding in Spring" bears testimony to the statement that the West Indian writer has a genius for the comic. It reminds us also of the very thin line between the comic and the tragic. *A. R.*

A Wedding in Spring

London was their first lesson in cities. The solitude and hugeness of the place had joined their lives more closely than ever; but it was the force of similar childhoods which now threatened to separate them: three men and a woman, island people from the Caribbean, who waited in separate rooms of the same basement, sharing the nervousness of the night.

The wedding was only a day away.

Snooker thought he could hear the sweat spilling out of his pores. Talking to himself, old-woman-like in trouble, he started: "Is downright, absolute stupid to make me harness myself in dis mornin' costume. . . . I ain't no Prince Philip or ever want to be. . . ."

A pause drew his attention to the morning suit he had rented. The top hat sat on its crown, almost imitating itself. It provoked Snooker. He watched it, swore at it, then stooped as though he was going to sit on it.

"Now what you think you doin'?"

Snooker was alerted. He heard the closing creak of the door and the blurred chuckle of Knickerbocker's voice redeeming the status of the top hat.

Snooker was silent. He watched Knickerbocker hold the top hat out like some extraordinary fruit in his hand.

"Is what Beresford think it is at all?" he said, turning his back on the suit to face Knickerbocker. "My body, not to mention my face, ain't shape for dis kind o' get-up."

"Even de beggar can be king," said Knickerbocker, "an' dis is de kind o' headpiece kings does wear." He cuddled the top hat to his chest. "An' tomorrow," he added, lifting his head towards Snooker, "I goin' to play king."

"You goin' to play jackass," Snooker said sharply.

"So what?" Knickerbocker smiled. "Christ did ride on one."

"Is ride these clothes goin' ride you tomorrow," said Snooker, " 'cause you ain't got no practice in wearin' them."

"You goin' see who ride what," said Knickerbocker, "I sittin' in de back o' dat limousine jus' so, watch me, Snooker." He was deter-

44

mined to prove his passion for formal dress. He had lowered his body on to the chair, fitting the top hat on his head at precisely the angle his imagination had shaped. He crossed his legs, and plucked at the imaginary seams of his morning trousers. The chair leaned with him while he felt the air for the leather rest which would hold his hand.

Snooker refused to look. But Knickerbocker had already entered the fantasy which the wedding would make real. His head was loud with bells and his eyes turned wild round the crowd, hilarious with praise, as they acknowledged his white gloved welcome. Even the police had removed their helmets in homage to the splendour which he had brought to a drab and enfeebled London. He was teaching the English their own tune. So he didn't hear Snooker's warning until the leather rest refused his hand and the crowd vanished into the shadows which filled the room. The chair had collapsed like a pack of cards under Knickerbocker's body. He looked like a cripple on his back.

Now he was afraid, and he really frightened Snooker too, the way he probed his hands with fearful certainty under and across his thighs. His guess was right. There was a split the size of a sword running down the leg and through the crutch of the only pair of trousers he owned.

"You break up my bes' chair," Snooker said sadly, carrying the top hat like wet crockery across the room. It had fallen into the sink.

The crisis had begun. Knickerbocker crouched on all fours, his buttocks cocked at the mirror, to measure the damage he had done. The basement was still: Knickerbocker considering his black exposure while Snooker collected the wreckage in both hands, wondering how he could fit his chair together again. They didn't speak, but they could hear, behind the door, a quiet tumble of furniture, and after an interval of silence, the sullen ticking of the clock in Flo's room.

She was alone, twisting her hair into knotty plaits that rose like spikes out of her skull. She did not only disapprove of her brother's wedding but she also thought it a conspiracy against all they had learnt. Preoccupied and disdainful, she saw the Vaseline melt and slip like frying lard over her hands. The last plait done, she stuck the comb like a plough into the low shrub of hair at the back of her neck. She scrubbed her ears with her thumb; stretched the under

45

lid of each eye to tell her health; and finally gave her bottom a belligerent slap with both hands. She was in a fighting mood.

"As if he ain't done born poor," she said, caught in that whispering self-talk which filled the basement night. "Borrowin' an' hockin' every piece o' possession to make a fool o' himself, an' worse still dat he should go sell Snooker his bicycle to rent mornin' suit an' limousine. Gran Gran. . . . Gawd res' her in de grave, would go wild if she know what Beresford doin' . . . an' for what . . . for who he bringin' his own downfall."

It was probably too late to make Beresford change his mind: what with all those West Indians he had asked to drop in after the ceremony for a drink: the Jamaican with the macaw face who arrived by chance every Sunday at supper time, and Caruso, the calypsonian, who made his living by turning every rumour into a song that could scandalize your name for life. She was afraid of Caruso, with his malicious tongue, and his sly, secretive, slanderous manner. Moreover Caruso never travelled without his gang: Slip Disk, Toodles and Square Dick; then there were Lice-Preserver, Gunner, Crim, Clarke Gable Number Two, and the young Sir Winston. They were all from "back home", idle, godless, and greedy. Then she reflected that they were not really idle. They worked with Beresford in the same tyre factory.

"But idle or no idle," she frowned, "I ain't want Beresford marry no white woman. If there goin' be any disgrace, let me disgrace him first."

She was plotting against the wedding. She wanted to bribe Snooker and Knickerbocker into a sudden disagreement with her brother. Knickerbocker's disapproval would have been particularly damaging since it was he who had introduced the English girl to Beresford. And there was something else about Knickerbocker that Flo knew.

The door opened on Snooker who was waiting in the passage for Knickerbocker. Flo watched him in the dark and counted three before leaning her hand on his head. Her anger had given way to a superb display of weakness: a woman outraged, defenceless, and innocent of words which could tell her feeling.

"Snooker."

"What happen now?"

"I want all you two speak to Beresford," she said. Her voice was a whimper appropriate with grief.

46

"Let the man make his own bed," said Snooker, "is he got to lie down in it."

"But is this Englan' turn his head an' make him lose his senses." Flo crouched lower, tightening her hand against Snooker's neck.

"He kept his head all right," said Snooker, "but is the way he hearken what his mother say, like he walkin' in infancy all life long."

"Ma wasn't ever goin' encourage him in trouble like this," Flo said.

"Is too late to change anything," said Snooker, "except these kiss-me-tail mornin' clothes. Is like playin' ju-ju warrior with all that silk cravat an' fish-shape' frock they call a coat. I ain't wearin' it."

"Forget 'bout that," said Flo, "is the whole thing we got to stop complete."

Knickerbocker was slipping through the shadows, silent and massive as a wall which now rose behind Flo. The light made a white mask over his face. Flo seemed to feel her failure, sudden and complete. Knickerbocker had brought a different kind of trouble. He was fingering the safety-pins which closed the gap in his trousers. He trusted Flo's opinion in these details. He stooped forward and turned to let her judge whether he had done a good job.

"Move you tail out of my face," she shouted, "what the hell you take me for?"

Knickerbocker looked hurt. He raised his body to full height, bringing his hands shamefully over the safety-pins. He couldn't understand Flo's fury: the angry and unwarranted rebuke, the petulant slam of the door in his face. And Snooker wouldn't talk. They stood in the dark like dogs shut out.

Beresford was waiting in the end room. He looked tipsy and a little vacant under the light; but he had heard Flo's voice echoing down the passage, and he knew the others were near. It was his wish that they should join him for a drink. He watched the bottle making splinters with the light, sugar brown and green, over the three glasses and a cup. The label had lost its lettering; so he turned to the broken envelope on his stomach and went on talking to himself.

All night that voice had made dialogue with itself about his bride. His mood was reflective, nostalgic. He needed comfort, and he turned to read his mother's letter again.

. . . concernin the lady in question you must choose like i would have you in respect to caracter an so forth. i excuse and forgive your long silence since courtship i know takes time. pay my well-meanin and prayerful respects to the lady in question. give flo my love and my remembrance to snooker and knick. . . .

The light was swimming under his eyes; the words seemed to harden and slip off the page. He thought of Flo and wished she would try to share his mother's approval.

. . . if the weddin come to pass, see that you dress proper. i mean real proper, like the folks in that land would have you. hope you keepin the bike in good condition. . . .

The page had fallen from his hand in a moment of distraction. He was beginning to regret that he had sold the bicycle to Snooker. But his mood didn't last. He heard a knock on the door and saw Knickerbocker's head emerge through the light.

"Help yuhself, Knick."

Beresford squeezed the letter into his pocket while he watched Knickerbocker close in on the table.

"I go take one," Knickerbocker said, "just one."

"Get a next glass if the cup don't suit you."

"Any vessel will do," Knickerbocker said.

Knickerbocker poured rum like water as though his arm could not understand the size of a drink. They touched cup and glass, making twisted faces when the rum started its course down their throats.

"Where Snooker?"

"Puttin' up the bike," Knickerbocker said. "But Flo in a rage."

"She'll come round all right," said Beresford. "Is just that she in two minds, one for me an' one 'gainst the wedding."

"You fix up for the limousine?"

"Flo self do it this mornin'," said Beresford, "they comin' for half pas' four."

"Who goin' partner me if Flo don't come to the church?"

"Flo goin' go all right," said Beresford.

"But you never can know with Flo."

Beresford looked doubtful, but he had to postpone his misgivings.

Knickerbocker poured more rum to avoid further talk, and Beresford held out his glass. They understood the pause. Now they were quiet, rehearsing the day that was so near. The room in half light and liquor was preparing them for melancholy: two men of similar tastes

village camaraderie/
chauvinism

temporarily spared the intrusion of female company. They were a club whose rules were part of their instinct.

"Snooker ask me to swap places wid him," Knickerbocker said.

"He don't want to be my best man?" Beresford asked.

"He ain't feel friendly with the morning suit," Knickerbocker said.

"But what is proper is proper."

"Is what I say too," Knickerbocker agreed. "If you doin' a thing, you mus' do it as the done thing is doed."

Beresford considered this change. He was open to any suggestion.

"Snooker or you, it ain't make no difference," he said.

"Then I goin' course wid you to de altar," Knickerbocker said.

Was it the rum or the intimacy of their talk which had dulled their senses? They hadn't heard the door open and they couldn't guess how long Flo had been standing there, rigid as wire, with hands akimbo, and her head, bull shaped, feeding on some scheme that would undo their plans.

"Get yuhself a glass, Flo," Beresford offered.

"Not me, Berry, thanks all the same."

"What you put your face in mournin' like that for?" Knickerbocker said. He was trying to relieve the tension with his banter. "Those whom God join together . . . ."

"What you callin' God in this for?" Flo charged. "It ain't God join my brother wid any hawk-nose English woman. Is his stupid excitement."

"There ain't nothin' wrong wid the chick," Knickerbocker parried.

"Chick, my eye!" Flo was advancing towards them. "He let a little piece o' left-over white tail put him in heat."

"Flo!"

Beresford's glass had fallen to the floor. He was standing, erect, wilful, his hands nervous and eager for action. Knickerbocker thought he would hit her.

"Don't you threaten me wid any look you lookin'," Flo challenged him. "Knickerbocker, here, know what I sayin' is true. Look him good in his face an' ask him why he ain't marry her."

"Take it easy, Flo, take it easy," Knickerbocker cautioned. "Beresford marryin' 'cause he don't want to roam wild like a bush beast in this London jungle."

"An' she, you know where she been roamin' all this time?" Flo answered. Knickerbocker fumbled for the cup.

49

"Is jus' what Seven Foot Walker tell you back in Port-o'-Spain," Beresford threw in.

Whatever the English girl's past, Beresford felt he had to defend his woman's honour. His hands were now steady as stone watching Flo wince as she waited to hear him through.

"That man take you for a long ride, Flo, an' then he drop you like a latch key that won't fit no more. You been in mournin' ever since that mornin' he turn tail an' lef' you waitin'. An' is why you set yuh scorpion tongue on my English woman."

"Me an' Seven Foot Walker . . ."

"Yes, you an' Seven Foot Walker!"

"Take it easy," Knickerbocker begged them. "Take it easy . . ."

"I goin' to tell you, Berry, I goin' to tell you . . ."

"Take it easy," Knickerbocker pleaded, "take it easy . . ."

Flo was equipped for this kind of war. Her eyes were points of flame and her tongue was tight and her memory like an ally demanding vengeance was ready with malice. She was going to murder them with her knowledge of what had happened between Knickerbocker and the English girl. Time, place, and circumstance: they were weapons which now loitered in her memory waiting for release. She was bursting with passion and spite. Knickerbocker felt his loyalty waver. He was worried. But Flo's words never came. The door opened and Snooker walked in casual as a bird, making music on his old guitar. He was humming: "Nobody knows the trouble I've seen". And his indifference was like a reprieve.

"The limousine man outside to see you," he said. "Somebody got to make some kind o' down payment."

The crisis had been postponed.

Very un-
English
Image

London had never seen anything like it before. The Spring was decisive, a hard, clear sky and the huge sun naked as a skull eating through the shadows of the afternoon. High up on the balcony of a fifth-floor flat an elderly man with a distressful paunch was feeding birdseed to a flock of pigeons. He hated foreigners and noise, but the day had done something to his temper. He was feeling fine. The pigeons soon flew away, cruising in circles above the enormous crowd which kept watch outside the church; then closed their ranks and settled one by one over the familiar steeple.

The weather was right; but the crowd, irreverent and forgetful in their fun, had misjudged the meaning of the day. The legend of

English reticence was stone-cold dead. An old-age pensioner with no teeth at all couldn't stop laughing to the chorus, a thousand times chuckled: "Cor bli'me, look at my lads." He would say, "'Ere comes a next in 'is tails, smashers the lot o' them," and then: "Cor bli'me, look at my lads." A contingent of Cypriots on their way to the Colonial Office had folded their banners to pause for a moment that turned to hours outside the church. The Irish were irrepressible with welcome. Someone burst a balloon, and two small boys, swift and effortless as a breeze, opened their fists and watched the firecrackers join in the gradual hysteria of the day.

Snooker wished the crowd away; yet he was beyond anger. Sullen and reluctant as he seemed he had remained loyal to Beresford's wish. His mind alternated between worrying and wondering why the order of events had changed. It was half an hour since he had arrived with the bride. Her parents had refused at the last moment *prejudice* to have anything to do with the wedding, and Snooker accepted to take her father's place. He saw himself transferred from one role to another; but the second seemed more urgent. It was the intimacy of *friendship* their childhood, his and Beresford's, which had coaxed him into wearing the morning suit. He had to make sure that the bride would keep her promise. But Beresford had not arrived; nor Knickerbocker, nor Flo.

Snooker remembered fragments of the argument in the basement room the night before; and he tried to avoid any thought of Flo. He looked round the church and the boys from "back home" looked at him and he knew they, too, were puzzled. They were all there: Caruso, Slip Disk, Lice-Preserver, and an incredibly fat woman whom they called Tiny. Behind him, two rows away, he could hear Toodles and Square Dick rehearsing in whispers what they had witnessed outside. There had been some altercation at the door when the verger asked Caruso to surrender his guitar. Tiny and Slip Disk had gone ahead, and the verger was about to show his *farce* firmness when he noticed Lice-Preserver who was wearing full evening dress and a sword. The verger sudenly changed his mind and indicated a pew, staring in terror at the sword that hung like a frozen tail down Lice-Preserver's side. Snooker closed his eyes and tried to pray.

But trouble was brewing outside. The West Indians had refused to share in this impromptu picnic. They had journeyed from Brixton and Camden Town, the whole borough of Paddington and the Holloway Road, to keep faith with the boys from "back home".

51

One of the Irishmen had a momentary lapse into prejudice and said something shocking about the missing bridegroom. The West Indians bristled and waited for an argument. But a dog intervened, an energetic, white poodle which kicked its hind legs up and shook its ears in frenzy at them. The poodle frisked and howled as though the air and the organ music had turned its head. Another firecracker went off, and the Irishman tried to sing his way out of a fight. But the West Indians were showing signs of a different agitation. They had become curious, attentive. They narrowed the circle to whisper their secret. "Ain't it his sister standin' over yonder?"

They were slow to believe their own recognition.

"Is Flo, all right," a voice answered, "but she not dress for the wedding."

"Seems she not goin'," a man said as though he wanted to disbelieve his suspicion.

"An' they wus so close," the other added, "close, close, she an' that brother."

Flo was nervous. She stood away from the crowd, half hearing the rumour of her brother's delay. She tried to avoid the faces she knew, wondering what Beresford had decided to do. Half an hour before she left the house she had cancelled the limousine and hidden his morning suit. Now she regretted her action. She didn't want the wedding to take place, but she couldn't bear the thought of humiliating her brother before this crowd. The spectacle of the crowd was like a rebuke to her own stubbornness.

She was retreating further away. Would Beresford find the morning suit? And the limousine? He had set his heart on arriving with Knickerbocker in the limousine. She knew how fixed he was in his convictions, like his grandfather whose wedding could not proceed; had, indeed, to be postponed because he would not repeat the words: *All my worldly goods I thee endow.* He had sworn never to part with his cow. He had a thing about his cow, like Beresford and the morning suit. Puzzled, indecisive, Flo looked round at the faces, eager as they for some sign of an arrival; but it seemed she had lost her memory of the London streets.

The basement rooms were nearly half a mile from the nearest tube station; and the bus strike was on. Beresford looked defeated. He had found the morning suit, but there was no way of arranging for another limousine. Each second followed like a whole season of waiting. The two men stood in front of the house, hailing cabs, pleading for lifts.

"Is to get there," Beresford said, "is to get there 'fore my girl leave the church."

"I goin' deal wid Flo," Knickerbocker swore. "Tomorrow or a year from tomorrow I goin' deal wid Flo."

"How long you think they will wait?"

Beresford had dashed forward again, hailing an empty cab. The driver saw them, slowed down, and suddenly changed his mind. Knickerbocker swore again. Then: a moment of revelation.

prejudice

"Tell you what," Knickerbocker said. He looked as though he had surprised himself.

"What, what!" Beresford insisted.

"Wait here," Knickerbocker said, rushing back to the basement room. "I don't give a goddam. We goin' make it."

The crowd waited outside the church, but they looked a little bored. A clock struck the half-hour. The vicar came out to the steps and looked up at the sky. The man in the fifth floor flat was eating pork sausages and drinking tea. The pigeons were dozing. The sun leaned away and the trees sprang shadows through the early evening.

Someone said: "It's getting on."

It seemed that the entire crowd had agreed on an interval of silence. It was then the woman with the frisky white poodle held her breast and gasped. She had seen them: Beresford and Knickerbocker. They were arriving. It was an odd and unpredictable appearance. Head down, his shoulders arched and harnessed in the morning coat, Knickerbocker was frantically pedalling Snooker's bicycle towards the crowd. Beresford sat on the bar, clutching both top hats to his stomach. The silk cravats sailed like flags round their necks. The crowd tried to find their reaction. At first: astonishment. Later a state of utter incomprehension.

They made a gap through which the bicycle free-wheeled towards the church. And suddenly there was applause, loud and spontaneous as thunder. The Irishman burst into song. The whole rhythm of the day had changed. A firecracker dripped flames over the church steeple and the pigeons dispersed. But crisis was always near. Knickerbocker was trying to dismount when one tail of the coat got stuck between the spokes. The other tail dangled like a bone on a string, and the impatient white poodle charged upon them. She was barking and snapping at Knickerbocker's coat tails. Beresford fell from the bar on to his knees, and the poodle caught the end of his silk cravat. It turned to threads between her teeth.

The crowd could not determine their response. They were hysterical, sympathetic. One tail of Knickerbocker's coat had been taken. He was aiming a kick at the poodle; and immediately the crowd took sides. They didn't want harm to come to the animal. The poodle stiffened her tail and stood still. She was enjoying this exercise until she saw the woman moving in behind her. There was murder in the woman's eyes. The poodle lost heart. But the top hats were her last temptation. Stiff with fright, she leapt to one side seizing them between her teeth like loaves. And she was off. The small boys shouted: "Come back, Satire, come back!" But the poodle hadn't got very far. Her stub of tail had been safely caught between Flo's hand. The poodle was howling for release. Flo lifted the animal by the collar and shook its head like a box of bones.

Knickerbocker was clawing his rump for the missing tail of the morning coat. Beresford hung his head, swinging the silk cravat like a kitchen rag down his side. Neither could move. Flo's rage had paralysed their speech. She had captured the top hats, and it was clear that the wedding had now lost its importance for her. It was a trifle compared with her brother's disgrace.

The vicar had come out to the steps, and all the boys from "back home" stood round him: Toodles, Caruso, and Square Dick, Slip Disk, Clarke Gable Number Two, and the young Sir Winston. Lice-Preserver was carrying the sword in his right hand. But the poodle had disappeared.

Flo stood behind her brother, dripping with tears as she fixed the top hat on his head. Neither spoke. They were too weak to resist her. She was leading them up the steps into the church. The vicar went scarlet.

"Which is the man?" he shouted. But Flo was indifferent to his fury.

"It don't matter," she said. "You ju' go marry my brother."

And she walked between Knickerbocker and her brother with the vicar and the congregation of boys from "back home" following like a funeral procession to the altar.

Outside, the crowd were quiet. In a far corner of sunlight and leaves, the poodle sat under a tree licking her paws, while the fat man from the fifth-floor flat kept repeating like an idiot to himself: "But how, how, how extraordinary!"

Peter Cowan

'Wherever we look,' Peter Cowan wrote in a book-review published in the Australian periodical *Westerly*, No. 2, 1967, 'we are coldly set to erase our natural environment. How can we assume a tomorrow? In this inevitable spread of urbanisation how can people value wildlife, a natural environment they have never seen?'

A rubbish-dump is the setting for the story by Patrick White, but its implications for Australian civilization figure even more visibly in Peter Cowan's work. Sarsaparilla, for Patrick White, is as much a state of mind as it is a place on a map. Cowan, on the other hand, is even more concerned with the physical consequences of suburbia, with the way in which the inexorable march of bricks and mortar across the landscape encroaches upon and blots out the natural resources of the countryside and all wildlife. White's attitude to the quality of life in suburbia is fundamentally an ambivalent one, recognizing its mediocrity at the same time as it seeks to discover the underlying 'mystery and the poetry'; Cowan's is much more unreservedly one of outright condemnation. The characters in his novel *Seed*, for example, live in the outskirts of Perth, and the book is deeply critical of the whole of their materialistic ethos, of which the suburb itself, where they live, is the concrete embodiment.

Peter Cowan's work, in fact, reminds us very forcibly of an essential feature of Australian life today that is only too easily forgotten by non-Australians. Despite its vastness and the great empty spaces at the heart of the continent, or *because* of them, Australia nowadays is one of the most highly urbanized and suburbanized nations in the world; eighty-five per cent of the country's twelve and a half million inhabitants are concentrated in metropolitan areas. These facts are never far from Cowan's awareness as a writer (he has himself worked both on the land and in the town), and they form the background to "The Tractor". The major theme is established in the very first sentence in which the girl watches her fiancé walking towards 'the slightly ornate suburban-style house' *incongruously* set down on the bare rise in the midst of the Australian landscape.

The story has one main focus of interest: our attention is concentrated upon the two chief characters' reaction to the central situation, and this situation, in turn, defines their relationship to each other. A most carefully constructed short story in which every aspect is dovetailed together, it is probably the most meticulously wrought in this anthology, and stands at the opposite pole to the looseness and episodic structure of Mordecai Richler's. "The Tractor" is really a moral fable written to illustrate a thesis, to which all the characters and events are moulded in order to demonstrate the predominant concept. To the farmers the land is something that must be cleared and "developed"; to the girl and to the hermit, living in instinctive communion with nature, it represents the natural values of a life about to be laid waste by the machines of modern society.

So far the story would seem to be simply a romantic assertion of the values of unspoilt nature, but towards the end it suddenly takes a sharply ironical curve back upon itself. The girl herself is from the city and, despite all her feeling for the bush and her passionate desire to protect it from despolation, she proves ultimately to be even more of a stranger to it than the farmers who are intent only upon clearing it. In her attempt to warn the hermit she loses her way in the bush and finds herself alone in an environment which, she becomes aware, is an essentially alien one: 'it was like nothing she could encompass'. And when she does eventually come across him, it is only to be confronted by the fact that he is in possession of a 'knowledge which was not hers' and lives in a world utterly different from the one she is familiar with. There is no easy solution to the problems propounded by "The Tractor", and it is one of the major achievements of the story that it shows full awareness of this fact.

D. H.

The Tractor

She watched him coming back from the gate, walking towards the slightly ornate suburban-style house she felt to be so incongruous set down on the bare rise, behind it the sheds and yards and the thin belt of shade trees. Yet he and his family were proud of it, grateful for its convenience and modernity, and had so clearly not understood her first quizzical remarks that she had never repeated them.

He stood on the edge of the veranda, and she saw in his face the anger that seemed to deepen because he knew the feeling to be impotent.

She said, "What is it?"

"Mackay's two big tractors—that they were going to use for the scrub-clearing—they've been interfered with. Sand put into the oil. The one they started up will cost a few hundred to repair."

"But no one would do that," she said, as if already it were settled, her temporizing without point.

"We know who did it."

"Surely he didn't come right up to the sheds—as close as that to the house——"

"No. They left the tractors down in the bottom paddock. Where they were going to start clearing."

"And now—they can't?"

"Now they can't. Not till the tractor's repaired."

She looked towards the distant line of the low scrub that was deepening in colour as the evening came. She said, "That is what he wanted."

"What he wants is to make as much trouble as he can. We haven't done anything to him."

"You were going to clear the land along the bottom paddock at the back of Mackay's. Where he lives."

"Where he lives?"

"You told me he lived in the bush there."

"He lives anywhere. And he takes the ball floats off the taps in the sheep tank and the water runs to waste, and he breaks the fences when he feels like it, and leaves the gates open——"

"You think he does this deliberately?"

"How else?"

"Oh," she said, "yet it is all so ruthless."

"You mean what he does?"

"No. You only ever think of what he does."

"Well, I'll admit he's given us a few things to think about."

"Clearing with those tractors and the chain," she said. "Everything in their path goes—kangaroos—all the small things that live in the scrub—all the trees——"

He looked at her as if her words held some relevance that must come to him. He said, "We clear the land. Yes."

"You clear it," she said. "It seems to be what is happening everywhere today."

"I don't know what you mean, Ann," he said.

She got up from the chair by the steps. "Perhaps he feels something should be left."

"Look," he said, "maybe you teach too much nature study at school. Or you read all this stuff about how we shouldn't shoot the bloody 'roos—so that when some crazy swine wrecks our property you think he's some sort of a——"

"Some sort of a what?"

"I don't know," he said, aware she mocked him. "Better than us."

"No," she said. "Perhaps just different."

"Different all right."

"What are you going to do?"

"Get the police," he said. "They don't take much notice most of the time, but they will of this." He looked at her as if he would provoke the calm he felt to be assumed. "We'll burn him out if we can't get him any other way."

She looked up quickly and for a moment he was afraid.

"You wouldn't do that."

"He's gone too far this time," he said stubbornly.

The long thin streamers of cloud above the darkening line of scrub were becoming deep and hard in colour, scarlet against the dying light. He watched her face that seemed now calm, remote, as if their words were erased. She was small, slight, somehow always neat, contained. Her dark hair was drawn straight back, her brows clearly marked, lifting slightly so that they seemed to give humour sometimes to her serious expression, her firm mouth.

"I'd better go, Ken."

"The family expect you for tea."

"It's Sunday night. I've to work in the morning. I have some things to prepare."

"Look," he said. "If it's this business——"

"No. I'm just tired. And I've assignments to mark."

"All right," he said.

As they drove she watched the long shadows that spread across the road and over the paddocks from the few shade trees, the light now with a clarity denied through the heat of the day. She would have liked to make some gesture to break the tension between them, to explain to him why she had been unwilling to stay and listen to the inevitable talk of what had happened. But to tell him that at such times she became afraid, as if she could never become one of them, certain that the disagreements now easily enough brought to a truce must in the end defeat them, would not lessen their dissension.

He said suddenly, "You're worried about it, aren't you?"

She knew he referred to themselves, as if he had been aware of her own thoughts.

"Yes," she said. "Sometimes."

"It could be all right, Ann. You'd come to like it here."

"In so many ways I do."

"It's nothing like it used to be. This light land has come good now. We've done well. We've got everything—you wouldn't be without anything you'd have in the city."

"I know that, Ken," she said.

"But you're not sure of it."

She thought he perhaps did this deliberately, seeking to provoke an issue on material grounds, these at least being demonstrable of some conclusion, that he was lost, unwilling, in the face of their real uncertainty. He was more perceptive, she knew, than he cared to reveal, but he had a stubbornness she felt was perhaps impossible to defeat. Before it, she relented a little.

"Not sure of some things. You must give me time. After all, I—hadn't thought to live here. It's different for you."

The few high trees stood out darkly above the low thick scrub, and beyond she could see the roofs of the town.

He said, "This other business will probably be over next week, anyhow."

She supposed he deliberately minimized this which perhaps he did not understand, preferring evasion, the pretence that when it was settled it would not matter. As to him it might not. But he was so clearly afraid that she would escape. She reached out quickly and touched his hand.

He stopped the car before the house near the end of the main street, where she boarded. Farther down, near the club, she could see the cars parked, and people moving without haste along the pavements.

There was no wind, and in the darkness the street was hot, as if the endless heat of summer was never to be dissipated. As he closed the door of the car he said, "I have to go out to the paddock on the way back. It won't take long."

She made no comment and he said, as if to prevent her censure, "I've got to take some stuff from the store out there."

"They haven't found him?"

"No. The police think he's moved out. But we know he hasn't. He makes fools of them in the bush. They've been looking since Sunday, but they've given it up now. Anyhow, you could walk right past him at three feet. And there are no tracks."

"To be able to dodge them like that he must know all this country very well."

"I suppose he does."

"Almost—more than that. He must understand it."

"He doesn't seem to do anything else all day."

She smiled. "Well, do you?"

"I'm not sure what you mean by that. You mean we don't understand it?"

"Perhaps in a different way. You're making it something you can understand."

"Here we go again." He banged his hand against the steering wheel. "We never take a trick. Why don't you go and live with this character?"

She laughed suddenly. "I'm sorry, Ken. But how long has he been here? That's a harmless enough question!"

"He's been around here something like ten years. I remember when I was at school. He's mad."

She said, "All those who oppose us are mad."

"Well," he said, "we're going to get him out this time. We're taking shifts down at the tractors, and we've got a watch on a camp of his we found."

"A camp?"

60

"Made out of boughs." His voice was grudging. "Pretty well made. You could live in it. We flushed him out, because he left some food, and a radio."

"That's not in keeping—a radio."

"It doesn't work. May never have been any good. But it might be only that the batteries are flat. We'll find out. But he could have camps like that all through the bush. We'll be lucky if he comes back to this one."

They turned off through a fence gate, and down along a track that followed a side fence. He switched off the car lights and drove slowly.

"He'll hear the car," he said. "Still, the lights are a give-away."

Suddenly they were close to the dark thick scrub, and then she saw the forms of the tractors, gaunt, high, like grotesque patches of shadow. Two men moved up to the car. One of them started to say something, then saw her, and paused.

He said, "He came back, Ken. Got the food. We never saw him."

They carried rifles, and suddenly she began to laugh. They looked at her with a surprise that had not yet become hostility.

"It—it just seems funny," she said weakly.

"It's not funny," Ken said. She was aware of their anger.

"We'll get him," the man she recognized as Don Mackay said. "We'll get him this time."

She was reminded suddenly of the boys at school in the playground at the lunch period, confronted by some argument that physical force could not immediately solve. Even their voices sound alike, she thought. Perhaps it is not so serious. But when they had taken the box Ken handed out to them, they stepped back from the car and she saw again the guns they carried, and the parallel frightened her.

"How long will they be repairing the tractor?" she asked.

"End of the week." His voice was brusque. She knew she had belittled him before his friends. She moved closer to him as he drove, and he looked briefly at her small, serious face shadowed in the half-light of the car.

"We'll go through there next week. I wish he'd get between the tractors when they're dragging the chain, that's all."

"Is he armed?"

"Yes," he said. "He is. He's lived off the land for years. And by taking food. He might be dangerous now."

She said slowly, "I wonder what made him begin to live like that?"

"No one will know that."

"You'll have to take care."

"There'll be a few of us there to watch for him."

"Actually, he hasn't ever threatened anyone, has he?"

"No. But he's never damaged anything big like this. And the police have never bothered about him before, either. You can see why. He's made fools of them."

"And of you."

"All right. And of us."

"Oh, Ken," she said, "I'm sorry. It's—it's just that I wish somehow you could just let him be."

"And have him do what he likes?"

"Well, he's not done anything much."

"Only wrecked a tractor."

"He would hate the tractors," she said, as if she no longer spoke to him, but was trying to work something out to her own satisfaction.

"Well, it's a reason why we can't leave him there."

"I suppose," she said, "you have to clear that land?"

"Of course. We clear some land every year. It's a tax deduction. And we need it the way taxation is."

"So there can't be anybody who wants things to stay the way they are for a while?"

He looked at her strangely. "Stay the way they are?"

If it was not what she meant she could not perhaps find words that were any more adequate. It was not a simple thing of statement, of definition, this that she felt. She saw with a sudden desolating clarity the grey sprawl of suburbs crossed by the black lines of roads, the cluster of city buildings that clawed up like a sudden focus, the endless tawdry, over-decorated little houses like the one he and his family had placed on the long low rise of land from which almost all else had been erased. As though, she thought painfully, he hated this land she had herself, incongruously enough, come to feel for in the brief time she had been close to it. And it was perhaps worse that he did not see what he was doing, himself a part of some force beyond him. Duped by pride. It was as if she had made some discovery she could not communicate to him and that set them apart.

She said desperately, "Do we have to change everything? Wipe out everything so that everlastingly we can grow things, make things, get tax deductions? You don't even leave a few acres of timber, some-where for animals and birds——"

"Animals and birds," he said. "You can't stop progress."

"The unanswerable answer," she said. Before them the shade trees showed briefly along the road as it turned near the farm. "So we must all conform."

He slowed the car for the house gate, and in the headlights she saw the façade of the house as if they had turned into a suburban street. As he stopped the motor the silence held them. For a moment they did not move, then he drew her against him, his arm lightly about her shoulders, the gesture token of a security they might both have willed, denying the words with which they had held themselves separate.

"Maybe," he said slowly, "it's because you're so crazy I have to have you. You—you're different——"

"I'm sorry, Ken. Because I'm afraid I do love you—I suppose I have to have you, too."

"And you'd rather you didn't."

"Perhaps," she said, "I would rather I didn't."

"It's a mess, isn't it?"

"It might sort out," she said, and she laughed with him. At the house the front door opened briefly, the light shining across the entrance porch as someone looked out at the car.

At the week-end she had arranged to stay at the farm, and she expected him to call for her soon after breakfast. She put her small case on the veranda, but as he did not come she went back inside. Idly, rather irritated at his lateness, she took out her paints and began to work on the flower illustrations she was making. She had begun to paint the native flowers, their grotesque seeds and leaves, to use for her teaching, but the work had begun to absorb her, and she spent whatever time she could searching for new examples. Many, at first, she could not identify. Now, though she told no one, she had begun to hope the paintings might be publishable if she could complete series of different areas.

It was mid-morning when she heard him outside. In the car as they drove he said, "Some of the fences were broken, out by Had-ley's boundary. We've been too busy this week to look down there, and the sheep had gone through into the scrub. We got most of them back."

"You lost some?"

"Some."

"I'm sorry," she said, as if somehow it were her fault.

"He knows we're going to clear that land, and he's out to do as much damage as he can first."

She had no wish to draw him, as if she deliberately sought their disagreement, but it seemed she must form the words, place them before him, his evasion too easy.

"You're sure about it, Ken, aren't you? That he's just getting his own back? That it's as simple as that?"

"It's obvious. He's done pretty well so far."

"And that's the only side there is to it?"

"What else could there be? He can't expect to stop us."

"He might know that."

"Well—that proves it."

"No—perhaps we've all got to make a gesture of some sort. For the things we believe in."

He shook his head. "You put it your way if you like. But what I believe in is using that land."

"Yes, Ken."

"We can't all be dreamers." And then, refusing to be further drawn, he laughed. "It's funny the way I've got caught up with one. Perhaps it will sort out, like you said. You do the dreaming. I'll do the work."

She ran her hands lightly over her arms, smiling at him. "You think we might convert one another?"

"It's a risk we'll have to take."

"Yes. I suppose we're young enough."

"I'll be out a bit this week-end, Ann. We've got to stop this somehow. While we've a few sheep left."

He went out late in the afternoon, and she helped his mother in the kitchen. The older woman had a quietness and a kind of insight that she found attractive, and they had always got on well together, though sometimes Ann was irritated by her acceptance of the men's decisions and views, as if this was something she no longer questioned, or perhaps, Ann thought, she had never questioned.

When Ken came back she heard him talking to his father on the veranda, and then the older man's voice raised in disagreement, though she could distinguish only a few of the words. She went out through the kitchen door and the men stopped talking.

As she came towards them Ken said, "We've found one of his camps. Ted and Don found it, but this time they turned off and kept away. They didn't go near enough for him to realize they'd seen it. We made that mistake last time."

"Where is this?" she said.

"It's new. So he may still be there. It's down in the paddock off the side road to Mackay's. Straight in from the dam. About half a mile north in the scrub."

"There."

"Yes. By the new land. Where we were going to build." He looked at her as if she might have contradicted him. "When we were married."

"What will you do?"

His father said, "I told them to get the police."

"He walked away from the police last time." For a moment his eyes met the girl's. "And us. All right. We were no better. And the reporters came up from town. Photographers all over the place. A seven-day wonder for the suburbanites."

"It's not something that happens every day," she said. "Naturally, it was news."

"They'll make it news again, if we let them. But this time it will be different. We don't do anything until tomorrow night. That way he won't be suspicious if he sees our tracks near the camp. Then Sunday night we'll make a line north of the camp, and if the wind's right we'll burn back towards the firebreak along the paddock. He'll have to break out through the paddock. We'll have a chance that way."

"I think it's too big a risk," his father said. "You'll burn the whole of that country. You can't do it."

"We were going to clear it, anyway."

"You can't start a fire like that."

"If we try to close in on the camp he'll hear us."

"You could still get him. There's enough of you."

"He'd go between us in the bush. No matter how close we were. You know that. No one's been able to get a sight of him in the bush. The police had trackers there last week. They found plenty of tracks. But he kept as far ahead or behind them as he liked. No," he said, "he's made fools of us long enough. I think we've got a chance now."

He turned suddenly towards the girl and she stood beside him, not moving. His words seemed to her to hold a kind of defiance as if he did not himself believe in them, and she thought that it was not simply that he doubted their ability to carry out the plan, but that he did not really believe in the idea of the fire himself. That if she or his father did not further pursue it he might be glad to drop it. But she could not be certain, and before she could speak, as if he intended to prevent her words, he said, "Let's forget this now, Ann. We'll go over to Harris's after tea. They've got a bit of a show on there for May's birthday."

Almost all those she had come to know seemed to have found their way to the party. And all of them discussed the hermit, as they called him; she realized it was general knowledge that he was expected to be caught soon. She listened to the undercurrent of derision that the police with all their resources had been mocked by this man it seemed none of them had seen, as if in this they were on his side. Some of the older people she spoke to claimed to have caught glimpses of him when, some years earlier, he had taken food quite freely for a time from the farmhouses. Some claimed to know his name. But it seemed to her, as she mixed with them and listened to them, that none of them really cared. She felt they simply accepted the idea that he must be denied, driven from cover and killed if necessary, as they might have accepted the killing of a dingo or a fox, a creature for them without motive or reason. When she tried to turn their words, to question them, they looked at her with a kind of surprise, or the beginning of suspicion, perhaps in doubt of her as a teacher of their children. And she saw that quite quickly they exhausted the topic, turning to the enjoyment of the evening, as if already the whole thing was disposed of. In the end she thought it was their lack of involvement, their bland rejection of responsibility, that irritated her to the point of anger, so that she was forced to hold herself from rudeness.

It was late when they returned, and in her room, after she had changed, she stood for a time by the window in the darkness. There was a small moon that seemed scarcely to break the dark ground shadow, and beyond the paddocks she could not see where the scrub began. Her sense of anger had given place to dejection and a kind of fear. She tried to imagine the man who in the darkness slept in what they had described as his camp, something she could picture only as a kind of child's cubby house in the thick scrub. But she could form no picture of him as a physical being, only that it seemed to her he must possess imagination and sensibility beyond that of his

66

pursuers, that he must be someone not difficult to talk to, someone who would understand her own feeling about these things for which he was persecuted. And who might even, she thought, be glad to know, however briefly, that they were shared. She was aware of a sense of disloyalty, but the image persisted, and it was suddenly monstrous that the darkness of the scrub should be swept by the glare of fire, as she would see it from the window where she stood now, the man stumbling from it in some unimaginable indignity. And though she had doubted the men's intention to carry out their plan, it seemed now in the darkness only too probable that in anger they might do what she, and perhaps they, feared. And it was impossible. Her hands felt the cold of the sill, she was aware of the faint wind that blew in through the window, cool upon her skin, and she could hear it in the boughs of the few shade trees behind the house.

On Sunday, in the afternoon, Ken left to make arrangements with the other men. His parents were resting, but she knew they would not question her going out, they were used to her wandering about the farm, looking for the plants she wished to paint. She went down through the yard gate, across the paddock towards the track that led out to the belt of scrub and timber. It seemed, in the heat, farther than she had expected.

She walked along the side fence, where the brush began, feeling that it would hide her if any of the men were watching. If she met them she would say she had come to look for Ken. She could see the dam ahead, the smooth red banks rising steeply, to one side a few thin trees, motionless in the heat.

At the dam she paused. The side track to Mackay's had turned some distance back to the left. In front of her, facing north, the scrub was thick, untouched, she was suddenly reluctant to go beyond the fence on the far side of the dam.

She pushed the wires down and stepped through. She began to pick her way through the scrub, choosing the small, most imperceptible pockets where the bushes were thinner. It was only after a time, when she could no longer see the dam or the trees beside it, that she realized her method of walking had led her away from a straight line. She had no clear idea how far she had come. She went on until she was certain she had covered half a mile, but as she stopped it was suddenly clear she could have deviated in any direction.

The bushes grew upward on their thin sparse stems to a rounded umbrella-like top, the leaves tough, elongated and spindly. They stretched away like endless replicas, rising head-high, become too thick for her to go farther. As she looked about it seemed improbable she had come so far. In the heat the scrub was silent. Along the reddish ground, over the thin stalks, the ants moved, in places she had walked round their mud-coloured mounds. She looked down at the ground, at the hard brittle twigs and fallen leaves, some of them already cemented by the ants. In a kind of fear she began to walk.

A short distance to the right a thin patch of trees lifted above the bushes, and though she thought it was the wrong direction she began to push her way towards it. The trees were like some sharp variation in the endless grey pattern of the brush that rose about her.

Beneath them the bark and leaves were thick upon the ground. She stood in the patch of shade, and she tried to reason that she could not have come far, that she could find her way back if she was careful. And in the silence she thought again, as she had the night before, of the man she had come to warn. It had seemed that if she could explain to him, he must understand, and that perhaps he would go. She had relied on there being understanding between them, that at least in these things they must feel alike. So that it had seemed her words would have effect. Now, in the heat and the silence, it was a dream, holding in this place no reality. She could never have thought to do it. And it was here he had spent ten years. It was like nothing she could encompass. She felt a sharp, childish misery, as if she might have allowed herself tears.

It occurred to her that if she could climb one of the trees she might gain an idea of direction. But the trunks were slippery, without foothold, and at the second attempt she fell, twisting her leg. She leant against the trunk, afraid of the pain, trying to deny it, as if she would will herself to be without injury that might imprison her.

She was not aware of any movement or sound, but she looked up, and turned slightly, still holding to the smooth trunk. He was standing just at the edge of the clump of trees. He might have been there all the time. Or been attracted by the noise she had made.

She said weakly, "I—didn't see you——"

His face held no expression she could read. His hair was grey and short, and she was vaguely surprised, as if she had imagined something different, but cut crudely, and streaked across his head by sweat. He was very thin, all the redundant flesh might long ago have been burnt from him, his arms stick-like, knotted and black. His hands held a rifle, and she knew a sudden fear that he would kill her, that somehow she must place words between them before he took her simply as one of his persecutors.

She said quickly, "I came to warn you—they have found your camp—tonight they mean to drive you out towards the paddock——"

But they were not the words she had planned. His eyes gave her no sign. They were very dark, sharp somehow, and she knew suddenly they were like the eyes of an animal or a bird, watchful, with their own recognition and knowledge which was not hers. The stubble of beard across his face was whitish, his skin dark from the sun.

"I—if only you would go from here," she said. "They only want you to go—they don't understand——"

The words were dead in the heat and the silence. She saw the flies that crawled across his face.

"I wanted to help you," she said, and she despised herself in her terror. Only his hands seemed to move faintly about the rifle. His stillness was insupportable. Abruptly she began to sob, the sound loud, gulping, ridiculous, her hands lifting to her face.

He seemed to step backwards. His movement was somehow liquid, unhuman, and then she thought of the natives she had once seen in the north, not the town natives whose movements had grown like her own. But with a strange inevitability he moved like an animal or the vibration of the thin sparse trees before the wind. She did not see him go. She looked at the boles of the trees where he had stood, and she could hear her own sobbing.

Some time in the afternoon she heard the sudden sound of shots, flat, unreal, soon lost in the silence. But she walked towards where the sound had seemed to be, and after a time, without warning she came on the track that ran towards Mackay's place. She had gone only a short distance when she heard the voices, and called out. The men came through the scrub and she saw them on the track. She began to run towards them, but checked herself. Farther down she saw a Landrover and one of the police. Ken said, "We missed you —we've been searching—it was only that Ted saw where you'd walked down the fence—"

She said, "The shots—I heard them—"

"We were looking for you. We didn't see him. He tried to get past us, then shot at Don—we had to shoot."

She did not speak and he said, "We had to do it, Ann. We sent for the police. But where were you? How did you get out here?"

There was nothing she could tell him. She said, "I was looking for you, I think."

The Landrover had drawn up beside them, and the driver opened the door for her. They moved back down the dry rutted track where the thin shade had begun to stretch in from the broken scrub.

Mordecai Richler

'No matter how long I continue to live abroad,' Mordecai Richler writes in *Canadian Literature*, No. 41, 'I do feel forever rooted in St. Urbain Street [Montreal]. This was my time, my place, and I have elected myself to get it exactly right.' Although he has been living for several years in Spain, France and England and some of his novels have a European background, it is still to Canada that the best of his work, in particular, *The Apprenticeship of Duddy Kravitz*, published in 1959, returns for its setting.

The book is really a twentieth-century picaresque novel. Like "The Summer My Grandmother was Supposed to Die" it is full of acutely observed realistic detail, which again and again the reader feels Richler succeeds in getting 'exactly right'. As in all of his work, the novel shifts rapidly from episode to episode and is held together both by the richly ironic tone, in which the wit constantly flashes forth, and by the presence in all these episodes of the central character. Duddy Kravitz exerts a continual fascination upon the reader. Brought up in the same Jewish quarter of Montreal as Richler himself, his chief aim, when he grows up, is to buy land for development as an economic investment, and thus acquire a middle-class position in society. If a search for stability and for permanent values in life is a major concern in Richler's fiction, Duddy Kravitz has his own interpretation of these assets. Shrewd, with only his native wits to rely upon, resourceful, able to exploit every situation to his own advantage, Duddy has all the resilience of a rubber ball, and the harder he is hit the more vigorously he rebounds.

Richler's short story so closely resembles this novel in its vitality of narration, in its satirical tone and attitude, but most of all in the vividness of its rendering of life in the Jewish quarter, that "The Summer My Grandmother was Supposed to Die" could easily be an early stage in Duddy Kravitz's apprenticeship. Moreover, if Patrick White in "Down at the Dump" has very mixed feelings about the narrowly confined and restricted life of the Australian suburb, so too has Richler about the even more closely knit and inward-looking Jewish community. The Jewish upbringing with its rigidly ordained customs, its strict adherence to tradition, its strongly defined pattern of family life provides a fertile field for the satirist, as Philip Roth has demonstrated in an American context. This is no less the case for Mordecai Richler. It is the mould which shapes this entire story; it also provides the source of much of Richler's comedy. Rebellious, irreverent and wickedly funny, it paradoxically reveals the strength and stability of the Jewish tradition at the same moment as it is most iconoclastic about it. The characters in the story are sharply and swiftly etched in, bawdiness is quickly touched upon, the Jewish speech idiom with its inverted syntax is rapidly caught, comic episode follows comic episode in headlong succession, and the whole story is driven on in a vividly colloquial style which, with its verve and unflagging energy, splendidly sustains the pace to the very end.

All these contribute to the highly entertaining comic effect. But is entertaining comedy the sole impression the story leaves? 'I would say that any serious writer', Richler states in the article already mentioned, 'is a moralist, and only incidentally an entertainer.' It is really the central fact of the old woman, paralysed by a stroke, and helplessly suffering death by slow degrees, while, at the same time, ordinary life with all its rich vitality and comedy continues around her, that provides the undertones of the story. These undertones are in no way muffled by the comedy; instead, the two play against and accentuate each other. So that eventually, as well as being alive with comedy, the story is also instinctive with humanity. *D. H.*

The Summer My Grandmother
was Supposed to Die

Dr. Katzman discovered the gangrene on one of his monthly visits. "She won't last a month," he said.

He repeated that the second month, the third, and the fourth, and now she lay dying in the heat of the back bedroom.

"If only she'd die," my mother said. "Oh God, why doesn't she die? God in heaven, what's she holding on for?"

The summer my grandmother was supposed to die we did not chip in with the Breenbaums to take a cottage in the Laurentians. It wouldn't have been practical. The old lady couldn't be moved, the nurse came daily and the doctor twice a week, and so it seemed best to stay in the city and wait for her to die or, as my mother said, pass away. It was a hot summer, her bedroom was just behind the kitchen, and when we sat down to eat we could smell her. The dressings on my grandmother's left leg had to be changed several times a day and, according to Dr. Katzman, her condition was hopeless. "It's in the hands of the Almighty," he said.

"It won't be long now," my father said, "and she'll be better off, if you know what I mean."

"Please," my mother said.

A nurse came every day from the Royal Victorian Order. She arrived punctually at noon and at five to twelve I'd join the rest of the boys under the outside staircase to look up her dress as she climbed to our second-storey flat. Miss Monohan favoured lacy pink panties and that was better than waiting under the stairs for Cousin Bessie, for instance. She wore enormous cotton bloomers, rain or shine.

I was sent out to play as often as possible, because my mother felt it was not good for me to see somebody dying. Usually I'd just roam the scorched streets shooting the breeze. There was Arty, Gas sometimes, Hershey, Stan, and me. We talked about everything from A to Z.

"Why is it," Arty wanted to know, "that Tarzan never shits?"

"Dick Tracy too."

"Or Wonder Woman."

"She's a dame."

"So?"

"Jees, wouldn't it be something if Superman crapped in the sky? He could just be flying over Waverly Street when, whamo, Mr. Rabinovitch catches it right in the kisser."

Mr. Rabinovitch was our Hebrew teacher.

"But there's Tarzan," Arty insisted, "in the jungle, week in and week out, and never once does he need to go to the toilet. It's not real, that's all."

Arty told me, "Before your grandma dies she's going to roll her eyes and gurgle. That's what they call the death-rattle."

"Aw, you know everything. Big shot."

"I *read* it, you jerk," Arty said, whacking me one, "in Perry Mason."

Home again I'd find my mother weeping.

"She's dying by inches," she said to my father one stifling night, "and none of them even come to see her. Oh, such children! They should only rot in hell."

"They're not behaving right. It's certainly not according to Hoyle," my father said.

"When I think of all the money and effort that went into making a rabbi out of Israel—the way Mother doted on him—and for what? Oh, what's the world coming to? God."

"It's not right."

Dr. Katzman was amazed. "I never believed she'd last this long. Really, it must be will-power alone that keeps her going. And your excellent care."

"I want her to die, Doctor. That's not my mother in the back room. It's an animal. I want her to please please die."

"Hush. You don't mean it. You're tired." And Dr. Katzman gave my father some pills for my mother to take. "A remarkable woman," he said. "A born nurse."

At night in bed my brother Harvey and I used to talk about our grandmother. "After she dies," I said, "her hair will go on growing for another twenty-four hours."

"Sez who?"

"Arty. It's a scientific fact. Do you think Uncle Lou will come from New York for the funeral?"

"Sure."

"Boy, that means another fiver for me. You too."

"You shouldn't say things like that, kiddo, or *her ghost will come back to haunt you.*"

"Well," I said, "I'll be able to go to her funeral, anyway. I'm not too young any more."

I was only six years old when my grandfather died, and I wasn't allowed to go to his funeral.

I have only one memory of my grandfather. Once he called me into his study, set me down on his lap, and made a drawing of a horse for me. On the horse he drew a rider. While I watched and giggled he gave the rider a beard and the round fur-trimmed cap of a rabbi.

My grandfather was a Zaddik, one of the Righteous, and I've been told that to study Talmud with him had been a rare pleasure. I wasn't allowed to go to his funeral, but years later I was shown the telegrams of condolence that had come from Eire and Poland and Israel and even Japan. My grandfather had written many books: a translation of the Zohar into modern Hebrew—some twenty years' work—and lots of slender volumes of sermons, chassidic tales, and rabbinical commentaries. His books had been published in Warsaw and later in New York. He had been famous.

"At the funeral," my mother told me, "they had to have six motorcycle policemen to control the crowds. It was such a heat that twelve women fainted—and I'm *not* counting Mrs. Waxman from upstairs. With her, you know, *anything* to fall into a man's arms. Even Pinsky's. And did I tell you that there was even a French-Canadian priest there?"

"No kidding?"

"The priest was a real big *knacker*. A bishop maybe. He used to study with the *zeyda*. The *zeyda* was some personality, you know. Spiritual and wordly-wise at the same time. Such personalities they don't make any more. Today, rabbis and peanuts are the same size."

But, according to my father, the *zeyda* (his father-in-law) hadn't been as famous as all that. "There are things I could say," he told me. "There was another side to him."

My grandfather had come from generations and generations of rabbis, his youngest son was a rabbi, but none of his grandchildren would be one. My brother Harvey was going to be a dentist and at the time, 1937, I was interested in flying and my cousin Jerry was already a communist. I once heard Jerry say, "Our grandpappy wasn't all he was cracked up to be." When the men at the kosher bakeries went on strike he spoke up against them on the streets where they were picketing and in the *shule*. It was of no consequence to him that they were grossly underpaid. His superstitious followers had to have bread. "Grandpappy," Jerry said, "was a prize reactionary."

A week after my grandfather died my grandmother suffered a stroke. Her right side was completely paralysed. She couldn't speak. At first, it's true, my grandmother could say a few words and move her right hand enough to write her name in Hebrew. Her name was Malka. But her condition soon began to deteriorate.

My grandmother had six children and seven step-children, for my grandfather had been married before. His first wife had died in the old country. Two years later he had married my grandmother, the only daughter of the richest man in the village, and their marriage had been a singularly happy one. My grandmother had been a beautiful girl. She had also been a wise, resourceful, and patient wife. Qualities, I fear, indispensable to life with a Zaddik. For the synagogue had paid my grandfather no stipulated salary and much of the money he had picked up here and there he had habitually distributed among rabbinical students, needy immigrants, and widows. A vice, and such it was to his hard-pressed family, which made him as unreliable a provider as a drunkard. And indeed, to carry the analogy further, my grandmother had had to make many hurried trips to the pawnbroker with her jewellery. Not all of it had been redeemed, either. But her children had been looked after. The youngest, her favourite, was a rabbi in Boston, the eldest was the actor-manager of a Yiddish theatre in New York, and another was a lawyer. One daughter lived in Toronto, two in Montreal. My mother was the youngest daughter, and when my grandmother had her stroke there was a family meeting and it was decided that my mother would take care of her. This was my father's fault. All the other husbands spoke up—they protested their wives had too much work, they could never manage it—but my father detested quarrels, and he was silent. So my grandmother came to stay with us.

Her bedroom, the back bedroom, had actually been promised to me for my seventh birthday. But all that was forgotten now, and I had to go on sharing a bedroom with my brother Harvey. So naturally I was resentful when each morning I left for school my mother said, "Go in and kiss the *baba* goodbye."

All the same I'd go into the bedroom and kiss my grandmother hastily. She'd say "Buoyo-bouyo," for that was the only sound she could make. And after school it was, "Go in and tell the *baba* you're home."

"I'm home, *baba*."

During those first hopeful months—"Twenty years ago who would have thought there'd be a cure for diabetes?" my father asked, "where there's life there's hope, you know"—she'd smile at me and try to speak, her eyes charged with effort. And even later there were times when she pressed my head urgently to her bosom with her surprisingly strong left arm. But as her illness dragged on and on and she became a condition in the house, something beyond hope or reproach, like the leaky icebox, there was less recognition and more ritual in those kisses. I came to dread her room. A clutter of sticky medicine bottles and the cracked toilet chair beside the bed; glazed but imploring eyes and a feeble smile, the wet slap of her lips against my cheeks. I flinched from her touch. After two years of it I protested to my mother. "Look, what's the use of telling her I'm going or I'm here. She doesn't even recognize me any more."

"Don't be fresh. She's your grandmother."

My uncle who was in the theatre in New York sent money regularly to help support my grandmother and, for the first few months, so did the other children. But once the initial and sustaining excitement had passed and it became likely that my grandmother might linger in her invalid condition for two or maybe even three more years, the cheques began to drop off, and the children seldom came to our house any more. Anxious weekly visits—"and how is she today, poor lamb?"—quickly dwindled to a dutiful monthly looking in, then a semi-annual visit, and these always on the way to somewhere.

"The way they act," my father said, "you'd think that if they stayed long enough to take off their coats we'd make them take the *baba* home with them."

When the children did come to visit, my mother made it difficult for them.

"It's killing me," she said. "I have to lift her on to that chair three times a day maybe. Have you any idea how heavy she is? And what makes you think I always catch her in time? Sometimes I have to change her bed twice a day. That's a job I'd like to see your wife do," she said to my uncle, the rabbi.

"We could send her to the Old People's Home," the rabbi said.

"Now there's an idea," my father said.

But my mother began to sob. "Not as long as I'm alive," she said. And she gave my father a stony look. "Say something."

"It wouldn't be according to Hoyle."

"You want to be able to complain to everyone in town about all the other children," the rabbi said. "You've got a martyr complex."

"Everybody has a point of view, you know. You know what I mean?" my father said. "So what's the use of fighting?"

Meanwhile, Dr. Katzman came once a month to examine my grandmother. "It's remarkable, astonishing," he'd say each time. "She's as strong as a horse."

"Some life for a person," my father said. "She can't speak—she doesn't recognize anybody—what is there for her?"

The doctor was a cultivated man; he spoke often for women's clubs, sometimes on Yiddish literature and other times, his rubicund face hot with impatience, the voice taking on a doomsday tone, on the cancer threat.

"Who are we to judge?" he asked.

Every evening, during the first months of my grandmother's illness, my mother read her a story by Sholem Aleichem. "Tonight she smiled," my mother would say. "She understood. I can tell." And my father, my brother, and I, would not comment. Once a week my mother used to give the old lady a manicure. Sunny afternoons she'd lift her into a wheel chair and put her out in the sun. Somebody always had to stay in the house in case my grandmother called. Often, during the night, she would begin to wail unaccountably, and my mother would get up and rock the old lady in her arms for hours. But in the fourth year of my grandmother's illness the strain and fatigue began to tell on my mother. Besides looking after my grand-mother—"and believe you me," the doctor assured her with a clap on the back, "it would be a full-time job for a professional nurse"—she had to keep house for a husband and two sons. She began to quarrel with my father and she became sharp with Harvey and me. My father started to spend his evenings playing pinochle at Tansky's Cigar & Soda. Weekends he took Harvey and me to visit his brothers and sisters. And everywhere he went people had little bits of advice for him.

"Sam, you might as well be a bachelor. You're just going to have to put your foot down for once."

"Yeah, in your face maybe."

My cousin Libby, who was at McGill, said, "This could have a very damaging effect on the development of your boys. These are their formative years, Uncle Samuel, and the omnipresence of death in the house . . ."

"What you need," my father said, "is a boy friend. *And how.*"

At Tansky's Cigar & Soda it was, "Come clean, Sam. It's no hardship. If I know you, the old lady's got a big insurance policy and when the time comes . . ."

My mother lost lots of weight. After dinner she'd fall asleep in her chair in the middle of Lux Radio Theatre. One minute she'd be sewing a patch on my breeches or be making a list of girls to call for a bingo party (proceeds for the Talmud Torah), and the next she'd be snoring. Then, one morning, she just couldn't get out of bed, and Dr. Katzman came round a week before his regular visit. "Well, well, this won't do, will it?" He sat in the kitchen with my father and the two men drank apricot brandy out of small glasses.

"Your wife is a remarkable woman," Dr. Katzman said.

"You don't say?"

"She's got a gallstone condition."

My father shrugged. "Have another one for the road," he said.

"Thank you, but I have several more calls to make." Dr. Katzman rose, sighing. "There she lies in that back room, poor old woman," he said, "hanging desperately onto life. There's food for thought there."

My grandmother's children met again, and the five of them sat around my mother's bed embarrassed, irritated, and quick to take insult. All except my uncle who was in the theatre. He sucked a cigar and drank whisky. He teased my mother, the rabbi, and my aunts, and if not for him I think they would have been at each other's throats. It was decided, over my mother's protests, to send my grandmother to the Old People's Home on Esplanade Street. An ambulance came to take my grandmother away and Dr. Katzman said, "It's for the best." But my father had been in the back bedroom when the old lady had held on tenaciously to the bedpost, not wanting to be moved by the two men in white—"Easy does it, granny," the younger one had said—and afterwards he could not go in to see my mother. He went out for a walk.

"She looked at me with such a funny expression," he told my brother. "Is it my fault?"

My mother stayed in bed for another two weeks. My father cooked for us and we hired a woman to do the housework. My mother put on weight quickly, her cheeks regained their normal pinkish hue and, for the first time in months, she actually joked with Harvey and me. She became increasingly curious about our schools and whether or not we shined our shoes regularly. She began to cook again, special dishes for my father, and she resumed old friendships with women on the parochial school board. The change reflected on my father. Not only did his temper improve, but he stopped going to Tansky's every other night, and began to come home early from work. Life at home had never been so rich. But my grandmother's name was never mentioned. The back bedroom remained empty and I continued to share a room with Harvey. I couldn't see the point and so one evening I said, "Look, why don't I move into the back bedroom?"

My father glared at me across the table.

"But it's empty like."

My mother left the table. And the next afternoon she put on her best dress and coat and new spring hat.

"Where are you going?" my father asked.

"To see my mother."

"Don't go looking for trouble."

"It's been a month. Maybe they're not treating her right."

"They're experts."

"Did you think I was never going to visit her? I'm not inhuman, you know."

"All right, go," he said.

But after she'd gone my father went to the window and said, "Son-of-a-bitch."

Harvey and I sat outside on the steps watching the cars go by. My father sat on the balcony above, cracking peanuts. It was six o'clock, maybe later, when the ambulance turned the corner, slowed down, and parked right in front of the house.

"Son-of-a-bitch," my father said. "I knew it."

My mother got out first, her eyes red and swollen, and hurried upstairs to make my grandmother's bed.

"I'm sorry, Sam, I had to do it."

"You'll get sick again, that's what."

"You think she doesn't recognize people. From the moment she saw me she cried and cried. Oh, it was terrible."

"They're experts there. They know how to handle her better than you do."

"Experts? Expert murderers you mean. She's got bedsores, Sam. Those dirty little Irish nurses they don't change her linen often enough, they hate her. She must have lost twenty pounds there."

"Another month and you'll be flat on your back again."

"Sam, what could I do? Please Sam."

"She'll outlive all of us. Even Muttel. I'm going out for a walk."

She was back and I was to blame.

My father became a regular at Tansky's Cigar & Soda again and every morning I had to go in and kiss my grandmother. She began to look like a man. Little hairs had sprouted on her chin, she had a spiky grey moustache and, of course, she was practically bald. This near-baldness, I guess, sprang from the fact that she had been shaving her head ever since she had married my grandfather the rabbi. My grandmother had four different wigs, but she had not worn one since the first year of her illness. She wore a little pink cap instead. And so, as before, she said, "buoyo-buoyo," to everything.

Once more uncles and aunts sent five-dollar bills, though erratically, to help pay for my grandmother's support. Elderly people, former followers of my grandfather, came to inquire after the old lady's health. They sat in the backroom with her for hours, leaning on their canes, talking to themselves, rocking, always rocking to and fro. "The Holy Shakers," my father called them, and Harvey and I avoided them, because they always wanted to pinch our cheeks, give us a dash of snuff and laugh when we sneezed, or offer us a sticky old candy from a little brown bag with innumerable creases in it. When the visit was done the old people would unfailingly sit in the kitchen with my mother for another hour, watching her make lockshen or bake bread. My mother always served them lemon tea and they would talk about my grandfather, recalling his books, his sayings, and his charitable deeds.

And so another two years passed, with no significant change in my grandmother's condition. But fatigue, bad temper, and even morbidity enveloped my mother again. She fought with her brothers and sisters and once, when I stepped into the living-room, I found her sitting with her head in her hands, and she looked up at me with such anguish that I was frightened.

"What did I do now?" I asked.

"If, God forbid, I had a stroke, would you send me to the Old People's Home?"

"Don't be a joke. Of course not."

"I hope that never in my life do I have to count on my children for anything."

The summer my grandmother was supposed to die, the seventh year of her illness, my brother took a job as a shipper and he kept me awake at night with stories about the factory. "What we do, see, is clear out the middle of a huge pile of lengths of material. That makes for a kind of secret cave. A hideout. Well, then you coax one of the *shiksas* inside and hi-diddle-diddle."

One night Harvey waited until I had fallen asleep and then he wrapped himself in a white sheet, crept up to my bed, and shouted, "Bouyo-bouyo."

I hit him. He shouted.

"Children. Children, please," my mother called. "I must get some rest."

As my grandmother's condition worsened—from day to day we didn't know when she'd die—I was often sent out to eat at my aunt's or at my other grandmother's house. I was hardly ever at home. On Saturday mornings I'd get together with the other guys and we'd walk all the way past the mountain to Eaton's, which was our favourite department store for riding up and down escalators and stealing.

In those days they let boys into the left-field bleachers free during the week and we spent many an afternoon at the ball park. The Montreal Royals, part of the Dodger farm system, was some ball club too. There was Jackie Robinson and Roy Campanella, Honest John Gabbard, Chuck Connors, and Kermit Kitman was our hero. It used to kill us to see that crafty little hebe running around there with all those tall dumb *goyim*. "Hey, Kitman," we'd yell. "Hey, hey, sho-head, if your father knew you played ball on *shabus*——" Kitman, unfortunately, was all field and no hit. He never made the majors. "There goes Kermit Kitman," we'd yell, after he'd gone down swinging again, "the first Jewish strike-out king of the International League." This we usually followed up by bellowing some choice imprecations in Yiddish.

It was after one of these games on a Friday afternoon, that I came home to find a small crowd gathered in front of the house.

"That's the grandson."

"Poor kid."

Old people stood silent and expressionless across the street staring at our front door. A taxi pulled up and my aunt hurried out, hiding her face in her hands.

"After so many years," somebody said.

"And probably next year they'll discover a cure. Isn't that *always* the case?"

I took the stairs two at a time. The flat was full. Uncles and aunts from my father's side of the family, odd old people, Dr. Katzman, Harvey, neighbours, were all standing around and talking in hushed voices in the living-room. I found my father in the kitchen, getting out the apricot brandy. "Your grandmother's dead," he said.

"She didn't suffer," somebody said. "She passed away in her sleep."

"A merciful death."

"Where's Maw?"

"In the bedroom with . . . you'd better not go in," my father said.

"I want to see her."

My mother's face was long with grief. She wore a black shawl, and glared down at a knot of handkerchief clutched in a fist that had been cracked by washing-soda. "Don't come in here," she said.

Several bearded, round-shouldered men in black shiny coats stood round the bed. I couldn't see my grandmother.

"Your grandmother's dead."

"Daddy told me."

"Go and wash your face and comb your hair. You'll have to get your own supper."

"O.K."

"One minute. The *baba* left some jewellery. The ring is for Harvey's wife and the necklace is for yours."

"Who's getting married?"

"Better go and wash your face. And remember behind the ears, Muttel."

Telegrams were sent, long-distance calls were made, and all through the evening relatives and neighbours came and went like swarms of fish when crumbs have been dropped into the water.

"When my father died," my mother said, "they had to have *six* motorcycle policemen to control the crowds. Twelve people fainted, such a heat . . ."

The man from the funeral parlour came.

"There goes the only Jewish businessman in town," my Uncle Harry said, "who wishes all his customers were Germans."

"This is no time for jokes."

"Listen, life goes on."

My Cousin Jerry had begun to use a cigarette holder. "Everyone's going to be sickeningly sentimental," he said. "Soon the religious mumbo-jumbo starts. I can hardly wait."

Tomorrow was the Sabbath and so, according to the law, my grandmother couldn't be buried until Sunday. She would have to lie on the floor all night. Two old grizzly women in white came to move and wash the body and a professional mourner arrived to sit up and pray for her.

"I don't trust his face," my mother said. "He'll fall asleep. You watch him, Sam."

"A fat lot of good prayers will do her now."

"Will you just watch him, please."

"I'll watch him, I'll watch him." My father was livid about my Uncle Harry. "The way he's gone after that apricot brandy you'd think that guy never saw a bottle in his life before."

Harvey and I were sent to bed, but we couldn't sleep. My aunt was sobbing over the body in the living-room—"That dirty hypocrite," my mother said—there was the old man praying, coughing, and spitting into his handkerchief each time he woke; and hushed voices and whimpering from the kitchen, where my father and mother sat. Harvey was in a good mood, he let me have a few puffs of his cigarette.

"Well, kiddo, this is our last night together. Tomorrow you can take over the back bedroom."

"*Are you crazy?*"

"You always wanted it for yourself."

"She died in there, but. You think I'm going to sleep in there?"

"Good night. Happy dreams, kiddo."

"Hey, let's talk some more."

Harvey told me a ghost story. "Did you know that when they hang a man," he said, "the last thing that happens is that he has an orgasm?"

"A what?"

"Forget it. I forgot you were still in kindergarten."

"I know plenty. Don't worry."

"At the funeral they're going to open her coffin to throw dirt in her face. It's supposed to be earth from Eretz. They open it and you're going to have to look." Harvey stood up on his bed, holding his hands over his head like claws. He made a hideous face. "Bouyo-buoyo. Who's that sleeping in my bed? Woo-Woo."

My uncle who was in the theatre, the rabbi, and my aunt from Toronto, all came to Montreal for the funeral. Dr. Katzman came too.

"As long as she was alive," my mother said, "he couldn't even send five dollars a month. Some son! What a rabbi! I don't want him in my house, Sam. I can't bear the sight of him."

"You don't mean a word of that and you know it," Dr. Katzman said.

"Maybe you'd better give her a sedative," the rabbi said.

"Sam. Sam, will you say something, please."

My father stepped up to the rabbi, his face flushed. "I'll tell you this straight to your face, Israel," he said. "You've gone down in my estimation."

"Really," the rabbi said, smiling a little.

My father's face burned a deeper red. "Year by year," he said, "your stock has gone down with me."

And my mother began to weep bitterly, helplessly, without control. She was led unwillingly to bed. While my father tried his best to comfort her, as he said consoling things, Dr. Katzman plunged a needle into her arm. "There we are," he said.

I went to sit in the sun on the outside stairs with Arty. "I'm going to the funeral," I said.

"I couldn't go anyway."

Arty was descended from the tribe of high priests and so was not allowed to be in the presence of a dead body. I was descended from the Yisroelis.

"The lowest of the low," Arty said.

"Aw."

My uncle, the rabbi, and Dr. Katzman stepped into the sun to light cigarettes.

"It's remarkable that she held out for so long," Dr. Katzman said.

"Remarkable?" my uncle said. "It's written that if a man has been married twice he will spend as much time with his first wife in heaven as he did on earth. My father, may he rest in peace, was married to his first wife for seven years and my mother, may she rest in peace, has managed to keep alive for seven years. Today in heaven she will be able to join my father, may he rest in peace."

Dr. Katzman shook his head, he pursed his lips. "It's amazing " he said. "The mysteries of the human heart. Astonishing."

My father hurried outside. "Dr. Katzman, please. It's my wife. Maybe the injection wasn't strong enough? She just doesn't stop crying. It's like a tap. Could you come please?"

"Excuse me," Dr. Katzman said to my uncle.

"Of course."

My uncle approached Arty and me.

"Well, boys," he said, "what would you like to be when you grow up?"

Lee Kok Liang

Lee Kok Liang is not a writer who is widely known outside his own country, Malaysia, but his collection of short stories, *The Mutes in the Sun*, has been sufficient to establish his reputation very firmly there. Several of his stories are played out against a background of considerable violence, others are concerned with the disillusioning experience youth undergoes in its encounter with the adult world. He also has a deep, almost Lawrencian awareness of the body as a living organism registering physical sensation: characters in his stories often feel physically long before reacting to an experience by conscious thought or speech. This, in turn, has a direct effect on the formal structure of "When the Saints Go Marching": there is less use of dialogue and more purely narrative description in this story than in practically any other in this anthology. Moreover, no small part of the effectiveness displayed in the treatment of the theme of sensuality here is due to the fact that the core of the character's relationships is not so much indicated by speech as by their visceral reactions to each other:

> Holding the cup with both hands, she drank the water slowly, pressing the rim hard against the bridge of her nose. After a while she found difficulty in breathing and water ran down her cheeks. She began squeezing the cup. Forgetting his resolution he tried to snatch the cup away and as he touched her, she screamed, jerking her head away.

Lee Kok Liang also shows again and again in his work a striking ability to convey the feel of place that extends far beyond merely using this as local colour.

All these aspects are combined in "When the Saints Go Marching". Here, however, the main character, Kung Ming, is not a youth but a middle-aged man, and the "local colour" is provided by the fact that the events are chronicled against a wider political background. It is the anniversary of Independence Day. A day which also brings round for Kung Ming, once again, the anniversary of the betrayal of his wife and the violation of the innocent trust his young sister-in-law had reposed in him that had caused her to commit suicide.

Time determines the skilfully handled narrative structure as we move from present to past and back again; thus the whole story acquires a density of meaning which is only gradually revealed to the reader. But time also becomes a major theme. 'The luminous hands of his watch quivered in the dark as he wound it for the next day.' The country may be celebrating its independence, but when the saints go marching in, Kung Ming will not be among their number. He is not even aware of taking part in a public festival; instead he lives in a private hell—of his own making. *D. H.*

When the Saints Go Marching

Lifting up his left hand, Kung Ming glanced at his watch. 5.30 p.m. He still had time.

As his car slipped out from the shade, the sun pounced, scattering sparks of tiny lights on the dark surface of the bonnet. In anticipation he had already screwed up his eyes. Holding the wheel with one hand, he dragged out his handkerchief and quickly wiped the back of his head. The sweat trickled down the sides of his face and ran down his neck. He threw down his handkerchief on the floor of the car and, picking up the dark glasses on the seat, adjusted them over his eyes. The road was now climbing gradually with gentle twists. When he reached the main curve, he checked his watch with the time on the new clock-tower on a hillock that pierced the glassy sky.

In the distance at the end of the road because of the dust, the dark scaly roof of his house rose and floated like the hull of some ancient junk above the thick line of tea-leaf hedge. His house stood on higher ground backing into the hills.

When he saw the roof, he felt a slight throb at his temples. The blood of his old age. The throbs had grown in intensity. Kung Ming sat straight stiffening his back. Without realizing it, he tensed his knees as the great roof grew in size and dirtiness. It sloped sharply down, mottled with blotches that the rains had left like stains of sweat. His face became cold and tremors spread out from the base of his spine in tiny wavelets. He held his breath as the pain came into his right temple, like a hammer blow. Two days ago, he had stared helplessly at the roof. It seemed to move as though riding on a crest of some unseen wave as he approached, and threatened to heave itself over the tall hedge. He had found the strength, however, to pull the car to a stop before it could crash into an embankment.

This time, however, the tremors subsided before they reached his shoulder blades. His breath came out in one great sigh and he drove his car across the road and brought it to a gentle halt in front of the heavy wooden gates. He waited till the giddiness had passed before getting down. He unlocked the gates and drove his car silently up the short incline of the concrete driveway. He turned off the engine, and, feeling the exhaustion and heat suddenly coming over him, rested his forehead on the back of his arm, smelling the heavy odour of his armpits. When he opened his eyes, he saw how dark and coarse his hand had become; the skin on the back was covered with tiny white flakes where he had scratched himself; short straight hairs emerged from beds of pores; and one dark purple vein swelled in his loose skin. With an effort he pushed himself up and got down. He walked to the gates and shut them carefully, using one foot to press down on the iron bolt. The sun boiled on the back of his neck as he bent down to examine the nuts that held the panels together. And then, straightening up, he turned his steps to the house that he had built when he first arrived with his young wife. They had come from Java to settle in this land and he had chosen this patch on the slope of the hill because it was cheap and much cooler than those parts of the city on the coast. He had built with many sons in mind. A very large house. As solid as the rain trees.

The front of the house took up nearly three-quarters of the width of the land with four windows on the lower and upper storeys. A huge wooden porch stood before the entrance of the house. The upper storey was not used and he had the stairs leading to it boarded up, and when he re-wired his house, he prevented the workmen from going upstairs. Sometimes at nights he heard the thumps of musangs on the upper floor. The concrete drive, the tall hedge, the zinc fencing on the sides and back, the heavy gates, were fairly recent.

As he neared the porch, the pink chintz curtain of the nearest window stirred as though disturbed by a breeze. He paused in his steps, narrowing his eyes, as he caught a glimpse of a figure behind the curtain. Gingerly he stepped into the coolness of the porch and sat down on the threshold of the door, removing his shoes. Silence.

"Who's there? Is it you?" he said after a while, trying to keep his voice steady.

There was no answer.

"Who's there?" he called again. Moving into the gloom of the hall, he made out the figure of the new servant, Ah Nooi.

"Are you alone?" He tried to keep the annoyance from his voice.

The girl nodded her head vigorously and looked away. Still in her teens and dark with the sun, she stood with stooping shoulders by the window. A look of nervousness brushed across her features. She tightened her hold on the curtain as she tried to stifle a shiver which was going through her body.

"Was it you who was looking out of the window just now?" he repented his sternness and asked her in a gentle voice. She looked so young in that yellow dress, holding the curtain with a large awkward hand. As she shifted her legs, the light filtered through the curtain touching her young breasts. Small, curving softly and growing every moment. He glanced away sharply. The tips of his fingers tingled as though he was having his first cigarette of the day. He moved his right hand and pretended to adjust the clip of his pen on his pocket. "You can go," he said sharply, forcing himself to be stern. "And don't peep next time." He walked across the hall and switched on the ceiling fan.

But she remained where she was, looking at him, trembling at the corners of her mouth, as though she was going to say something. The sun now glided on to her neck, burning on a mole below her ear, not black but pink like a tiny open wound. She hesitated and then quickly released the curtain, lowering her head as she walked away. As she passed the green door at the other end of the hall, she quickened her steps and disappeared to the back of the house. He followed her passage across the hall and then moved his eyes back to the green door. It was shut.

When she had gone he sat down on an arm-chair, placing his left hand on his lap where he could see the face of his watch. The fan cooled him. After a while, he removed his shirt and took off his singlet and padded to his room on the other side of the corridor that led to the back of the house. He opened his wardrobe and touched his clothes, feeling their crispness. Lifting up his shirt, he brought it to his nose, sniffing the clean smell of the cotton. How well she had ironed his things. It was a pity that her own dress had always looked unwashed and a size too big for her. He wondered if he should buy a few dresses for her. How frightened she looked a moment ago when he first saw her. But there was something in her timid expression which set her apart from the rest. If she were a flower, he would nurse her and wait till she bloomed. And if she could have been his daughter how proud he would have been. But whenever he thought of speaking to her about her dress, a sense of guilt invaded his feelings and he could not utter a word, although he had meant to be kind to her.

Pulling up a chair close to the window he sat leaning with his head on the window-pane, trying to look into the kitchen from his room. He had finished one cigarette and was about to light another when he glanced at his watch. With a start he got up, and walked out of his room and went to the kitchen. She was not there. From the refrigerator he poured ice-cold water into a jug and carried it to the green door. Quietly he took out a bunch of keys and stood with an ear pressed against the door. The hands of his watch pointed to six o'clock and he waited till the second hand quivered towards the figure twelve, before he inserted the key and pushed the door slowly ajar.

The windows of this room were closed. Standing in the doorway he looked towards the bed in the corner of the room. There was no movement. Tiptoeing across the room he pulled the cord of the venetian blinds slowly. The room brightened. He straightened himself and walked over to the bed and sat down on the edge, balancing on one buttock, staring at his wife.

She was flat on her back, breathing regularly. As the bed sank under his weight, she stirred and crossed her ankles. Her face looked small in the pale light—bloodless and full of wrinkles which seamed her cheeks with tiny white scratches. Her eyes were not completely closed and he could see parts of the eye-balls moving loosely beneath the crescent slits, disturbing the swell of her egg-shell lids. Her hair was white, shot with dark streaks at the sides. It was strange sitting like this examining her for a new set of wrinkles.

The muscles of his buttocks began to ache and he had to shift his weight. The movement disturbed her; she opened her eyes, rolling her pupils upwards and then with a small sigh turned over on her side and curled herself into a ball. Her sarong crept up her legs, revealing her calves, lemony-pale and somehow still firm-looking. He ran the pads of his fingers over them lightly trying to recapture those early days. His nails must have scratched her skin, for she shot out her legs and brought her hand to her mouth gasping. She did not recognize him at first, staring wildly.

"Did I disturb you?" He leant over, taking her hand away from her mouth. "I'm sorry." She pushed herself up to look at him. "No, don't get up. Go back to sleep. I'm here now." He smiled with a twitch.

She fell back, yawning and stretching her legs. When she subsided into the bed, she looked straight up at the ceiling and drew in her lower lip, biting it hard between her teeth. His hand moved quickly but before he could touch her, she released her lip. It sprang out, very pink. Raising herself on her elbows, she again scrutinized his face and with one hand clutched the the loose folds of his shirt. He remained still with the tense smile.

"Water, water, I want water." There was no recognition in her voice.

"Yes, yes. Now, will you please lie down. I'll get you the water." Controlling the tremor which fanned out from the base of his spine, he gently freed his shirt from her clutch and tightened the smile on his face. At the touch of his hands she averted her face; the bone suddenly bulged out like a cord smoothing away the wrinkles on the side of her neck.

When he returned with the jug and a plastic cup, leaving the door ajar, he found her in the same position. He called out to her softly, deciding not to touch her again, "Look. Water. I've brought you water. Drink it."

Holding the cup with both hands, she drank the water slowly, pressing the rim hard against the bridge of her nose. After a while she found difficulty in breathing and water ran down her cheeks. She began squeezing the cup. Forgetting his resolution he tried to snatch the cup away and as he touched her, she screamed, jerking her head away. The water spilled. Wet lines ran down the front of her blouse. Swiftly he withdrew his hand and stood up, looking at her with his false smile; he clenched his fists hard against his thighs. For a long time he held his breath. How far did her scream carry this time, how far? The house had grown quiet suddenly. Where was the maid cowering this time? A wave of bitterness battered his thoughts. His temples throbbed. Hadn't he suffered enough? For something he never wanted to happen? A quiver of cold fury rippled through his frame. But he felt, as he did many times before, so helpless, standing before her like this, and when calmness returned, a new sort of bitterness and contempt lingered like a harsh taste in his throat. He savoured this strange taste, and then the usual trickle of resignation percolated through his body, softening his bones and ageing his muscles. Everything seemed so hopeless and grey. They were now in the last years of their lives, and if he could have borne out so far, a little more could hardly do any more damage. He had to take care of her as there was no one else.

It was a mistake to try to take her cup away. Yes, his mistake. He relaxed his fists and his shoulders slumped. Now he could look at her properly. Strange how her face had sunk so much, leaving only the bones sharply defined. One afternoon, when he returned to his office earlier than usual during lunch-break, he had walked past the small store-room and as he was moving away he overheard an argument about where a woman shrank when she got old. A stray sentence had stuck in his mind. "My auntie says lah", came a shrill voice, holding back laughter—and then a pause, "that when a woman grows old, she shrinks from her face downwards, because we develop so much later below lah." The laughter burst out laced with giggles. He walked away quickly.

His wife lay quietly on her pillow as though the scream had exhausted her. She began to twine several strands of hair round her little finger, slow careful movements and started to hum with small mewing noises. The light had shifted across the room and a patch of brightness lay on the front of her blouse like a cat, licking the dry wrinkled throat. She had grown suddenly so old in the last five years. Was it due to some cancerous bleeding that had drained her insides and robbed her flesh of moisture? The professor of medicine at the University of Singapore had examined her and could find nothing organically wrong with her. He had discussed her with the professor as she lay inert on the couch, deep in artificial sleep. And on the journey home, she had been sitting quietly on her seat until a group of young men and women flushed with celebrating Independence Day came noisily into their carriage. She stirred uneasily and began brushing the left side of her face with her hand as though flies had settled on her flesh. He, however, had become strangely excited with watching the boisterous crowd; especially the appearance of those young girls in their short skirts who moved about so confidently along the corridors, their faces alive, that hot afternoon, washed with perspiration. When he went out to get her water, he had to squeeze through a crowd of young girls and as his thighs brushed against their hips his nose caught their hot young smells and the blood rose suddenly in him, making him weak. On his return, his wife probably sensed his excitement for she sat up straight and moved away, refusing to drink. Carefully he took out his handkerchief, surreptitiously rolling it into a ball and held it ready hidden in his palm, waiting for her to scream. Instead, she unpinned her hair and twined the strands round her fingers which she held up spread-eagled in front of her. And when the girls passed along they giggled at the sight and he became very bitter.

94

He felt very tired watching her now, repeating her hand movements, playing with her hair as she lay in her bed. The small of his back ached and he had to arch his spine to get some relief. If only for a moment he could rest his head and go to sleep, unthinking. Where did a man shrink first?

"Come," he said, shaking the thought from his mind, "Let's go out to the garden. The alamanders are out. Come." He must get her out of this room. The thought of those girls had unsettled him.

But she was not listening. She had closed her eyes and was rolling a corner of her blanket between her fingers as though making little balls out of the material.

"Come, please," he pleaded, "really the alamanders are so beautiful. Bright, bright yellow." He drew in a deep breath. The room seemed to be full of the smell of young bodies. Startled, he looked at her guiltily. But she was still rolling the corner of her blanket.

"Please come." He began to wonder about his sense of smell. She dropped the blanket and her hand went to her hair. "Will you come?" A tightness entered into his voice. Watching her, he thought how ugly she had become with that permanent mask of slumbering hatred. A sullen vindictive repose covered her face, and at any moment her features could distort. Thinking of this, an idea formed in his mind, and the more he considered it, the more excited he grew. It became urgent now to get her out of this room. He glanced at his watch. There was still time enough. But first he must lull her, remove her truculence. "All right then," he said, "since you're so worried about your hair, I'll get you a brush. And then you'll look beautiful." It had no relation to what she was doing but from experience he learnt that saying anything that came into his head attracted her attention. He was not wrong.

As he was speaking she swiftly cupped her hand over her mouth. A weird smile spread across her cheeks, stopping at the brink of her vacant eyes. A slight titter came and went. Years ago when he took her out to her first function in a mixed group, some silly Englishman as they were leaving had complimented her in Malay and she had stood still, looking surprised, craning her head, not knowing what to do, and then all of a sudden, she raised her hand and pressed her handkerchief on her mouth, giggling. He felt embarrassed. The same sensation affected him now, only it carried on its fringes glutinous substances of concealed hatred and contempt. Still, he kept the tensed smile on his face. She nodded her head.

Leaving her, he walked to the dressing-table on the other side of the room, bending over and rummaging the drawers for her hair brush. The mirror had been removed. One day when he had come home late, stopping at the hotel, he had found her standing before the mirror. One of her hands was badly cut, bleeding, and the floor was strewn with broken pieces of mirror. It had taken him a long time to coax her to bed and after the doctor had given her some tranquillizers he sat in the arm-chair, keeping watch over her. He swore to himself then that he would never stop at the hotel again. It was another of his mistakes.

"I've found it." He held up the brush and turned round. The prepared smile vanished from his face. She was not in her bed. He rushed forward and went down on his knees looking for her under the bed. The blood went to his head and he got up with difficulty, closing his eyes as he gripped the edge of the bed for purchase, till the spell of giddiness had passed. What a fool he was not to have locked the door.

As he stood up he swayed slightly on his feet before he could make for the door. Slowly he pushed his head out, watching for the slightest movement. Silently he prayed that she would not get into one of her hysterical fits so soon this evening. The saliva gathered in his mouth as he held his breath. When he was certain that his wife was not in the hall, he left the room, taking care to lock the door. Creeping on his toes he made for the kitchen.

When he walked in, Ah Nooi was in the act of slicing up the vegetables, squatting on the floor with her bare feet wide apart. She had her back to him. Tiny prickly sensations ran through his loins when he noticed how heavily her round buttocks pressed on the bottom of her yellow trousers. Perhaps she sensed she was not alone for she swung round with a gasp and dropped the knife on the board. Telling himself that he must keep calm, he glanced round the kitchen with a preoccupied air and without looking at her, quietly retreated heading for the garden in front.

Luckily he had taken the precaution, when the first signs appeared, of building a high zinc fence round three sides of the house. The front hedge was two feet thick and he could not remember how many cart-loads of cow-dung he had had to use. But before the present wooden gates were put up, there was a low swing gate with a latch that could be easily opened. She had disappeared one evening, leaving the swing gate wide open. The searchers had climbed all over the slope of the hill and for a time he avoided leading them in the direction of the great rain-tree which had a stumpy crooked branch growing very low above the huge granite rock at its foot. But, when they could not find her, he mentioned the tree to them, and pleading exhaustion, remained seated on a fallen trunk as they trooped off in a short file carrying torch-lights. He counted their steps until they disappeared from sight. A great shout arose when they saw her standing with upraised arms on the dark rock, trying to touch that crooked branch. And when they brought her back to him she had not stopped screaming and he broke down before the others weeping as he pinned his arms round her. Years ago.

The wooden gates had now become brown; green moss grew between the joints. At a glance, he saw that they were still shut and so he remained standing under the porch. The garden was made up of a green lawn, planted with the finest grass he could buy, studded with delicious fruit trees, small, heavy with dark leaves. The brilliant yellow alamanders, with the rusty seed-pods grew close to the gates. The five varieties of hibiscus bushes held out blood-waxy flowers in the middle of the lawn, and he had lined the borders with red-bricks: next to the alamander, its branches sweeping over the brick border, a gnarled-looking frangipani tree sent its white flowers parachuting to earth at slow intervals. The air had grown cooler and the sun was in the upper branches of the trees.

"Come out," he raised his voice, pointing his hand vaguely at the the trees, "I've seen you." He paused, listening. "You're cheating," he continued, "I've seen you. Won't play any more if you're like that." He then turned his head slowly from left to right and then looked up at the sky. Pale violet, almost pinkish grey, with the sinking sun. "Come out." He shouted again, swallowing his saliva, and then made as if he wanted to walk back into the house. He gave his watch a quick nervous glance.

Before his voice had died away, her laughter shrilled out from behind one of the hibiscus bushes at the far end of the lawn. She stood up, shaking the leaves, with her hair falling over her face. A smile crinkled the mask and then she became sullen. He walked slowly towards her, stopping to pluck the tiny garnet-coloured flowers that grew along the borders.

"Naughty. Naughty. Why didn't you come out before?" He pressed the flowers into her hand. She held them high up and crushed their petals in both hands. She laughed again as she looked at the purplish stains on her palms. He whipped out his handkerchief and nervously wiped her hands. As he did so, he noticed through the corners of his eyes, a tiny movement behind the curtain of the window next to the porch.

"Ah Nooi. Ah Nooi," he called. "Bring out the mat."

The shadow moved away from the curtain.

And then she came out, a flash of bright yellow, holding the mat rolled under her arm, and walked towards them with her head lowered. As she neared them, she dropped the mat, standing still. His wife stared at the servant girl, moving her lips silently and clenching her hands. For a moment he was afraid that his wife would chase the girl as she had done to another girl the previous year, but all his wife did this time was to spit out. "I don't like young girls. They're so bitchified." Her voice hissed. But the girl did not stir. "Go now. You can go now", he said hurriedly, not wanting a scene so soon. How slim her waist was when the girl turned her body away.

"Come let's sit down." He unrolled the mat on the grass.

Without taking her eyes off the retreating figure, his wife sat down stiffly. Her face had become remote.

From his pocket he eased out the pack of cards which he had snatched from a table when he was looking for her in the house. Arching the two halves between his thumbs and forefingers, he brought the cards close together and released them in a series of snaps. The expression on her face changed as she watched him. He shuffled the cards and placed them in a row before him face upwards. She followed the movements of his hands and when he stopped, without a word she leant over and picked out a jack. He nodded and smiled. Three months ago she could not distinguish the cards at all. He had got the idea from a Digest magazine. None of the doctors in the city could do anything for her except to write out prescriptions for tranquillizers and to tell him to keep her calm. As for that mental institution, Tanjong Nyiur Hospital, it was like a prison or worse; he could never send her there, even though some of the doctors were willing to certify her. Some of his business associates had said that great things would happen after Independence and since then he had paid several visits to Tanjong Nyiur, hoping to see changes made. He had been there several times for the past six years without much hope.

Another shuffle and the cards flashed deftly down the mat like the wings of birds. This time however she did not touch the cards. Raising his head, he looked at her. Mouth pouting, dry brownish lips corded with wrinkles, she sucked and blew; her cheeks swelled and collapsed in tight balloon curves and flabby hollows, the bones protruding under the withered flesh. The phrase of that young girl at his office stabbed into his mind and with a shock, he realized that they had been talking about his wife. She had once gone to his office a few days before he overhead the conversation, dressed like a young girl, and when he looked into her eyes, he knew that she was in one of her moods. After he had calmed her down, he led her out from his room. It was on one of those grey hot afternoons when everyone sat listless behind their desks, expecting time to pass. He sweated under the armpits. And as they were going through the main office, his wife broke away from him and ran up to one of the girls and slapped her on the cheek. The girl gave a gasp, trying to stand up. His wife pushed her down and, screaming, pinched her breasts. "Indecent! Indecent!" There was a startled silence. With the help of the office boy, he got her out of the building. That afternoon he did not return to his office.

"All right, pick out a king," he said, controlling his feelings; his wife blew her cheeks. A ball of hardness grew in him and his voice became thin. The memory of what had happened in the office made him suddenly bitter.

Perhaps she sensed the change in him for she stopped at once. A look of wariness came into her expression. Her eyes darkened and glowed in the fading light, her right hand trembled as she stretched and curled her fingers spasmodically. She sat very still. He did not know whether she was going to cry or shout at him.

"Come on", he urged, thinning his voice farther, enjoying his bitterness.

A tremor twitched the muscles of her left cheek, and as she nervously extended her right hand, she gazed at him with unmoving eyes. He noticed her gaze and resorted to the trick of staring through her, keeping his head immobile. She surrendered this time and quietly she lowered her head, keeping her hand poised above the cards. Suddenly the silence was broken by a high warble of the yellow bird flying towards the hill. She pulled her hand back and lifted her head, following the flight of the bird. A look of horror inched into her face when she noted the direction of its flight, swooping low towards the great trees.

"See there is a . . ." He tried to distract her for he too had seen where the bird was heading for. Before he could finish, she lunged forward and swept the cards from the mat. She beat the grass with both fists, crying.

"It's all right. Don't cry. It's all right." His bitterness fled. He sensed the great grief that bound them together. It made him so impotent when it came so unexpectedly. For once he felt genuinely contrite. He put out his hand and laid it trembling on her shoulder. She calmed down at once. "Come, lie down. You'll feel much better." So long as she could not see the hill, her calmness would remain.

She allowed him to push her down without a struggle. Stretched out on the mat she crossed her arms over her stomach staring at the sky. He began talking to her, little phrases which she liked to hear, at the same time running his fingers gently over her forehead, keeping his eyes closed. When he opened his eyes she was asleep. It was getting dark. Above, the sky turned dark-violet, streaked with clouds. The air stopped moving and the earth was releasing its warmth in slow humid layers. Cars hummed steadily on the road leaving washes of sound; their headlamps speckling the hedge, blowing patches of fireflies against the dark leaves, as they swept past. The slopes of the hill absorbed the fading twilight; cauliflower tops of the trees submerged as the shadows of the night crept up towards the peak. And that yellow bird was probably nesting in some great tree on a quivering branch, looking at the dark rocks below. In the dusk, the frangipani tree bled at slow intervals small white drops from a dark body.

And Siew Choo, he thought, in her white pyjama dress under the frangipani, watching the flare of the dying sun behind the back of the hill, had stood like an apparition petrified amongst these fallen flowers. He had nearly startled her, walking up to her from the darkened house, to call her in. Young, very much younger than his wife, Siew Choo had come to stay with them waiting for her wedding day to arrive. He was to be her wedding witness, since his father-in-law was already dead and there was no male line in her family. There was still some two months before the wedding. But she had wanted to see his wife who had left home when she was still a child.

Perhaps excited by the beauty of the hill, she talked freely to him, in the garden before coming into the house. He found it a strange experience to be able to talk freely to a young woman.

His wife's health had been failing for some time; mysterious backaches and night sweats, and she had left the girl in his care. Sometimes he took Siew Choo to the city, shopping with her, and he was gradually fascinated by her quiet manners. Every evening, after food, they would go out into the garden, his wife excusing herself. He did not remember much of their conversation. Mostly about trivial matters which seemed to amuse her. The girl was greedy for knowledge about the outside world and soon lost her initial shyness. He could look at her without embarrassing her. A pair of dark eyes reflecting the lights of the night, delicate oval face, and a voice that tinkled. She was a much finer version of his wife and was surprisingly gentle. His wife had a certain streak of hardness, malevolence slumbering under a parchment of restraint. The girl reminded him of the soft breast of a yellow bird.

He could not exactly remember how it had happened. One evening as they were playing cards, his fingers accidentally brushed against the back of her hand. Cool. He felt instantly as though a spark had fallen on his flesh. The small of his back tensed. From that night, he had avoided seeing her, repressing his feelings that took on a strange disturbing quality. But after a few nights of indecision, he dismissed the incident from his mind, or rather, tried to look upon it as something not to worry about. After all it was an accident.

The girl was at first puzzled and could not understand the change in him. Her laughter still tinkled. Slowly however she became aware of his gaze, and then, a worried look knitted her brows when he did not look away quickly enough. She appeared to be frightened of him. But so long as he could pick out from the heavy night air the young tangerine smell that came from her, it did not bother him if the girl thought him strange.

On the day Independence was proclaimed he had joined in the celebrations, quaffing drinks with his business associates at the bar, exchanging innuendos with the waitresses, and when he came home later than usual, balancing himself on the balls of his feet as he got down from the car, he had found her under the frangipani tree, face lifted to the sky, watching the fireworks. The marchers had long ago passed the house. He walked softly to her side. She asked him what was going on in the city. It was the drinks of course. His skin prickled in the cool air and strange feelings, released by brandy, swept through him until he felt dizzy to the finger-tips. It was the thought of those girls in the city with their excited faces that made him do it. He caught hold of her, giddiness sweeping into his head as he kissed her. She gave out a cry. The fireworks opened out an umbrella of light in the sky, sputtering the darkness with dots of iridescence, and, as she managed to push him away, they saw the the figure of his wife facing them under the porch. The girl broke away and ran into the house past his wife. Oh so very stupid of her. He could have found excuses if she had not run that night.

Far into the night the fireworks popped, but an uneasy silence hovered over the house. He slept fitfully on the couch under the fan instead of going to his room. His wife had flung his things out. Once he thought in his dreams he saw a dark shadow bending over him, as he turned over on his side, touching him on his cheek. Towards early morning when he could not sleep, he got up and walked for a long time in the hall. And then he peered into his room; his wife was still sound asleep. He resumed his pacing and finally went to the other room, trembling as he pushed the door open. But Siew Choo's bed was empty. He wandered through the house searching for her quietly and then went out into the garden. As he was about to return, he saw that the swing gates were unlocked. The road outside was deserted. Feeling unwell, he returned to the hall. Half-an-hour had passed before he could bring himself to wake up his wife. And when they got a search party going, it was already light. In a tight group, they scoured about the slopes of the hill. It was his wife who saw her swinging from the stumpy crooked branch of the rain-tree, a small white figure dangling above the dark rock. Her screams shattered the quietness of the hill as she ran forward and tried to pull the girl down. He led his wife home and called for a doctor.

Of course he was genuinely contrite. In his mind he questioned fate. It was after all such a small trivial thing and why should it end in this way. Somehow Kung Ming never accepted the fact that life was shaped in the same way that the night was enlarged by a single solitary quiver from the cricket's throat.

That was seven years ago. The cold night air froze his face and he shivered. The luminous dial of his watch showed 7.45 p.m. His wife was still sleeping on the mat. The road had become quiet all of a sudden. Slowly, a new sound arose. Faintly at first, from a distance, the strains of music approached. His wife was still asleep and he debated with himself. Should he allow it to happen. Turning his head he saw the lights in the hall shining through the pink curtains, and biting his lips, he prayed silently that what he wanted to happen would not happen. After Siew Choo's death, he had collapsed inside;

the dam had broken, and the pure stream was now an evil flood. He put his head on his knees, pressing hard against the knee-caps till his forehead hurt. It was too late now. He raised his head and looked in the direction of the hedge. Sequinned with probing lights of the gas-lamps held by the approaching marchers the hedge quivered in the breeze like a serpent. The sounds of the parade rose, filling the air. Voices in songs. Trumpets. Brassy martial airs. And suddenly like a sword, the voice from a microphone lashed out. A sharp strident command was issued. "Independence. Long Live Our Nation." A great shout came from the crowds, "Independence! Independence!"

His wife sat up with a start, looking to the left and right, without understanding anything. Suddenly high up in the dark sky the first fireworks hung out their branches, exploding. A swelling roar came from the marchers. For a moment his wife remained stunned and then with a huge leap she ran into the house, screaming.

When he rushed after her into her room she had thrown herself into her bed, her face distorted.

"Ah Nooi. Ah Nooi", Kung Ming yelled above her screams. "Come here quick." He then flung himself against his wife and pinned her down as she started to rise. Turning his head he saw the maid staring at them from the doorway. "Quick, get me the bottle of pills and a cup of water. Quick!" he shouted to the frightened girl. The girl hurried away and came back with the bottle and the plastic cup. "Come closer." He waved his free hand. "Now press her down when I give her the medicine." He prayed silently that she would not run away. The girl obeyed him.

When his wife saw who was holding her, obscenities frothed from her mouth. The girl turned pale. Trying to keep his fingers from jerking, he unscrewed the cap and poured out the pills into his palm. And then leaning over, he slapped his wife several times, and using his thumb and forefinger as pincers, dug into her cheeks, forcing her to open her mouth. She made a gurgling sound and with surprising strength, twisted over on her side, wrenching her face from his grasp, dragging the girl with her. The sudden movement threw him off his balance and he found himself with his chest on top of the shoulders of the girl. Another struggle as his wife tried to get up. The buttocks of the girl heaved and crushed against his belly. A tremor prickled his loins. Bringing his left hand over the girl's head he held the cheeks of his wife in a pincer grip again. Slowly he forced the mouth to open. With the other hand he shook the pills into the quivering mouth and closed his hand over it, pinching her nose with the other hand. His wife swallowed the pills as though she was retching. The girl was now crying. In the confusion he stroked the curve of her buttocks, trembling and feeling weak. For a long time the three of them remained locked together. With a shock he realized that he was kissing the bright pink mole below the girl's ear licking it with the top of his tongue. His nose was inhaling her lemony smell as though he was a dog. He was rubbing himself on her. And then a wave of giddiness swept over him. He regained control of himself shifting his body from hers, and heard himself say in a strained voice, "You can go now." His wife lay below him now, pinned down by his weight. The girl moved, pressing against him; the bed creaked, one of the springs snapping into place as she climbed down. When he turned his face he met the curious embarrassed gaze of the girl who remained standing by the side of the bed. Her eyes glowed with understanding. "You can go. I'm all right. I'm all right," he repeated, averting his face. She walked away, hunched slightly. When she had gone, he wept quietly over his wife who was now lying still as if dead.

The parade was over half-an-hour ago. Quietly he got up from the bed and went out to the garden retrieving the fallen cards and rolling up the mat. It was a moonless night and the fireworks still banged overhead. He felt weak and rested against a tree. A large waxy flower brushed his check and fell on to the ground.

As he started to walk back, the light from the girl's room went out. He shut his eyes as the tremors began, indecisive, pausing on the edge of the lawn; with an effort he resumed his walk. He switched off the hall lights, listening attentively for her sounds. A quiver from the throat of a cricket trembled in the air; dove-grey lizards moved lazily on the ceiling boards, seeking their victims. Who was it last time. Was it Ah Pin who stammered as she hurriedly locked her door, or Ah Kim with heavy knowing glances when she ironed clothes and then tried to blackmail him, or Ah Poh who banged on the front gates wanting to get out? So many, it seemed.

Feeling tired, he went to his wife's room and crumpled into the arm-chair, staring at her vague form on the bed. Thank heaven to-morrow was a holiday. He closed his eyes, fighting against the pull of dark dreams that had become frequent. The musangs ran softly across the upper floor of his house. In a queer way he was happy, he thought to himself, he had a house and no money worries. Independence had brought him greater riches. If only Siew Choo was alive. The luminous hand of his watch quivered in the dark as he wound it for the next day.

Wilson Harris

Wilson Harris is one of the most challenging and rewarding novelists writing in the Commonwealth today. If ready-made concepts were not so alien to his art, we might say that he has introduced a kind of 'permanent revolution' in Caribbean writing. Contrary to what is often said of him, he is not a pure aesthete but an intensely committed writer who compels the reader to reject, as he does, prejudice and preconceived ideas, and demands his active participation in the discovery of man. "Kanaima" illustrates the outstanding qualities of Harris's work: the freedom of the imagination, the power to epitomize and control his material, and his coherent use of symbols.

In *The Marches of El Dorado* Michael Swan writes that Kanaima 'is perhaps the most potent force in all Indian life . . . it is still very much alive among the Indians as the source of death and evil". While remaining faithful to the traditional character of the evil spirit, Wilson Harris has discovered a new significance in his role. "Kanaima" describes a struggle between life and death in the Guyanese landscape which is gradually transmuted into a struggle between life and death of a spiritual and universal significance. The setting is the dying village of Tumatumari. Though it is described as a 'standing death' it contains potentialities of life, concrete in the waterfall with its 'violent inner concentration and energy'. However, this symbol of 'something alive and vibrant and wholehearted' is an untamed, and therefore wasted, life force.

The Indians who came to the empty and lifeless village in search of 'a new encampment', i.e., of a new life, are themselves flying from death, which for some time has pursued them in several forms; the last of these, a destructive fire, is interpreted by them as a spiritual warning. Yet, wherever they go, they see death as something outside themselves. The 'barren', African pork-knocker (a gold- or diamond-miner) who meets them personifies the death which results from the gold-miners' exclusive concern for material riches, from their 'expending nearly every drop of heart's blood in the fever and lust of the diamond bush'. Because Jordan and his companion are inhospitable and selfish, we have the impression at first that they merely want to get rid of the Indians, until we realize that Jordan too is afraid of death and aware of its hold over his own life. Both the Indians and the Africans submit to what they interpret as the inevitability of fate and through their passivity and resignation acquiesce in the power of death.

The way to death is described in the imagery of a snake coiling through the story like the trail through the forest, and repeatedly showing its ugly head. It is a manifestation of primeval undifferentiated life as well as a life-giving principle. The snake of Tumatumari is dead since it is with its skin that the trail is compared, while its entrails, which used to contain its fertilizing power, are 'dangling and rotting' like 'husks of vine' in the forest. But the snake is also a symbol of the inferior psyche, of the unconscious, and as such is associated with the fire that destroys the Indians' village, with the garment of Kanaima and with the 'trailing darkness' that envelops Tumatumari when Kanaima is among them. As a symbol, the snake shows affinity with the shadow, itself an expression of man's personal unconscious and of the negative, dark side of his personality. Now it is as a shadow that Kanaima appears, shaped by the two shadows of the pork-knockers and making one with the shadows of the forest, which participates in their death in life. The shadow of Kanaima is inseparable from the earth, the primeval mother; its cloak sweeps 'into a black hole in the ground', and though moving freely in death, is incapable of an upward movement.

As soon as Kanaima materializes on the scene, it is shown literally feeding on the meat of life. The signs of possible rebirth are still present: the fire lifts a tongue up to heaven, and the sound of the falls with their potential fertility is heard by the Indian headman. But he remains aware of death only. Arriving at Tumatumari, he and his companions had felt that 'the world they knew was dying everywhere and no one could dream what would take its place'. Now he sees that 'all the trails were vanishing into a running hole in the ground', i.e., were all leading to death instead of ascending to life. But unexpectedly, the struggle between life and death is brought to a climax in the person of his wife, who has misjudged the trail (the snake, the shadow: death). The headman perceives then 'the cloud of unknowing darkness' (their own ignorance or want of spiritual light). Recognizing Kanaima in the watchman, in nature, in everything that surrounds them, the Indians are struck by 'what they knew all along'. At last they acknowledge the presence of the Lord of Death among themselves. If they have been unable to escape his threatening shadow, if death was at each place they were coming to, it was because they were carrying it within themselves. Now their fate is being played out in one of their own, who acts as a 'vessel of experience', as Harris would say, 'the *groping* muse of all their humanity'.

Passing through the jaws of a monster is one way of gaining access to heaven or to real life. As the woman climbs upon the 'staircased-teeth' (the ladder leading to life), the roaring jaws of the waterfall, now a potential instrument of death, are the gateway to salvation for herself and her companions. If Kanaima alone knows whether she will reach the cliff top, it is because their unconscious, or the deathly part in them, is still all-powerful and still takes precedence over their conscious self.

Though apparently pessimistic, the story implies that the characters can free themselves from the all-pervasive influence of death. Life and death are inseparable but the Guyanese or, for that matter, universal man, can either choose between looking up to 'the golden mountains of heaven' or allowing themselves to be dragged into 'the hole in the ground'. Tumatumari means 'sleeping rocks' and rocks are said to be the source of life. Whatever is asleep can always be awakened. *H. M.-J.*

Kanaima

Tumatumari is a tiny dying village on a hill on the bank of the Potaro River, overlooking roaring rapids. The bursting stream foams and bunches itself into a series of smooth cascading shells enveloping backs of stone. Standing on the top of the hill one feels the gully and river sliding treacherously and beautifully as though everything was slipping into its own curious violent inner concentration and energy, and one turns away and faces the tiny encampment and village with a sensation of loss—as of something alive and vibrant and wholehearted, whose swift lure and summons one evades once again to return to the shell of this standing death.

A beaten trail that keeps its distance from the dangerous brink of the gorge winds its spirit over the hill, through the village, like the patient skin of a snake, lying on the ground with entrails hanging high as husks of vine, dangling and rotting in the ancient forest.

The village seems to hold its own against the proliferation of the jungle with great difficulty, dying slowly in a valiant effort to live, eternally addressed by the deep voice of the falls, conscious too of a high far witness across the slanting sky—a blue line of mountains upholding a fiction of cloud.

A tiny procession—about a dozen persons in all, mostly women and children—was making its way across the trail. The man who led them, a rather stocky Indian, had stopped. His face bore the mooning fateful look of the Macusi Indians, travelling far from home. They lived mostly in the high Rupununi savannahs stretching to Brazil, a long way off, and the village encampment at Tumatumari was composed of African and Negro pork-knockers, most of whom were absent at this time, digging the interior creeks for diamonds. They had left a couple of old watchmen behind them at Tumatumari but otherwise the village (which they used as a base camp) was empty. The leader of the newcomers reconnoitred the situation, looking around him with brooding eyes, rolling a black globule and charm on his tongue, and exhibiting this every now and then against his teeth under his curling lips with the inward defiance of an experienced hunter who watches always for the curse of men and animals.

The six o'clock parrots flew screeching overhead. The Indians looked at the sun and corrected their mental timepiece. It could not have been later than four. The sky was still glowing bright on the mountain's shoulder. In the bush the hour was growing dark, but here on the snake's trail which coiled around the huts and the shuttered houses the air still swam with the yellow butter of the sun.

One of the old decrepit watchmen left by the Negro pork-knockers was approaching Macusis. He shambled along, eyeing the strangers in an inhospitable, barren way. "Is no use," he said when he reached them, shaking his head at them with an ominous spirit, "Kanaima been here already." The Indians remained silent and sullen, but in reality they were deeply shaken by the news. They started chattering all of a sudden like the discordant premature parrots that had passed a few moments ago overhead. The sound of their matching voices rose and died as swiftly as it had begun. Their stocky leader with the black fluid beetle on his tongue addressed the old watchman, summoning all the resources of the pork-knocker's language he was learning to use. "When Kanaima"—he spoke the dreadful name softly, hoping that its conversion into broken English utterance deprived it of calling all harm, and looking around as if the ground and the trees had black ears—"when Kanaima come here?" he asked. "And which way he pass and gone?" His eyes, like charms betokening all guarded fear, watched the watchman before him. They glanced at the sky as if to eclipse the sentence of time and looked to the rim of the conjuring mountains where the approach of sunset burned indifferently, as though it stood on the after-threshold of dawn. rather than against the closing window of night.

"He gone so—that way." The old Negro pointed to the golden mountains of heaven. "He say to tell you"—his voice croaked a little—"he expect you here today and he coming tonight to get you. He know every step of the way you come since you run away from home and is no use you hiding any more now. I believe"—he dropped his voice almost to a whisper—"I believe if you can pass him and shake him off your trail in the forest tonight—you got your only chance."

The Indians had listened attentively and their chattering rose again, full of staccato wounded cries above the muffled voice of the waterfall, dying into helpless silence and submersion at last. "We got take rest," the leader of the party declared heavily and slowly, pronouncing each word with difficulty. He pointed to everyone's condition, indicating that they stood on the very edge of collapse. They had come a long way—days and weeks—across steep ridges and through treacherous valleys. They must stop now even if it was only for four or five hours of recuperative sleep. The burden of flight would be too great if they left immediately and entered the trail in the night.

"Is no use," the old man said. Nevertheless he turned and shambled towards a shattered hut which stood against the wall of the jungle. It was all he was prepared to offer them. The truth was he wanted them to go away from his village. His name was Jordan. Twenty years of pork-knocking—living on next to nothing, expending nearly every drop of heart's blood in the fever and lust of the diamond bush—had reduced him to a scarecrow of ill-omen always seeing doom, and Kanaima, the avenging Amerindian god, who could wear any shape he wished, man or beast, had come to signify —almost without Jordan being aware of it—the speculative fantasy of his own life; the sight of strange Indians invariably disturbed him and reminded him of the uselessness of time like a photograph of ghosts animated to stir memories of injustice and misfortune. He always pictured them as bringing trouble or flying from trouble. They were a conquered race, were they not? Everybody knew that. It was best to hold them at arm's length though it seemed nothing could prevent their scattered factions from trespassing on ground where he alone wanted to be.

The light of afternoon began to lose its last vivid shooting colour, the blazing gold became silver, and the resplendent silver was painted over by the haze of dusk. In the east the sky had turned to a deep purple shell, while an intensity of steel appeared in the west, against which—on the topmost ridge of the ghostly mountains— the trees were black smudges of valiant charcoal emphasising the spectral earth and the reflection of fury. A few unwinking stars stood at almost vanishing point in the changing spirit of heaven.

The Indians witnessed the drama of sunset, as if it were the last they would see, through the long rifts in the roof of the house, and out beyond the open places in the desolate walls. The stupor of their long day enveloped them, the ancient worship of the sun, the mirage of space and the curse of the generations.

Kanaima had been on their heels now for weeks and months.

Their home and village, comprising about sixty persons, had been stricken. First, there had been an unexpected drought. Then the game had run away in the forest and across the savannahs. After that, people had started dropping down dead. Kanaima planted his signature clear at last in the fire he lit no one knew when and where; it came suddenly running along the already withered spaces of the savannahs, leaving great black charred circles upon the bitten grass everywhere, and snaking into the village compound where it lifted its writhing self like a spiritual warning in the headman's presence before climbing up the air into space.

They knew then it was no use quarrelling with fate. Day after day they had travelled, looking for somewhere to set up a new encampment, their numbers dwindling all the time, and every situation they came to, it was always to find that Kanaima had passed through before them. If it was not nature's indifference—lack of water or poor soil—they stumbled upon barren human looks and evil counsel, the huts they saw were always tumbling down, and the signs upon the walls they visited were as arid and terrible as flame, as their own home had looked when they had left to search for a new place. It was as if the world they saw and knew was dying everywhere, and no one could dream what would take its place. The time had surely come to stop wherever they were and let whatever had to happen, happen.

It was a hot, stifling night that fell pitch-black upon them. Jordan and the other aged watchman the pork-knockers had left at Tumatumari had nevertheless lit a fire in the village, over which they roasted a bush cow they had shot that morning. It was rare good fortune at a time when the country was yielding little game. The flame blazed steadily, painting a screen on the trees and the shadows of the two men seemed to race hither and thither out of a crowded darkness and back into multitudes still standing on the edge of the forested night. It seemed all of a sudden that another man was there in the open, a sombre reticent spectator. His shadow might have been an illusion of a glaring moment on the earth, or a curious blending of two living shapes into the settlement of a third moving presence.

He was taller than the two blind watchmen over whom he stood. He studied them from behind a fence of flaming stakes, a volcanic hallucinated gateway that might have belonged to some ancient overshadowed primeval garden. It was as if, though he stood near, he was always too far for anyone to see his flowing garb. It appeared as if his feet were buried in a voluminous cloak whose material swept into a black hole in the ground, yet when he moved it was with perfect freedom and without a sign of stumbling entanglement. He occasionally glided over the enfolding majestic snake of his garment that obeyed his footsteps.

All at once sparks flew and his shadow seemed to part the two men in a rain of comets, despatching one with a great leg of beef to the hut where the Indians were, while with another imperious gesture his muffled hand turned the roasting cow into a comfortable position for the one who remained by the fire to slice a share of the breast for dinner. It was the tenderest part of the meat and the stranger devoured a ghostly portion. A distant breeze stirred the whole forest and the fire lifted a tongue up to heaven as though a nest of crucial stars remaining just above a mass of dark trees had finally blown down on earth's leaves.

All around the fire and under the stars the night had grown blacker than ever. The crowding phantoms of the bush had vanished, turning faceless and impotent and one with Kanaima's cloak of trailing darkness: the strong meat of life over which the lord of death stood had satisfied them and driven them down into the blackest hole at his feet. The aged watchmen too had their fill and seemed unable to rise from their squatting heels, dreaming of a pile of diamonds under the waterfall. The Macusi headman came to the door of the hut and stood looking towards every hidden snake and trail in the jungle. His companions were sound asleep after their unexpected meal. They had picked the bone clean and then tossed it into the uncanny depths of the lost pit outside their window. Even if they had wanted to resume their journey, the headman felt, it was impossible to do so now. The sound of the Tumatumari Falls rose into the air like sympathetic magic and universal pouring rain. But not a drop descended anywhere out of a sky which was on fire, burning with powder and dust choked with silver and gold, a great pork-knocker's blackboard and riddle, infinitely rich with the diamonds of space and infinitely poor with the wandering skeletons of eternity.

The headman let his chin drop slowly upon his breast, half-asleep in awe and with nameless fatigue and misery. It was no use complaining he said to himself. Tumatumari was the same as every other village through which they had come, uniform as the river's fall and the drought standing all over the forgotten land from which the had fled, insignificant as every buried grave over which they had crossed. All the trails were vanishing into a running hole in the ground and there was nothing more to do than wait for another joint of roasting meat to fall upon them from the stars that smoked over their head.

There was a movement in the hut behind him, the shaking of a hammock, and a woman appeared in the door beside him. He recognised her in the dim light. She was his wife. She said something to him and began descending the steps, rolling a little like a balloon and half-crouching like an animal feeling for sand before it defecates.

The headman suddenly raised an alarm. He realised she had taken the wrong direction, her eyes half-bandaged by sleep. She had misjudged the trail and had blundered towards the waterfall. His voice was hardly out of his throat when her answering shriek pierced him. She had come to the yawning blind gully, had tried to scramble for the foothold she was losing, and had only succeeded in slipping deeper and deeper. The headman continued to shout, running forward at the same time. He perceived the cloud of unknowing darkness where the chasm commenced and far below he felt he saw the white spit of foam illuminated by starshine, blue and treacherous as a devil. The voices of his companions had followed him and were flying around him like a chorus of shrieks, and it seemed their cry also came from below. The two village-watchmen had also been aroused and they were heaving at the low fire, squandering a host of sparks, until they had acquired flaming branches in their hands. They began to approach the gully. The flaring billowing light forked into the momentous presence of their infused companion, the shadow of the god who had attended the feast. He had been crouching at the fire beside them as though he presided over each jealous spark, his being shaped by the curious flux of their own bodies which wove his shape on the ground. Now his waving cloak swirled towards the great pit and it seemed that no one realized he was there until the headman of the Macusis saw him coming at last, a vast figure and extension of the dense frightful trees shaking everywhere and shepherding the watchmen along.

"Kanaima," he screamed. The whole company were startled almost out of their wits, and Jordan—who had met the Indians that afternoon when they arrived in the village—gasped, "I tell you so." He repeated like a rigmarole, "I tell you so."

Then indeed, as if they were proving what they had known all along, they perceived him, his head raised far in the burning sky and his swirling trunk and body sliding over the illuminated cloud above the waterfall. Yet in spite of themselves they were all drawn towards the precipice and the roaring invisible rainfall in the night. The flaring torches in their hands picked out the snaking garment which streamed upon the hideous glitter of the angry river, whose jaws gaped with an evil intent. They were lost in wonder at which they saw. The woman who had fallen hung against the side of the cliff, half-sitting upon a jutting nose of rock, her hands clasping a dark trailing vine that wreathed itself upwards along a ragged descending face in the wall. The torches lit up her blind countenance and her pinpoint terrified eyes were enabled to see grinning massive teeth in the face on the wall. Tremblingly holding the vine—as if it were a lock of beloved hair—she began to climb upon the staircased-teeth, brushing lips of stone that seemed to support her, and yet not knowing whether at any moment she would be devoured by falling into the roaring jaws of death.

The watchers waited and beheld the groping muse of all their humanity: Kanaima alone knew whether she would reach the cliff top.

Frank Sargeson

I began to read all the New Zealand fiction I could lay my hands on; and it seemed to me that virtually always the formal language of the English novelists had been used to deal with the material of New Zealand life . . . and for the first time so far as I can remember I asked myself the question whether there might not be an appropriate language to deal with [that] material.

(from the New Zealand periodical, *Landfall*, No. 74)

The language of Frank Sargeson's short stories seems as apparently plain and straightforward as does his whole art as a short story writer. At first glance no story in this anthology looks more unassuming or seems written with less art. 'When I called at that farm they promised me a job for two months so I took it on, but it turned out to be tough going,' one begins, or, 'It was during the slump, when times were bad'. The characteristic quiet note is struck from the start, the voice is never raised, even the violence, cruelty and passion found in several of the stories is described in the same low-key, dispassionate monotone. But this language, down-to-earth and colloquial, firmly rooted in the idiom of New Zealand speech, is deceptively simple, for it is, in reality, a skilfully devised literary medium kept within carefully circumscribed limits. The art of Sargeson's stories is essentially an art of understatement which restricts itself to the surface and leaves the reader to plumb the depths. For it is not only what is said that matters, of even greater importance is what remains unsaid. Thus Ted in "A Man and His Wife", baulked from finding an outlet for his feelings in his marriage, is forced to find some form of emotional release by keeping at first a dog, which is killed, and then a canary. The depth of his feelings, when he loses even that and returns to his wife, is merely implied in the flat exchange of remarks with which the story concludes. 'I've still got the wife, he said. Yes, I said. The wife never let me down, he said. No, I said.'

'An appropriate language to deal with the material of New Zealand life'; several critics in Sargeson's own country have been concerned with the question of how much of the material is authentically New Zealand. And it is true that the world of his short stories seems a restricted one, mainly populated by social misfits and underdogs. But, like Hemingway's characters, they are inarticulate men, not without feelings, but unable to express them. The limitations of their understanding is demarcated by the limits of their speech. Like Ted and the narrator of this story they often feel an instinctive but tacit comradeship with each other, similar to the "mateship" that is also found in Australian life and literature, especially in Henry Lawson's work. But, whereas for the Australian men in the outback mateship was an answer to the loneliness of the vast solitudes surrounding them on all sides, in Sargeson's work solitude is a state of mind. It is the hardship of their lives that brings his characters together ('along the street you'd meet too many who were as hard put to it as you were yourself'), and it is also this relationship which helps alleviate these conditions ('that's one thing the slump did, it put a certain sort of comradeship into life that you don't find now').

As the tone here indicates, however, this is not a bond of personal relationship that is idealized in any way. Sargeson is too much of a realist, too aware of some of the conditions of modern man, whether in New Zealand or elsewhere, for that to happen. If his characters can become "cobbers", they can also drift apart again as casually as they do in this story, leaving them alone and rootless in a New Zealand and in a country of the mind where, even while they are at home, they are still inescapably solitary and alien. *D. H.*

A Man and His Wife

It was during the slump, when times were bad. Bad times are different from good times, people's habits aren't quite the same. When the slump was on you didn't have to worry about certain things. The way you were dressed, for instance. Along the street you'd meet too many who were as hard put to it as you were yourself. That's one thing the slump did, it put a certain sort of comradeship into life that you don't find now.

During the slump people had to live where they could, and a lot of them lived in sheds and wash-houses in other people's backyards. I lived in an old shed that had once been a stable, and it was all right except for the rats. It was out towards the edge of the town, and there were two of us living there, and my cobber was on relief work like myself. There'd been some trouble between him and his wife, so when he had to get out he came and lived with me. It cut the rent in half, and there was room enough. And Ted was quite a good hand at rigging up a table and suchlike out of any odds and ends he could pick up. He got quite a lot of pickings from a rubbish tip that was handy, and with me giving him a hand we made a fireplace and got the place pretty snug, which it needed to be for the winter. It wasn't a bad sort of life. We never went short of tucker, though a few times we had to raid a Chinaman's garden after we'd spent all our money in the pubs. As a single man, I'd only get about a day and a half's relief work a week, and drew fourteen shillings. Ted got more but of course there was his wife, and he had to part up.

I knew Ted only casually until I struck him on relief. He hadn't long been in the town. He'd had a good job in a pub, but he went on the booze once too often. To start with he wasn't so hot with a shovel, and the gang used to pull his leg, but he was a good-tempered bloke, and as I say there grew up that comradeship when the slump was on. It was pretty hard for him when his wife got her separation, because it was all in the paper, and everybody started making jokes. When she got in Court his wife certainly got going about the sort of husband he was. Besides always getting drunk, she said, he kept a dog, and he'd talk to the dog when he'd never talk to her. He was always taking the dog for walks too, and once when she tried to go along as well he locked her in the wash-house and never let her out until he came home. Well, our gang certainly thought up plenty of jokes about that dog.

When he came to my place, Ted brought the dog. It was nothing special, just a dog, but Ted was certainly fond of it. He had it sleeping at the foot of his bed, and I only put up with it because it was good for the rats. But later on it got under a bus along the road and that was the finish. Ted took it pretty hard, but he wasn't the sort that ever says much. He never told me anything about the trouble he'd had with his wife. There are men who'll talk to you about such things, but it's more often you find women that way. And Ted's wife was the sort. She'd call sometimes to collect her money, though if Ted saw her coming up the road he'd hook off if he could before she got near. And if he couldn't I'd hook off while they had their barney. But usually Ted would have a fair idea when she was coming and wouldn't be around, and then Mrs. Watts would talk to me. She was quite all right, quite a nice woman, though always a bit on edge so to speak. She'd say quite a lot. Ted spent too much money on drink, she said, but it was the dog that was the trouble. A man ought to put his wife first, she said. She wouldn't have minded so much if it had been another woman. She couldn't understand it, she said. Well, maybe I couldn't either, so I felt sorry for Mrs. Watts. But I felt sorry for Ted too, so I never told her when the dog was done in. I thought maybe things would come right if they were just left alone.

It didn't work out though, because one day Ted came home with a canary, and he certainly began to think the world of that canary. It just about made me think that he might be a bit unnatural, though I didn't think he was, because one night when some of the gang were round and we were all a bit stonkered, Ted told about how his missis once ran a fish shop and had a girl serving behind the counter for a pound a week. And it was only a shame she was worth the money, Ted said. His wife used to complain that the pound made too big a hole in the profits, but as for him he reckoned the girl was well worth the money. But of course we all chipped in to say he was a dirty old man, and it was no wonder his missis had kicked him out.

But about the canary. Ted loved that bird. He worshipped it. And anyway, it certainly could sing. Ted'd make himself late for work in the morning talking to it and seeing it was all O.K., and he paid a neighbour's little girl sixpence a week to always run over and put the cage inside the window if it came on to rain. And when we got home it was no good expecting him to lend a hand because he'd just want to sit down and kid to the bird. I'd tell him he was a goat, but it did no good. Even when the dinner was cooked it was no good telling him to come and eat, he'd sooner just sit there and kid to the bird.

There was another thing too. Ted'd get all hot and bothered if anybody began to take too much of an interest in his bird. He didn't mind me so much, though I sort of felt I had to keep off the grass. It was when there was a crowd round that he'd get properly hot and bothered. We'd have some rare old times some evenings when there was a crowd round, usually some of the boys in the gang. We'd fill up the baby. We had a big demijohn that we used to call the baby, and we'd all put in and then toss to see who'd go and get her filled up. And an old suitcase that Ted'd got from the rubbish tip came in handy for the purpose. Well, evenings when we'd had the baby filled would get Ted all hot and bothered. Because once they were a bit stonkered the boys would want to have a bo-peep at the bird while he was asleep. If you were careful you could look under the cloth Ted put over the cage at night and see him standing on one leg with his head tucked in, and his feathers all fluffed up. And it was certainly great to see him sleeping there, specially considering the noise and the smoke. He'd always be a bit unsteady on his one leg and the boys'd argue about that, some saying it was because of his heart beating, and others that he was only balancing. But of course Ted'd be all on edge trying to keep everybody away, and he'd go crook if somebody moved the cloth too much and woke the poor little blighter up, which was usually what happened.

Well, for months on end Ted just about lived for that canary. Then later on he decided it didn't get enough exercise inside the cage, so he tried a stunt. We'd shut the door and the window and Ted'd let the bird out of the cage, and it certainly seemed to enjoy the outing. And Ted thought he was a clever bloke when he'd taught it to sit on his shoulder, though when he put seed in his hair to get it to go on top it wasn't a success, because the bird got its feet tangled, and I had to cut off some hair to get it away, which reminded me how once on a sheep farm I found a little skeleton tangled in the wool on a sheep's back. In the end though, Ted did a stupid thing, he left the window open while the bird was having its outing. I said wasn't he taking a risk, but he said no, the bird loved him too much ever to fly away. And certainly for a time it just did its usual stuff, sitting on Ted's shoulder and hopping about on the table. Though when it decided to go it didn't waste any time. It up and nipped out that window just as fast as if it was a sparrow that had blown in by mistake. For a time it hung about in a tree while Ted walked round and round underneath with the cage in his hand. And watching the pair of them I thought the bird was rubbing it in, because up in the tree it sounded to me as if it was singing better than ever it did before.

The next morning Ted was gone before I was awake. The cage was gone too, and Ted never turned up at work and lost a day's pay. It was no good though, he never found the bird. Later on we talked it over and I said he'd better try another dog, but he said no. I've still got the wife, he said. Yes, I said. The wife never let me down, he said. No, I said. It was all I could think of to say. He put his things together and went right away, and it wasn't long before I was going round regularly twice a week for a game of cards with the pair of them. But right until the finish of the slump I was living on my own, and occasionally I'd sort of wish that Ted hadn't been so careless with his canary.

Amos Tutuola

Tutuola's world is that of the myths and legends of the Yoruba. But to say that he simply retells the tales of his people is to do him an injustice; just as it is to say that he is heavily indebted to Bunyan or to Jung. For Tutuola's genius is essentially an individual one; what he has done is to take the old myths and legends and reshape them according to his own personal vision. That it is his own experience and vision of life that he presents is emphasized by his answer when asked why he had described the various towns in the Bush of Ghosts in a particular order. Tutuola replied, ' "That is the order in which I came to them." '

This extract is one incident from Tutuola's masterpiece, *The Palm-Wine Drinkard*, a novel which tells the story of the Drinkard's quest for his dead tapster. It follows the pattern of all great quest literature, Departure–Initiation–Return, and like all epics of this nature it is a journey of self-discovery, to find the true meaning of existence. The Palm-Wine Drinkard's journey is not just a journey into the African jungle any more than the expedition of Patrick White's great quest-hero Voss was merely one into the Australian desert. Both are journeys of self-discovery. The geographical exploration is a metaphor for the exploration of the individual life.

Following the quest pattern the hero sets out alone, for as Kierkegaard has reminded us, 'on the mystical pilgrimage one cannot have company.' During the journey he encounters all the familiar figures of the heroic quest. The Complete Gentleman is just one of the many grotesque characters, that he, like all such pilgrims (Ulysses, Jason, Sir Gawain, Christian), has to meet. These are the monsters of the primitive imagination, familiar to us all in one form or another, and representing man's deepest fears. The girl's father is the well-known figure of the task-master, and when the Drinkard has successfully completed his task, he is rewarded, like so many of his counterparts, with a helpmate.

The book is rich in episodes such as we find in this extract and the Drinkard undergoes many such adventures before he descends like Orpheus to the underworld, to the Town of the Deads. It is here that his initiation takes place and he learns the true meaning of life and death. He returns home with a new understanding of the meaning of existence and with this dearly bought knowledge he is able to restore harmony between the villagers and the gods.

One must, of course, be struck by Tutuola's language. It is not pidgin English but neither is it, of course, standard English. Indeed Tutuola's language has proved a source of embarrassment to some Africans who would not wish the rest of the world to think that this was how *they* spoke. Such people are probably very much like the West Indians who object to dialect in books read outside the West Indies. V. S. Naipaul comments on these people and this attitude in *The Middle Passage*: ' "They must be does talk so by you. . . . They don't talk so by me." '

Behind Tutuola's English is the vernacular; he reminds us that he is telling an ancient tale and 'translating' it for our benefit when his Drinkard says, '[I] changed myself to a very small bird which I could describe as a 'sparrow' in English language.' We must remember that the literature of Tutuola's vernacular belongs to the oral tradition, behind the written word we hear the voice of the story-teller; the tiny asides, the simplicity and directness with which the tale is told, the rhythms which are essentially the rhythms of speech; all these are there to remind us of the oral tradition from which the tale has sprung.

Exciting event after exciting event are crowded on to his pages and in the telling of these we fall readily under the charm and enchantment of the story-teller, for that is what Tutuola is, a born story-teller. In these stories we find a delightful mixture of ancient and modern. Rolling skulls are likened to petrol drums rolling along a road, the bombers won't bomb the complete gentleman because of his beauty. This mixture and intrusion of the modern serves to remind us that this is in actual fact Tutuola's own personal experience, this is a twentieth-century man re-enacting the old myth. By exercising the imaginative genius which he possesses and by embracing the new as well as the old he has been able to give a new life and flavour to the old.

The archetypal pattern and characters give his tale a universal validity. Tutuola's world is that of the imagination, of the universal subconscious. By reshaping the old legends and images for his own purpose he has reminded us that it is in the world of myth that men of all ages find the answers to the meaning of existence. It is his own vision of life presented in a language that all men can read. He reminds us of the validity of Jung's statement, 'He who speaks to us in primordial images speaks in a thousand voices'. *A. R.*

The Complete Gentleman

Then I left the town without knowing where my tapster was, and I started another fresh journey.

When it was the fifth month since I had left that town, then I reached another town which was not so big, although there was a large and famous market. At the same time that I entered the town, I went to the house of the head of the town who received me with kindness into his house; after a little while he told one of his wives to give me food and after I had eaten the food, he told his wife to give me palm-wine too; I drank the palm-wine to excess as when I was in my town or as when my tapster was alive. But when I tasted the palm-wine given to me there, I said that I got what I wanted here. After I had eaten the food and drunk the palm-wine to my satisfaction, the head of the town who received me as his guest asked for my name, I told him that my name was called "Father of gods who could do anything in this world". As he heard this from me, he was soon faint with fear. After that he asked me what I came to him for. I replied that I was looking for my palm-wine tapster who had died in my town some time ago. Then he told me that he knew where the tapster was.

After that he told me that if I could help him to find out his daughter who was captured by a curious creature from the market which was in that town, and bring her to him, then he would tell me whereabouts my tapster was.

He said furthermore that as I called myself "Father of gods who could do anything in this world", this would be very easy for me to do; he said so.

I did not know that his daughter was taken away by a curious creature from the market.

I was about to refuse to go and find out his daughter who was taken away from the market by a curious creature, but when I remembered my name I was ashamed to refuse. So I agreed to find out his daughter. There was a big market in this town from where the daughter was captured, and the market-day was fixed for every 5th day and the whole people of that town and from all the villages around the town and also spirits and curious creatures from various bushes and forests were coming to this market every 5th day to sell or buy articles. By 4 o'clock in the evening, the market would close for that day and then everybody would be returning to his or her destination or to where he or she came from. But the daughter of the head of that town was a petty trader and she was due to be married before she was taken away from the market. Before that time, her father was telling her to marry a man but she did not listen to her father; when her father saw that she did not care to marry anybody, he gave her to a man for himself, but this lady refused totally to marry that man who was introduced to her by her father. So that her father left her to herself.

This lady was very beautiful as an angel but no man could convince her for marriage. So, one day she went to the market on a market-day as she was doing before, or to sell her articles as usual; on that market-day, she saw a curious creature in the market, but she did not know where the man came from and never knew him before.

THE DESCRIPTION OF THE CURIOUS CREATURE

He was a beautiful "complete" gentleman, he dressed with the finest and most costly clothes, all the parts of his body were completed, he was a tall man but stout. As this gentleman came to the market on that day, if he had been an article or animal for sale, he would be sold at least for £2000 (two thousand pounds). As this complete gentleman came to the market on that day, and at the same time that this lady saw him in the market, she did nothing more than to ask him where he was living, but this fine gentleman did not answer her or approach her at all. But when she noticed that fine or complete gentleman did not listen to her, she left her articles and began to watch the movements of the complete gentleman about the market and left her articles unsold.

By and by the market closed for that day then the whole people in the market were returning to their destinations, etc., and the complete gentleman was returning to his own too, but as this lady was following him about in the market all the while, she saw him when he was returning to his destination as others did, then she was following him (complete gentleman) to an unknown place. But as she was following the complete gentleman along the road, he was telling her to go back or not to follow him, but the lady did not listen to what he was telling her, and when the complete gentleman had tired of telling her not to follow him or to go back to her town, he left her to follow him.

"Do Not Follow Unknown Man's Beauty"

But when they had travelled about twelve miles away from that market, they left the road on which they were travelling and started to travel inside an endless forest in which only all the terrible creatures were living.

"Return the Parts of Body to the Owners; or Hired Parts of the Complete Gentleman's Body to be Returned"

As they were travelling along in this endless forest then the complete gentleman in the market that the lady was following, began to return the hired parts of his body to the owners and he was paying them the rentage money. When he reached where he hired the left foot, he pulled it out, he gave it to the owner and paid him, and they kept going; when they reached the place where he hired the right foot, he pulled it out and gave it to the owner and paid for the rentage. Now both feet had returned to the owners, so he began to crawl along on the ground, by that time, that lady wanted to go back to her town or her father, but the terrible and curious creature or the complete gentleman did not allow her to return or go back to her town or her father again and the complete gentleman said thus:—"I had told you not to follow me before we branched into this endless forest which belongs to only terrible and curious creatures, but when I became a half-bodied incomplete gentleman you wanted to go back, now that cannot be done, you have failed. Even you have never seen anything yet, just follow me."

When they went furthermore, then they reached where he hired the belly, ribs, chest, etc., then he pulled them out and gave them to the owner and paid for the rentage.

Now to this gentleman or terrible creature remained only the head and both arms with neck, by that time he could not crawl as before but only went jumping on as a bull-frog and now this lady was soon faint for this fearful creature whom she was following. But when the lady saw every part of this complete gentleman in the market was spared or hired and he was returning them to the owners, then she began to try all her efforts to return to her father's town, but she was not allowed by this fearful creature at all.

When they reached where he hired both arms, he pulled them out and gave them to the owner, he paid for them; and they were still going on in this endless forest, they reached the place where he hired the neck, he pulled it out and gave it to the owner and paid for it as well.

"A FULL-BODIED GENTLEMAN REDUCED TO HEAD"

Now this complete gentleman was reduced to head and when they reached where he hired the skin and flesh which covered the head, he returned them, and paid to the owner, now the complete gentleman in the market reduced to a "SKULL" and this lady remained with only "Skull". When the lady saw that she remained with only Skull, she began to say that her father had been telling her to marry a man, but she did not listen to or believe him.

When the lady saw that gentleman became a Skull, she began to faint, but the Skull told her if she would die she would die and she would follow him to his house. But by the time that he was saying so, he was humming with a terrible voice and also grew very wild and even if there was a person two miles away he would not have to listen before hearing him, so this lady began to run away in that forest for her life, but the Skull chased her and within a few yards, he caught her, because he was very clever and smart as he was only Skull and he could jump a mile to the second before coming down. He caught the lady in this way: so when the lady was running away for her life, he hastily ran to her front and stopped her as a log of wood.

By and by, this lady followed the Skull to his house, and the house was a hole which was under the ground. When they reached there both of them entered the hole. But there were only Skulls living in that hole. At the same time that they entered the hole, he tied a single Cowrie on the neck of this lady with a kind of rope, after that, he gave her a large frog on which she sat as a stool, then he gave a whistle to a Skull of his kind to keep watch on this lady whenever she wanted to run away. Because the Skull knew already that the lady would attempt to run away from the hole. Then he went to the back-yard to where his family were staying in the day time till night.

But one day, the lady attempted to escape from the hole, and at the same time that the Skull who was watching her whistled to the rest of the Skulls that were in the back-yard, the whole of them rushed out to the place where the lady sat on the bull-frog, so they caught her, but as all of them were rushing out, they were rolling on the ground as if a thousand petrol drums were pushing along a hard road. After she was caught, then they brought her back to sit on the same frog as usual. If the Skull who was watching her fell asleep, and if the lady wanted to escape, the cowrie that was tied on her neck would raise up the alarm with a terrible noise, so that the Skull who was watching her would wake up at once and then the rest of the Skull's family would rush out from the back in thousands to the lady and ask her what she wanted to do with a curious and terrible voice.

But the lady could not talk at all, because as the cowrie had been tied on her neck, she became dumb at the same moment.

THE FATHER OF GODS SHOULD FIND OUT WHEREABOUTS THE DAUGHTER OF THE HEAD OF THE TOWN WAS

Now as the father of the lady first asked for my name and I told him that my name was "Father of gods who could do anything in this world", then he told me that if I could find out where his daughter was and bring her to him, then he would tell me where my palm-wine tapster was. But when he said so, I was jumping up with gladness that he should promise me that he would tell me where my tapster was. I agreed to what he said; the father and parent of this lady never knew whereabouts their daughter was, but they had information that the lady followed a complete gentleman in the market. As I was the "Father of gods who could do anything in this world," when it was at night I sacrificed to my juju with a goat.

And when it was early in the morning, I sent for forty kegs of palm-wine, after I had drunk it all, I started to investigate whereabouts was the lady. As it was the market-day, I started the investigation from the market. But as I was a juju-man, I knew all the kinds of people in that market. When it was exactly 9 o'clock a.m., the very complete gentleman whom the lady followed came to the market again, and at the same time that I saw him, I knew that he was a curious and terrible creature.

"The Lady was not to be Blamed for following the Skull as a Complete Gentleman"

I could not blame the lady for following the Skull as a complete gentleman to his house at all. Because if I were a lady, no doubt I would follow him to wherever he would go, and still as I was a man I would jealous him more than that, because if this gentleman went to the battlefield, surely, enemy would not kill him or capture him and if bombers saw him in a town which was to be bombed, they would not throw bombs on his presence, and if they did throw it, the bomb itself would not explode until this gentleman would leave that town, because of his beauty. At the same time that I saw this gentleman in the market on that day, what I was doing was only to follow him about in the market. After I looked at him for so many hours, then I ran to a corner of the market and cried for a few minutes because I thought within myself why was I not created with beauty as this gentleman, but when I remembered that he was only a Skull, then I thanked God that He had created me without beauty, so I went back to him in the market, but I was still attracted by his beauty. So when the market closed for that day, and when everybody was returning to his or her destination, this gentleman was returning to his own too and I followed him to know where he was living.

"Investigation to the Skull's Family's House"

When I travelled with him a distance of about twelve miles away to that market, the gentleman left the real road on which we were travelling and branched into an endless forest and I was following him, but as I did not want him to see that I was following him, then I used one of my juju which changed me into a lizard and followed him. But after I had travelled with him a distance of about twenty-five miles away in this endless forest, he began to pull out all the parts of his body and returned them to the owners, and paid them.

After I had travelled with him for another fifty miles in this forest, then he reached his house and entered it, but I entered it also with him, as I was a lizard. The first thing that he did when he entered the hole (house) he went straight to the place where the lady was, and I saw the lady sat on a bull-frog with a single cowrie tied on her neck and a Skull who was watching her stood behind her. After he (gentleman) had seen that the lady was there, he went to the back-yard where all his family were working.

"THE INVESTIGATOR'S WONDERFUL WORK IN THE SKULL'S FAMILY'S HOUSE"

When I saw this lady and when the Skull who brought her to that hole or whom I followed from the market to that hole went to the back-yard, then I changed myself to a man as before, then I talked to the lady but she could not answer me at all, she only showed that she was in a serious condition. The Skull who was guarding her with a whistle fell asleep at that time.

To my surprise, when I helped the lady to stand up from the frog on which she sat, the cowrie that was tied on her neck made a curious noise at once, and when the Skull who was watching her heard the noise, he woke up and blew the whistle to the rest, then the whole of them rushed to the place and surrounded the lady and me, but at the same time that they saw me there, one of them ran to a pit which was not so far from that spot, the pit was filled with cowries. He picked one cowrie out of the pit, after that he was running towards me, and the whole crowd wanted to tie the cowrie on my neck too. But before they could do that, I had changed myself into air, they could not trace me out again, but I was looking at them. I believed that the cowries in that pit were their power and to reduce the power of any human being whenever tied on his or her neck and also to make a person dumb.

Over one hour after I had dissolved into air, these Skulls went back to the back-yard, but there remained the Skull who was watching her.

After they had returned to the back-yard, I changed to a man as usual, then I took the lady from the frog, but at the same time that I touched her, the cowrie which was tied on her neck began to shout; even if a person was four miles away he would not have to listen before hearing, but immediately the Skull who was watching her heard the noise and saw me when I took her from that frog, he blew the whistle to the rest of them who were in the back-yard.

Immediately the whole Skull family heard the whistle when blew to them, they were rushing out to the place and before they could reach there, I had left their hole for the forest, but before I could travel about one hundred yards in the forest, they had rushed out from their hole to inside the forest and I was still running away with the lady. As these Skulls were chasing me about in the forest, they were rolling on the ground like large stones and also humming with terrible noise, but when I saw that they had nearly caught me or if I continued to run away like that, no doubt, they would catch me sooner, then I changed the lady to a kitten and put her inside my pocket and changed myself to a very small bird which I could describe as a "sparrow" in English language.

After that I flew away, but as I was flying in the sky, the cowrie which was tied on that lady's neck was still making a noise and I tried all my best to stop the noise, but all were in vain. When I reached home with the lady, I changed her to a lady as she was before and also myself changed to man as well. When her father saw that I brought his daughter back home, he was exceedingly glad and said thus:—"You are the 'Father of gods' as you had told me before."

But as the lady was now at home, the cowrie did not stop making a terrible noise once, and she could not talk to anybody; she showed only that she was very glad she was at home. Now I had brought the lady but she could not talk, eat or loose away the cowrie on her neck, because the terrible noise of the cowrie did not allow anybody to rest or sleep at all.

"THERE REMAIN GREATER TASKS AHEAD"

Now I began to cut the rope of the cowrie from her neck and to make her talk and eat, but all my efforts were in vain. At last I tried my best to cut off the rope of the cowrie; it only stopped the noise, but I was unable to loose it away from her neck.

When her father saw all my trouble, he thanked me greatly and repeated again that as I called myself 'Father of gods who could do anything in this world' I ought to do the rest of the work. But when he said so, I was very ashamed and thought within myself that if I return to the Skulls' hole or house, they might kill me and the forest was very dangerous travel always, again I could not go directly to the Skulls in their hole and ask them how to loose away the cowrie which was tied on the lady's neck and to make her talk and eat.

"BACK TO THE SKULL'S FAMILY'S HOUSE"

On the third day after I had brought the lady to her father's house, I returned to the endless forest for further investigation. When there remained about one mile to reach the hole of these Skulls, there I saw the very Skull who the lady had followed from the market as a complete gentleman to the hole of Skull's family's house, and at the same time that I saw him like that, I changed into a lizard and climbed a tree which was near him.

He stood before two plants, then he cut a single opposite leaf from the opposite plant; he held the leaf with his right hand and he was saying thus:—"As this lady was taken from me, if this opposite leaf is not given her to eat, she will not talk for ever," after that he threw the leaf down on the ground. Then he cut another single compound leaf from the compound plant which was in the same place with the opposite plant, he held the compound leaf with his left hand and said that if this single compound is not given to this lady, to eat, the cowrie on her neck could not be loosened away for ever and it would be making a terrible noise for ever.

After he said so, he threw the leaf down at the same spot, then he jumped away. So after he had jumped very far away (luckily, I was there when he was doing all these things, and I saw the place that he threw both leaves separately) then I changed myself to a man as before, I went to the place that he threw both leaves, then I picked them up and I went home at once.

But at the same time that I reached home, I cooked both leaves separately and gave her to eat; to my surprise the lady began to talk at once. After that, I gave her the compound leaf to eat for the second time and immediately she ate that too, the cowrie which was tied on her neck by the Skull, loosened away by itself, but it disappeared at the same time. So when the father and mother saw the wonderful work which I had done for them, they brought fifty kegs of palm-wine for me, they gave me the lady as wife and two rooms in that house in which to live with them. So, I saved the lady from the complete gentleman in the market who afterwards reduced to a "Skull" and the lady became my wife since that day. This was how I got a wife.

Randolph Stow

In a footnote to his story, "Magic", Randolph Stow has said:

> The story is expanded from the first half of the 'sulumwoya' myth of the Trobriand Islands, originally recorded by Malinowski and included in the *Sexual Life of the Savage*. An almost identical version was given to me by an informant in the same village in 1959.

The "sulumwoya" myth is one of great poignancy. It is the myth of the origins of love and is concerned with the supreme sexual taboo of the Trobriander islanders, that of incest between brother and sister, and with the power of the magic of love.

For the Trobriander his sister is the very symbol of all that is sexually forbidden. Play between brother and sister, even when they are very young is frowned upon, and when the boy grows up he must leave the family home and go and sleep in bachelor quarters. The lure of forbidden fruit however, is a strong one; we may consciously repress what is forbidden but the subconscious is not so easily tamed. And so the Trobriander will sometimes dream that he has had sexual relations with his sister, a dream which will make him perhaps troubled, or sad or ashamed. This dream is conceived, as are all love dreams, as a manifestation of magic, just as love itself is attributed to the same source. The Trobriander believes that this magic is so strong that it can break even the strongest taboo of all, that of the brother–sister incest.

The magic of love has its own special ritual. The first of the rites involves, amongst other things, the boy bathing so as to make himself beautiful and attractive to the girl; the second ritual is to offer the girl something to eat which has been charmed; in the next rite a herb is mixed with coconut oil and if possible this should be smeared on her body, particularly her breasts. The remaining rite is the all powerful one. It is the rite that uses the "sulumwoya", the aromatic mint plant, which plays a central role in the myth of the origins of love. The mint plant is boiled in coconut oil, the aim is that this oil may be spilt on her so that the perfume will enter her nostrils and infect her with its magic. This is the culminating act of love magic; when it has been administered the woman will have desire only for the maker of the love potion and nothing will override this desire. All love, all attraction, is attributed to the magic of love; should incest occur, whether in myth, dream or reality, the excuse given is that there must have been an accidental misuse of the magic.

The myth itself tells of one such incestuous relationship brought about by the sister accidentally knocking her brother's love potion over. The tragic climax is the death of the lovers. The interesting item in the aftermath tells how they were eventually discovered and sprouting from their bodies was the sulumwoya plant, the symbol of love and source of the most effective love potion of all. The great irony, of course, is that love and the magic of love derive from the most strongly forbidden of all love relationships. Stow has followed the original myth quite closely but he has made his own special contribution to it by adding what Malinowski regretted was missing from the original recounting, namely, any explicit allusion to the psychology of the actors and a description of the setting.

Few writers today have greater descriptive powers than Randolph Stow. He is a master at evoking a landscape which comes completely to life, so much so that we feel ourselves present in it, and respond, not only visually but with all our senses. Normally it is the vast, arid landscape of Australia that he presents. This story shows us that he has an eye and feeling that will respond just as readily to the lush fertile richness of the thick tropical forests, the shimmering light of the coral reef, the air heavy with the perfume of tropical flowers. It is his close observation and care for the tiniest of details which do much to create this sense of atmosphere. Stow is a poet as well as a prose writer and there is a poet's sensitivity to sound behind his choice of words; "sloshing" suggests all the abundance and fertility of the tropics. There is a delicate suggestiveness behind his description of the two drops of water trickling down Soulava's breast. Lalami we feel is watching as closely as we are. Soulava's destruction of the hibiscus flower seems to be a symbolic foreshadowing of her own destruction. And, as always with Stow, the landscape reflects the emotions of the actors and the whole atmosphere of the work. No incident, no detail is without significance.

Just as his landscape is one rich in detail so too are his characters rich in psychological realism. The young couple are aware of the underlying tension, a tension felt more intensely in the stillness of the day. There is deep human psychology in the reluctance to mention names, fearing that their hidden fears and desires will assume reality if brought out into the open. What pervades the whole story is the sense of inevitability, the brother and sister are moving on to a doom over which they have no control. Lalami tries at first to refute what has been ordained; he is aware, however, that refutation is merely a token gesture, and he waits for what he says is *not* true, and yet knows *is* true, with both excitement and dread. This suggests the dual aspect of the situation for Lalami; the horror at the thought of breaking the strongest of all taboos, the excitement at the thought of partaking of the most forbidden of all fruits. His comment when they finally succumb, "O—my sister", reveals both aspects.

The inevitability is not the only thing one senses; we are also aware of the attraction each feels for the other. We are tempted to ask was it all due to chance or did Soulava make a potion for Lalami in the first place. We shall never know the answer but the fact that we ask the question tells us how well Stow has succeeded in peopling this myth with recognizable human beings. By doing this, and also through his description of the landscape, he has added a new richness and dimension to a myth of great primitive beauty. *A. R.*

Magic

The boy came from the grotto with the filled water-bottles quietly sloshing in the basket on his arm and his hair wet from bathing. He was pushing back his hair with a comb of long palm spines.

When he saw the girl he stopped. He had been smiling to himself, because he felt healthy and cool, but now his smile became hesitant.

Out of no curiosity, but because it was the greeting of the country, he asked: "Where are you going?"

"I am walking," said the girl, "that is all." She did not return his smile, and looked unhappy; unsure, uneasy, for all her beauty.

"I am fetching the water," he said.

"That should be my work," she said. "It is women's work."

"But you are ill. Our mother told me."

"It is true," she said, listlessly, rubbing her forehead. "My head aches. It is very hot."

"Go to the house," he said, "lie down."

"No," she said. "I am better. I will go to the garden."

Then they stood wavering, because they did not often speak to one another, and did not know what to say.

"I am thirsty," she said, at last. "Give me some water."

He took a coconut water-bottle from the basket and held it out to her, and she took it, touching his fingers in passing. She unstoppered the bottle and drank from it, tilting her head. Two trickles of water escaped from the corners of her mouth and flowed down her body, over the brown breasts, to the waistband of her skirt.

"Enough," he said, suddenly impatient, taking back the bottle from her. "I shall have to fill it again if you drink everything."

She turned away from him and sat down in the grass. "You are bad-tempered now," she said, meekly.

"No," he said, "no. Only——" But he could not truly say what she had done that he resented. And the stillness of the day seemed to expect something of him. He did not want to be there. He wanted to be alone, or else with many people.

"I will take the water to our mother," he said. And waited for something. But nothing happened.

The girl, Soulava, sat in the grass, chewing a stem of it. She did not speak again. She only watched him, sidelong, as he hitched the basket over his shoulder and set off down the path at a half trot. The plume of the grass-stalk that hung from her lips moved as she gnawed at it. Tiny seeds fell, and clung to the trails of water drying on her dark skin.

"You are a silent man today," the mother said.

She was outside, kneading sago dumplings in the shadow of the yam store, and he was in the dark dwelling house, where he had taken the water-bottles.

"What are you doing?" she called to him.

"Nothing," he said. And he came out, after a moment, and squatted in the shade behind her, combing his hair.

Although he no longer lived with her and his sister, preferring to share a house with the other unmarried boys, he would do occasional services for her, such as this carrying of the water, and would use her house as a repository for valuable and secret things.

"Will you not speak one word?" said the woman. "Are you ill?"

"No," he said. "I did not sleep in the night, not much. That is all."

"Why?" she demanded. "Eh, I know. It is these girls."

"There were no girls," he answered, half angry.

She hissed between her teeth, in amusement and disbelief.

"It is true," he said. "Not one girl. Truly, I could not sleep because—because of my dreaming."

He spoke reluctantly, frowning down at the four teeth of his comb, which he was twanging with his thumb.

"Eh," said the woman, "if they will not come and scratch at the house-wall, then they will come in dreams."

"I do not understand your mind," he murmured.

"Supposing you dream of a girl——"

"Supposing."

"Then that one who comes to you is one who has made magic, so that you will dream of her. That is true."

"It is not true," he said, softly and sullenly, twanging his comb. "I understand magic. You are wrong."

Then she shrugged, reflecting perhaps that one could not speak to a son with the same freedom as to a nephew, and said nothing more.

"It is not true," he whispered to himself, staring at his own fingers, and seeming from his face to think deeply, in some mood between excitement and dread.

The girls were languid, oppressed by the still heat, and by the heavy sweetness of the bwita tree. Their backs were to the bark of it, their laps heaped with its flowers: waxy yellowed ficus flowers, of a penetrating fragrance, from which their hands, having nothing else to do, were working garlands. As little worth comment had happened on that morning they had not spoken for some time, but were still and comfortable in their thoughts, which the flowers in their hands had turned to the subject of their own beauty, and the boys who might know that beauty when they looked at it.

Only Soulava was not quiet, but threaded her garland with an irritable carefulness, and glanced up now and again at the path that went by the tree.

"Soulava, who do you think will come?" one of the girls asked her.

And another called out, laughing; "Where will you meet him? In the bush?"

Soulava said nothing, but scowled, under her curling hair.

Because they were bored, and because they liked to talk about the boys, they teased her.

"Soulava, who is your friend?" they had to know. "What is his name?"

"I have no friend," she said, intent on her garland.

"She is lying," they called to one another. Now the langour was going out of them, and their voices and their laughter grew shrill.

"I have no friend," she repeated, with an edge of anger, but softly.

"Lying," they told each other, "lying." And one quieter girl, whose name was Davatabuna, whispered to them: "Her friend is Tomdiyu."

Then they all echoed it, shrilly. "Her friend is Tomdiyu."

The girl did not raise her head or speak, a long time, and they would have forgotten about her and sunk back into their thoughts and into the torpor of the day. But she could not be still. Her hands fumbled at the flowers. At last she turned her head a little, looking sidelong from under her dark brows at the girl beside her, and asked in her turn: "Who is your friend, Davatabuna?"

"I have no friend," said Davatabuna.

"You are lying," said Soulava, speaking very quietly, and trembling a little.

"I am not lying," Davatabuna said, and smiled to herself.

"You are lying," Soulava said, suddenly angry, standing up and scattering loose flowers from her skirt.

They were all laughing at her, although they did not understand.

"I have no friend," Davatabuna said again. "Who is my friend? Tell me, who is my friend?"

"You know."

"Tell me."

"You know."

"She is mad," Davatabuna said. "What is his name?"

"I will not say his name," Soulava said, turning away.

"Eh, Soulava," they called after her. "What is the matter? Where are you going, Soulava? Tomdiyu is coming."

She swore at them, swinging her skirt. "*Inam!*" she shouted, and went away from their piercing laughter; across the brown earth and outcropping coral of the yam gardens, between the vine-covered poles and the bordering leaves of taro and tapioca. And so on, through other gardens several years fallow, where scrub was beginning to spring again, among convolvulus and vincas and painted-lady.

The sultry sky glared white. A harsh brightness came off the exposed coral. She rubbed her eyes, because of the light, and because she was close to crying.

But on the path to the village, lined with palms and hibiscus, it was all coolness and greenness, and the trodden-down grass was smooth to her feet. So she walked more slowly there, no longer running away, because she thought no one could see her.

But someone had, through the bushes at a bend in the path, and called to her. "O! Soulava!"

Then she would have turned back. But he shouted: "Where are you going?" So she went on, dragging her feet, and came around the turn to where Tomdiyu was, squatting under a palm with his lime-gourd between his feet.

"Where are you going?" he called again, as she came in sight.

"To the village," she said, "that is all."

She would not go near him, but chose to lean against a palm on the other side of the path.

"Will you chew?" he asked, holding out his hand with two green nuts in the palm.

"No," she said, looking at her feet.

He laughed at her then, his face splitting open, showing his mouth bright red with betelnut. "I think you are afraid," he said.

"Why should I be afraid?" she asked, indifferently.

"You are afraid I will work magic."

She said, with a trace of contempt: "You know no magic."

"You are wrong," he said. "I know strong magic."

"Who has taught you this?"

"No one has taught me. I am a true magician."

Her hands could not leave exploring the corky bark of the tree behind her, and she would not look at him. "I know who has taught you," she said.

"Who, then?"

"I know."

"You are lying," he said, but good-humouredly.

"I will not say his name."

"He has no name, this one."

"He is," she said, scowling, "he is—Davatabuna's friend."

"Eh," he said, spitting red juice on the path, "he is a true magician, that one."

Then her voice got quieter, and began to tremble again. "You know nothing," she accused him. "You do not know Davatabuna's friend."

"You are wrong," he said. "I know him."

"Then, what is his name?"

"If you know, you say."

"You do not know," she cried out, as if he had mortally offended her.

"You are mad," he said, with affection. "The whole village knows this man. He is Lalami. He is your brother."

Then he stood up, reaching down for his lime-gourd. "I am going to the beach," he said, standing in the path.

She stayed where she was, leaning against the palm-trunk and hanging her head.

"Soulava," he said, half joking, "are you my friend?"

"No," she said. "Go away. I have no friend."

"Eh," he said, "you are a bad-tempered woman." And he went away from her and around the turn of the path. A long mocking ululation came back from him, lingering among the columns of the palms.

"*Inam!*" she whispered after him, pushing herself away from the treetrunk and starting out along the path to the village again. Her sullen head was bent and she kicked at the coconut husks in her way. Once she reached out and roughly tore off a hibiscus flower, which she shredded between her fingers, leaving behind her a brief trail of crimson fragments on the green path.

Under a palm at the edge of the beach Tomdiyu found Lalami. He was making a fishing net, the smooth shuttle flickering through the loops of pandanus string.

"O! *So!*" Tomdiyu called to him. "Hey, friend."

The boy hardly bothered to look up, knowing the voice. "Where are you going?" he asked, as a matter of course.

"Any fish?"

"No. Later."

Tomdiyu squatted beside him, taking his lime-gourd from the string bag that hung from his shoulder, and his betelnut, wrapped up in a pepperleaf. "You want to chew?"

"Eh," said the boy, putting down the shuttle and taking a green nut and a piece of the leaf.

"You are working hard," said Tomdiyu.

"Eh."

"You will be an important man, later on."

The boy laughed, tearing the green husk from the betelnut with his teeth.

"Master of the canoes, or magician of the garden, maybe."

"Truly I do not know," the boy said, scooping lime from the gourd with his piece of leaf, and putting leaf and all into his mouth.

"You know strong magic."

"Maybe."

"Some people tell me you know strong magic. Love magic."

"Some people talk a lot."

"Will you teach me some magic?"

"I know no magic," the boy said. "That is true."

"I will give you a big reward."

The boy stared at the sea, and thought of his future. He would be an important man, later on. Master of the canoes, or magician of the gardens. In time, when his uncle died, he would be headman of the village. He would marry, before long. He would marry Davatabuna, because she was gentle, and because she had four brothers to fill her yam house every season.

"What reward?" he asked.

"I will give you—eh, five baskets of yams."

The boy hissed with contempt. "I want no yams," he said. "I have plenty of yams."

"Then what do you want?"

The boy was brooding over his future. "Your uncle," he said, "your uncle has the arm-shell called Nula'ota. I want that."

"You are mad," said Tomdiyu, laughing in his surprise. "He will not give that away. He cannot."

"Eh," said the boy, picking up his shuttle again, "I know no magic. That is true. I am sorry for you."

"You are a mean man," Tomdiyu said, and jabbed with a stick in the sand.

Watching his own swift hands, thinking of the future, the boy smiled.

At length, idly, he asked: "Who would you make magic on?"

"I will not tell you," Tomdiyu said.

"I know," said the boy.

"You are lying."

"I know."

"Who, then?"

"I will not say her name," said the boy, and seemed not greatly interested.

Tomdiyu looked at him, and then at the sea. "Hey, friend," he said, after a time. "Are you my friend?"

"Eh," said the boy, abstracted.

"I will tell you her name."

"All right," said the boy.

"Come here," Tomdiyu said, "listen." He put his mouth close to Lalami's ear.

"I am listening. Say it."

"It is Soulava," said Tomdiyu, and snorted with uneasy laughter.

Slowly the boy got to his feet, the net and shuttle still in his hands. He could not speak, it seemed, for a while.

"What is wrong with you?" Tomdiyu asked, looking up, anxious.

"I might hit you in the belly," said the boy, in a thick whisper.

"Hey, friend——"

"Get out," the boy shouted. "Get out." And then, as Tomdiyu would only stare at him, and he himself did not know what to do, he began to go away, because only movement could help him in such bewilderment.

By his canoe, pulled up on the sand, he stopped, and threw the net into it. He looked at the sea, hot and still. The day at any moment might break into a storm. And his bright future might crack in his hands. He might fall from a palm and die, like Nesai, or be carried away in his canoe and never seen again, like Simsim. Or in anger he might kill someone, or be killed. The world lay in wait for him, from the sea, with its spirits like living stones, to the night sky with its flying witches. "My mind is very heavy," he said aloud, in growing dread.

Widespaced palms made up the outer circle of the village, fencing in the darker and denser ring of mangoes and areca palms and ancient shade trees, which in turn sheltered and contained the third circle of dwelling houses, and the clustered yam houses where the woman was.

In the steamy air the village smelt of fowl-dung and wood-smoke and boiling yams. The light gave a steely tinge to the sago-leaf roofs, and discovered traces of copper in the palms. There was no stir in the blue smoke that rose from under the woman's cooking pot, or in the trees, or in the clump of poinsettia burning like a bonfire at the centre of the village. It was so still that the screech of a pair of lorries in the bush beyond made the woman start and look up.

"Eh," she said, seeing the girl. "Where have you been?"

"In the garden, that is all."

The woman was sitting in the blurred shadow of the yam house, with a board across her knees. She was preparing a new skirt, scraping away at the fibres of a banana leaf with a tooth-edged shell.

"Who have you seen?" she asked, automatically.

"No one," said the girl. "Some girls. Tomdiyu, on the path."

Her mother laughed. "Your friend?"

"No," said the girl, angrily. "He is not my friend."

Her mother made a sound that was both soothing and mocking.

"I have no friend!"

"*Des*," said the woman, "Enough."

The girl leaned against a jutting log of the yam house and looked at her feet.

"I am thirsty," she said.

"There is water," said the woman. "Your brother fetched it."

"Give me some."

"I am sitting here," said the woman, "with the board across my knees. What is wrong with you? You get the water."

"I do not know where to find it," said the girl.

"You are a fool. It is in the house."

Because she was in a bad humour the girl knocked against her mother's shoulder as she passed her, and tore the strip of palm-frond that fastened the door of the house. "*Inam*," she swore to herself, fumbling in the darkness for the water-bottles. "*Kai inam*," she swore at the water-bottles as her hands found them.

A small pot hanging by cords from the ridge-pole struck her head as she straightened.

Ah, she breathed, for it had startled her.

Something was dripping from the swinging pot. It was dripping into her hair. She put up her hand to feel this wetness, and put her wet fingers against her nostrils. It is *bulami*, she thought; coconut cream. She tasted it.

It is *bulami*, she thought. And dropped the water-bottle.

Aii, she cried, in her terror.

Magic. It is magic.

My brother.

She came from the house staring, blind. It was all so silent. It was waiting.

But the woman did not look up.

"Where is the water?" she asked. "Give me some."

"It is in the house," the girl said, trembling. "I did not remember—"

"You are a fool," said the mother.

The girl stood, shaking, at the side of the yam house, where her mother could not see her. She put her hands to her face, digging the nails into her forehead.

"Where is my brother?" she asked—crying out, but muffled.

"You are a fool," said the woman. "How should I know where your brother is?"

"I want to talk to him."

"Perhaps he is on the beach," said the woman. "He will come soon."

"I am going," said the girl. She began to run, between the houses, towards the path from the village.

"Where are you going?" the woman called after her, lifting her head for a moment and holding the scraping shell poised. "Eh, truly, my children are mad." And she went back to her scraping, making a soft sound.

The girl ran down the path between the palms and the hibiscus, past the gardens, through the sweet-smelling scrub. The path climbed to the coral ridge of the island's coast, dank philodendron-choked forest. On its sodden floor a monitor lizard took flight and ran from her into a tree.

Now slimy moss coated the roots and the ragged coral, so that she stumbled and fell, and a projecting root caught in the waistband of her skirt and tore it. She left it there, and went naked. Because she was mad, with the magic.

She went stumbling, crying, on the jagged path. Crying: Lalami. Crying: Magic. In the padded silence, which the far hush of the sea could hardly penetrate.

He heard his name, and turned; standing on the pale sand, by his canoe, at the water's edge.

He saw her body, running between the palms and the tall scrub at the fringe of the beach. Her naked body, as in his dream. His sister.

He could not move for trembling; for dread, and for resignation, because the world had been lying in wait for him, and had chosen this means.

"O Lalami," she cried, in her madness.

It was no hope that gave him strength to run from her, only the pain in his mind that was asking for time. Though his legs trembled, it was astonishing how swiftly the sand passed under his feet, and how clearly he noted every stick and shell and fragment of coral, every coconut husk and scuttling hermit crab, every crevice and ledge of the grey headland that rose up to block him.

Then I must die, he perceived, without grief or surprise.

The shallow water was tepid to his skin. Spurs of coral jabbed him. He was stumbling, plodding, ploughing his way through the pale water towards the dark water between the two reefs.

I must die, he realized.

His eyes were on the darker sea, stretching away to the sharp edge of the world.

That way the coral caught him and tripped him, and he lay sprawled in the shallow water, and forgot.

He watched her as she followed. She was crying. "O Lalami."

No words would come to him. He raised himself and knelt in the water. He tried with his eyes to say what there were no words for, since no one had ever found need of them.

And she knelt with him, weeping. "I am mad."

"O," he said, trembling.

"It is the magic," she whispered. "In the house. Your magic, Lalami."

"O," he said. "O—my sister."

He could find no other words, at that time, and ceased to try.

So the frigate-birds went wheeling over their silence, and over the white reef and over the dark sea, that had taken so many island people by ways they knew nothing of.

In time she rose from the water and went, stumbling and weeping, to the cave at the foot of the headland, and lay down there on the damp sand, in cold that struck to the bone, though the world outside withered in the heat. She lay with her back to the cold rock, her eyes to the cave opening and the sea.

Presently he followed, stepping over the line of wrack that the tide had left. The light from the sea polished his wet skin.

"Your shame," he said, gently. "It is very great."

"Our shame," she said. "Our shame."

He lay beside her, holding her shivering body.

"We shall die," she said, unresenting.

He knew it. They would never leave the cave, to eat or to drink, but would die there, of their shame.

"We shall die," he said, with tenderness; "but later. Later."

So they held one another, in the cold cave looking out across the sea to Kitava and Iwa and Gawa and Yanaba and Muruya and all islands to the eastward, where fires were being lit and pots boiled and doors of the safe houses pulled to, one by one, against the dark.

Janet Frame

Janet Frame, a New Zealand writer, has probably more compelling personal reasons for writing than any other author in this anthology. Having spent eight years of her life in a mental hospital she consulted yet another doctor, and 'was astonished and grateful to hear him refute all previous commandments—"Why mix, why conform? I think you need to write to survive'." And later in the same article in the New Zealand periodical *Landfall*, No. 73, she states:

> Though I began writing when I was a child and have never really stopped writing, I think I really began when my need to write was understood. . . . Freedom to write is a very narrow freedom among the many personal imprisonments suffered by those who want to write, yet it is the master key, and if a writer has determination enough to turn the key . . . then he may be able to put his dreamed works into words.

From these circumstances come some of her chief concerns as an author, which can also be traced in "A Boy's Will": her preoccupation with the inner life, her absorbed interest in that very narrow border-land between fantasy and reality in which much of her work takes place, and the attempt to chart the internal processes of a personality divided between the claims of normal life and the pressing need not to mix or to conform.

'Write to survive'; but it remains at best a survival subject to constant threat from all sides. It is this awareness of undefinable menace hanging over life, waiting to strike at any moment, that both affords a major theme in her work and is the source from which it derives much of its inspiration and power. Of the "Two Sheep" one does indeed succeed in escaping death, but,

> if you notice him in a flock, being driven along a hot dusty road, you will be able to distinguish him by his timidity, his uncertainty, the frenzied expression in his eyes when he tries, in his condemned silence, to discover whether the sky is at last free from

hawks, or whether they circle in twos and threes above him, waiting to kill him.

If Peter Cowan's story "The Tractor" is a moral fable illustrating a preconceived thesis, "Two Sheep" is pure fable embodying a highly personal vision of life. Several of Janet Frame's stories are cast in this form (one of her collections, *Snowman Snowman*, is subtitled *Fables and Fantasies*), and her attraction to this type of narrative goes back to her very early childhood. In the *Landfall* article she writes:

> I made my first story on the banks of the Mataura river after a meal of trout and billy tea. 'Once upon a time there was a bird. One day a hawk came out of the sky and ate the bird. The next day a big bogie came out from behind the hill and ate up the hawk for eating up the bird.' The story's not unusual told by a child of three. . . . I keep that story in mind as an example of a time in my life when I did not waste words.

"Two Sheep" is told in a bare poetic style that still, so many years later, does not waste a single word. Without a trace of sententiousness or sentimentality, it yet does much more than merely set out a simple and demonstrable moral truth. It proves nothing whatsoever, but it does constitute a whole desperate philosophy of life.

The fact that "A Boy's Will", although by the same author, is so completely different in presentation serves as an illustration of the range and resources of the short-story form. Taking as its starting-point Longfellow's words from his poem "My Lost Youth", 'A boy's will is the wind's will, And the thoughts of youth are long, long thoughts', the style itself develops this theme. Metaphor and imagery combine with a loose, fluid, syntactical structure to give an effect as highly poetical as Tutuola's "The Complete Gentleman". But, whereas in his case there lies a long oral folk-tradition behind it, with Janet Frame there is a distinctly literary influence, especially that of Virginia Woolf. If Tutuola in a sense is speaking aloud to an audience, Janet Frame is recording the boy's unspoken thoughts to himself. The story traces the flow of the boy's consciousness, one in which fantasy and day-dream continually mingle and run together with memories of the past and with immediate experience like coloured patterns in a kaleidoscope. Nevertheless, although the depiction of an ever-changing mood replaces the narration of a chronological sequence of events, there is still a development in the story. For, if the boy refuses to conform, and rebels against his mother's insidious tyranny, he also ultimately finds a truth in a vision of life which is not essentially dissimilar from that in the "Two Sheep":

> He understood now what the television preachers meant when they insisted the skies had opened. He believed them. He saw his mother with a stone in her eyes and a bone in her throat. Stone and bone were his future. *D. H.*

Two Sheep

Two sheep were travelling to the saleyards. The first sheep knew that after they had been sold their destination was the slaughter-house at the freezing works. The second sheep did not know of their fate. They were being driven with the rest of the flock along a hot dusty valley road where the surrounding hills leaned in a sun-scorched wilderness of rock, tussock and old rabbit warrens. They moved slowly, for the drover in his trap was in no hurry, and had even taken one of the dogs to sit beside him while the other scrambled from side to side of the flock, guiding them.

"I think," said the first sheep who was aware of their approaching death, "that the sun has never shone so warm on my fleece, nor, from what I see with my small sheep's eye, has the sky seemed so flawless, without seams or tucks or cracks or blemishes."

"You are crazy," said the second sheep who did not know of their approaching death. "The sun is warm, yes, but how hot and dusty and heavy my wool feels! It is a burden to go trotting along this oven shelf. It seems our journey will never end."

"How fresh and juicy the grass appears on the hill!" the first sheep exclaimed. "And not a hawk in the sky!"

"I think," replied the second sheep, "that something has blinded you. Just look up in the sky and see those three hawks waiting to swoop and attack us!"

They trotted on further through the valley road. Now and again the second sheep stumbled.

"I feel so tired," he said. "I wonder how much longer we must walk on and on through this hot dusty valley?"

But the first sheep walked nimbly and his wool felt light upon him as if he had just been shorn. He could have gambolled like a lamb in August.

"I still think," he said, "that today is the most wonderful day I have known. I do not feel that the road is hot and dusty. I do not notice the stones and grit that you complain of. To me the hills have never seemed so green and enticing, the sun has never seemed so warm and comforting. I believe that I could walk through this valley forever, and never feel tired or hungry or thirsty."

F

"Whatever has come over you?" the second sheep asked crossly. "Here we are, trotting along hour after hour, and soon we shall stand in our pens in the saleyards while the sun leans over us with its branding irons and our overcoats are such a burden that they drag us to the floor of our pen where we are almost trampled to death by the so dainty feet of our fellow sheep. A fine life that is. It would not surprise me if after we are sold we are taken in trucks to the freezing works and killed in cold blood. But," he added, comforting himself, "that is not likely to happen. Oh no, that could never happen! I have it on authority that even when they are trampled by their fellows, sheep do not die. The tales we hear from time to time are but malicious rumours, and those vivid dreams which strike us in the night as we sleep on the sheltered hills, they are but illusions. Do you not agree?" he asked the first sheep.

They were turning now from the valley road, and the saleyards were in sight, while drawn up in the siding on the rusty railway lines, the red trucks stood waiting, spattered inside with sheep and cattle dirt and with white chalk marks, in cipher, on the outside. And still the first sheep did not reveal to his companion that they were being driven to certain death.

When they were jostled inside their pen the first sheep gave an exclamation of delight.

"What a pleasant little house they have led to us! I have never seen such smart red-painted bars, and such four-square corners. And look at the elegant stairway which we will climb to enter those red caravans for our seaside holiday!"

"You make me tired," the second sheep said. "We are standing inside a dirty pen, nothing more, and I cannot move my feet in their nicely polished black shoes but I tread upon the dirt left by sheep which have been imprisoned here before us. In fact I have never been so badly treated in all my life!" And the second sheep began to cry. Just then a kind elderly sheep jostled through the flock and began to comfort him.

"You have been frightening your companion, I suppose," she said angrily to the first sheep. "You have been telling horrible tales of our fate. Some sheep never know when to keep things to themselves. There was no need to tell your companion the truth, that we are being led to certain death!"

But the first sheep did not answer. He was thinking that the sun had never blessed him with so much warmth, that no crowded pen had ever seemed so comfortable and luxurious. Then suddenly he was taken by surprise and hustled out of a little gate and up the ramp into the waiting truck, and suddenly too the sun shone in its true colours, battering him about the head with gigantic burning bars, while the hawks congregated above, sizzling the sky with their wings, and a pall of dust clung to the barren used-up hills, and everywhere was commotion, pushing, struggling, bleating, trampling.

"This must be death," he thought, and he began to struggle and cry out.

The second sheep, having at last learned that he would meet his fate at the freezing works, stood unperturbed now in the truck with his nose against the wall and his eyes looking through the slits.

"You are right," he said to the first sheep. "The hill has never seemed so green, the sun has never been warmer, and this truck with its neat red walls is a mansion where I would happily spend the rest of my days."

But the first sheep did not answer. He had seen the approach of death. He could hide from it no longer. He had given up the struggle and was lying exhausted in a corner of the truck. And when the truck arrived at its destination, the freezing works, the man whose duty it was to unload the sheep noticed the first lying so still in the corner that he believed it was dead.

"We can't have dead sheep," he said. "How can you kill a dead sheep?"

So he heaved the first sheep out of the door of the truck onto the rusty railway line.

"I'll move it away later," he said to himself. "Meanwhile here goes with this lot."

And while he was so busy moving the flock, the first sheep, recovering, sprang up and trotted away along the line, out the gate of the freezing works, up the road, along another road, until he saw a flock being driven before him.

"I will join the flock," he said. "No one will notice, and I shall be safe."

While the drover was not looking, the first sheep hurried in among the flock and was soon trotting along with them until they came to a hot dusty road through a valley where the hills leaned in a sun-scorched wilderness of rock, tussock, and old rabbit warrens.

By now he was feeling very tired. He spoke for the first time to his new companions.

"What a hot dusty road," he said. "How uncomfortable the heat is, and the sun seems to be striking me for its own burning purposes."

The sheep walking beside him looked surprised.

"It is a wonderful day," he exclaimed. "The sun is warmer than I have ever known it, the hills glow green with luscious grass, and there is not a hawk in the sky to threaten us!"

"You mean," the first sheep replied slyly, "that you are on your way to the saleyards, and then to the freezing works to be killed."

The other sheep gave a bleat of surprise.

"How did you guess?" he asked.

"Oh," said the first sheep wisely, "I know the code. And because I know the code I shall go around in circles all my life, not knowing whether to think that the hills are bare or whether they are green, whether the hawks are scarce or plentiful, whether the sun is friend or foe. For the rest of my life I shall not speak another word. I shall trot along the hot dusty valleys where the hills are both barren and lush with spring grass."

"What shall I do but keep silent?"

And so it happened, and over and over again the first sheep escaped death, and rejoined the flock of sheep who were travelling to the freezing works. He is still alive today. If you notice him in a flock, being driven along a hot dusty road, you will be able to distinguish him by his timidity, his uncertainty, the frenzied expression in his eyes when he tries, in his condemned silence, to discover whether the sky is at last free from hawks, or whether they circle in twos and threes above him, waiting to kill him.

A Boy's Will

All the wild summer holidays Peter was angry. The rain came down heavily almost every day but it was not the rain that angered, it was people—family, visitors, neighbours who moved judging, complaining in their subtropical sweat and steam with their damp skin clinging to the new plastic-covered chairs in the sitting room and their voices tired and their eyes puzzled when they looked at him, as if they did not understand; and then he grew puzzled too for he did not know what they were trying to understand.

He wanted to be left alone. His fourteen years belonged to him like trophies. He sensed that this, his fifteenth year, would be so much prized by himself and others that he would need to fight to preserve it for himself. Everyone had suddenly become intensely interested, seeming to want to share him and explore him. In the first week of the holidays when in answer to his mother's question, "Where have you been?" he said, "Nowhere," his aunt Lily who had come to stay began to chant with an inexplicable triumph in her thick country throat,

"Where have you been?—Nowhere.—What did you do?—Nothing."

"It's begun, Cara," she said softly. She was standing by the telephone pressing her hand gently upon the cradle, circling her index finger on the black polished curves.

"It's begun, Cara."

Her hand quivered as she spoke.

What did she mean by her chant? "Nowhere, nothing, no-one?"

Why did everyone know so much about him? About his future too, what he would become, where he would live, how he would feel in his most secret self?

His aunt had said,

"In a few years, Cara, he'll want to break away. You can see the signs already."

His mother replied.

"As I've told you, Lily, it's a scientific career for him. With his I.Q."

His I.Q. was high. He'd heard them say it was so high it couldn't be marked. His mother had said in tones of awe as if she had been describing an elusive beast instead of his intelligence that it was so high it had "gone off the page," while Aunt Lily had replied in a sour dry voice,

"These tests are not as reliable as they were once thought to be." Then his aunt Lily sighed as if she wanted something that would never be given to her and though he possessed skates, a transistor, a half-share with his brother Paul in a dinghy and there were few things he wanted desperately, he identified the feeling Aunt Lily had and he felt sorry for her with her hairy chin and her footballer's legs. When she came to stay everyone always told her, "You're one of the family, Lil, you're one of the family", but it was said so often that nobody seemed to believe it any more and she was really not one of the family, she laughed too loudly and her clothes were funny and she was just a woman living by herself in a room, in Wellington: in a room, not even in a house. It was when she came to stay that Peter's mother talked about him and Paul and their young sister Emily, describing what they had said or done, how from the very first he'd shown signs of exceptional intelligence, how he'd skipped classes at school, had learned to play the piano and was now on to Chopin Waltzes and Beethoven's Moonlight Sonata.

When Aunt Lily arrived Peter had to play all his music to her.

"Play the Beethoven," his mother said, closing her eyes and humming, "De-De-De, De-De-De, De-De-De. . . ."

"Now the Minute Waltz again, Peter. (He does this well because it ties in with his mathematics.)"

Peter felt his fingers moving stiffly. He'd been shirking his practice. His aunt murmured in her sour dry voice,

"He's good technically but he thumps."

He heard his mother's quick intake of breath and her protective,

"He hasn't always thumped. He hasn't been practising. You should have heard him . . ."

and his aunt's cold reply,

"Anyone really interested in music practises all the time."

His mother sighed then.

"There are so many demands made on him, with his intelligence. . . ."

He played his pieces, too, when a family friend arrived by plane from America, and though the friend had been flying all night and his eyes were dark with wanting to sleep he sat on one of the new plastic-covered chairs listening to the messy blurr of notes made by Peter's unpractised fingers.

The expression masked on his face he said calmly,

"That's all right."

Peter saw his mother frown, searching the remark for the comforting word "brilliant". Not finding it, she looked lonely and Peter, turning and seeing her face and knowing what she wanted, felt miserable. He finished in a hurried swallow of notes banging the final chords down like a window sash and taking the kid's toy, an American police car, the visitor had given him he escaped through the kitchen and downstairs to the garage where, his misery giving way to anger, he leapt up and down on the lid of an applebox until it snapped beneath him, sharply, satisfyingly.

Auckland this summer was a factory of storms. Lightning, thunder, rain swept from West to East, Tasman to Pacific, rolling big smoke-white clouds like a bushfire in the sky with tongues of lightning darting and stabbing and the thunder exploding and more rain like sheets of aluminium falling. Peter dealt with each storm by recording it, calculating, experimenting. He collected and measured the rain in his rain-gauge, he read his barometer, his maximum and minimum thermometer, and then after such close disciplined reading he spent hours reading the sky, in agreeable free translation. His teacher had written on his School Report, "What has happened to Peter's reading? Must read more." Peter had not explained that he suddenly found clouds more interesting than words. Clouds, light, heat, sound. On their Christmas trip round the East Coast in the family car he carried his barometer like a book on his lap, reading it.

"He'll be a meteorologist," his mother said, almost destroying his new passion with the weight of her tomorrow.

He made a sundial too and set it on one of the fenceposts but there had been so much rain and so little sun that its applebox surface was sodden. Only once or twice at the beginning of the holidays he had been able to read the time by the shadow but now, when the holidays were nearly over, that time seemed so long ago, a time when he had not been angry, when his anger did not seize him so completely that he threw things or slapped his young sister, prompting his mother's cry,

"Peter, stop bullying. Remember you're fourteen to her eleven. Be your age."

His brother Paul, two years older, had a job for the holidays and would let no-one forget that he earned five pounds a week and was grown up. He was studying photography, too, and spent his spare time shut in the downstairs bathroom with a sheet of cardboard over the window and the slit under the door sealed with newspaper, developing and enlarging films. With his savings and his earnings he'd bought himself an enlarger, all the James Bond paperbacks, two books of science fiction, a bottle of Cedar Wood pre-electric shave lotion, and he'd had his trousers tapered. One Saturday early in the holidays he'd gone with Peter for a train-ride to Swanson where they sat in the Domain sheltering under the macrocarpa trees, licking icecreams, jelly-tipped on sticks, and reading comics bought at the railway bookstall. It rained, they came home early, and on the way home Paul made it clear that he hadn't gone out with Peter for the day that he'd *taken* Peter, and as they loitered up the drive, preparing answers to embarrassing questions they might be asked, Paul said, "I'll never go anywhere with you again. You act like a kid."

Now, in the weekends, Paul went to the pictures with a girlfriend and Peter saw little of him except when they watched television.

There had been a fuss about that too. His aunt Lily nearly died when she saw the new television set. She had cried out as if she were in danger.

"What about the children? For their sake. . . ."
Peter's mother flushed.

"Ted and I made the decision. It's easy for you as you've no children."

Aunt Lily nodded meekly.

"I just hoped," she said quietly, "that it wouldn't draw the children too much."

Draw? Once when he had a boil on his neck his mother had put a poultice on it, as she said, to "draw" it. She had burned the poultice in the oil drum at the back of the section.

Certainly they watched television at first. They enjoyed the easy programmes, those with the laughs, and escaped when the serious news appeared showing jungle warfare, poverty, disease, famine. But that, too, had been at the beginning of the holidays before Peter began to get angry. Now he seldom watched except for the programme starring the cowboy who gambled. Peter knew all the poker terms. I'll raise you, he'd say coolly to an imaginary opponent. He'd seen a programme, too, about the chances of a fly settling on a certain lump of sugar and he'd worked out the probability and had even snared Paul's interest in this, though what was the use when all their windows and doors had insect screens and flies never landed on the sugar?

It was just before he began to make his kite that he heard his mother saying to Aunt Lily,

"Do you notice how impatient he's getting? His intelligence will be no use if he has no patience. Paul is the one who perseveres. Paul will go far."

"You mean he's the plodding type?"

Peter saw his mother's shocked face as she absorbed all that plodding implied. Oh no, her children were bright, quick, surely they would never plod.

"I think *persevere* is the word. Peter will find life hard if he has no patience. He's grown so quick-tempered!"

Peter pulled a face to himself. Who did they think they were to try to live his life for him?

"This interest in the weather. It could be permanent. I rang up the Department."

He heard his aunt's manuka-stick voice,

"The experts now say. . . ."

He did not wait to hear what the experts now said. He escaped from the top of the stairs down to the garage and ten minutes later Emily came upstairs crying.

"Peter thumped me!"

Peter sat on an upturned applebox in the garage. He could imagine his mother's exclamation,

"Thumped you!"

And her tender admonition afterwards,

"Peter, you must be kind to your little sister. Boys must be gentle with girls."

How could he explain that the thumping had been Emily's fault? They'd all watched a programme on television the night before where there was an old woman, so old and tired that she had to be moved from her little house to be put among the old people, and the film showed her arriving with the few belongings she'd been allowed to bring with her, and one was a photograph of herself as a young girl, and just when she was deciding where to hang it in her new bedroom, a big nurse in a white fly-a-way hat had rushed into the room, admired the photograph, said the woman had not grown a day older, then she'd seized the photograph and the old woman stood looking unhappy and lonely with her arms dangling and her hands empty. But that had been last night on television. Now, this morning, Emily had taken an open page of Peter's Boy's Book of Outdoor Hobbies and drawn a picture of the old woman clinging to her treasure while the nurse tried to take it from her. Peter had no quarrel with Emily's drawing. The programme had frightened him, too, for old age was part of tomorrow and tomorrow was like one of those tools that clamped down and screwed tight, permanently fixing everything beneath it. But Emily had drawn the picture where she shouldn't have, over the diagram of the kite that Peter planned to make, and surely a thump was small punishment for such a crime?

The Boy's Book of Outdoor Hobbies was one of the few consolations Peter had during the holidays. He had worked carefully through it, making the sundial, the wind gauge, other interesting items not connected with the weather. He had skipped the chapter on Photography and Radio for these were Paul's interests and it was better, at this stage, to know nothing about them than try to compete with Paul's accurate detailed knowledge. With an elder brother in the family it was a case of the younger taking the leftovers or perishing in the comparisons that would follow.

"When Paul takes photographs he——"

"Paul knows how to fix the tv when it breaks down——"

Peter had decided, therefore, as his next project, to make a box kite.

He rubbed angrily at the pencilled lines of the old woman and the photograph and the wicked nurse. Emily ought to have known better. The figures quite covered his diagram and measurements. And even if he managed to decipher them and make his kite would the weather be clear for kite-flying? Rain steamed in the sky, the leaves of the big subtropical flowers grew glossy, their stems grew tall, the bush on the hills had a milky green appearance as if rain and milk had fallen together from the sky.

Peter found paste, bamboo sticks, string, a roll of blue and white crepe paper left over from someone's attempt at fancy dress, and forgetting about Emily and the old woman and thumping and the weather and his future he began to make his kite.

Just then he heard his mother and aunt coming downstairs.

"In this gap between showers I'll show you the passion fruit growing by Emily's playhouse."

His mother looked into the garage.

"What are you doing, Peter? Oh, making a kite."

She turned apologetically to Aunt Lily.

"I suppose it's a childish thing for him to make. For all his intelligence he's young for his age."

"All normal boys like kites," Aunt Lily said smoothly.

They crossed the lawn to the playhouse where Emily with the innocent gaze of one who has been thumped and avenged peeped out at them.

"Aren't they big? It will be ages before they ripen. I've always wanted to grow passion fruit."

"I love passion fruit."

They were coming back across the lawn. Peter's mother seized the opportunity to scold him for his treatment of Emily.

"We can't have these rages, Peter."

He heard her saying with sadness in her voice as they climbed the stairs,

"Though he has always played the piano best when he's been angry. I'm sorry he's giving it up. Ted's sorry too. I don't know what's come over the boy these holidays. There was a drop in his school work, too, at the end of last year. The teacher remarked on it. He doesn't seem to have the patience."

"You have to have patience," Aunt Lily said, snapping shut the insect-screen door.

It took Peter several hours to make his kite. He knew he was perhaps the only boy in the street making a kite; he knew also that as soon as it was launched everyone would be flying kites and no doubt some would break the rules, flying theirs in forbidden places like the street where entanglement in the wires would cause electro-cution and death. Peter had been warned. There was not much his mother and his father and his teachers had not warned him about. When he thought of his kite as an instrument of death he began to breathe quickly and his hands grew cold and he could not believe that anything so beautiful could help to destroy. It was a box kite, blue and white, as light as a bird's wing on bamboo-stick bones. None of the other boys in the street would make a box kite; theirs would be the usual kind, flat, a skeleton cross of sticks fleshed with brown paper or plastic with a sharp nose and tail and though it would fly the flight would be a plunging swooping movement as if it were not at home in the sky and longed to descend to earth whereas the box kite, Peter knew, would float and drift without panic or restlessness, like a cloud. To Peter, the clouds that passed overhead during all the wild stormy rainy holidays had been unlike any others he had known; or perhaps his feeling for them had changed. In a mysterious way they seemed to contain promises of a wall or window opening beyond into the light. Sometimes in the evening the sun setting in secret appeared to grow so full of light that it could not contain itself and burst through, suddenly, thrusting like a shaft through the big soft clouds down, down into the earth. Watching, Peter knew a feeling of strength, of himself powered by light, of a discovery that he could not understand or control. He felt after closely reading, translating the sky day after day night after night (the "holiday reading" *Under the Greenwood Tree*, *Great Expectations*, lay unopened on his bookshelf) that the clouds in their lightness would offer no resistance when the time came for the moment, *his* moment, to burst through. Without being able to articulate his dream he thought that the moment might come when he flew his blue and white box kite.

When that evening he drew aside the curtains in the sitting room he could not suppress his joy when he saw the clear bright sky.

"Ooh Mum, it'll be fine tomorrow. Isn't the sky lovely?" he called.

He frowned when he heard her comment.

"Come and look at the sky everyone. Peter says come and look at the sky."

And her loudly whispered aside to his father.

"It's the poet in him, Ted. Peter's discovered the wonders of Nature."

Peter felt the rage growing in him. It was *his* sky, *his* light, *his* clouds. He had impulsively let others intrude to claim them.

Before the whole family could surge about the drawn curtain he swung it back across the window.

"It's gone now," he said sullenly.

"Will you fly your new kite tomorrow?" his mother asked, and turning to his father said proudly,

"Peter made such a beautiful kite today. Not the ordinary sort of kite, either."

And then turning to Aunt Lily,

"He's clever with his hands as well."

Peter decided then that he would not make an event of the flight. If the next day were fine he would sneak out, launch the kite, fly it to his satisfaction, then come home without any of the family knowing what had happened. At the back of the house there was a play-ground as big as two paddocks where the Catholic children played games and where during the holidays the grass had grown as tall as wheat and had browned without sun as everyone's skin, too, had turned brown in the humid sunless weather. Day by day the rain lashed the grass and the strong winds rippled it and the cloud-shapes twisted across it in plaited shadows. It was an ideal place to fly a kite. Peter dreamed of it as he lay in bed. He would run through the grass with his kite flying behind and above him. He would not feel any more the irritating rage and impatience that kept overwhelming him for there would be nothing to rage over, then, flying his kite, with his face looking up at the clouds and the sky that swung like a vast ship's deck under the surge of the sky's waves. He could almost feel that he might be standing in the sky, sailing through it, steering his path on a voyage of discovery.

The day was fine, the sky clear except for cottontails of cloud and rather more wind than Peter had hoped for. He did not hurry to get up. He sneaked a plate of Weetbix from the kitchen to his bed-room, ate most of it, then lay waiting for Paul and his father to go to work and for Emily to go about her recent domestic craze of making clothes for her teenage doll. Then, when Peter was sure the coast was clear he made ready his kite but his plans for secrecy were destroyed when he met his mother by the kitchen door. She was standing, waiting, while the washing eddied in its white machine. Did all mothers know how to destroy in such subtle ways? Surely she too had not been thinking all night of whether today would be fine for kite-flying? Surely mothers had other things to think of besides their children and their abilities, their intelligence, and what the future held for them in such proud frightening store?

"A nice day to fly your kite, Peter."

He grunted. Then, remembering his manners, he said,

"I think I'll try it in the Catholic playground."

"Good!" his mother said, seeming to think, but not saying, that once he had flown his kite he might go on to activities more suited to his intelligence. Her eyes as she looked at him were heavy as if his future lay inside them like a dark stone.

He climbed through the fence and ran into the playground. The kite obeyed at a touch, stumbled in a jaggling way, at first, over the long grass until it caught and was caught by the passing wind when it began to float like a feather then to turn and swim lightly like a fish in buoyant air, while Peter ran, his feet and legs soaked in the long wet grass, the grass-seeds like clusters of shot stinging his knees; feeling the kitestring as if, tied to himself, it were a part of his own body. He knew a pleasurable feeling at once of lightness and of anchorage, as if his fastrunning legs were tangled for ever in the twisted stems of grass while another part of himself were floating lightly up near the shredded white clouds; then suddenly he found himself out of breath, with running and flying, and he was sobbing with his eyes full of stinging tears, and he stopped running and stood still while the kite jerked and laboured above him, no longer flying with freedom and grace. He felt the tears falling down his face. He was aghast at his weeping but he could not stop it, and all the while he clung fast to the kite string feeling the weight like that of a restless wing upon his arm. It was then that a stronger gust of wind came buffeting, gashing the fragile blue and white crepe paper body, and as the kite drifted down the blue and white paper trailed behind it like shreds of skin. It fell a few yards from where Peter was standing. For a moment he stood still. Then slowly he wound the string and calmly picked up the broken kite. He felt no rage at its breaking. He carried it over the playground, through the gap in the back fence and was crossing the lawn when his mother, hanging out the washing, saw him and cried out, her face full of sympathy,

"Oh Peter, your lovely kite! What happened to it?"

Peter's voice was calm.

"The wind was too strong."

"What a shame!"

His mother spoke into the white flapping sheets. He knew that when she went upstairs she would say to Aunt Lily who would be reading her share of the morning paper,

"Peter's kite is broken, his lovely kite!"

Perhaps she might also say,

"More tantrums, I suppose. That boy. For all his intelligence, that boy. . . ."

That boy. He was that boy. He was intelligent. He had been in the Silver class at Intermediate and his brother, for all his photography and repairing of radios, had been in the Bronze, and his sister—well, sisters were not the same.

That boy.

Immune, he went to the garage. He understood now what the television preachers meant when they insisted the skies had opened. He believed them. He saw his mother with a stone in her eyes and a bone in her throat. Stone and bone were his future and she could never remove them nor perhaps would he want her to. He did not want her to grow old, or go to an institution and have her treasure snatched from her. He felt suddenly protective towards her. He looked at her standing passively on the lawn while the flying sheets and towels slapped at her face and he felt a surge inside him as if he still anchored the blue and white kite and the kite itself flew on towards the hidden sun.

"Now keep your temper, Peter. Just because your kite's broken don't go throwing things around or interfering with Emily's playhouse!"

Shrugging his shoulders as he'd seen his father do, Peter laid the kite gently on the garage floor. Then taking the remaining whole pieces of crepe paper he began patiently to renew and repair the broken body.

Andrew Salkey

One of the most popular folk tales of the West Indies is the story of Anancy. It is a story belonging originally to the Ashanti tribe and one they brought with them to the New World.

Anancy is a spider and as such is physically weak, but he is a very cunning fellow and through his wily ways he is always able to get the better of those who are stronger than he is. This suggests the reason for his popularity, for to the slaves he must have symbolized the resilience of the spirit and the hope that they too would eventually conquer. It is an interesting example of how the West Indian retained from his African heritage what remained relevant to him under new conditions.

This is the "background" to Andrew Salkey's story. The word, background, is used, for though Salkey has named his story "Anancy" and though he deals with a spider and uses the traditional form and style, the tale he tells is not a traditional Anancy one. His version is both personal and experimental. Like a number of writers today, Tutuola, for example, whose heritage provides a rich storehouse of folklore, Salkey has made use of the traditional but has reshaped it in order to explore new experiences and analyse new problems. The problem he explores here is that of the Black man in the New World; what he attempts to analyse is "the complex fate of the West Indian", the fate of a man caught between two worlds. It is, in the words of Ivan Van Sertima:

> The conflict of a people attracted at one and the same time to Western influence and the barbaric roots and memories of earlier Africa, the conflict of origins in the Old World and a home in the New, between the ancestral past and all its ghosts and the living and challenging present.
>
> (from *Caribbean Writers*)

Recent years have seen the pilgrimage of many back to Africa but much has happened since the first middle passage. Deprived of community life, oppressed first by slavery then by poverty, subjected to new languages, religions, social and climatic conditions, we have the feeling that too much has gone between, and that the Black West Indian no longer belongs in Africa either. The dilemma of the "halfie" finds its most notable expression in the hero of Denis Williams's novel, *Other Leopards*, Lionel Lobo Froad. He says,

'I am a man, you see, plagued by these two names, and this is their history: Lionel, the who I was, dealing with Lobo, the who I continually felt I ought to become.'

It is this conflict and dilemma that Salkey explores in his fable. The fact that the dilemma of the twentieth-century West Indian is explored through the means and in the way of the old African legend emphasizes the duality. As in Tutuola's story we have the mixture of traditional and modern. Ghosts spin like electric fans, bodies splinter fine like icing sugar or showers of confetti. Lizards, scorpions and cobra snakes, occupants of the pagan underworld, are hungry as the Christians who spent forty days in the wilderness.

Anancy is the Black West Indian living in the New World who makes a voyage of self-discovery to Africa, to the underworld where his spirit resides. He makes it because he 'is all that he is' and when he arrives the 'small small ghost's' recognition of him makes it quite clear that he has returned to his ancestral home. In all such quests there is a conflict of body and spirit and so we are prepared for the moment when Anancy must fight his spirit which resides here in Africa. This is not just a collision of body and spirit but of two worlds, and when his spirit is victorious the words of Mother Johnson from *A Quality of Violence*, Salkey's first novel, ring in our ears. Addressing the Jamaican villagers she says, ' "I'm you' conqueror. And you know why? Because Africa is me. I black true. I stone strong." ' The ghost's remark, ' "Who ever heard of anybody fighting against his own life!" ' reminds us how foolish it is for the Black West Indian to think he can defeat the African presence within him.

But in spite of the victory of his spirit Anancy does not remain in Africa. He returns home, for though Africa may be his spiritual home, many factors have been at work over the centuries to distance him from his ancestors. In *A Quality of Violence* Miss Mellie's reply to Mother Johnson is of interest. She says,

'We do not frighten by white fowl talk or Africa or slave power! We don't belong to them things. We is people that you always living-off of. We is people who live on the land in St. Thomas, not Africa.'

The answer to the dilemma, it seems, lies midway between the two points of view.

Though Anancy returns to the West Indies there is no desertion on the part of his spirit, indeed there cannot be for it is integral to his very existence. Africa and the spirit of Africa remain a part of him, the most vital part, his soul. This is the idea behind the epigram from Horace that Salkey uses in his first novel, 'They change their climate, not their soul, who run beyond the sea.' The West Indian must create a new consciousness but Africa will ever be part of it.

In political terms, for Anancy has been called a political spider, we could say that the story emphasizes that the spirit of the African West Indian, like that of Anancy, will, in spite of slavery and oppression, remain undefeated. It also reminds the Black man that power alone is not sufficient. But this I believe is a much too narrow interpretation. In its broadest sense Anancy's quest is one of a man in search of his origins, of his past. It expresses the hope that having come to terms with this past he may have a greater understanding of the present and perhaps an even greater hope for the future. *A. R.*

Anancy

I'm going to tell you a story about a spider. The spider's name is Anancy. The story is such a wonder story that not even Anancy himself would want to tell it. And that's the mystery of things, believe me.

Well, now, Anancy was a real big spider, the kind of spider with heaps of shoulder muscles, a black-hairy chest and a night-black frighten-children beard on his chin. Anancy was really a frightened-up spectacle of all things powerful and massive. He was a miracle of terror. All the same, though, he had a certain sort of high-class dignity together with all the strong presence that most spiders carry around with them. And this high-class dignity, this sort of big-house pride, was also a form of strength. It was a strength in the way that veins and muscles in the arm are sure signs of stress, strain and strength.

When Anancy walked about the place, he looked like a sort of a war memorial rumbling and tumbling at earthquake time. Anancy was the kind of spider who could do plenty of things, like swim-in-river, climb tall-tall mountains and run long-long races. Anancy was also a great-time trickster and a giant-wrestler, as well. Total everybody called his name and still calling it in a hush-hush voice: "Who, Anancy? Man, Anancy is a giant wrestler! Anancy is a fair-ground of powers and muscles! Anancy is a spider is a champion is a strangler is a basinful of big-house pride is a real terror is a ocean of magic with him hands and feet!"

Now, one day some fat news reached Anancy and the news said that the ghosts from the far-far country parts were thinking of holding a real serious wrestling match; and because Anancy is all that he is, he decided sudden-like that he would go to the far-far country parts and take part in the match with the ghosts.

Well, when total everybody in Anancy's village heard what Anancy was going to do, some of his wrestler friends felt doubtful and tormented-up, some of his political spider friends started to put bets on him, some decided that they would pray plenty for Anancy, and some just stood shaking their head of worries and sighing heaps of sympathetic sighs.

But Anancy had a mother and a father. And he loved them in a great respectful way. But they didn't like the wrestling match idea, at all, at all. Anancy's mother started to tell Anancy that it is a foolish business for him to wrestle against ghosts because ghosts can read a spider's mind and they can see clear-like total everything that a spider's going to do before he actually does it.

All that Anancy said to that was: "One ghost is a hundred ghosts, and a hundred ghosts is only one ghost. A ghost is only a ghost to me."

But Anancy's mother and father were arguing with plenty love in their hearts for him. They kept reminding him of the days when he couldn't even see straight, of the days when the shadow of a hoe at the slant used to frighten him, of the days when the smallest noise used to make him draw up all his spider legs under himself and shudder. They tried hard to talk protection into him but all he said was: "I'm Anancy."

When his mother and father were pleading, all he was doing was stretching out his arms and yawning a wide tired yawn, and going on like he was bored and frightened about total nothing in the world.

Later on that same day, he went back to his mother and because she was so sad, Anancy whispered some nice-nice words in her ears, and the nice-nice words made her sad face light up with twinkle eyes and merry-merry heart. Then he gave her some corn meal and cassava flour and asked her to make some cassava cakes for him. He rubbed his arms with sweet herbs and he tensed up his muscles. Afterwards, he stepped outside and gave away some juicy mangoes and nuts to the children spiders who were always standing round his hut. He shut his door and rested himself for a while. Then he went up to his mother and asked her for the cassava cakes. She was looking pale and mournful as if she saw a funeral standing up in front of her instead of her own son. She cleared her throat and told him that the cassava cakes were not ready. Anancy wrinkled up his eyes and was angry bad-bad. He was puffing and blowing inside himself like a heap of brand-new bellows.

Well, Anancy didn't wait to hear what his mother was going to explain to him; he just ups and left her and ran down the road to meet his best friend, Brother Tacuma, who always travelled with him wherever he went. Brother Tacuma, was a calm-sea, thoughtful sort of spider, constantly walking by Anancy's side and constantly smiling through dark thinking eyes. This was so much Brother Tacuma's way of behaving that he got the name of "conscience of all spiders".

So now, Anancy and Brother Tacuma started to walk to the far-far country parts where the ghosts were waiting to open the wrestling match. So they were walking in all sorts of darkness in the forest; and different bad sounds and bird noises were making some terrible confusion in both their heads. Trees and leaves and twigs and branches were having some faces of evilness and dead-skull laughter. There was no brightfulness in the forest at all. Big lizards and scorpions and cobra-snakes were all over the place; and they were looking ugly and hungry like forty days in the wilderness.

When Brother Tacuma and Anancy got out of the forest they were so tired and full of sleepy eyes and tight muscles that total everything seemed to look like one big blur of confusion and hurricane happenings. Still, now that Anancy actually reached the far-far country of the ghosts, he ran into some good luck. He heard of a new rule that the ghosts had just passed. And this was it: "When anybody comes to wrestle with a ghost and the ghost beats up that person, the custom is for the conquering ghost to carry that person away and to dash that person's head against a sharp rockstone which is a special river rockstone fixed up for the purpose."

Now neither Anancy nor Brother Tacuma liked the new rule at all. Stomach turned over flip-flap when they saw what the ghosts were doing to the persons whom they were conquering. After watching those horrible happenings, up comes a small-small ghost to talk to Anancy and Brother Tacuma. Listen to how he's talking to them in a nose voice: "So you two small-time wrestlers come to the match. I recognise you, Anancy. You still among the living, eh? We'll have to see about that."

To that speech Anancy just bowed his head and started to stretch his muscles. That was how Anancy answered the small-small ghost. But the small-small ghost wasn't satisfied. Hear him: "Anancy! You think that pride is a good thing to have, eh? You think that pride is a good mirror for you to see yourself in properly? Up and down this country we break all such mirrors."

After a little foot shifting, clearing of throats, hustling here and there, things really began to look like business. Anancy started to fight, now. Even though it was broad daylight the silence that was surrounding everything and everybody was like the silence of a

Sunday morning. The first ghost contestant was a tall-tall ghost with hands and feet like an old-time electric fan, actually going on mad and circular like an old-time electric fan. The first ghost was tough like a crocodile skin and stiff like ice; and because he was stiff like ice, he was also slippery out of this world. But Anancy moved up and down like he was a great jack-in-the-box in a trance. He dived into the ghost, twisted him up and twisted him round, and before you could say Jack Mandora, he dropped him like a piece of rolled-up silver paper. After that, he grabbed the ghost and dashed him down on the river rockstone. As soon as the ghost touched the rockstone, he was splintered fine like icing sugar; and just as white as that.

Brother Tacuma started to feel a proud feeling for Anancy. He just looked at Anancy and smiled a lovely-brother-smile at him.

Then another ghost came out and challenged Anancy with plenty hot breathing, insults and wild nose-talking. This ghost had four heads, a big central head with three other heads sitting on it. Anancy looked at him, cute-like. Anancy moved up and down the wrestling ring and began to spin himself like a bright spinning two-and-six piece. When he was doing that the four-headed ghost began to get dizzy and all his eight eyes turned over and became jumbled up like plenty marbles twirling in a circle. After that, Anancy stepped heavy and stepped light and danced round and round until sudden-like the ghost's four heads dropped off. When they touched the ground, they rolled away in four different corners of the ring and the body of the ghost was crumpled up like dry grass.

Well, now, after that pretty victory, another ghost walked into the ring. This ghost had eight heads, and it could think eight times as fast as Anancy. But already Anancy was ready, and quick and brisk he was throwing his hands around the ghost's neck. As Anancy did that, the eight heads dropped off and rolled away like marbles. Then Anancy grabbed the next ghost who had ten heads and beat him up as if nothing happened.

He beat up the twelve-headed one, the fourteen-headed one, the sixteen-headed one, the eighteen-headed one and the twenty-headed one. You won't believe me when I tell you that the heads were rolling all over the place like wild red cabbage, and the eyes were blinking neons turning over and over, showing white, black and red. The whole place was a total of heads and eyes!

By this time, Anancy was really causing the ghosts a lot of worry head. So the ghosts who had promoted the wrestling match decided to hold a Ghosts United Conference. Big meeting of nose accents going on in deep session! After they had talked plenty Summit talking, they found the answer to the Anancy problem. And this was the answer to the problem: Anancy will have one last fight. And this time, Anancy must fight his own spirit. Imagine that, now! Anancy actually fighting Anancy! Yet, that's the mystery of things, believe me. Body against spirit! (Of course, this is one spirit that will have only one head.)

Well, both of them stood up and faced each other, the Anancy's body facing his own spirit. Their eyes made four as they looked at each other. All the total ghosts were holding a long low-breathing silence. Sudden-like, Anancy's spirit looked at Anancy's body, saw right through it and Anancy's body felt all crumpled-up-like.

After all the trembling brain and soul messages between body and spirit, Anancy's spirit made a flash-of-lightning movement and lifted up Anancy's body and dashed it against the rockstone. And Anancy's body was splintered up into small pieces like plenty showers of confetti.

So listen to the ghosts, now: "Ai-ya-ai! At last it's come to pass! At last! Who ever heard of anybody fighting against his own life! Serve him right! Serve him damn right! Proud and stupid spider!"

After that, the chief of the ghosts walked into a thick clump of bush-john, picked some berries off the bush-john tree, and squeezed the juice into the eyes of all the dead ghosts. Quick-like, all of the conquered ghosts jumped up and began to live again and talk in their old-time nose voices.

Brother Tacuma who was watching the chief ghost, decided to do total everything he saw the chief ghost do. So Brother Tacuma went into the thick clump of bush-john, picked some berries off it and squeezed the juice into Anancy's right eye, then, into his left eye. As soon as he did that, quick-like, Anancy came back to life and returned to his normal spider self. Yet, even though Anancy was restored to his living body again, he was feeling very angry and he started to grumble and quarrel with his spirit for being a Judas person to him. He told his spirit that he hated the bad treachery which it did to his body. And the row lasted for a long time.

When the ghosts returned to find Anancy and to pick up his pieces and to eat him for supper, they didn't see him at all. But they heard him far off. They heard him shouting out loud in the distance, quarrelling with his spirit and running away as fast as he could go from the far-far country parts. So the ghosts decided to chase Brother Tacuma and Anancy.

The ghosts were running mad races and Anancy and Brother Tacuma were running even faster. The ghosts started catching up, now. The speed is pure power-house speed between them! But Anancy and Brother Tacuma were getting nearer home, now. The ghosts opened out to a bigger speed and the forest was making plenty celebrating noises like hurricane wind.

Anancy and Brother Tacuma turned the last corner and headed for the door that led into Anancy's mother's hut. The ghosts were coming quicker, now. They were flying low like madness and cursing-hot fever. Then, Anancy, sudden-like, from nowhere, started to feel weak and he felt like all his total courage and power was oozing out of him. As he was having that weak sensation, he gave up the high speeding and he began to slow down. As he was slowing down, quick-like, something burst way deep down inside him. Anancy's spirit, who had been having a big disagreement with Anancy's body, decided to show that he was no Judas person at all. So Anancy's spirit (one-time conqueror and only conqueror of Anancy) shot out of Anancy's sweating body and began to tackle the ghosts. Anancy's spirit performed some terrible wrestling tricks on the ghosts. After about the count of twelve, most of the ghosts who were chasing Anancy cried out in plenty aches and pain and they turned round the other way and ran back to the far-far country parts; all the same, many of them couldn't move because they were too battered and splintered.

As soon as the ghosts were no more, Anancy's spirit made a real flying come-back to Anancy's body. And as that was happening a joyous, heaven-come-down-to-earth smile spread itself all over Anancy's face. Brother Tacuma saw the joyous, heaven-come-down-to-earth smile on Anancy's face and he, too, felt a happy feeling swelling deep down inside himself. And Anancy made Brother Tacuma know that a person is truly strong only after that person's spirit has proved him.

Ezekiel Mphahlele

I can hear the big curfew bell at the police station peal 'ten to ten, ten to ten, ten to ten' for the Black man to be out of the streets to be at home to be out of the policeman's reach. Year after year the sound of the bell floats in the air at ten minutes to ten and the Black man must run home and the Black man must sleep or have a night special permit. The police whistle is very near now and the hunted man must be in Second Avenue but the bell goes on pealing lustily and so Black man you must run wherever you are, run.

(from Down Second Avenue)

With Mphahlele's work we enter a world utterly different from those depicted by Ngugi, Achebe or Tutuola, one governed by a racial doctrine which determines every action, segregates man from man, and leaves the *kaffir* a fugitive with no place to run to.

Even though most of Mphahlele's fiction derives from the same experience of apartheid in South Africa which is so movingly and so painfully described in his autobiographical *Down Second Avenue*, nevertheless the prose-style of the short stories is surprisingly lacking in the searingly vivid quality and the acrid bitterness of that work. One notes – also in "The Living and the Dead" – an impoverishment of language, a use of cliché, a dullness and monotony which offer a great contrast to the disciplined grace of Achebe's prose, for example, or the exuberant torrent of Tutuola's.

The reasons for this must again be sought in the different world of South Africa, the setting for the story. If Mphahlele is speaking directly in his autobiographical work, he is using language in his fiction as an instrument to depict the stock reaction and engrained bigotry of the whites and to show the enforced dullness and monotony of the black people. Both the autobiography and the fiction are written in character:

The workers' rush was over. Only a few women sat on the benches on the platform. One was following his movements with her eyes. She sat there, so fat, he observed, looking at him. Just like a woman. She just sat and looked at you for no reason; probably because of an idle mind; maybe she was thinking about everything.

Thus the very prose-style of the story becomes an implicit indictment of the social system it is concerned to reflect. Art is sacrificed to depicting the realities of life.

But the indictment of apartheid does not cease there. Against his will Stoffel does become involved in the fate of these black people, despite all the 'ready-made attitudes, stock attitudes that various people had each in their own time planted in him', and contrary to his avowed belief that 'black was black, white was white—that was all that mattered'. The story seems indeed to be leading up to a dramatic—and sentimental—conversion. But in the end the reader is deceived: Stoffel remains the same person. Mphahlele's bitter personal experience combines with his artistic awareness to make this a better story, and one truer to life. It becomes a story that forces us to ask ourselves how, given these circumstances, could things really be different? And this question is also a measure of the story's value as literature. *D.H.*

The Living and the Dead

Lebona felt the letter burning in his pocket. Since he had picked it up along the railway it had nagged at him no end.

He would read it during lunch, he thought. Meantime he must continue with his work, which was to pick up rubbish that people continuously threw on the platform and on the railway tracks. Lebona used a piece of wire with a ball of tar stuck on at the end. One didn't need to bend. One only pressed the ball of tar on to a piece of paper or any other rubbish, detatched it and threw it into a bag hanging from the shoulder.

A number of things crossed Lebona's mind: the man who had died the previous afternoon. Died, just like that. How could a man just die like that—like a rat or a mere dog?

The workers' rush was over. Only a few women sat on the benches on the platform. One was following his movements with her eyes. She sat there, so fat, he observed, looking at him. Just like a woman. She just sat and looked at you for no reason; probably because of an idle mind; maybe she was thinking about everything. Still he knew if he were a fly she might look at him all day. But no, not the letter. She mustn't be thinking about it. The letter in his pocket. It wasn't hers—no, it couldn't be; he had picked it up lower down the line; she could say what she liked, but it wasn't her letter.

That man: who would have thought a man could die just as if death were in one's pocket or throat all the time?

Stoffel Visser was angry; angry because he felt foolish. Everything had gone wrong. And right through his university career Stoffel Visser had been taught that things must go right to the last detail.

"Calm yourself, Stoffel."

"Such mistakes shouldn't ever occur."

"Don't preach, for God's sake!"

Doppie Fourie helped himself to more whisky.

"It's all Jackson's fault," Stoffel said. "He goes out yesterday and instead of being here in the evening to prepare supper he doesn't come. This morning he's still not here, still not here, and I can't get my bloody breakfast in time because I've to do it myself, and you know *I must* have a good breakfast every day. Worse, my clock is out of order, buggered up, man, and the bloody Jackson's not here to wake me up. So I oversleep—that's what happens—and after last night's *braaivleis*, you know. It's five o'clock on a Friday morning, and the bastard hasn't turned up yet. How could I be in time to give Rens the document before the Cape Town train left this morning?"

"Now I think of it, Stoffel," said Fourie, "I can't help thinking how serious the whole thing is. Now the Minister can't have the report to think about it before the session begins. What do we do next?"

"There'll still be time enough to post it by express mail."

Doppie Fourie looked grave.

"You don't have to look as if the sky was about to fall," he said, rather to himself than his friend. "Have another whisky."

Stoffel poured one for himself and his friend. "What a good piece of work we did, Doppie!"

"Bloody good. Did you see this?" Fourie held out a newspaper, pointing his trembling finger at a report. The item said that Africans had held a "roaring party" in a suburban house while the white family were out. There had been feasting and music and dancing.

"See, you see now," said Stoffel, unable to contain his emotion. "Just what I told these fellows in the commission. Some of them are so wooden-headed they won't understand simple things like kaffirs swarming over our suburbs, living there, gambling there, breeding there, drinking there and sleeping there with girls. They won't understand, these stupid fools, until the kaffirs enter their houses and boss them about and sleep with white girls. What's to happen to white civilisation?"

"Don't make another speech, Stoffel. We've talked about this so long in the commission I'm simply choking with it."

"Look here, Doppie Fourie, *ou kêrel*, you deceive yourself to think I want to hear myself talk."

"I didn't mean that, Stoffel. But of course you have always been very clever. I envy you your brains. You always have a ready answer to a problem. Anyhow I don't promise to be an obedient listener tonight. I just want to drink."

"C'mon, *ou kêrel*, you know you want to listen. If I feel pressed to speak you must listen, like it or not."

Doppie looked up at Stoffel, this frail-looking man with an artist's face and an intellect that seldom rose to the surface. None of our Rugby-playing type with their bravado, Doppie thought. Often he hated himself for feeling so inferior. And all through his friend's miniature oration Doppie's face showed a deep hurt.

"Let me tell you this, *rooinekke*," Stoffel said, "you know I'd rather be touring the whole world and meeting people and cultures and perhaps be learning some art myself—I know you don't believe a thing I'm saying—instead of rotting in this hole and tolerating numskulls I'm compelled to work with on committees. Doppie, there must be hundreds of our people who'd rather be doing something else they love best. But we're all tied to some bucking bronco and we must like it while we're still here and work ourselves up into a national attitude. And we've to keep talking, man. We haven't much time to waste looking at both sides of the question like these stupid *ou kêrel*. That's why it doesn't pay any more to pretend we're being just and fair to the kaffir by controlling him. No use even trying to tell him he's going to like living in enclosures."

"Isn't it because we know what the kaffir wants that we must call a halt to his ambitious wants? The danger, as I see it, *ou kêrel*, isn't merely in the kaffir's increasing anger and desperation. It also lies in our tendency as whites to believe that what we tell him is the truth. And this might drive us to sleep one day—a fatal day, I tell you. It's necessary to keep talking, Doppie, so as to keep jolting the whites into a sharp awareness. It's dangerously easy for the public to forget and go to sleep."

Doppie clapped his hands in applause, half-dazed, half-mocking, half-admiring. At such times he never knew what word could sum up Stoffel Visser. A genius?—yes, he must be. And then Stoffel would say things he had so often heard from others. Ag, I knew it—just like all of us—ordinarily stubborn behind those deep-set eyes. And thinking so gave Doppie a measure of comfort. He distrusted complex human beings because they evaded labels. Life would be so much nicer if one could just take a label out of the pocket and tack it on the lapel of a man's coat. Like the one a lady pins on you to show that you've dropped a coin into her collecting box. As a badge of charity.

"We can't talk too much, *ou kêrel*. We haven't said the last word in that report on kaffir servants in the suburbs."

Day and night for three months Stoffel Visser had worked hard for the commission he was secretary of—the Social Affairs Commission of his Christian Protestant Party. The report of the commission was to have been handed to Tollen Rens, their representative in Parliament, who, in turn, had to discuss it with a member of the Cabinet. A rigorous remedy was necessary, it was suggested, for what Stoffel had continually impressed on the minds of his cronies as "an ugly situation". He could have chopped his own head off for failing to keep his appointment with Tollen Rens. And all through Jackson's not coming to wake him up and give him the breakfast he was used to enjoying with an unflagging appetite.

"Right, Stoffel, see you tomorrow at the office." Doppie Fourie was leaving. Quite drunk. He turned on his heel a bit as he made for the door, a vacant smile playing on his lips.

Although the two men had been friends for a long time, Doppie Fourie could never stop himself feeling humiliated after a serious talk with Stoffel. Visser always overwhelmed him, beat him down and trampled on him with his superior intellect. The more he drank in order to blunt the edge of the pain Stoffel unwittingly caused him, the deeper was the hurt Doppie felt whenever they had been talking shop. Still, if Fourie never had the strength of mind to wrench himself from Stoffel's grip, his friend did all he could to preserve their companionship, if only as an exhaust-pipe for his mental energy.

Stoffel's mind slowly came back to his rooms—Jackson in particular. He liked Jackson, his cook, who had served him with the devotion of a trained animal and ministered to all his bachelor whims and eating habits for four years. As he lived in a flat, it was not necessary for Jackson to clean the house. This was the work of the cleaner hired by Stoffel's landlord.

Jackson had taken his usual Thursday off. He had gone to Shanty-Town, where his mother-in-law lived with his two children, in order to fetch them and take them to the zoo. He had promised so many times to take them there. His wife worked in another suburb. She couldn't go with them to the zoo because, she said, she had had the children's sewing to finish.

This was the second time that Jackson had not turned up when he was expected after taking a day off. The first time he had come the following morning, all apologies. Where could the confounded kaffir be? Stoffel wondered. But he was too busy trying to adjust his mood to the new situation to think of the different things that might have happened to Jackson.

Stoffel's mind turned around in circles without ever coming to a fixed point. It was this, that, and then everything. His head was ringing with the voices he had heard so many times at recent meetings. Angry voices of residents who were gradually being incensed by speakers like him, frantic voices that demanded that the number of servants in each household be brought down because it wouldn't do for blacks to run the suburbs from their quarters in European backyards.

But there were also angry voices from other meetings: if you take the servants away, how are they going to travel daily to be at work on time, before we leave for work ourselves? Other voices: who told you there are too many natives in our yards? Then others: we want to keep as many servants as we can afford.

And the voices became angrier and angrier, roaring like a sea in the distance and coming nearer and nearer to shatter his complacency. The voices spoke different languages, different arguments, often using different premises to assert the same principles. They spoke in soft, mild tones and in urgent and hysterical moods.

The mind turned around the basic arguments in a turmoil: you shall not, we will; we can, you can't; they shall not, they shall; why must they? Why mustn't they? Some of these kaffir lovers, of course, hate the thought of having to forego the fat feudal comfort of having cheap labour within easy reach when we remove black servants to their own locations, Stoffel mused.

And amid these voices he saw himself working and sweating to create a theory to defend ready-made attitudes, stock attitudes that various people had each in their own time planted in him: his mother, his father, his brothers, his friends, his schoolmasters, his university professors and all the others who claimed him as their own. He was fully conscious of the whole process in his mind. Things had to be done with conviction or not at all.

Then, even before he knew it, those voices became an echo of other voices coming down through the centuries: the echo of gun-fire, cannon, waggon-wheels as they ground away over stone and sand; the echo of hate and vengeance. All he felt was something in his blood which groped back through the corridors of history to pick up some of the broken threads that linked his life with a terrible past. He surrendered himself to it all, to this violent desire to remain part of a brutal historic past, lest he should be crushed by the brutal necessities of the present, he should be forced to lose his identity:

Almighty God, no, no! Unconsciously he was trying to pile on layers of crocodile hide over his flesh to protect himself against thoughts or feelings that might some day in the vague future threaten to hurt.

When he woke from a stupor, Stoffel Visser remembered Jackson's wife over at Greenside. He had not asked her if she knew where his servant was. He jumped up and dialled on his telephone. He called Virginia's employer and asked him. No, Virginia didn't know where her husband was. As far as she knew her husband had told her the previous Sunday that he was going to take the children to the zoo. What could have happened to her husband, she wanted to know. Why hadn't he telephoned the police? Why hadn't he phoned Virginia in the morning? Virginia's master asked him these and several other questions. He got annoyed because he couldn't answer them.

None of the suburban police stations or Marshall Square Station had Jackson's name in their charge books. They would let him know "if anything turned up". A young voice from one police station said perhaps Stoffel's "kaffir" had gone to sleep with his "maid" elsewhere and had forgotten to turn up for work. Or, he suggested, Jackson might be under a hang-over in the location. "You know what these kaffirs are." And he laughed with a thin sickly voice. Stoffel banged the receiver down.

There was a light knock at the door of his flat. When he opened with anticipation he saw an African standing erect, hat in hand.

"Yes?"

"Yes, *Baas*."

"What do you want?"

"I bring you this, *Baas*," handing a letter to the white man, while he thought: *just like those white men who work for the railways. . . it's good I sealed it . . .*

"Whose is this? It's addressed here, to Jackson! Where did you find it?'

"I was clean the line, *Baas*. Um pick up papers and rubbish on railway line at Park Stish. Um think of something as um work. Then I pick up this. I ask *my*-self, who could have dropped it? But . . ."

"All right, why didn't you take it to your boss?"

"They keep letters there many months, *Baas*, and no one comes for them." His tone suggested that Stoffel should surely know that.

The cheek he has, finding fault with the way the white man does things.

"You lie! You opened it first to see what's inside. When you found no money you sealed it up and were afraid your boss would find out you had opened it. Not true?"

"It's not true, *Baas*, I was going to bring it here whatever happened."

He fixed his eyes on the letter in Stoffel's hand. "Truth's God, *Baas*," Lebona said, happy to be able to lie to someone who had no way of divining the truth, thinking at the same time: *they're not even decent enough to suspect one's telling the truth!*

They always lie to you when you're white, Stoffel thought, *just for cheek.*

The more Lebona thought he was performing a just duty the more annoyed the white man was becoming.

"Where do you live?"

"Kensington, *Baas*. Um go there now. My wife she working there."

Yet another of them, eh? Going home in a white man's area—we'll put a stop to that yet—and look at the smugness on his mug!

"All right, go." All the time they were standing at the door, Stoffel thought how the black man smelled of sweat, even although he was standing outside.

Lebona made to go and then remembered something. Even before the white man asked him further he went on to relate it all, taking his time, but his emotion spilling over.

"I feel very sore in my heart, *Baas*. This poor man, he comes out of train. There are only two lines of steps on platform, and I say to *my*-self how can people go up when others are coming down? You know, there are iron gates now, and only one go and come at a time. Now other side there's train to leave for Orlando."

What the hell have I to do with this? What does he think this is, a complaints office?

"Now, you see, it's like this: a big crowd go up and a big crowd want to rush for their train. Um look and whistle and says to *my*-self how can people move in different ways like that? Like a river doing against another!"

One of these kaffirs who think they're smart, eh.

"This man, I've been watching him go up. Then I see him pushed down by those on top of steps. They rush down and stamp on him and kick him. He rolls down until he drops back on platform. Blood comes out mouth and nose like rain and I says to *my*-self, oho he's dead, poor man!"

I wish he didn't keep me standing here listening to a story about a man I don't even care to know! . . .

"The poor man died, just like that, just as if I went down the stairs now and then you hear um dead."

I couldn't care less, either . . .

"As um come here by tram I think, perhaps this is his letter."

"All right now, I'll see about that."

Lebona walked off with a steady and cautious but firm step. Stoffel was greatly relieved.

Immediately he rang the hospital mortuary, but there was no trace of Jackson. Should he or should he not read the letter? It might give him a clue. But, no, he wasn't a *kaffir!*

Another knock at the door.

Jackson's wife, Virginia, stood just where Lebona had stood a few minutes before.

"He's not yet here, Master?"

"No." Impulsively he showed her to a chair in the kitchen. "Where else could he have gone?"

"Don't know, Master." Then she started to cry, softly. "Sunday we were together, Master, at my master's place. We talked about our children and you know one is seven the other four and few months and firstborn is just like his father with eyes and nose and they have always been told about the zoo by playmates so they wanted to go there, so Jackson promised them he would take them to see the animals." She paused, sobbing quietly, as if she meant that to be the only way she could punctuate her speech.

"And the smaller child loves his father so and he's Jackson's favourite. You know Nkati the elder one was saying to his father the other day the day their grandmother brought them to see us—he says I wish you die, just because his father wouldn't give him more sweets, Lord he's going to be the rebel of the family and he needs a strong man's hand to keep him straight. And now if Jackson is—is— oh Lord God above."

She sobbed freely now.

"All right. I'll try my best to find him, wherever he may be. You may go now, because it's time for me to lock-up."

"Thank you, Master." She left.

Stoffel stepped into the street and got into his car to drive five miles to the nearest police station. For the first time in his life he left his flat to look for a black man because he meant much to him— at any rate as a servant.

Virginia's pathetic look; her roundabout unpunctuated manner of saying things; the artless and devoted Virginia; the railway worker and his I-don't-care-whether-you're-listening manner; the picture of two children who might very well be fatherless as he was driving through the suburb; the picture of a dead man rolling down station steps and of Lebona pouring out his heart over a man he didn't know. . . . These images turned round and round into a complex knot. He had got into the habit of thinking in terms of irreconcilable and contradictions and opposition and categories. Black was black, white was white—that was all that mattered.

So he couldn't at the moment answer the questions that kept bobbing up from somewhere in his soul; sharp little questions coming without ceremony; sharp little questions shooting up, sometimes like meteors, sometimes like darts, sometimes climbing up like a slow winter's sun. He was determined to resist them. He found it so much easier to think in categories and to place people.

His friend at the police station promised to help him.

The letter. Why didn't he give it to Jackson's wife? After all, she had just as much right to possess it as her husband?

Later he couldn't resist the temptation to open the envelope; after all, it might hold a clue. He carefully broke open the flap. There were charming photographs, one of a man and woman, the other of two children, evidently theirs. They were Jackson's all right.

The letter inside was written to Jackson himself. Stoffel read it. It was from somewhere in Vendaland; from Jackson's father. He was very ill and did not expect to live much longer. Would Jackson come soon because the government people were telling him to get rid of some of his cattle to save the land from washing away, and will Jackson come soon so that he might attend to the matter because he, the old man, was powerless. He had only the strength to tell the government people that it was more land the people wanted and not fewer stock. He had heard the white man used certain things to stop birth in human beings, and if the white man thought he was going to do the same with his cattle and donkeys—that would be the day a donkey would give birth to a cow. But, alas, he said, he had only enough strength to swear by the gods his stock wouldn't be thinned down. Jackson must come soon. He was sending the photographs which he loved very much and would like them to be safe because he might die any moment. He was sending the letter through somebody who was travelling to the gold city.

The ending was:

May the gods bless you my son and my daughter-in-law and my lovely grandsons. I shall die in peace because I have had the heavenly joy of holding my grandsons on my knees.

It was in a very ugly scrawl without any punctuation marks. With somewhat unsteady hands Stoffel put the things back in the envelope.

Monday lunch-time Stoffel Visser motored to his flat, just to check up. He found Jackson in his room lying on his bed. His servant's face was all swollen up with clean bandages covering the whole head and cheeks. His eyes sparkled from the surrounding puffed flesh.

"Jackson!"

His servant looked up at him.

"What happened?"

"The police."

"Where?"

"Victoria Police Station."

"Why?"

"They call me monkey."

"Who?"

"White man in train."

"Tell me everything, Jackson." Stoffel felt his servant was resisting him. He read bitterness in the stoop of Jackson's shoulders and in the whole profile as he sat up.

"You think I'm telling lie, Master? Black man always tell lie, eh?"

"No, Jackson. I can only help if you tell me everything." Somehow the white man managed to keep his patience.

"I take children to zoo. Coming back I am reading my night-school book. White man come into train and search everyone. One see me reading and say what's this monkey think he's doing with a book. He tell me stand up, he shouts like it's first time for him to talk to a human being. That's what baboons do when they see man. I am hot and boiling and I catch him by his collar and tie and shake him. Ever see a *marula* tree that's heavy with fruit? That's how I shake him. Other white men take me to place in front, a small room.

Everyone there hits me hard. At station they push me out on platform and I fall on one knee. They lift me up and take me to police station. Not in city but far away I don't know where but I see now it must have been Victoria Station. There they charge me with drunken noise. Have you a pound? I say no and I ask them they must ring you, they say if I'm cheeky they will hell me up and then they hit and kick me again. They let me go and I walk many miles to hospital. I'm in pain." Jackson paused, bowing his head lower.

When he raised it again he said, "I lose letter from my father with my beautiful pictures."

Stoffel sensed agony in every syllable, in every gesture of the hand. He had read the same story so many times in newspapers and had never given it much thought.

He told Jackson to lie in bed, and for the first time in four years he called a doctor to examine and treat his servant. He had always sent him or taken him to hospital.

For four years he had lived with a servant and had never known more about him than that he had two children living with his mother-in-law and a wife. Even then they were such distant abstractions— just names representing some persons, not human flesh and blood and heart and mind.

And anger came up in him to muffle the cry of shame, to shut out the memory of recent events that was battering on the iron bars he had built up in himself as a means of protection. There were things he would rather not think about. And the heat of his anger crowded them out. What next? He didn't know. Time, time, time, that's what he needed to clear the whole muddle beneath the fog that rose thicker and thicker with the clash of currents from the past and the present. Time, time. . . .

And then Stoffel Visser realized he did not want to think, to feel. He wanted to do something. . . . Jackson would want a day off to go to his father. . . . Sack Jackson? No. Better continue treating him as a name, not as another human being. Let Jackson continue as a machine to work for him. Meantime, he must do his duty—dispatch the commission's report. That was definite, if nothing else was. He was a white man, and he must be responsible. To be white and to be responsible were one and the same thing. . . .

Mavis Gallant

Mavis Gallant has been described by her fellow-countryman, Mordecai Richler, as Canada's most compelling short-story writer since Morley Callaghan. Her work is a bitter indictment of some aspects of twentieth-century civilization.

The world of her stories is one of broken marriages, divorces, half-sisters and half-brothers, step-mothers and step-fathers, "guests". A complete 'set of parents' rarely exists. The victim of this society can occasionally be the parent being sent on from Regan to Goneril, but more often it is the child, 'the result, the product, the thing we, [the parents], have left.' Children are objects to be picked up and dropped at random. A common attitude is the one revealed by the mother in the story "Malcom and Bea";

> He, [the son,] was hers like the crickets she kept in plastic cages and fed on scraps of lettuce . . . like the birds she buys on the Quai de la Corse in Paris and turns out to freeze or starve or be pecked to death.

One of the sharpest criticisms of these parents is in the story "The Rejection". Because of her own rejection the child has just abandoned her pet armadillo. We hear:

> . . . the frantic note of the creature abandoned; there was no mistaking the hysteria and terror, the fear that no one would ever come for it again.
> "Go back and get him," he [the father] said.
> " 'I don't want him.'
> "You can't leave him,' said the man. 'You've taken him out of his own life and made a pet of him. You can't abandon him now. You're responsible for him."

The father goes on to tell the child. ' "If she [the mother] knew you had abandoned that creature, she might tell you that there are two sorts of people, that the world is divided." ' The bitter irony, of course, is that the mother has treated the child in exactly the same way: what is perhaps most frightening is the father's unawareness of the parallel. The world of these people is that one depicted in the short story "Saturday" in which ' "Il n'y a pas assez lumière" ', and where ' "Nobody cares' is just a family phrase." ' It is characterized by its rootlessness, its barrenness and, most of all, by the absence of love.

' "There are two sorts of people . . . the world is divided" '; "Orphans' Progress" illustrates this statement and in doing so suggests a parallel to Patrick White's "Down at the Dump". The former life of the children is in many aspects similar to the life led by the Whalley children; the mother, like Daise Morrow, possesses qualities of warmth and generosity; the men she attracts are like Ossie, 'men without wits, money, affection or a job'. It is a life of love, a life which '(to the children)' seemed safe. But the other sort of people view it differently. Blake's lines 'Both read the Bible day and night, But thou read'st black where I read white', come to mind when we read the story:

"All of yez slept in the one bed," said the maid.
"Yes, we slept together."

Again and again the 'two sorts of people' present us with different viewpoints of one and the same situation; from the inside the life might appear safe but from without it was a perilous one not fit for children. So social welfare, the state's substitute for love, removes the children. As usual they have no say in the matter, the children are never the prime movers, they are always the object of the action, pawns in a game played between adults. The life to which they are removed is one of cold respectability, as sterile as Mrs. Hogben's and symbolized by the coldness of a room in which 'even the maid said her feet were cold'. They are given food, baths, 'sheltered conditions" but not love; the uprooting from their old life had meant 'the end of love'.

There is a special Canadian aspect to the conflict between these two worlds, the old life is associated with French-speaking Quebec and the new with English-speaking Ontario. The children are soon given to understand 'that French was an inferior kind of speech', and with smug complacency the new guardians congratulate themselves that if the children had faults, 'Ontario could not be blamed'. But for all Ontario's faults, it did not subject the children to cruelty which was reserved for the next move. One consolation remained to them now, they were still together. But they are deprived even of that when they are finally placed in a convent. It is in this narrow, warped, institutionalized world, in which all human values are denied, that the dehumanization process is completed.

In an article in *Canadian Literature*, No. 41, Donald Stephens comments on developments in the Canadian short story from around 1955 onwards. One of these developments he said is that 'the story was [no longer] told by carefully engineered plot, but by the subtle implication of selected isolated incidents'. It is the technique employed by Mavis Gallant in this story: both the story and Mildred herself progress from:

"To the day I die," said the social worker from Montreal to her colleague in Ontario, "I won't forget the screams of Mildred when she was dragged out of that pigsty".

to:

"Look, Mildred," said her father, and let the car slow down on a particular street. The parents craned at a garage, and at some dirty-legged children with torn sneakers on their feet. Mildred glanced up, and then back at her book. She had no reason to believe she had seen the place before, or would ever again. *A. R.*

Orphans' Progress

When the Collier children were six and ten, a social worker came to the place where they were living in Montreal, and shortly after that they were taken away from their mother, whom they loved without knowing what the word implied, or even that it existed, and sent to their father's mother in Ontario. Their father was dead. Their mother was no longer capable of looking after them properly. When women turn strange, it happens very rapidly. The first sign is lack of care about clothes and hair, and all at once they are sluts. Drinking slides in. They attract frightening men—at first men without wits, money, affection, or a job, compared with whom the woman seems a monument of character and strength. At the end, the men around them are almost respectable (by contrast) but very unkind. I have more than once seen women get into this state, and the common factors were drink, and dirt, and weeping, and rages, and being preyed upon, and finally seeming so sexually innocent that one is frightened. One says she is alcoholic, she is manic-depressive, the children should be taken away. Yes, they are seeing things they shouldn't, and not getting proper food, and in moral and perhaps physical danger (someday she will set the place on fire); but if the mother still has her qualities—those that attracted, say, her friends or her husband in the first place: warmth, generosity—do you take them away for their own good? One day someone tells—a janitor's wife, an anonymous friend of the husband—and the life that seems safe from inside (to the children) but perilous from without is destroyed. Whether it is the right thing or the wrong thing as far as the children are concerned, it is the end of love.

The children's grandmother was scrupulous about food, and made them drink goat's milk. Two goats were brought by station wagon from fifty miles away. The girls went with the driver to get them. A man in a filling station was frightened by the goats, because of their oblong eyes. The girls were not reflected in the goats' eyes, as they were in each other's. What they remembered afterward of this period when they were living with their grandmother was goat's milk, goat eyes, and the frightened man.

From their grandmother they learned that their mother was French-Canadian but had spoken French and English to them. They had called her Mummy, a habit started when their father was still alive, for he had not learned French. They understood—from their grandmother, and their grandmother's maid, and the social worker who came from Montreal to see their grandmother but had little to say to them—that French was an inferior kind of speech. At first, when they were taken away from their mother, Cathie, the elder girl, would wake up at night holding her head, her elbows on her knees, saying in French, "My head hurts," but a few minutes later, the grandmother having applied cold wrung-out towels, she would say in English, "It's better."

Mildred had pushed out two front teeth by sucking her thumb. She had been sucking her thumb forever, even before they were taken away from their mother. Ontario could not be blamed. Nevertheless, their grandmother told the social worker about it, and the social worker wrote it down.

They did not know, and never once asked, why they had been taken away. When the new social worker, the one in Ontario, said to Cathie, "Were you disturbed because your mother was unhappy?" Cathie said, "She wasn't." When the girls were living with their mother, they knew that sometimes she listened and sometimes could not hear; all the same, she was there. They slept in the same bed, all three. Even when she sat on the side of the bed with her head hanging and her undone jagged-cut hair hiding her eyes, mumbling complaints that were not their concern, the children were close to her and did not know they were living under what would later be called "unsheltered conditions". They didn't know that they were uneducated, and dirty, and in danger. Now they learned that their mother never washed her neck and hair, that she dressed in layers of woollen stuff, covered with grease, and wore men's shoes because some man had left them behind and she liked the shape or the comfort of them. They did not know, until they were told, that they had never been properly fed.

"We ate chicken," said Cathie.

"They say she served it up half raw," said their grandmother's maid. "Surrvet" said the maid for "served", and that was not the way their mother had spoken. "The sheets was so dirty the dirt was like clay. All of yez slept in the one bed," said the maid.

"Yes, we slept together."

The apartment—a loft, they were told, over a garage, not an apartment at all—must still exist, it must be somewhere, with the piano that Mildred, the little one, had banged on with her palms flat. What about the two cats that were always fighting or playing, depending on their disposition? The children's drawings were pinned up on the wall, and there were other pictures.

"When one of the pitchers was moved, there was a square mass of bugs," said the grandmother's maid. "The same shape as the pitcher."

"To the day I die," said the social worker from Montreal to her colleague in Ontario, "I won't forget the screams of Mildred when she was dragged out of that pigsty." This was said in the grandmother's parlour, where the three women—the two social workers and the grandmother—sat with their feet freezing on the linoleum floor. The maid heard, and told the children. She had been in and out, serving coffee, coconut biscuits, and damson preserves in custard made of goat's milk. The room was heated one or twice a year—even the maid said her feet were cold. But "To the day I die" was a phrase worth hearing. She liked the sound of that, and repeated it to the children. The maid was from a place called Waterloo, where, to hear her tell it, no one behaved strangely and all the rooms were warm.

Thumb-sucker Mildred did not remember having screamed, or anything at all except the trip from Montreal by train. "Boy, is your grandmother ever a rich old lady!" said the maid from Waterloo. "If she wasn't, where'd you be? In an orphung asylum. She's a Christian, I can tell you."

They went to school in Ontario now, with children who did not have the same accent or the same vocabulary as children in Montreal. When their new friends liked something, they said it was "smart". A basketball game was "smart", and so was a movie—it did not mean "elegant", it just meant "all right". Ice cream made out of goat's milk was not "smart"; it tasted of hair.

The children's grandmother died when they were seven and eleven, and beginning to speak in the Ontario way. One day when the maid was angry at their grandmother over something, she said, "She's a damned old sow. It's in the mattress and she's lying on it. You can hear the bills crackle when you turn the mattress Saturdays. I hope they find it when she dies is all I can say."

The girls saw their grandmother dead, in the bed, on the mattress.

The person crying hardest in the room was the maid. She had suddenly dyed her hair dark red, and the girls did not know her, because of her tears, and her new clothes, bought for the funeral, and because of the way she fondled and kissed them. "We'll never see each other again," said the maid.

Now that their grandmother had died, the girls went to live with their mother's brother and his wife and their many children, in a section of Montreal called Ahuntsic. They did not see anything that reminded them of Montreal, and did not recall their mother. The parlour here was full of cut glass, which was daily rubbed and polished. The girls slept on a pull-out divan and wrangled about bed-clothes. Cathie wanted them pushed down between them in a sort of trough, because she felt a draught, but Mildred complained that the blankets thus arranged were tugged away from her side. She was not properly covered, and afraid of falling on the floor. One of their relations (they had any number here, on their mother's side) made them a present of a box of chocolate almonds, but the cousins they lived with bought exactly the same box, so as to tease them, and started eating the whole box. When Cathie and Mildred rushed to see if their own box was still where they had hidden it, they were bitterly mocked. Every scrap of food they put in their mouths was taken from the mouths of cousins, so they were told. Their cousins made them afraid of ghosts. They put out the lights and said, "Look out, she is coming to get you, all in black!" And when Mildred began to whimper, Cathie said, "Our mother wouldn't try to frighten us." She had not spoken of their mother until now. One of the cousins said, "I'm talking about your old grandmother. Your mother isn't dead." They were shown their father's grave, and made to kneel and pray. Their lives were in the dark now, in the dark of ghosts, whose transparent shadows stood round their bed. Soon they lived in the black of nuns. Language was black, until they forgot their English. Until they spoke French, nothing but French, the family pretended not to understand them, and stared as if they were peering in the dark. They very soon forgot their English.

They could not stay here with these cousins forever, for the flat was too small. When they were eight and twelve, their grandmother's will was probated, the money their grandmother had left them was made available, and they were sent away to school. For the first time in their lives now, the girls did not sleep in the same bed. Mildred slept in a dormitory with the little girls, where a green light burned overhead and a nun rustled and prayed or read beside a green lamp all night long. Mildred was bathed once every fortnight, wearing a rubber apron so that she would not see her own body. In the morning she dressed like the other little girls, sitting on the floor, and hidden by the beds so that they would not see one another. Her thumb, sucked white, was taped to the palm of her hand. She caught glimpses of Cathie sometimes during recreation periods, but Cathie was one of the big girls, and important. She did not play, as the little ones did, but walked up and down with the supervisor, walking backward as the nun walked forward.

One day, looking out of a dormitory window, Mildred saw a roof-top and an open skylight. She said to a girl standing nearby, "That's our house." "What house?" "Where Mummy lives." She said that sentence—three words—in English. She had not thought or spoken "Mummy" since she was six and a half. It turned out that she was lying about the house. Lying was serious; she was made to promenade through the classrooms carrying a large pair of shears and the the sign "I AM A LIAR." She did not know the significance of the shears, nor, it seemed, did the nun who decreed the punishment. It had always been associated with lying, and (the nun suddenly remembered) had to do with cutting out the liar's tongue. The tattling girl who had told about "where Mummy lives" was punished, too, and made to carry a wastebasket from room to room with "I AM A BASKET CARRIER" hung round her neck. This meant talebearer. Everyone was in the wrong.

Cathie was not obliged to wear a rubber apron in her bath but a muslin shift. She learned the big girls' trick, which was to take it off and dip it in water and then bathe in the ordinary way. When Mildred came round carrying her scissors and her sign, Cathie had had her twice-monthly bath and felt damp and new. She said to someone, "That's my sister," but "sister" was a dark, scowling little thing. "Sister" got into still more trouble. A nun, a stray from Belgium, perhaps as one refugee to another, said to Mildred, swiftly drawing her into a broom cupboard, "Call me *Maman*." "*Maman*," said the child, to whom "Mummy" had meaning until the day of the scissors. Who was there to hear what was said in the broom cupboard? What basket-carrier repeated that? Somebody. It was forbidden for nuns to have favourites, forbidden to have pet names for nuns, and the Belgian stray was sent to the damp, wet room behind the chapel and

195

given flower-arranging to attend to. There Mildred found her, by chance, and the nun said, "Get away! Haven't you made enough trouble for me?"

Cathie was told to pray for Mildred, the troublemaker, but forgot. The omission weighed on her. She prayed for her mother, grandmother, father, herself (with a glimpse in the prayer of her own future coffin, white), and for the uncles and aunts and cousins she knew and those she had never met. Her worry about forgetting Mildred in her prayers caused her to invent a formula: "Everyone I have ever known who is dead or alive, anyone I know now who is alive but might die, and anyone I shall ever know in the future." She prayed for her best friend, who wanted, like Cathie, to become a teacher, and for a nun with a moustache, who was jolly, and for her confessor, who liked to hear her playing the "Radetzky March" on the piano. Her hair grew lighter and was brushed and combed by her best friend.

Mildred was suddenly taken out of school and adopted. Their mother's sister, one of the aunts they had seldom seen, had lost a daughter by drowning. She said she would treat Mildred as she did her own small son, and Mildred, who wished to leave the convent school but did not know if she cared to go and live in a place called Chicoutimi, did not decide. She made the grown-ups decide, and let them take her away.

When the girls were fifteen and nineteen, and Mildred's last name was Desaulniers and not Collier, the sisters were made to meet. Cathie had left school and was studying nursing, but she came back to the convent when she had time off, not because she did not have anywhere else to go but because she did not want to go to any other place. The nuns had said of Cathie, laughing, "She doesn't want to leave—we shall have to push her out." When Cathie's sister, Mildred Desaulniers, came to call on her, the two girls did not know what to say. Mildred wore a round straw hat with a clump of plastic cherries hanging over the brim; her adoptive brother, in long trousers and bow tie, did not get out of the car. He was seven, and had slick, wet-looking hair, as if he had been swimming. "Kiss your sister," said Mildred's mother to Cathie, admonishingly. Cathie did as she was told, and Mildred immediately got back in the car with her brother and snatched a comic book out of his hands.

"Look, Mildred," said her father, and let the car slow down on a particular street. The parents craned at a garage, and at some dirty-legged children with torn sneakers on their feet. Mildred glanced up, and then back at her book. She had no reason to believe she had seen the place before, or would ever again.

V. S. Naipaul

A stranger could drive through Miguel Street and just say 'Slum!',
because he could see no more. But we, who lived there, saw our
street as a world, where everybody was quite different from everybody else. Man-Man was mad; George was stupid; Big Foot was
a bully; Hat was an adventurer; Popo was a philosopher; and
Morgan was our comedian.

(from Miguel Street)

Miguel Street is both the name Naipaul has given to his imaginary
street in a Port-or-Spain slum, and the title of his novel, which con-
sists of a series of sketches in which he describes the inhabitants and
their fortunes. "Man-man" is one of these sketches.

In his book *The Middle Passage* Naipaul maintains that 'slavery,
the mixed population, the absence of national pride and the closed
colonial system have to a remarkable degree re-created the attitudes
of the Spanish picaroon world.' This, Naipaul points out, is an
ugly world in which you starve unless you steal and are beaten unless
you beat first. But he warns us that we must not condemn it out of
hand for to do so would be to ignore its most important quality,
tolerance, 'tolerance for every human activity'. The Trinidadian is
eccentric for there are no social conventions to which he must conform. The society in which he lives is a fragmented, inorganic one,
in which the one concern is with survival. 'Three hundred years of
slavery had taught him only that he was an individual and that life
was short.' 'But,' says Naipaul, 'everything that makes the Trinidadian an unreliable, exploitable citizen makes him a quick, civilized
person whose values are always human ones, whose standards are
only those of wit and style.'

This is the society and these are the individuals that Naipaul
describes in this story. Man-man is the typical picaroon hero living
by his wits. His eccentricity is taken for granted and his ability to
survive at the expense of others is not only accepted but admired.
The inhabitants take a pride in the ingenuity of their fellow citizen,
in his Anancy-like spirit, and the tolerance that Naipaul spoke about

is strongly in evidence. Any tendency towards malicious laughter is quickly crushed and when Hat complains that the crucifix is made of match-wood Edward quickly rebukes him and reminds him that though Man-man's cross might fall short of the ideal, ' "Is the heart and the spirit that matter." '

An emerging society, particularly the remnant of a colonial society, provides rich soil for frauds and opportunists and it appears from Naipaul's novels that the West Indies have had their fair share of such people. The political and religious opportunists are recurring figures in his works and have been the targets of some of his most savage satire. That the situation is a ripe one for the corrupt politician is clear enough, but the religious issue is perhaps not so obvious. What we must remember is that for centuries religion provided for many their one source of hope. We must also remember that the West Indian's religion, like so many other things, showed the influence of two cultures and was quite often a strange mixture of Christianity and paganism. This explains much of his fondness for the ecstatic cults that appealed to the emotions rather than to the intellect. In such a situation the way is wide open for the religious opportunist, particularly if he is able to provide entertainment in this life as well as hope for the life hereafter. A crucifixion would provide as good an entertainment as anything else to relieve the drab monotony of their lives. Christy Mahon, the playboy of the Western World, self-confessed murderer, proved a great success with the peasants of the Western Isles for much the same reasons. It would have been quite obvious to Man-man, that having lost his well-trained dog, the must lucrative occupation he could turn to would be that of mystic. In doing so he was following in the footsteps of one of Naipaul's most memorable characters, Ganesh Pundit, the mystic masseur and the greatest fraud of them all.

As a satirist Naipaul has few equals and we find him in his familiar role in this story: he uses the boy narrator as a distancing factor and this enables him to avoid the sentimental and to achieve a certain degree of objectivity. Naipaul grew up in Trinidad and the novel may be regarded as semi-autobiographical. However, the boy's insertion of the word 'now' in his comment 'But I am not so sure now that he was mad' reminds us that the boyhood experiences have been looked at in retrospect with the wisdom of the adult. Behind the innocence and naïveté of the boy's narration we hear the voice of the ironist aware of all the deeper nuances and meanings.

Naipaul uses another distancing factor, namely the use of standard English for the narrator and dialect for the other characters. Here where the norm is one of brutality, poverty and corruption it is Naipaul's task to suggest that another can exist. He does this through the boy. In another of the sketches Popo is drunk and the boy rejects him saying, 'I didn't like him when he was drunk.' Hat, however, rejoices, and says, ' "We was wrong about Popo. He is a man, like any of we." ' The two reactions and the two ways of expressing them reflect the different attitudes.

Like all satirists Naipaul is concerned with reform. In *The Middle Passage* he has written that 'nationalism is the only revitalizing force' in the West Indies and he believes that 'the West Indian . . . needs writers to tell him who he is and where he stands'. For the writer to be able to do this he must possess 'the most exquisite gifts of irony and perhaps malice, . . . of subtlety and brutality.' The gifts which Naipaul mentions are all ones which he possesses and which he has no hesitation in using. We find in this story, however, and in *Miguel Street* as a whole, another gift which is sometimes missing from Naipaul's work, that of compassion. There is no contempt for these people; on the contrary there is an underlying pity and a deep understanding of why they act as they do. Beneath the comedy there is a strong sense of the tragic; a sense that the laughter is there to cover up the cry.

Man-man's reaction to the stoning points out the great gap between human pretensions and reality which is another constant preoccupation of the satirist. But we feel in this case that Naipaul is not so concerned with pointing out the folly of Man-man; we sense rather an admiration for men, who under such conditions, still continue in their endeavours to survive. The story may be a condemnation of the forces which have created such a society. But it is above all a tribute to these people with no past and no hope for the future, it is a tribute to the ability of man, under the most appalling conditions, to go on living, and laughing. It reminds us that 'is the heart and the spirit that matter'. *A. R.*

Man-man

Everybody in Miguel Street said that Man-man was mad, and so they left him alone. But I am not so sure now that he was mad, and I can think of many people much madder than Man-man ever was.

He didn't look mad. He was a man of medium height, thin; and he wasn't bad-looking either. He never stared at you the way I expected a mad man to do; and when you spoke to him you were sure of getting a very reasonable reply.

But he did have some curious habits.

He went up for every election, city council or legislative council, and then he stuck posters everywhere in the district. These posters were well printed. They just had the word 'Vote' and below that, Man-man's picture.

At every election he got exactly three votes. That I couldn't understand. Man-man voted for himself, but who were the other two?

I asked Hat.

Hat said, "I really can't say, boy. Is a real mystery. Perhaps is two jokers. But they is funny sort of jokers if they do the same thing so many times. They must be mad just like he."

And for a long time the thought of these two mad men who voted for Man-man haunted me. Everytime I saw someone doing anything just a little bit odd, I wondered, "Is he who vote for Man-man?"

At large in the city were these two men of mystery.

Man-man never worked. But he was never idle. He was hypnotised by the word, particularly the written word, and he would spend a whole day writing a single word.

One day I met Man-man at the corner of Miguel Street.

"Boy, where you going?" Man-man asked. "I going to school," I said.

And Man-man, looking at me solemnly, said in a mocking way, "So you goes to school, eh?"

I said automatically, "Yes, I goes to school." And I found that without intending it I had imitated Man-man's correct and very English accent.

That again was another mystery about Man-man. His accent. If

incongruous

you shut your eyes while he spoke, you would believe an Englishman
—a good-class Englishman who wasn't particular about grammar—
was talking to you.

Man-man said, as though speaking to himself, "So the little man
is going to school."

Then he forgot me, and took out a long stick of chalk from his
pocket and began writing on the pavement. He drew a very big s in
outline and then filled it in, and then the c and the h and the o. But
then he started making several o's, each smaller than the last, until
he was writing in cursive, o after flowing o.

When I came home for lunch, he had got to French Street, and
he was still writing o's rubbing off mistakes with a rag.

In the afternoon he had gone round the block and was practically
back in Miguel Street.

I went home, changed from my school-clothes into my home-
clothes and went out to the street.

He was now half-way up Miguel Street.

He said, "So the little man gone to school today?"

I said, "Yes."

He stood up and straightened his back.

Then he squatted again and drew the outline of a massive l and
filled that in slowly and lovingly.

When it was finished, he stood up and said, "You finish your work.
I finish mine."

Or it was like this. If you told Man-man you were going to the
cricket, he could write CRICK and then concentrate on the E's until he
saw you again.

One day Man-man went to the big café at the top of Miguel Street
and began barking and growling at the customers on the stools as
though he were a dog. The owner, a big Portuguese man with hairy
hands, said, "Man-man, get out of this shop before I tangle with
you."

Man-man just laughed.

They threw Man-man out.

Next day, the owner found that someone had entered his café
during the night, and had left all the doors open. But nothing was
missing.

Hat said, "One thing you must never do is trouble Man-man. He
remember everything."

That night the café was entered again and the doors again left open.

The following night the café was entered and this time little blobs of excrement were left on the centre of every stool and on top of every table and at regular intervals along the counter.

The owner of the café was the laughing-stock of the street for several weeks, and it was only after a long time that people began going to the café again.

Hat said, "Is just like I say. Boy, I don't like meddling with that man. These people really bad-mind, you know. God make them that way."

It was things like this that made people leave Man-man alone. The only friend he had was a little mongrel dog, white with black spots on the ears. The dog was like Man-man in a way, too. It was a curious dog. It never barked, never looked at you, and if you looked at it, it looked away. It never made friends with any other dog, and if some dog tried either to get friendly or aggressive, Man-man's dog gave it a brief look of disdain and ambled away, without looking back.

Man-man loved his dog, and the dog loved Man-man. They were made for each other, and Man-man couldn't have made a living without his dog.

Man-man appeared to exercise a great control over the movements of his dog's bowels.

Hat said, "That does really beat me. I can't make that one out."

It all began in Miguel Street.

One morning, several women got up to find that the clothes they had left to bleach overnight had been sullied by the droppings of a dog. No one wanted to use the sheets and the shirts after that, and when Man-man called, everyone was willing to give him the dirty clothes.

Man-man used to sell these clothes.

Hat said, "Is things like this that make me wonder whether the man really mad."

From Miguel Street Man-man's activities spread, and all the people who had suffered from Man-man's dog were anxious to get other people to suffer the same thing.

We in Miguel Street became a little proud of him.

I don't know what it was that caused Man-man to turn good. Perhaps the death of his dog had something to do with it. The dog was run over by a car, and it gave, Hat said, just one short squeak, and then it was silent.

Man-man wandered about for days, looking dazed and lost.

He no longer wrote words on the pavement; no longer spoke to me or to any of the other boys in the street. He began talking to himself, clasping his hands and shaking as though he had ague.

Then one day he said he had seen God after having a bath.

This didn't surprise many of us. Seeing God was quite common in Port of Spain and, indeed, in Trinidad at that time. Ganesh Pundit, the mystic masseur from Fuente Grove, had started it. He had seen God, too, and had published a little booklet called *What God Told Me*. Many rival mystics and not a few masseurs had announced the same thing, and I suppose it was natural that since God was in the area Man-man should see Him.

Man-man began preaching at the corner of Miguel Street, under the awning of Mary's shop. He did this every Saturday night. He let his beard grow and he dressed in a long white robe. He got a Bible and other holy things and stood in the white light of an acetylene lamp and preached. He was an impressive preacher, and he preached in a odd way. He made women cry, and he made people like Hat really worried.

He used to hold the Bible in his right hand and slap it with his left and say in his perfect English accent, "I have been talking to God these few days, and what he tell me about you people wasn't really nice to hear. These days you hear all the politicians and them talking about making the island self-sufficient. You know what God tell me last night? Last night self, just after I finish eating? God say, 'Man-man, come and have a look at these people.' He show me husband eating wife and wife eating husband. He show me father eating son and mother eating daughter. He show me brother eating sister and sister eating brother. That is what these politicians and them mean by saying that the island going to become self-sufficient. But, brethren, it not too late now to turn to God."

I used to get nightmares every Saturday night after hearing Man-man preach. But the odd thing was that the more he frightened people the more they came to hear him preach. And when the collection was made they gave him more than ever.

In the week-days he just walked about, in his white robe, and he begged for food. He said he had done what Jesus ordered and he had given away all his goods. With his long black beard and his bright deep eyes, you couldn't refuse him anything. He noticed me no longer, and never asked me, "So you goes to school?"

The people in Miguel didn't know what to make of the change. They tried to comfort themselves by saying that Man-man was really mad, but, like me, I think they weren't sure that Man-man wasn't really right.

What happened afterwards wasn't really unexpected.

Man-man announced that he was a new Messiah.

Hat said one day, "You ain't hear the latest?"

We said, "What?"

"Is about Man-man. He says he going to be crucified one of these days."

"Nobody go touch him," Edward said. "Everybody fraid of him now."

Hat explained. "No, it ain't that. He going to crucify hisself. One of these Fridays he going to Blue Basin and tie hisself to a cross and let people stone him."

Somebody—Errol, I think—laughed, but finding that no one laughed with him, fell silent again.

But on top of our wonder and worry, we had this great pride in knowing that Man-man came from Miguel Street.

Little hand-written notices began appearing in the shops and cafés and on the gates of some houses, announcing Man-man's forthcoming crucifixion.

"They going to have a big crowd in Blue Basin," Hat announced and added with pride, "and I hear they sending some police too."

That day, early in the morning, before the shops opened and the trolley-buses began running in Ariapita Avenue, the big crowd assembled at the corner of Miguel Street. There were lots of men dressed in black and even more women dressed in white. They were singing hymns. There were also about twenty policemen, but they were not singing hymns.

When Man-man appeared, looking very thin and very holy, women cried and rushed to touch his gown. The police stood by, prepared to handle anything.

A van came with a great wooden cross.

Hat, looking unhappy in his serge suit, said, "They tell me it make from match-wood. It ain't heavy. It light light."

Edward said, in a snapping sort of way, "That matter? Is the heart and the spirit that matter."

Hat said, "I ain't saying nothing."

Some men began taking the cross from the van to give it to Man-man, but he stopped them. His English accent sounded impressive in the early morning. "Not here. Leave it for Blue Basin."

Hat was disappointed.

We walked to Blue Basin, the waterfall in the mountains to the north-west of Port of Spain, and we got there in two hours. Man-man began carrying the cross from the road, up the rocky path and then down to the Basin.

Some men put up the cross, and tied Man-man to it.

Man-man said, "Stone me, brethren."

The women wept and flung bits of sand and gravel at his feet.

Man-man groaned and said, "Father, forgive them. They ain't know what they doing." Then he screamed out, "Stone me, brethren!"

A pebble the size of an egg struck him on the chest.

Man-man cried "Stone, *stone*, STONE me, brethren! I forgive you."

Edward said, "The man really brave."

People began flinging really big stones at Man-man, aiming at his face and chest.

Man-man looked hurt and surprised. He shouted, "What the hell is this? What the hell you people think you doing? Look, get me down from this thing quick, let me down quick, and I go settle with that son of a bitch who pelt a stone at me."

From where Edward and Hat and the rest of us stood, it sounded like a cry of agony.

A bigger stone struck Man-man; the women flung the sand and gravel at him.

We heard Man-man's shout, clear and loud, "Cut this stupidness out. Cut it out, I tell you. I finish with this arseness, you hear." And then he began cursing so loudly and coarsely that the people stopped in surprise.

The police took away Man-man.

The authorities kept him for observation. Then for good.

James Ngugi

Like many others in this anthology James Ngugi, a writer from Kenya, is better known as a novelist, and the three novels he has written so far mirror very clearly the pattern of change that his country has undergone. *The River Between*, the first to be written, although the second to be published, describes the development of hostility between the Kikuyu inhabitants of two ridges of land. On one of these the people follow the traditional gods and myths and maintain the same way of life hallowed by age-old tribal customs; on the other, they become Christianized:

> When you stood in the valley, the two ridges . . . became antagonists. You could tell this, not by anything tangible but by the way they faced each other, like two rivals ready to come to blows in a life and death struggle for the leadership of this isolated region.

Waiyaki, the main character, is caught in this life and death struggle, and rent between a passionate devotion to Western education on the one hand, and an equally deep-rooted veneration for tribal values on the other.

In his essay, "Notes on the English Character", included in *Abinger Harvest*, E. M. Forster wrote that the English 'built up an Empire with a Bible in one hand, a pistol in the other, and financial concessions in both pockets'. In Ngugi's work, after the advent of the Bible in *The River Between* comes the era of the pistol. *Weep not Child* describes the struggle for independence led by the Mau Mau in Kenya during the State of Emergency in the nineteen-fifties. Christianity had been a disruptive force in the other novel, but the people in this one are united in suffering at the hands of the colonial power. In *A Grain of Wheat* history has moved a stage further, even if many of the links with the past still remain unbroken. The tone and theme of the book are indicated in Ngugi's foreword:

> Although set in contemporary Kenya, all the characters in this book are fictitious. . . . But the situation and the problems are real

—sometimes too painfully real for the peasants who fought the British yet who now see all that they fought for being put on one side.

Set in Kenya on the eve of Independence, the action of the novel weaves back and forth in time to show that, although the achievement of self-government may solve some problems, it also supplies fertile ground for the growth of others. Moreover, the origins of the Mau Mau movement itself, which has now triumphantly brought the country face to face with a new future, 'can, so the people say, be traced to the day the white man came to the country, clutching the book of God in both hands'.

In Ngugi's work as a whole there is a continual awareness that these successive stages in the history of his country are not isolated and distinct from each other; each stage only brings to the surface difficulties and dilemmas which have really been latent all the time. They are only different facets of the most basic problem of all, and their roots must be sought for in that clash of a conservative, traditional way of life with new ideas, new ways, and another ethos.

In "A Meeting in the Dark", John, the main character, has received a Western-style education, and is about to leave his parents and his tribe to pursue his studies further at Makerere university college (as Ngugi himself did), studies that will inevitably alienate him even more from tribal values and its traditions, without necessarily offering him alternative values more acceptable and enduring. Like Waiyaki in *The River Between*, he is not really a person with a recognizable individual identity; but this is not so much a criticism of Ngugi's art, it is more an inevitable consequence of the major preoccupation of the story. John is also an epitome of the man trapped between two irreconcilable worlds and torn by a conflict of cultures. And in "A Meeting in the Dark", again as in *The River Between*, it is Christianity that is the force splintering the closely knit tribal community and its heritage of belief into fragments. Brought up as a child of the Christian faith, John becomes a victim of its moral attitudes: 'The trouble with John was that his imagination magnified the fall from the heights of "goodness" out of all proportion.'

If the weakness of the story is its over-explicit quality (the inverted commas around 'goodness' are a finger lifted in admonishing emphasis at the reader, and one notes the betrayingly obtrusive slip into the present tense at the end in an attempt to convey dramatic immediacy), its strength and interest derive from the fact that it deals with a vitally central problem. The conflict here is the enduring fact, in many different guises, which has shaped for good or ill the conditions of the present. Nor is it one confined only to Kenya; Achebe's work in West Africa demonstrates this. *D. H.*

A Meeting in the Dark

He stood at the door of the hut and saw his old, frail but energetic father coming along the village street, with a rather dirty bag made out of a strong calico swinging by his side. His father always carried this bag. John knew what it contained: a Bible, a hymn-book and probably a notebook and a pen. His father was a preacher. He wondered if it had been he who had stopped his mother from telling him stories when he became a man of God. His mother had stopped telling him stories long ago. She would say to him, "Now, don't ask for any more stories. Your father may come." So he feared his father. John went in and warned his mother of his father's coming. Then his father entered. John stood aside, then walked towards the door. He lingered there doubtfully, then he went out.

"John, hei, John!"

"Baba!"

"Come back."

He stood doubtfully in front of his father. His heart beat faster and an agitated voice within him seemed to ask: Does he know?

"Sit down. Where are you going?"

"For a walk, Father," he answered evasively.

"To the village?"

"Well—yes—no. I mean nowhere in particular." John saw his father look at him hard, seeming to read his face. John sighed, a very slow sigh. He did not like the way his father eyed him. He always looked at him as though John was a sinner, one who had to be watched all the time. "I am," his heart told him. John guiltily refused to meet the old man's gaze and looked past him and appealingly to his mother who was quietly peeling potatoes. But she seemed oblivious of everything around her.

"Why do you look away? What have you done?"

John shrank within himself with fear. But his face remained expressionless. He could hear the loud beats of his heart. It was like an engine pumping water. He felt no doubt his father knew all about it. He thought: "Why does he torture me? Why does he not at once say he knows?" Then another voice told him: "No, he doesn't know, otherwise he would have already jumped at you." A consolation. He faced his thoughtful father with courage.

"When is the journey?"

Again John thought, why does he ask? I have told him many times.

"Next week, Tuesday," he said.

"Right. Tomorrow we go to the shops, hear?"

"Yes, Father."

"Then be prepared."

"Yes, Father."

"You can go."

"Thank you, Father." He began to move.

"John!"

"Yes?" John's heart almost stopped beating.

"You seem to be in a hurry. I don't want to hear of you loitering in the village. I know young men, going to show off just because you are going away? I don't want to hear of trouble in the village."

Much relieved, he went out. He could guess what his father meant by not wanting trouble in the village.

"Why do you persecute the boy so much?" Susan spoke for the first time. Apparently she had carefully listened to the whole drama without a word. Now was her time to speak. She looked at her tough old preacher who had been a companion for life. She had married him a long time ago. She could not tell the number of years. They had been happy. Then the man became a convert. And everything in the home put on a religious tone. He even made her stop telling stories to the child. "Tell him of Jesus. Jesus died for you. Jesus died for the child. He must know the Lord." She, too, had been converted. But she was never blind to the moral torture he inflicted on the boy (that was how she always referred to John), so that the boy had grown up mortally afraid of his father. She always wondered if it was love for the son. Or could it be a resentment because, well, they two had "sinned" before marriage? John had been the result of that sin. But that had not been John's fault. It was the boy who ought to complain. She often wondered if the boy had . . . but no. The boy had been very small when they left Fort Hall. She looked at her husband. He remained mute though his left hand did, rather irritably, feel about his face.

"It is as if he was not your son. Or do you . . ."

"Hm, Sister." The voice was pleading. She was seeking a quarrel

but he did not feel equal to one. Really, women could never understand. Women were women, whether saved or not. Their son had to
be protected against all evil influences. He must be made to grow in
the footsteps of the Lord. He looked at her, frowning a little. She
had made him sin but that had been a long time ago. And he had
been saved. John must not follow the same road.

"Look, Sister." He hastily interrupted. He always called her sister.
Sister-in-the-Lord, in full. But he sometimes wondered if she had
been truly saved. In his heart he prayed: Lord, be with our sister
Susan. Aloud, he continued, "You know I want the boy to grow in
the Lord."

"But you torture him so! You make him fear you!"

"Why! He should not fear me. I have really nothing against him."

"It is you. You have always been cruel to him. . . ." She stood up.
The peelings dropped from her frock and fell in a heap on the floor.
"Stanley!"

"Sister." He was startled by the vehemence in her voice. He had
never seen her like this. Lord, take the devil out of her. Save her this
minute. She did not say what she wanted to say. Stanley looked away
from her. It was a surprise, but it seemed he feared his wife. If you
had told the people in the village about this, they would not have
believed you. He took his Bible and began to read. On Sunday he
would preach to a congregation of brethren and sisters.

Susan, a rather tall, thin woman, who had once been beautiful, sat
down again and went on with her work. She did not know what was
troubling her son. Was it the coming journey? Still, she feared for him.

Outside, John was strolling aimlessly along the path that led from
his home. He stood near the wattle tree which was a little way from
his father's house and surveyed the whole village. They lay before
his eyes, crammed, rows and rows of mud and grass huts, ending in
sharply defined sticks that pointed to heaven. Smoke was coming out
of various huts. It was an indication that many women had already
come from the Shambas. Night would soon fall. To the west, the sun
—that lone day-time traveller—was hurrying home behind the misty
hills. Again, John looked at the crammed rows and rows of huts that
formed Makeno Village, one of the new mushroom "towns" that
grew up all over the country during the Mau Mau war. It looked so
ugly. A pain rose in his heart and he felt like crying—I hate you, I
hate you! You trapped me alive. Away from you, it would never have
happened. He did not shout. He just watched.

A woman was coming towards where he stood. A path into the village was just near there. She was carrying a big load of Kuni which bent her into an Akamba-bow shape. She greeted him. "Is it well with you, Njooni (John)?"

"It is well with me, Mother." There was no trace of bitterness in his voice. John was by nature polite. Everyone knew of this. He was quite unlike the other proud, educated sons of the tribe—sons who came back from the other side of the waters with white or Negro wives who spoke English. And they behaved just like Europeans! John was a favourite, a model of humility and moral perfection. Everyone knew that though a clergyman's son, John would never betray the tribe. They still talked of the tribe and its ways.

"When are you going to—to——"

"Makerere?"

"Makelele." She laughed. The way she pronounced the name was funny. And the way she laughed, too. She enjoyed it. But John felt hurt. So everyone knew of this.

"Next week."

"I wish you well."

"Thank you, Mother."

She said quietly, as if trying to pronounce it better, "Makelele." She laughed at herself again but she was tired. The load was heavy.

"Stay well, Son."

"Go well and in peace, Mother."

And the woman who all the time had stood, moved on, panting like a donkey, but she was obviously pleased with John's kindness.

John remained long, looking at her. What made such a woman live on day to day, working hard, yet happy? Had she much faith in life? Or was her faith in the tribe? She and her kind, who had never been touched by ways of the white man, looked as though they had something to cling to. As he watched her disappear, he felt proud that they should think well of him. He felt proud that he had a place in their esteem. And then came the pang. *Father will know. They will know.* He did not know what he feared most; the action his father would take when he knew, or the loss of the little faith the simple villagers had placed in him, when they knew. He feared to lose all.

He went down to the small local teashop. He met many people who all wished him well at the college. All of them knew that the priest's son had finished all the white man's learning in Kenya. He would now go to Uganda. They had read all this in the *Baraza*, a Swahili weekly paper. John did not stay long at the shop. The sun had already gone to rest and now darkness was coming. The evening meal was ready. His tough father was still at the table reading his Bible. He did not look up when John entered. Strange silence settled in the hut.

"You look unhappy." His mother first broke the silence.

John laughed. It was a nervous little laugh. "No, Mother," he hastily replied, nervously looking at his father. He secretly hoped that Wamuhu had not blubbed.

"Then I am glad."

She did not know. He ate his dinner and went out to his hut. A man's hut. Every young man had his own hut. John was never allowed to bring any girl visitor in there. Stanley did not want "trouble". Even to be seen standing with one was a crime. His father could easily thrash him. He feared his father, though sometimes he wondered why he feared him. He ought to have rebelled like all the other young educated men. He lit the lantern. He took it in his hand. The yellow light flickered dangerously and then went out. He knew his hands were shaking. He lit it again and hurriedly took his big coat and a huge *Kofia* which were lying on the unmade bed. He left the lantern burning, so that his father would see it and think him in. John bit his lower lip spitefully. He hated himself for being so girlish. It was unnatural for a boy of his age.

Like a shadow, he stealthily crossed the courtyard and went on to the village street.

He met young men and woman lining the streets. They were laughing, talking, whispering. They were obviously enjoying themselves. John thought, they are more free than I am. He envied their exuberance. They clearly stood outside or above the strict morality that the educated ones had to be judged by. Would he have gladly changed places with them? He wondered. At last, he came to the hut. It stood at the very heart of the village. How well he knew it—to his sorrow. He wondered what he should do! Wait for her outside? What if her mother came out instead? He decided to enter.

"Hodi!"

"Enter. We are in."

John pulled down his hat before he entered. Indeed they were all there—all except she whom he wanted. The fire in the hearth was dying. Only a small flame from a lighted lantern vaguely illuminated the whole hut. The flame and the giant shadow created on the wall seemed to be mocking him. He prayed that Wamuhu's parents would not recognize him. He tried to be "thin", and to disguise his voice as he greeted them. They recognized him and made themselves busy on his account. To be visited by such an educated one who knew all about the white man's world and knowledge and who would now go to another land beyond, was not such a frequent occurrence that it could be taken lightly. Who knew but he might be interested in their daughter? Stranger things had happened. After all, learning was not the only thing. Though Wamuhu had no learning, yet charms she had and she could be trusted to captivate any young man's heart with her looks and smiles.

"You will sit down. Take that stool."

"No!" He noticed with bitterness that he did not call her "mother".

"Where is Wamuhu?"

The mother threw a triumphant glance at her husband. They exchanged a knowing look. John bit his lips again and felt like bolting. He controlled himself with difficulty.

"She has gone out to get some tea leaves. Please sit down. She will cook you some tea when she comes."

"I am afraid . . ." he muttered some inaudible words and went out. He almost collided with Wamuhu.

In the hut: "Didn't I tell you? Trust a woman's eye!"

"You don't know these young men."

"But you see John is different. Everyone speaks well of him and he is a clergyman's son."

"Y-e-e-s! A clergyman's son? You forget your daughter is circumcised." The old man was remembering his own day. He had found for himself a good virtuous woman, initiated in all the tribe's ways. And she had known no other man. He had married her. They were happy. Other men of his *Rika* had done the same. All their girls had been virgins, it being a taboo to touch a girl in that way, even if you slept in the same bed, as indeed so many young men and girls did. Then the white men had come, preaching a strange religion, strange ways, which all men followed. The tribe's code of behaviour was broken. The new faith could not keep the tribe together. How could it? The men who followed the new faith would not let the girls be circumcised. And they would not let their sons marry circumcised girls. Puu! Look at what was happening. Their young men went away to the land of the white men. What did they bring? White women. Black women who spoke English. Aaa—bad. And the young men who were left just did not mind. They made unmarried girls their wives and then left them with fatherless children.

"What does it matter?" his wife was replying. "Is Wamuhu not as good as the best of them? Anyway, John is different."

"Different! Different! Puu! They are all alike. Those coated with the white clay of the white man's ways are the worst. They have nothing inside. Nothing—nothing here." He took a piece of wood and nervously poked the dying fire. A strange numbness came over him. He trembled. And he feared; he feared for the tribe. For now he saw it was not only the educated men who were coated with strange ways, but the whole tribe. The old man trembled and cried inside, mourning for a tribe that had crumbled. The tribe had nowhere to go to. And it could not be what it was before. He stopped poking and looked hard at the ground.

"I wonder why he came. I wonder." Then he looked at his wife and said, "Have you seen strange behaviour with your daughter?"

His wife did not answer. She was preoccupied with her own great hopes. . . .

John and Wamuhu walked on in silence. The intricate streets and turns were well known to them both. Wamuhu walked with quick light steps; John knew she was in a happy mood. His steps were heavy and he avoided people, even though it was dark. But why should he feel ashamed? The girl was beautiful, probably the most beautiful girl in the whole of Limuru. Yet he feared being seen with her. It was all wrong. He knew that he could have loved her; even then he wondered if he did not love her. Perhaps it was hard to tell but, had he been one of the young men he had met, he would not have hesitated in his answer.

Outside the village he stopped. She, too, stopped. Neither had spoken a word all through. Perhaps the silence spoke louder than words. Each was only too conscious of the other.

"Do they know?" Silence. Wamuhu was probably considering the question. "Don't keep me waiting. Please answer me," he implored. He felt weary, very weary, like an old man who had suddenly reached his journey's end.

"No. You told me to give you one more week. A week is over today."

"Yes. That's why I came!" John whispered hoarsely.

Wamuhu did not speak. John looked at her. Darkness was now

between them. He was not really seeing her; before him was the image of his father—haughtily religious and dominating. Again he thought: I, John, a priest's son, respected by all and going to college, will fall, fall to the ground. He did not want to contemplate the fall.

"It was your fault." He found himself accusing her. In his heart he knew he was lying.

"Why do you keep on telling me that? Don't you want to marry me?"

John sighed. He did not know what to do. He remembered a story his mother used to tell him. *Once upon a time there was a young girl . . . she had no home to go to and she could not go forward to the beautiful land and see all the good things because the Irimu was on the way. . . .*

"When will you tell them?"

"Tonight."

He felt desperate. Next week he would go to the college. If he could persuade her to wait, he might be able to get away and come back when the storm and consternation had abated. But then the government might withdraw his bursary. He was frightened and there was a sad note of appeal as he turned to her and said, "Look, Wamuhu, how long have you been pre—I mean, like this?"

"I have told you over and over again, I have been pregnant for three months and mother is being suspicious. Only yesterday she said I breathed like a woman with a child."

"Do you think you could wait for three weeks more?"

She laughed. Ah! the little witch! She knew his trick. Her laughter always aroused many emotions in him.

"All right," he said. "Give me just tomorrow. I'll think up something. Tomorrow I'll let you know all."

"I agree. Tomorrow. I cannot wait any more unless you mean to marry me."

Why not marry her? She is beautiful! Why not marry her? Do I love her or don't I?

She left. John felt as if she was deliberately blackmailing him. His knees were weak and lost strength. He could not move but sank on the ground in a heap. Sweat poured profusely down his cheek, as if he had been running hard under a strong sun. But this was cold sweat. He lay on the grass; he did not want to think. Oh, no! He could not possibly face his father. Or his mother. Or Reverend Carstone who had had such faith in him. John realized that, though he was educated, he was not more secure than anybody else. He was no better than Wamuhu. *Then why don't you marry her?* He did not

217

know. John had grown up under a Calvinistic father and learnt under a Calvinistic headmaster—a missionary! John tried to pray. But to whom was he praying? To Carstone's God? It sounded false. It was as if he was blaspheming. Could he pray to the God of the tribe? His sense of guilt crushed him.

He woke up. Where was he? Then he understood. Wamuhu had left him. She had given him one day. He stood up; he felt good. Weakly, he began to walk back home. It was lucky that darkness blanketed the whole earth and him in it. From the various huts, he could hear laughter, heated talks or quarrels. Little fires could be seen flickeringly red through the open doors. Village stars, John thought. He raised up his eyes. The heavenly stars, cold and distant, looked down on him impersonally. Here and there, groups of boys and girls could be heard laughing and shouting. For them life seemed to go on as usual. John consoled himself by thinking that they, too, would come to face their day of trial.

John was shaky. Why! Why! Why could he not defy all expectations, all prospects of a future, and marry the girl? No. No. It was impossible. She was circumcised and he knew that his father and the church would never consent to such a marriage. She had no learning —or rather she had not gone beyond standard four. Marrying her would probably ruin his chances of ever going to a university. . . .

He tried to move briskly. His strength had returned. His imagination and thought took flight. He was trying to explain his action before an accusing world—he had done so many times before, ever since he knew of this. He still wondered what he could have done. The girl had attracted him. She was graceful and her smile had been very bewitching. There was none who could equal her and no girl in the village had any pretence to any higher standard of education. Women's education was very low. Perhaps that was why so many Africans went "away" and came back married. He too wished he had gone with the others, especially in the last giant student airlift to America. If only Wamuhu had learning . . . and she was uncircumcised . . . then he might probably rebel. . . .

The light still shone in his mother's hut. John wondered if he should go in for the night prayers. But he thought against it; he might not be strong enough to face his parents. In his hut the light had gone out. He hoped his father had not noticed it. . . .

John woke up early. He was frightened. He was normally not superstitious, but still he did not like the dreams of the night. He

218

dreamt of circumcision; he had just been initiated in the tribal manner. Somebody—he could not tell his face, came and led him because he took pity on him. They went into a strange land. Somehow, he found himself alone. The somebody had vanished. A ghost came. He recognized it as the ghost of the home he had left. It pulled him back; then another ghost came. It was the ghost of the land he had come to. It pulled him from the front. The two contested. Then came other ghosts from all sides and pulled him from all sides so that his body began to fall into pieces. And the ghosts were unsubstantial. He could not cling to any. Only they were pulling him and he was becoming nothing, nothing . . . he was now standing a distance away. It had not been him. But he was looking at the girl, the girl in the story. She had nowhere to go. He thought he would go to help her; he would show her the way. But as he went to her, he lost his way . . . he was all alone . . . something destructive was coming towards him, coming, coming. . . . He woke up. He was sweating all over.

Dreams about circumcision were no good. They portended death. He dismissed the dream with a laugh. He opened the window only to find the whole country clouded in mist. It was perfect July weather in Limuru. The hills, ridges, valleys and plains that surrounded the village were lost in the mist. It looked such a strange place. But there was almost a magic fascination in it. Limuru was a land of contrasts and evoked differing emotions at different times. Once John would be fascinated and would yearn to touch the land, embrace it or just be on the grass. At another time he would feel repelled by the dust, the strong sun and the pot-holed roads. If only his struggle were just against the dust, the mist, the sun and the rain, he might feel content. Content to live here. At least he thought he would never like to die and be buried anywhere else but at Limuru. But there was the human element whose vices and betrayal of other men were embodied in the new ugly villages. The last night's incident rushed into his mind like a flood, making him weak again. He came out of his blankets and went out. Today he would go to the shops. He was uneasy. An odd feeling was coming to him—in fact had been coming—that his relationship with his father was perhaps unnatural. But he dismissed the thought. Tonight would be the day of reckoning. He shuddered to think of it. It was unfortunate that this scar had come into his life at this time when he was going to Makerere and it would have brought him closer to his father.

They went to the shops. All day long, John remained quiet as they moved from shop to shop buying things from the lanky but wistful Indian traders. And all day long, John wondered why he feared his father so much. He had grown up fearing him, trembling whenever he spoke or gave commands. John was not alone in this.

Stanley was feared by all.

He preached with great vigour, defying the very gates of hell. Even during the Emergency, he had gone on preaching, scolding, judging and condemning. All those who were not saved were destined for hell. Above all, Stanley was known for his great and strict moral observances—a bit too strict, rather pharisaical in nature. None noticed this; certainly not the sheep he shepherded. If an elder broke any of the rules, he was liable to be expelled, or excommunicated. Young men and women, seen standing together "in a manner prejudicial to church and God's morality" (they were one anyway) were liable to be excommunicated. And so, many young men tried to serve two masters by seeing their girls at night and going to church by day. The alternative was to give up church-going altogether. . . .

Stanley took a fatherly attitude to all the people in the village. You must be strict with what is yours. And because of all this he wanted his house to be a good example of this to all. That is why he wanted his son to grow upright. But motives behind many human actions may be mixed. He could never forget that he had also fallen before his marriage. Stanley was also a product of the disintegration of the tribe due to the new influences.

The shopping did not take long. His father strictly observed the silences between them and neither by word nor hint did he refer to last night. They reached home and John was thinking that all was well when his father called him.

"John."

"Yes, Father."

"Why did you not come for prayers last night?"

"I forgot . . ."

"Where were you?"

Why do you ask me? What right have you to know where I was? One day I am going to revolt against you. But, immediately, John knew that this act of rebellion was something beyond him—unless something happened to push him into it. It needed someone with something he lacked.

"I—I—I mean, I was . . ."

"You should not sleep so early before prayers. Remember to turn up tonight."

"I will."

Something in the boy's voice made the father look up. John went away relieved. All was still well.

Evening came. John dressed like the night before and walked with faltering steps towards the fatal place. The night of reckoning had come. And he had not thought of anything. After this night all would know. Even Reverend Carstone would hear of it. He remembered Reverend Carstone and the last words of blessing he had spoken to him. No! he did not want to remember. It was no good remembering these things; and yet the words came. They were clearly written in the air, or in the darkness of his mind. "You are going into the world. The world is waiting even like a hungry lion, to swallow you, to devour you. Therefore, beware of the world. Jesus said, Hold fast unto . . ." John felt a pain—pain that wriggled through his flesh as he remembered these words. He contemplated the coming fall. Yes! He, John, would fall from the Gates of Heaven down through the open waiting Gates of Hell. Ah! He could see it all, and all that people would say. All would shun his company, all would give him oblique looks that told so much. The trouble with John was that his imagination magnified the fall from the heights of "goodness" out of all proportion. And fear of people and consequences ranked high in the things that made him contemplate the fall with so much horror.

John devised all sorts of punishment for himself. And when it came to thinking of a way out, only fantastic and impossible ways of escape came into his head. He could not simply make up his mind. And because he could not, and because he feared Father and people and did not know his true attitude to the girl, he came to the agreed spot having nothing to tell her. Whatever he did looked fatal to him. Then suddenly he said:

"Look, Wamuhu. Let me give you money. You might then say that someone else was responsible. Lots of girls have done this. Then that man may marry you. For me, it is impossible. You know that."

"No. I cannot do that. How can you, you . . ."

"I will give you two hundred shillings."

"No!"

"Three hundred."

"No!" She was almost crying. It pained her to see him so.

"Four hundred, five hundred, six hundred." John had begun

calmly but now his voice was running high. He was excited. He was becoming more desperate. Did he know what he was talking about? He spoke quickly, breathlessly, as if he was in a hurry. The figure was rapidly rising—nine thousand, ten thousand, twenty thousand. . . . He is mad. He is foaming. He is quickly moving towards the girl in the dark. He has lain his hands on her shoulders and is madly imploring her in a hoarse voice. Deep inside him, something horrid that assumes the threatening anger of his father and the village, seems to be pushing him. He is violently shaking Wamuhu, while his mind tells him that he is patting her gently. Yes, he is out of his mind. The figure has now reached fifty thousand shillings and is increasing. Wamuhu is afraid. She extricates herself from him, the mad, educated son of a religious clergyman, and runs. He runs after her and holds her, calling her by all sorts of endearing words. But he is shaking her, shake, shake, her, her—he tries to hug her by the neck, presses. . . . She lets out one horrible scream and then falls on the ground. And so all of a sudden, the struggle is over, the figures stop, and John stands there trembling like the leaf of a tree on a windy day.

Soon everyone will know that he has created and then killed.

Hal Porter

Hal Porter is not only one of Australia's finest short-story writers but he has also written one of the very best of all Australian autobiographies. The title of the first volume of this work is *The Watcher on the Cast-iron Balcony*; the watcher is Porter, and it is in this role that we find him in both his autobiography and his fiction. The role itself creates a duality between Hal Porter, the writer and Hal Porter, the man. As the watcher, the artist, he is alone, isolated, detached, endeavouring always to be objective, to sift the real from the non-real. 'This watching, this down-gazing, this faraway staring, is an exercise in solitude and non-involvement.' But the community is there 'to rob him of aloneness and content.' (from *The Watcher*). For Porter is not only a spectator, he is also a participant; his fiction as well as his auto-biography is written out of his own personal experience. He comments on his method of writing:

> . . . pure fiction, and flights of fancy are utterly beyond me. As a result another preoccupation is necessary. This is with the mechanics of transmuting actual personal experience, or the witnessed experiences of others, into what reads (I pray!) like true to life fiction. . . . Many characters, settings, and situations, already tied up in a 'plot', are filched, holus-bolus, with the insolence of a shop-lifter, straight out of 'life'.
>
> (from *Southerly*, No. 1, 1969)

Of course, as an artist he will shape his material; he may be, as he writes in *The Paper Chase*, a 'restless picker-up' but he is also a 'ruthless pruner' and it is in the pruning that his imagination is at work; in the artist's sensitivity to the essentials, and in the ability to arrange 'the million bits of the answer into One Answer.' The One Answer is what Porter is seeking, the question he asks is: what is real? Rarely do his characters know the truth; like his mother in "Francis Silver" they live, and some of them even die, in their illusions.

223

In the second volume of his autobiography, *The Paper Chase*, Porter tells of his methods when he is looking back on past experience, as he is in this story. 'As always, when writing of a past self, I try to put down what is felt "then" even if "now" has changed the feeling.' The narration passes through several Hal Porters, the naïve boy, the romantic adolescent, the idealistic youth, the bitter and cynical young adult and the writer aware of 'one disconcerting, even disenchanting thing: what one oneself remembers is not what others remember'. The concern of the story is with the question of true identity, it deals with a moment of initiation when a youthful illusion is shattered by a harsh reality. Such moments occur quite frequently in Porter's work and the often savage and grotesque nature of the reversal suggests the bitterness of one who feels that perhaps life is a fraud.

Any reader must be immediately aware that Porter has an eye that is gluttonous for details. He has said in the article already mentioned:

In more intense forms of writing—the short story, for instance—effects must be made quickly, and often on many planes in immediately sequent sentences. Even if one splurge or over-express, one dares not falter on minutiae: dress, vehicles, customs, moral quirks, peculiar snobberies, atmospheric tone, and—above all—conversation. . . . To write down what is literally heard, to tape-record as it were in writing is to miss the point: the eye does not hear. The reader has to be tricked with a selection of words which 'look' like what is supposed to be 'heard'. Acquiring the necessary illusionist's skill, . . . has been another of my preoccupations.

When we listen to the voices in this story it becomes obvious that Porter has acquired this skill. If we had any doubts before we met him that Francis Silver was a dandy, the lisp immediately banished them.

Porter's remarks about the details remind us of a similar remark made by R. K. Narayan in a television interview in which he was discussing his writing. Narayan said, 'Take care of the details with minute attention and when assembled you discover you've written a novel.' Through his assembling of all the details Porter has recaptured an age for us and also the people who lived in it. In *The Paper Chase* he said, 'The quality of one's connection with people through their relation with things, tunes, scents, sounds, and so on is a subject of great allure, its existence a great blessing.' This is the special significance of things for Porter, they are 'evidences of humanity . . . threads resistant to time and space'. As such they are man's protection against mutability, against the destructive element in time, which so often creates an illusion out of what was once a reality. The details, the picture, the song, remain to defy time.

The destruction of the lock of hair signifies the destruction of yet another illusion for the young man. The stench reminds us of the ugliness, perhaps the evil of reality, the agony is that of a youth stripped of one more romantic ideal. He goes out cynically to perform his first adult chore, which ironically enough is to perpetuate an illusion. Only the watcher will remain aware of the reality. *A. R.*

Francis Silver

One grows relievedly older and less an amateur: the high noon of middle age is free of the eccentricities of the innocent, one's senses are correctly disposed, one does not permit oneself the pleasure of discreditable actions; altogether, reality has no frayed ends. One can, at worst, fortify oneself with memories. Nevertheless, there is one disconcerting, even disenchanting, thing: what one oneself remembers is not what others remember. In this, women as annalists are terrifying. One expects them to get their recollections as exact as the amount of salt in Scotch Broth. Beyond the practical area, of course, one has no illusions: if a woman talk about democracy or eternal peace or disarmament one sees instantly and with the most telling clarity that these things are pure nonsense. One does not, however, expect a handful of salt or no salt at all in either Scotch Broth or memories, but what one expects, and what one gets—oh, dear. Take my mother for example.

As eldest son of a family of seven I got the best of her memories, partly because mothers of that period had time to make their special offerings to first-born sons, partly because her enthusiasm and salesmanship were fresh. Among her recollections the most recurrent were of Francis Silver.

Right here, I must indicate that mother was multiloquous, gay and romantic. Whatever else a large family tore from her, it was not her vivacity. She sang all the time, particularly, I think I remember, on ironing day. The pattern of this day was that of a holy day; there was an inevitability, a feeling of religious ritual. It was always Tuesday, always Shepherd's Pie day. To mother's heightened singing the kitchen-range was stoked with red-gum until a mirage almost formed above its black-leaded surface on which the flat-irons had been clashed down. The piled-up clothes-basket and the kauri clothes-horse were brought into the kitchen; the beeswax in its piece of scorched cloth was placed ready. These preparations over, and while the irons were heating, a tranquil overture began. Mother and the washerwoman took each bed-sheet separately and, one gripping the bottom edge, one the top, retreated backwards, straining the sheet taut in a domestic tug-o'-war, inclining their heads to scan it for signs of wear then, this done, advancing towards each other with uplifted arms to begin the folding. These retreatings, advancings, inclinations and deft gestures, repeated sheet after sheet, had the air of an endless figure of a pavane in which, sometimes, I attempted to represent the absent washerwoman. It was while thus engaged, and later, while mother was ironing, and between her ironing-songs which were more poignantly yearning than, say, her friskier carpet-sweeping- or cake-mixing-songs, that I recall hearing much about Francis Silver.

As a young woman mother lived in a middle-class seaside suburb of Melbourne. Plane-trees lined the three-chain-wide streets from which cast-iron railings and gates, and paths of encaustic tiles of Pompeian design, separated two-storeyed brick houses overtopped by Norfolk Island Pines exuding sap like candle-grease. These houses had such names as *Grevillea, Emmaville, Dagmar* and *Buckingham*. Stucco faces of gravely Grecian cast stared in the direction of the beach on to which oranges thrown from P. and O. liners rolled in with sea-lettuce, bladderwrack and mussel-shells. A bathing enclosure advertised HOT SEA-BATHS and TOWELS AND BATHING-DRESS FOR HIRE. Mother strolled the Esplanade, tamarisk by tamarisk, or sipped Lemon Squash Spiders in the Jubilee Café with the apparently numerous young men who were courting her. Of these beaux, two young men, one from the country, one from another suburb, were favoured most. In marrying the country wooer, my father, and darning his socks and bearing his children and darning their socks, mother left the suburb for a country town set smack-flat on the wind-combed plains of Gippsland. She also left behind Francis Silver, whom she never saw again, at least not physically. He lived on, remarkably visible, in a special display-case of her memories.

Since the time of mother's young womanhood was pre-Great War there had been a conventional and profuse to-and-fro of postcards. She had garnered several bulging albums of them. The most elaborate cards, in an album of their own, were from Francis Silver. These had a sacred quality. In my eyes they belonged to Sunday. My parents were pagan enough to regard the church merely as a setting for wedding, baptism and funeral services, but, largely for us children, I suspect, though also because of what had been dyed into the texture of their late-Victorian childhoods, they were firm about the sanctity of Sunday. On this day mother played on the piano, or sang, hymns only. We were forbidden to whistle or go barefoot. Reading was restricted to *The Child's Bible, Sunday at Home* or *Christie's Old Organ*. Apart from meals of great size and gorgeousness the only permissible secular pleasures were to look through the stereoscope at Boer War photographs or at Francis Silver's postcards.

Hypocritically careful, we resisted licking our fingers to turn the interleaves of tissue paper because mother hovered wrestling with herself. Invariably, at last, she could resist herself no longer. Perhaps a postcard of stiffened lace, *moiré* rosettes and spangles would set her off. Her eyes and her voice would detach themselves in focus and tone from the present.

"Yes," she would say in this unique, entranced voice, "Francis Silver sent me that after we'd had a tiny tiff near the Williamstown Time-ball Tower. We had gone for a stroll to St. Kilda to listen to the German Band. When we got there the ferry-boat to Williamstown was at the pier—the dear old *Rosny*. It was such a perfect day we decided to go across to Williamstown. There was a little man on board playing a concertina. I had on—oh, I remember it so well—a white *broderie anglaise* dress, and a hat with enormous peach-coloured silk roses on it. And a parasol of the same peach with a picot-edged triple flounce. I'd made Francis Silver a buttonhole of Cecile Brunner roses. And when we were on our way back, he threw it from the *Rosny* into Port Phillip Bay because I wouldn't talk to him. It was all because I refused to give him my lace handkerchief as a keepsake. How silly it all was! I'd have given him the hanky if he hadn't said he was going to sleep with it under his pillow. And the next day he sent me this card. But I was quite firm, and didn't send the hanky. It was mean of me, I suppose, but I was terribly well-brought-up."

All mother's memories of Francis Silver were of this vague, passionless kind. The time seemed eternally three o'clock in the afternoon of a deliciously sunny day, band-music drifted cloudily in the background, no one hurried or raised voices, there were no inflamed rages or cutting malices. It was a delicate game of teasing played in Sunday clothes and while wearing mignonette. It had its fragile rules no one would be untamed enough to break. As people walking on the fresh boards of a new floor soil it in gingerly and gentle fashion, so did mother and Francis Silver serenely walk the floor of their affection.

From accounts as lame as this, of incidents as small, flat and point-less as this, it amazes me, now, that so vivid and important an image of Francis Silver became mine.

As I saw it, Francis Silver was extraordinarily handsome in a certain way. He had a shortish, straight nose, a little black moustache with curled-up ends, lips clearly cut as a statue's, white teeth, small ears with lobes, definite but not untidy eyebrows, tightly packed black wavy hair, and an olive skin. His hands were hairless and supple; the half-moons showed even at the roots of his little finger-nails. He had a light tenor voice he exhibited in such songs as *Only a Leaf, After the Ball, 'Neath the Shade of the Old Apple Tree,* and *She Lives in a Mansion of Aching Hearts*—songs laced with misunderstanding, regret and tears. He was a picture-framer go-ahead enough to have his own business. In the sense of handling Christmas supplement oleographs and "art photographs" of Grecian-robed women holding water-lilies or bunches of grapes he was artistic and sensitive. He smoked Turkish cigarettes, did not drink, was popular with other sensitive young men, wore a gold ring with a ruby in it, was very proud of his small feet, and loved the theatre.

Throughout the years, mother had provided these and many more details, partly by anecdote, partly by a system of odious comparisons ("Mr Willoughby's eyebrows are much untidier than Francis Silver's"), partly by setting a standard we fell far short of ("You must press back the quicks of your fingernails each time you dry your hands: the half-moons on Francis Silver's nails, even on the little fingers, showed clearly"). It was incredible what we children knew of him: he disliked mushrooms, tomatoes and ripe apricots, he had cut his hand at a Fern Tree Gully picnic, lost his father's gold watch in Flinders Lane, had four sisters, used Wright's Coal Tar Soap, and was double-jointed.

During all the years of talk not once did mother call him any-thing else but Francis Silver, never Mr. Silver, and certainly never Francis, despite the fact that, seemingly to us, she had given him every consideration as a possible husband. This possibility was never directly expressed. We presumed from constant obliquities. At one stage of my early adolescence, when I was sullenly inclined to regard father as the malice-riddled offspring of parents like Simon Legree and the Witch of Endor, I yearned to be the son of a merrier, more handsome and talented father. I knew exactly whom, and spent much time practising in various ornate handwritings names I greatly preferred to my own . . . Hereward Silver, Montmorency Silver, Shem Silver, Fluellen Silver.

My placid actual father (it was his placidity I regarded as a sinister malice) was as aware as he was of anything of mother's indestructible interest in Francis Silver. It was a sort of joke with him which, as children, we loved: Francis Silver was so often a bore.

"Woman, dear," father would, for example, say, seeing mother and some of us off at the railway station when we were going for a few days to Melbourne, "if you are not back by Friday, I'll assume you've put the children in a comfortable orphanage, and have run off with Francis Silver. I shall, therefore, set up house with Mrs. Tinsley." This, to us, was hilariously funny: Mrs. Tinsley was a gushing woman who irritated father so much that he went and talked to the pigs when she appeared. If mother displayed herself in a new hat or dress, badgering father for an opinion, he would say, "Now, woman, dear, you know you look very nice. You must have a photograph taken for Francis Silver."

"Jealous beast," mother would say.

This light-hearted chyacking about Francis Silver made him appear for ever twenty-four, for ever dashing, for ever harmless. He was the legendary Gentleman first to his feet when Ladies entered; he daily cleaned his shoes, and the *backs* of his shoes.

Once only did this image of him take on sootier colours, and throw a disturbing shadow. This happened the one time I ever heard my parents really quarrel. What the quarrel was about I shall never know. To my alarm I was trapped in its orbit without the nous to consider flight let alone perform the act of flight. There mother and father were, upbraiding each other ferociously, in the glare of kitchen daylight, she songless and shrill and stripped of her vivacity, he loud-mouthed and stripped of his dry-tongued placidity. At the height of heat mother dashed a colander of French beans to the linoleum and, crying out, "I wish I'd married Francis Silver!" rushed from her kitchen, slamming its door, then the vestibule door, next her bedroom door. Horrified as I was at the quarrel itself which seemed the disreputable sort of thing poor people, common people or drunk people did, I was more horrified at this vision of Francis Silver as a mother-stealer. I had the impression father was startled; the framework of his being somehow showed; he seemed much less a father, nuder of face, younger, like nothing so much as a bewildered man. I began to pick up the beans so as not to look at him directly, but I absorbed him foxily. He was, as it were, reassembling himself and dressing his face again, when the kitchen door opened quietly. The slam of the bedroom door had scarcely died but mother had done something neatening to her hair.

"I have," she said, "just caught a glimpse of myself in the glass." It was a girl's voice. She tried a smile. It was too weighed out of balance with uncertainty and rising tears to succeed. "I was quite hideous with temper. I'm sorry, Henry. Of course I didn't mean ... honestly . . . ."

"Woman, dear," said father, "Francis Silver would have been a lucky man if you had married him. Out to play, boy, out to play," he said, crossing to mother who began to cry. I knew he was going to sit her on his knee. That night we had festive jelly with bananas and a dash of port wine in for pudding: a sure indication that, although he wasn't mentioned, Francis Silver was still in the house. Nevertheless, it was several months before I forgot him as a peril and could see him again as the eternal charmer.

When mother died at the age of forty-one I was eighteen.

Several hours before she died, her singing forgone for ever, her gaiety tampered with by the demands of dying, I was alone with her for a while. After saying what, I supposed, all dying mothers say to eldest sons, most of it trite, she asked me to take Francis Silver the album of postcards he'd sent her twenty-odd years ago.

"I know what the girls are like," she said of my sisters. "They'll marry and have children, and let the children tear them up. I'm sure he'd like to have them. He's still alive, and still in the same place, I think. I've looked in the obituary notices every day for years."

I began to cry.

"Stop that," she said, as though I were breaking some deathbed rule, "and listen. There's something else. In my handkerchief-drawer there's a pink envelope with his name on it. It's got a lock of my hair in it. Before I married your father I was going to give it to Francis Silver. But I decided against it. Burn it, throw it away, anything. Don't tell your father. About the album doesn't matter. Not about the envelope. Be a good boy, and promise."

In agony I promised.

It was not until several months after the funeral that I told father of mother's wish about the postcards.

"Yes," he said, "your mother told me she'd spoken to you. Women," he said, giving me that two-coloured look which at one and the same time questioned my knowledge and informed my ignorance, "are strange, strange mortals, and this is a strange gesture. He was very devoted to your mother, and may like to have them as a memento."

"Would *you* like to take them? It might be better if you took them—more—more suitable." I was trying a man-to-man briskness.

Father looked me over, and came to his decision about what I was up to.

"Why?" he said. "Why on earth would it be more suitable? I've never met Francis Silver in my life. Anyway, you promised your mother, didn't you? Which issue are you trying to avoid?"

That my father did not know Francis Silver astonished me. Reading between the lines of mother's tales I had pictured Francis Silver and father, stiff-collared, in pointed button boots, carrying heart-shaped boxes of chocolates in their hands, and arriving (often) at the same moment on the basalt doorstep of mother's front door.

"I'm not avoiding anything," I lied. "Are you sure . . . are you absolutely sure you've never met him?"

"I am absolutely sure." He looked me over again. "I'll be looking forward to hearing about him. And, although I've never met him, I think, in the circumstances, it could not be considered too much if you conveyed my kind regards."

Despite my death-bed promise, I had had hopes of finding father willing to return the postcards to Francis Silver. I'd justified these hopes by telling myself that Francis Silver would be more touched by receiving the album from his widower rival than from the son of the woman he had hoped to marry, from the son he might have had himself. My father's defection meant I should have to keep my promise. About this I was not really happy. At eighteen I conceived myself cynical; disillusionment was daily bread.

The next time I travelled to Melbourne the album went with me. As well, I took the pink envelope which I had not destroyed—there had been no moral pause, no sense of treachery in the betrayal. On her deathbed, I told myself, mother had tangled her values, her judgment had been marred. I . . .*I* . . . considered that the anguished man I would be meeting would be doubly consoled by this more personal memento.

I had no sooner arrived at the Coffee Palace in which I was staying in the city than it became imperative to set about handing over the album and the envelope: mother had been dead for four months;

the cards with their velveteen forget-me-nots, their sequins, and intricately folded and embossed layers, the envelope scented from its long secret life in the handkerchief-drawer, were too precious and unfitting to lie about for even an hour on the public furniture of a room that had been occupied by unknown, impermanent, maybe sinful people. As though preparing to meet God or have an accident, I had a shower, and cleaned my teeth, for the second time that day, put on all my best clothes, my new shoes and tie, and took much trouble with my hair. With the envelope in a pocket, and carrying the album as though it were frangible time, and dreams of finest glass, I set out for Francis Silver's.

Since all this happened before World War II and post-war vandalism, the picture-framing shop had not been contemporarized: it was still turn-of-the-century elegant in a slightly abraded way. These etchings with the enormously wide creamy mounts and narrow black frames fashionable at the period were disposed behind the plate-glass on which, in Gothic gold-leaf, was the name I had heard all my life, the name in my mother's handwriting on the pink envelope containing the piece of her hair she'd called a lock. I went into the shop. There was no one behind the counter. The sound of elfin-cobbler hammering came from behind plush curtains, black, on which were *appliqued* pale gold lyres, and which obviously concealed a workroom. When I rang the small brass bell attached to the counter by a chain the tiny tap-tapping continued for a few moments, and then ceased. I heard no footsteps, but the curtains were parted. A short, fat man stood behind the counter.

"And what," he said in light and somehow wheedling voice, "can I do for *you*?" His small eyes (beady, I said to myself) stitched over me in an assessing way. He was the most strikingly clean-looking man I had ever seen, composed of the blackest black (his suit and tie and eyes and semi-circular eyebrows) and the whitest white (his shirt, the handkerchief protruding from one sleeve, the white slices of hair curving back from his temples).

"I should like to speak to Fr . . . to Mr Francis Silver, please."

He lowered his lids while pretending to pick something languidly from his sleeve, and to flick delicately with finger-tips at the spot nothing had been picked from.

"You are," he said, interested in the fact, "thpeaking to that very perthon."

I was not prepared for this, a disillusion not cut to my template.

233

My face must have run empty.

"I athure you," he said, "I *am* Franthith Thilver. Have I been recommended? You *mutht* tell me by whom. You want thomething framed?"

"My . . . my mother . . ." I said, and placed the album on the counter. "My mother sent this. Postcards."

"To be framed?"

He opened the album.

He turned over several pages. "My dear," he said. "My dear, how thcrumptious!"

I saw on his hand the ring with the ruby mother had told us about. I saw the fingernails with each half-moon, even on the little fingers, unmistakably revealed.

"Jutht look! I've theen nothing like thethe for . . ." He pushed out his lips in a depreciating smile, ". . . for more yearth than I care to thtate publicly. I uthed to have a pothitive mania for them."

"They are yours," I said. "They *were* yours. You sent them to my mother. Years ago," I finished uncertainly.

"I did? Gay, reckleth boy I wath! May one have little lookieth?" He took one of the cards and examined its back. "Tho I did! My handwriting hathn't changed a bit. How ekthordinary, how very ekthordinary! And now they are to be framed?"

"No," I said. "No, not framed. Mother thought you'd like to have them back."

I knew I was expressing mother's wish very badly, but could do nothing else: the situation had become bewildering not only to me but also to Francis Silver who said, "Oh!". There was, moreover, something beyond the bewilderment of a clumsy social situation; there was something wrong. Francis Silver had not asked me who had sent the postcards. Some film clogging natural curiosity, even polite enquiry, some flaw in his humanity, made him seem careless and carelessly cruel.

I did not want to say it but I said it: I told him my mother's maiden name.

He became fretful: the past was not for him. Nevertheless he acted good manners of a sort. "Now, let me thee," he said, and he put the tip of his forefinger on his forehead in an absurd thinking posture. He pouted.

"My dear," he presently said, "the mind ith blank. Abtholutely! Nothing thtirs in my little addled brain. I'm very, very naughty.

But you muthn't tell your mother. I thhould be *tho* humiliated. You mutht tell her I loved *theeing* them but I couldn't *deprive* her of them. It'th a wonderful collection and in *faultleth* condition. Oh, if only my friend Rekth were here . . . he *adorth* pothcardiana, if I may coin a phrathe, abtholutely adorth."

Scraps of the past were blowing about my brain like the litter at the end of a perfect picnic.

"And you don't remember my mother?"

He could have smacked me.

He tossed his eyes heavenwards, but not too high.

"Be reathonable, *pleathe!*" "More than twenty yearth! One would adore to remember, of courthe. But too much water under the bridge. There've been too many people, too many, many people. I *thaid* I wath terribly humiliated. I couldn't akthept them now, could I? You take them back. And thank your mother very, very much." He smiled a conspirator's smile, grasped my wrist and squeezed it boldly yet furtively. "I know you'll keep my ghathly thecret, just *know*. You've got a nithe kind fathe, haven't you? But there've really been too many people. I'm thure your mother ith ath charming ath you. But I don't remember her at all."

I detached myself. Without a word I left the shop.

The album of cards remained with whom I'd promised to give it.

By the time I had returned to the Coffee Palace through the sort of exquisite day I used to imagine a pretty mother and a jaunty Francis Silver flirting through along the sea-front, I had made up an outline of lies to satisfy and comfort my father for whom I felt the truth, as I saw it, to be of the wrong shape. By the time, days later, I was home with him, I hoped to have filled in that outline with unassailable detail: I dared not shock him. As my first adult chore, my initiation task, I would make a fitting Francis Silver for him, one that matched the Francis Silver of mother's recollections.

In the room at the Coffee Palace I looked at the pink envelope older than I. For one weak moment I felt like making a film-actor's gesture and kissing it. I remembered in time it was not mine to kiss. It was no one's. In that room with its Gideon Bible on the glass-topped bedside cabinet, its ecru net curtains, its oatmeal wallpaper and petty frieze of autumn Virginia Creeper, I burned the envelope. In its first resistance to flame it gave up its ingrained scent. It twisted, fighting the flame and itself. It emitted a stench of burning hair. It writhed and writhed in an agony I could not bear to watch.

Chinua Achebe

Chinua Achebe, a writer from Nigeria, laid the foundation for his deservedly high reputation with the publication of his first novel *Things Fall Apart* in 1958. Like most African authors today, Achebe is a deeply committed writer, and in recent years his work has taken a sharply satirical turn. This is particularly the case with *A Man of the People*, a novel set in post-Independence Nigeria. Like Naipaul in his novel, *The Suffrage of Elvira*, which has as its background the West Indies and the political and social problems in a former colonial country, Achebe is also deeply satirical of the corruption of self-seeking politicians and their system of government. 'It is a fat-dripping, gummy, eat-and-let-eat regime', one which 'inspired the common saying that a man could only be sure of what he had put away safely in his gut.' The novel culminates in an army coup and its closeness to contemporary events in Nigeria in 1966, the year in which it was published, does not need stressing.

There is no satire, however, in *Things Fall Apart*, nor is there any political engagement with contemporary events. It is set in Eastern Nigeria a half century or so ago, and in it the realistic detail, proverbs, folk-legend (that of the presiding deity of Umuru market recounted in "The Sacrificial Egg" is also found almost verbatim here), and descriptions of clan customs and beliefs are woven together without a trace of sentiment, but with such imaginative power and sympathetic understanding that the very texture of daily life in the Ibo community comes vividly alive on every page. But the fate of this community life, whose centre of traditional beliefs cannot hold against the new ideas and the new beliefs, is already indicated by the title. In the end the hero, Okonkwo, having made a useless gesture of defiance against the new order by helping to burn down a missionary centre, hangs himself. Unable to stem the tide of change he prefers death. *Things Fall Apart*; a certain similarity can be seen with the basic theme in Ngugi's otherwise very different story.

In "The Sacrificial Egg", in contrast to this novel, the two patterns of belief—or superstition—are woven into a seamless whole. Neither the one tradition nor the other triumphs. Sharply visualized realistic detail, evocative prose and legend also play their part here, not only in the description of the daily life of the market, but also in the account of Julius's meeting with the night-ghost—the same Julius 'whose education placed him above such superstitious stuff' as expounded by his devoutly Christian mother-in-law.

The story in itself is little more than a brief sketch, but by its controlled artistry and skilled organization (one notes how unobtrusively the crucial switch in time is managed) it becomes an extremely effective short story. Its power lies essentially in its very economy; nothing is elaborated or forced to any conclusion, and the reader is left to make of it what he will. As rounded and as complete as any story in this anthology, it leaves echoes reverberating in the reader's mind long after it has been finished. *D. H.*

The Sacrificial Egg

Julius Obi sat gazing at his typewriter. The fat chief clerk, his boss, was snoring at his table. Outside, the gatekeeper in his green uniform was sleeping at his post. No customer had passed through the gate for nearly a week. There was an empty basket on the giant weighing machine. A few palm kernels lay in the dust around the machine.

Julius went to the window that overlooked the great market on the banks of the Niger. This market, like all Ibo markets, had been held on one of the four days of the week. But with the coming of the white man and the growth of Umuru into a big palm-oil port, it had become a daily market. In spite of that, however, it was still busiest on its original Nkwo day, because the deity that presided over it cast her spell only on that day. It was said that she appeared in the form of an old woman in the centre of the market just before cockcrow and waved her magic fan in the four directions of the earth—in front of her, behind her, to the right, and to the left—to draw to the market men and women from distant clans. And they came, these men and women, bringing the produce of their lands: palm-oil and kernels, kola nuts, cassava, mats, baskets, and earthenware pots. And they took home many-coloured cloths, smoked fish, iron pots and plates.

Others came by the great river bringing yams and fish in their canoes. Sometimes it was a big canoe with a dozen or more people it it; sometimes it was just a fisherman and his wife in a small vessel from the swift-flowing Anambara. They moored their canoe on the bank and sold their fish, after much haggling. The woman then walked up the steep banks of the river to the heart of the market to buy salt and oil and, if the sales had been good, a length of cloth. And for her children at home she bought bean cakes or *akara* and *mai-mai*, which the Igara women cooked. As evening approached, they took up their paddles and paddled away, the water shimmering in the sunset and their canoe becoming smaller and smaller in the distance until it was just a dark crescent on the water's face and two dark bodies swaying forwards and backwards in it.

Julius Obi was not a native of Umuru. He came from a bush village twenty or so miles away. But having passed his Standard Six in a mission school in 1920 he came to Umuru to work as a clerk in the offices of the Niger Company, which dealt in palm-oil and kernels. The offices were situated beside the famous Umuru market, so that in his first two or three weeks Julius had to learn to work against the background of its noise. Sometimes when the chief clerk was away or asleep he walked to the window and looked down on the vast anthill activity. Most of these people were not there yesterday, he thought, and yet the market was as full. There must be many, many people in the world. Of course they say that not everyone who came to the great market was a real person. Janet's mother had said so.

"Some of the beautiful young women you see squeezing through the crowds are not real people but *mammy-wota* from the river," she said.

"How does one know them?" asked Julius, whose education placed him above such superstitious stuff. But he took care not to sound unbelieving. He had long learned that it was bad policy to argue with Ma on such points.

"You can always tell," she explained, "because they are beautiful with a beauty that is not of this world. You catch a glimpse of them with the tail of your eye, then they disappear in the crowd."

Julius thought about these things as he now stood at the window looking down at the empty market. Who would have believed that the great market could ever be so empty? But such was the power of *Kitikpa*, or smallpox.

When Umuru had been a little village, it had been swept and kept clean by its handful of inhabitants. But now it had grown into a busy, sprawling, crowded, and dirty river port. And *Kitikpa* came. No other disease is feared by the Ibo people as much as they fear *Kitikpa*. It is personified as an evil deity. Its victims are not mourned lest it be offended. It put an end to the coming and going between neighbours and between villages. They said, "*Kitikpa* is in that village," and immediately it was cut off by its neighbours.

Julius was worried because it was almost a week since he had seen Janet, the girl he was going to marry. Ma had explained to him very gently that he should no longer come to see them "until this thing is over by the power of Jehovah". Ma was a very devout Christian, and one reason why she approved of Julius for her only daughter was that he sang in the church choir.

"You must keep to your rooms," she had said. "You never know whom you might meet on the streets. That family has got it." She pointed at the house across the road. "That is what the yellow palm frond at the doorway means. The family were all moved away today in the big government lorry."

Janet walked a short way with him, and they said good night. And they shook hands, which was very odd.

Julius did not go straight home. He went to the bank of the river and just walked up and down it. He must have been there a long time, because he was still there when the *ekwe*, or wooden gong, of the night spirit sounded. He immediately set out for home, half walking and half running. He had about half an hour to get home before the spirit ran its race through the town.

As Julius hurried home he stepped on something that broke with a slight liquid explosion. He stopped and peeped down at the footpath. The moon was not yet up, but there was some faint light which showed that it would not be long delayed. In this light Julius saw that he had stepped on a sacrificial egg. There were young palm fronds around it. Someone oppressed by misfortune had brought the offering to the crossroads in the dusk. And he had stepped on it, and taken the sufferer's ill luck to himself. "Nonsense," he said and hurried away. But it was too late; the night spirit was already abroad. Its voice rose high and clear in the still, black air. It was a long way away, but Julius knew that distance did not apply to these beings. So he made straight for the cocoyam farm beside the road and threw himself on his belly. He had hardly done this when he heard the rattling staff of the spirit and a thundering stream of esoteric speech. He shook all over. The sounds came bearing down on him. And then he could hear the footsteps. It was if twenty men were running together. In no time at all the sounds had passed and disappeared in the distance on the other side of the road.

As Julius stood at the window looking out on the empty market he lived through that night again. It was only a week ago, but already it seemed to be separated from the present by a vast emptiness. This emptiness deepened with the passage of time. On this side stood Julius, and on the other Ma and Janet, who were carried away by the smallpox.

Notes on Contributors

ACHEBE, Chinua: Born 1930 in Ogidi, Eastern Nigeria. Educated at Government College, Umuahia, and at University of Ibadan. Worked for the Nigerian Broadcasting Corporation and became Director of External Broadcasting.

Published works: Novels: *Things Fall Apart*; *No Longer at Ease*; *Arrow of God*; *A Man of the People*.

COWAN, Peter: Born 1914 in Perth, Western Australia. Worked as clerk and farm worker. Later graduated at University of Western Australia where he is now teaching in the English department.

Published works: Short stories: *Drift*; *The Unploughed Land*; *The Empty Street*. Novels: *Summer*; *Seed*.

FRAME, Janet: Born 1924 in Dunedin, New Zealand. Studied at Otago University, spent a number of years in England and then returned to her own country.

Published works: Short stories: *The Lagoon and other stories*; *Snowman Snowman: Fables and Fantasies*; *The Reservoir: Stories and Sketches*. Novels: *Owls Do Cry*; *Faces in the Water*; *The Edge of the Alphabet*; *Scented Gardens for the Blind*; *The Adaptable Man*; *A State of Siege*; *The Rainbirds*; *Intensive Care*. Poetry: *The Pocket Mirror*.

GALLANT, Mavis: Born 1922 in Canada but now living in Paris. She has had many of her short stories published in *The New Yorker*.

Published works: Short Stories: *An Unmarried Man's Summer*. Novels: *The Other Paris*; *My Heart is Broken*; *Green Water, Green Sky*; *A Fairly Good Time*.

HARRIS, Wilson: Born 1921 in British Guyana. Educated in his native country. Worked in Guyana as a land surveyor before settling in London, where he lives at present.

Published works: Novels: *Palace of the Peacock*; *The Far Journey of Oudin*; *The Whole Armour*; *The Secret Ladder*; *Heartland*; *The Eye of the Scarecrow*; *The Waiting Room*; *Tumatumari*; *Ascent to Omai*. Poetry: *Season to Eternity*.

LAMMING, George: Born 1927 in Barbados. Educated in the West Indies, he taught for a number of years in Trinidad and moved to England in 1950 where he has been living ever since. He has described himself as "peasant by birth, colonial by education" and though he has lived in exile since 1950 his roots, he believes, still lie in the West Indies and close to the soil.

Published works: Novels: *In The Castle of My Skin*; *The Emigrants*; *Of Age and Innocence*; *Season of Adventure*. Non-fiction: *The Pleasures of Exile*.

LEE KOK LIANG: Born 1927 in Malaya. Educated English and Chinese secondary schools, at Melbourne University, and at Lincoln's Inn, London. Is now an advocate and solicitor living in Penang, Malaysia.

Published works: Short stories: *The Mutes in the Sun*.

MPHAHLELE, Ezekiel: Born 1919 in Pretoria, South Africa. Took external degrees University of South Africa. Left the country in 1957 for Nigeria where he was a lecturer at University of Ibadan. Subsequently lived in Paris, London, and the United States. Now professor of English in Zambia.

Published works: Short Stories: *Man Must Live*; *The Living and the Dead*; *in corner b*. Autobiography: *Down Second Avenue*. Nonfiction: *The African Image* (collection of political and literary essays). Editor: *African Writing Today*; joint editor with E. A. Komey: *Modern African Stories*.

NAIPAUL, Vidia S.: Born 1932 in Trinidad. He received his education in Trinidad and at Oxford University and has been resident in England for a considerable number of years. Apart from writing he has also been a free-lance broadcaster and a reviewer of fiction, particularly for *The New Statesman*.

Published works: Short Stories: *A Flag on the Island*. Novels: *The Mystic Masseur*; *The Suffrage of Elvira*; *Miguel Street*; *A House for Mr. Biswas*; *Mr. Stone and the Knights Companion*; *The Mimic Men*. Non-fiction: *The Middle Passage*; *An Area of Darkness*; *The Loss of Eldorado*.

NARAYAN, R. K.: Born 1907 in Madras he was educated at Maharaja's College in Mysore, the town in which he has spent most of his life. He was awarded India's Padma Bushman award for distinguished service of a high order, and has also received an honorary doctorate from Leeds University.

Published works: Short stories: *An Astrologer's Day*; *Gods, Demons and Others*. Novels: *Swami and Friends*; *The Bachelor of Arts*; *The Dark Room*; *The English Teacher*; *Mr. Sampath*; *The Financial Expert*; *Waiting for Mahatma*; *The Guide*; *The Man-eater of Malgudi*; *The Sweet Vendor*.

NGUGI, James: Born 1938 at Limuru, Kenya. Educated in Kenya, at Makerere University College, and at Leeds University. Now a lecturer in English at University College, Nairobi.

Published works: Novels: *Weep not, Child*; *The River Between*; *A Grain of Wheat*.

PORTER, Hal: Born 1917 in Melbourne. He has taught in various states in Australia and also in Japan. He has also been a librarian, a producer-actor, and lecturer in Australian literature for the Department of External Affairs.

Published works: Short stories: *A Bachelor's Children*; *The Cats of Venice*. Novels: *The Tilted Cross*; *A Handful of Pennies*. Poetry: *The Hexagon*; *Elijah's Ravens*. Drama: *The Tower*; *The Professor*. Autobiography: *The Watcher on the Cast-iron Balcony*; *The Paper Chase*. Non-fiction: *Stars of Australian Stage and Screen*; *The Actors: An Image of the New Japan*.

RICHLER, Mordecai: Born 1931 in Montreal, Canada. Left for Europe in 1951, lived in France, Spain, England, United States, Israel, and now lives in England.

Published works: Novels: *The Acrobats*; *Son of a Smaller Hero*; *A Choice of Enemies*; *The Apprenticeship of Duddy Kravitz*; *The Incomparable Atuk*; *Stick Your Neck Out*; *Cocksure*. Non-fiction: *Hunting Tigers Under Glass: Essays and Reports*. Also author of articles and reviews contributed to various periodicals. Author of television plays and written film scenarios.

SALKEY, Andrew: Born in Colon, Panama, of Jamaican parents. Educated in Jamaica and at London University. Free-lance broadcaster, interviewer and scriptwriter, mainly for the External Services of the B.B.C. in London, where he has lived for nineteen years.

Published works: Novels: *A Quality of Violence*; *Escape to an Autumn Pavement*; *The Late Emancipation of Jerry Stover*; *The Adventures of Catullus Kelly*. Children's novels: *Hurricane*; *Earthquake*; *Drought*; *Riot*; *Jonah Simpson*. Editor: *West Indian Stories*; *Stories from the Caribbean*; *Caribbean Prose*; *Caribbean Essays*; *Breaklight*.

SARGESON, Frank: Born 1903 in Hamilton, New Zealand. Qualified as a solicitor but did not go on with that profession. Made a short trip to Europe during his youth, but otherwise has remained in New Zealand.

Published works: Short stories: *Collected Stories*. Novels: *I Saw in My Dream*; *I for One*; *Memoirs of a Peon*; *The Hangover*; *Joy of the Worm*. Drama: *Wrestling with the Angel: Two Plays*. Editor: *Speaking for Ourselves: A Collection of Australian and New Zealand Stories*. Also author of essays and articles mainly on literary subjects contributed to various periodicals.

STOW, Randolph: Born 1935 in Western Australia. He has been, at various times, lecturer at the universities of Adelaide, Western Australia and Leeds, a worker at an aboriginal mission station in North Western Australia, and a patrol officer in New Guinea. He is at present living in England.

Published works: Novels: *A Haunted Land*; *The Bystander*; *To the Islands*; *Tourmaline*; *The Merry-Go-Round in the Sea*. Poetry: *Act One*; *Outrider*; *A Counterfeit Silence*. Children's novel: *Midnite*.

TUTUOLA, Amos: Born 1920 in Abeokuta, Western Nigeria. Received education up to primary level only and is now employed by the Nigerian Broadcasting Company, Lagos, as a storeman.

Published works: Novels: *Palm-Wine Drinkard*; *My Life in the Bush of Ghosts*; *Simbi and the Satyr of the Dark Jungle*; *The Brave African Huntress*; *Feather Woman of the Jungle*; *Ajaiyi and His Inherited Poverty*.

WHITE, Patrick: Born 1912 in London of Australian parents. He received his early education in Australia and then in his own words was "ironed out in an English public school and finished off at King's, Cambridge". During the war he was an R.A.F. Intelligence officer in Greece and the Middle East. After demobilization he returned to Australia and settled on a farm at Castle Hill.

Published works: Short stories: *The Burnt Ones*. Novels: *Happy Valley*; *The Living and the Dead*; *The Aunt's Story*; *The Tree of Man*; *Voss*; *Riders in the Chariot*; *The Solid Mandala*; *The Vivisector*. Poetry: *The Ploughman and Other Poems*. Drama: *Four Plays*.